PRETTIES IN PINK

ELISE NOBLE

Published by Undercover Publishing Limited

v1

ISBN: 978-1-912888-50-4

Edited by Nikki Mentges, NAM Editorial

Cover design by Abigail Sins

www.undercover-publishing.com

www.elise-noble.com

If not now...
...then when?

1

HALLIE

I so, so nearly made it out of the office.

Eight o'clock in the evening, the report was finished, my laptop was packed into my oversized purse, my car keys were in my hand, and...Knox was standing in the doorway.

His expression said that I wouldn't be going home anytime soon. He looked...spooked. And Knox was a former Navy SEAL, so he didn't spook easy.

"Dan said you might still be here."

Daniela di Grassi was my boss and mentor at Blackwood Security. Through several strokes of luck, both bad and good, I'd ended up working in the Investigations division, and she'd taken me under her wing. For a girl who'd lived on a diet of true-crime podcasts and coffee for years, it was a dream job.

"What's up?" I asked Knox, although I wasn't sure I wanted to know. After twelve hours in the office spent wrapping up a corporate fraud case that had involved not only Investigations but our Forensic Accounting and Cyber teams as well, I needed dinner and then bed. But we'd located three million bucks' worth of stolen assets—more than the client had been hoping for—so I was looking forward to the meeting with him tomorrow.

As long as I could get some sleep, that was.

Knox dropped into the empty chair at the next desk. Not a good sign. "Just got a call from one of my buddies in the teams. He's overseas right now, but he's got a family situation here in Virginia. Asked for my help."

What did that have to do with me? "Go on."

"His little brother got arrested." Knox paused for a second. "Actually, Micah's not so little anymore. He's also their younger sister's legal guardian, and the Department of Social Services got involved. They've put Fenika into a residential home while they search for a temporary guardian, and she's freaking out."

"And you need me to help you find her?"

"Nah, I know where she is. I was hoping you'd come with me to visit her."

"But I've never met her."

"I've never met her either—that's the problem. Figured maybe she'd feel more comfortable with a woman around." Knox offered a winning smile, and it was gold-medal-worthy. "Buy you dinner on the way back? Cal just wants to know she's okay."

How long would it take? An hour? Two? I knew how it felt to be alone and in trouble.

"It'll cost you a pizza from Il Tramonto."

Oh, that smile only got wider. "Appreciate it."

"Are we taking your car or mine?"

"I rode in on the bike today, but if you want to wrap your thighs around me, I have no objections."

When I first arrived at Blackwood, the office banter had freaked me out a bit. Hell, the sheer number of men had left me twitchy. But as I'd settled in, I'd grown to understand the place. Visit the finance department, and the quiet, industrious atmosphere made you want to whisper every word. The Security and Monitoring division, which provided everything from mall cops to event staff to home alarm systems—the bread-and-butter team, Dan called it—was always serious and professional. But climb up the ladder to Investigations or Cyber or Executive Protection, and the atmosphere grew more casual. For the people on the top rung—Emmy Black's Special Projects division—Blackwood wasn't just a job, it was a way of life. Lines between work and friendship got blurred. Those folks were a team in every sense of the word.

And by virtue of my unconventional route into Blackwood—I'd skipped the interview process and gotten rescued from a sex trafficking ring by the company's directors —I'd found myself a member of that exclusive club. Still very much the newbie, but...accepted. Until I came to Blackwood, I'd felt as if it was me against the world. Now? Now it was *us* against the world.

Knox, he was an incorrigible flirt, sometimes filthy with it, but also a gentleman. He'd never act on any of his innuendos. Well, I guess he might if I invited him to? But I never had and I never would. I didn't date, or hook up, or anything in between. The mere thought of being naked with a man again left me nauseated.

But the flirting? It was safe. Even fun.

"Aw, honey, you don't have enough to hold on to."

Knox laughed as I'd known he would. "Got your keys? If you drop me at my place afterward, I can catch a ride with Cade in the morning."

I drove a Honda compact, nothing flashy but a huge step up from the clunker I'd owned in Kentucky before my foray into hell. Back then, I'd scraped by as a waitress, working sixty hours a week to survive but not really live. The Honda was my most extravagant purchase to date—an old Blackwood pool car with a few nicks and scratches but a solid engine.

Even though the work parking lot was well lit, the mid-October darkness was never far away, and I felt safer with Knox by my side as I hurried across the damp asphalt. He folded himself into the passenger seat as I slipped behind the wheel.

"What did the guy do, anyway?" I asked. "The little brother?"

Knox's smile disappeared. "Cal said the cops accused him of taking a girl."

The blood in my veins turned to ice. I'd figured on burglary or a bar brawl, but abduction? I knew first-hand the toll that took, and any sympathy I might have had for a man who'd made a stupid mistake flittered away in the evening chill.

"Did he do it?"

"Cal says no way, but..." Knox shrugged. "I only met Micah a time or two. Can't say he struck me as the type, but we all wear masks, don't we?"

Yes, we did.

"Is Cal a good friend?"

Knox nodded as I started the engine. "Had my back for two years."

"What happened to his parents? I mean, for his brother to have custody of their sister?"

"His father was never on the scene. His mom, she died in a hit-and-run right after Cal completed BUD/S."

"Bud-what?"

"Basic Underwater Demolition SEAL training. He was committed to the Navy, had good money coming in, so Micah dropped out of college to take care of Fenika. The way Cal talks about him, the kid's a saint."

4

"What about the girl? The one he kidnapped?"

"We can't be certain that he did it."

"Okay, what about the girl he was *accused* of kidnapping?"

"Cal doesn't know much. Fen didn't have many details, and like I said, she was freaking out. They've been trying to get ahold of Cal for three days, but he was out of range."

I assumed "out of range" meant he'd been on some hush-hush mission that nobody was allowed to discuss.

"Is he coming home?"

"Not at the moment. He can't. Hell, he wasn't even meant to call me, and if he gets distracted, that could cost lives." Knox cursed under his breath. "I said I'd do what I could, okay? But I know nothing about the legal system."

"Other than how to circumvent it on occasion?"

That got me a half-smile. "Yeah, maybe."

Fenika Ganaway was a petite Black girl who scuttled out a side door of the residential centre to meet us by a bench in the courtyard. Her skinny jeans were on the wrong side of baggy, and she kept her hands stuffed into the pockets of an NYU hoodie that dwarfed her. I couldn't see much of her face since the hood was up, but her tears glistened under the streetlights.

"We have a nine o'clock curfew," she said right away. A stickler for the rules? "You're Knox?"

"Yeah, and this is Hallie."

They stared at each other, two strangers, neither of them sure where to start.

"Could you tell us what happened?" I asked gently. "Knox spoke to Cal, but I don't think he had all the details."

"I don't have the details either!"

"Micah got arrested?"

"They came to the apartment and took him. For questioning, they said, but he didn't come back, and these people..." She jerked her head toward the squat brick building next to us. "These people say he's gotta stay in jail."

"Have you spoken to him since?"

"One time. He told me to be strong and everything would get fixed, that he hadn't done anything and the cops would work that out, so why isn't he here?"

"What did they accuse him of doing?"

Yes, Knox had already told me, but I wanted to hear it in Fenika's own words.

"They said he took some girl, but that's bullshit." She shook her head. "Micah wouldn't lay a finger on anyone, let alone a kid."

"A kid?"

I began to get a bad, bad feeling about this.

"A rich little white girl got snatched outta her bed, so who do they blame?"

"Vonnie Feinstein? Are you talking about Vonnie Feinstein?"

The story had been all over the news for the past week. Eight-year-old Vonnie had disappeared from her bed in a well-heeled Richmond suburb sometime between nine p.m. and the early hours. Her devastated parents had been interviewed on every news channel, and half of the state's paparazzi were camping outside their home. Nick, one of Blackwood's directors, lived less than a mile away, and he said it was a circus. The cops thought Micah Ganaway was involved in Vonnie's disappearance?

Fenika nodded. "That's what they said her name was, but he never met her. I mean, why would he? Those kinda people don't eat dinner at Burger Ace."

"That's where he works?"

"Worked. When he didn't show up for Saturday's shift, his boss fired him on Twitter." A choke-sob burst from Fenika's throat. "I got no clue how we're gonna pay the rent, and the landlord's an asshole. Like, a *real* dick. He'll kick us out for sure, and what'll happen to our stuff? These people won't let me go home, not even to get more clothes. They just made me stuff whatever I could carry into a trash bag and drove me here. When will Micah come back? I need him to come back."

"Did he hire a lawyer?" I asked.

"He said the cops found him one, but the guy didn't seem much good."

"So, a public defender?"

"I guess. Not as if we have enough money to pay for an attorney ourselves, is it? What can I do? How can I get him out of there? You don't know my brother the way I do—there's no way he'd have hurt anyone. I feel real bad for that little girl's family, but they're trying to pin this on the wrong person."

And if that was true, then whoever took Vonnie Feinstein was still walking free.

If that was true.

I'd never even met Micah Ganaway. He could be a sociopath for all I knew. The only evidence we had to the contrary was the word of two people, one of whom was technically still a child.

But I also knew what it was like to be accused of a crime I didn't commit.

"There isn't much we can do tonight, but we'll speak to some people in the morning, okay? Find out what's going on. Do you know the lawyer's name?"

She shook her head again. "Do I have to stay here? They said I did, but I'm sixteen. I can take care of myself. Been doing that for years while Micah's out at work, anyway." Her voice hitched. "And the other kids, they're mean."

Sixteen, but in that moment, she sounded so much younger. And scared. Wouldn't anyone be if their whole family had been torn away from them? Even if Micah was guilty, Fenika didn't deserve to be collateral damage.

"We'll look into that too, but there are rules the Department of Social Services needs to follow."

"Rules suck." She turned to Knox. "You know Cal from the Navy?"

"We served together."

"Is he coming home? I asked him, but he wouldn't give me a straight answer."

"I'm sure he's doing everything he can to get away, but it's difficult for him to jump on a plane from...out there."

A silhouette appeared in the doorway, a stocky woman. "Curfew!"

"Don't make me go back in there. *Please.*" A note of panic came into Fenika's voice. "Take me with you?"

If we did that, the cops would be investigating two child abductions instead of one. "Just stay here for a few more days while we ask questions. This might all get cleared up tomorrow."

"We'll come back," Knox promised. "Whatever happens, we'll come back." Uncertainty crept into his voice as he glanced my way. "Won't we?"

Why not? It wasn't as if I had a social life. Mercy, my bestie, spent her days plotting how to spend a billion dollars of stolen cash—not even kidding—and my other roommate was a parrot.

And besides, I was curious. You see, Vonnie Feinstein wasn't the only little girl to have disappeared from her bed. Five years ago, Mila Carmody had vanished into the dark, and despite an extensive investigation by both Blackwood and the police, no trace of her had ever been found. Cold cases were my bedtime reading, and that one...that one had stuck. The media were already speculating about a connection, and the possibility intrigued me.

"Sure, I'll come back."

And Knox could buy me dessert too.

2

HALLIE

"How was the meeting with Hamble Corp?" Dan asked. "The CEO tried to poach Georgia for his finance team, but apart from that? Good."

"Hope she turned him down."

"Very diplomatically."

Georgia had been a lucky find. She'd started out as a client for Nick's Executive Protection team, but after being shot at and rescued, she'd ended up dating one of Emmy Black's exes. Now she used her accounting skills to ferret out fraud and money laundering schemes for Blackwood. Only part-time because she had a daughter now, but Dan said one of Georgia was worth two of most other people, so the arrangement worked well.

"Can't imagine Georgia being anything but diplomatic. She *is* a senator's daughter, after all."

"True. How was your vacation?"

Dan had flown back from Florida early this morning, and if the colour of her face was any indication, she'd spent most of the past week on the beach.

"Hot." She passed a hand over her forehead and grinned.

"In and out of the bedroom. To think I once thought monogamy would be a fate worse than death. And speaking of hot, did Knox find you yesterday?"

"Dan! You're practically married."

"Does that make me blind? Knox?"

"Did you watch the news while you were away? Or were you too preoccupied with Ethan's naked ass?"

"I can multitask," Dan said, but she quickly screwed up her face. "He hates when I do that."

Too much information. "Okay, so what story's been front and centre this week?"

"That guy who tried to get a gator to open his can of beer, but it bit off his—"

"Euew, no!"

"Chill, they reattached it."

"That's not what I'm talking about."

"Okay, do you mean the woman who got confused between hairspray and bear mace?"

How was that even possible? "Not that either."

"The home invasion gang that gorged themselves on illegal moonshine and then fell asleep, Goldilocks-style?"

We were going to be here all day, weren't we? "Vonnie Feinstein?"

"Oh, *Virginia* news. I've been watching Florida news." Then the wheels turned. "Shit, Knox's friend is involved in that?"

"His friend's brother. Maybe. It's kind of a mess. Now that the Hamble Corp meeting's over, I was planning to spend my lunch break tracking down Micah Ganaway's attorney."

"Micah Ganaway? As in Calvin Ganaway? His brother?"

"Cal, yes. You know him?"

"I know Emmy wants him for her Special Projects team."

"He's that good?"

"Apparently. Which means that if he leaves the SEALs,

he'll have a dozen job offers on the table, and we want him to pick us. So when you start digging into this, think of it as a reverse job interview."

"Digging into this? I only said I'd find the name of the public defender as a favour to Knox."

"What cases do you have on your docket?"

"Uh..."

Dan patted me on the shoulder. "Emmy encourages us to take on pro bono work from time to time."

"Are you serious?"

"Consider it a challenge."

"But...but...Micah Ganaway's in jail. Where do I start? How can I even ask him what happened?"

"Easy. First, you drive to Queen of Tarts and buy a dozen mixed donuts, and on the way back, you drop by the Grindhouse and pick up a triple espresso with caramel syrup. Then you take the whole lot up to Emmy's office, smile sweetly, and ask her to make you an appointment."

"At the jail?"

Dan just stared at me.

"Uh, I'll get my car key."

Every man had his price, so Emmy said, and the Richmond City Sheriff had been bought for a "reasonable" donation to the Sport4Kids community project. I was undecided on the ethics of that. Sure, there was a degree of corruption involved, but hey, they were kids. And didn't every child deserve the chance to play softball?

Dubious morals aside, my name was on Micah Ganaway's visitor list for tomorrow morning, thirty minutes max. Thankfully, Emmy had bought two seats at the table, and Dan had agreed to come with me, primarily out of a desire for justice—missing kids were the worst type of crime, and the Mila Carmody case had been one of hers—but partly out of curiosity.

After all, didn't everyone want to meet a celebrity?

The news about Micah Ganaway's arrest had broken this afternoon. Details of his arraignment had leaked, and now the whole world knew he'd been charged with the abduction of Vonnie Feinstein, missing and now presumed dead. The media circus had moved from Rybridge to the Richmond City Detention Center, and now we'd have to run the gauntlet of cameras before we could get inside.

"Good thing Emmy's not with us," Dan muttered. "She'd rather break in than walk past that crowd."

"At least they don't know who we're here to visit."

"Let's keep it that way for as long as possible."

The jail's dress code specified modesty. No tight-fitting pants, no exposed cleavage, all skirts to be at least knee-length. Dan had run into a department store on the way and bought a whole new outfit, and now she kept pulling at the turtleneck as if it were strangling her. At least they brought out a female deputy to search us. If a man had put his hands on me that way, I'd probably have puked.

A quarter-hour later, we got our first good look at Micah Ganaway. The pictures splashed across the news didn't do him justice, or had the reporters picked the most unflattering ones out of spite? Smooth light brown skin, neatly cropped hair, an athletic physique, and cheekbones to die for. But the eyes... The eyes were all kinds of hurt and angry and scared. Bewildered. And when he turned them on us, confused.

"I'm in the wrong place."

The deputy looked at us, then back to Micah. "These people are on your defence team, that's what Sheriff Bailey said. Your investigators?"

The deputy turned to Dan for confirmation, and she nodded. "That's right. His brother hired us."

Micah took a seat at the table, and his cuffs clanked against the metal surface. "*You're* private investigators?"

Dan folded her arms. "Oh, I'm sorry, were you expecting someone with a dick?"

Right away, he backed down. "Cal said he'd called a buddy of his, and I just figured..."

"The buddy called us. I'm Dan, and this is Hallie. And since we've only got half an hour together, you need to start talking. What happened?"

"Ask the cops. I didn't know nothing about nothing until they broke the damn door down."

"I'm asking you. Why did they break down your door and not somebody else's? There must have been a reason."

"You think they need a reason?" Micah looked both of us over. "Yeah, figures. Not like they'd come to *your* door."

"Time's ticking."

"They keep asking me where the girl is. That little girl who disappeared. And I keep telling them I don't know. She's a kid, man. I'd never touch a kid. That's messed up."

"So why do they think you did? You've been charged with her abduction, so there must be some kind of evidence."

"Because I went for a walk. A damn walk. I was in her neighbourhood, and some busybody thought I looked 'suspicious...'" He raised his hands, I guessed to make those air quotes, but quickly remembered they were cuffed together. Lowered them again. "So she made a note of my licence plate, and when the cops spoke to her about the kid, she told them I'd been there."

"This was on the day Vonnie disappeared?" *Vonnie*. Dan used her name to humanise her. I noted Micah had avoided doing that.

"The day before, that's what they said."

"Do you often walk in her neighbourhood?"

"Naw, first time and last time."

"So why did you walk there that day?"

"The light was good. I was driving through, and the light was good, so I stopped to take pictures. I'm a photographer. I mean, I work in a restaurant most of the time, but someday, I want to be a pro photographer. I got a website. Sell prints to make a few extra bucks. Do weddings too, birthdays, proms, anniversaries... And dogs. Took some photos of a dog in Bryan Park a year ago, and the lady wanted them printed onto canvas for her wall. Told all her friends about me, and suddenly I'm the dog photographer. Money's decent, though." He'd been smiling as he spoke about his work, but now his expression soured. "*Was* decent. Ain't nobody gonna hire me after this."

"So the light was good, and you stopped to take pictures. What did you take pictures of?"

"The sunset, mainly. Trees, the skyline. A group of boys playing soccer. Caught them in silhouette against the horizon. Gave them my card, told them the pictures would be on my website in a couple weeks, and they said they'd take a look."

"And this was in Rybridge Fields?"

"Yeah?" Micah shrugged. "I guess. Big green space with soccer pitches and nature trails. Lotta dogs, and half of them were wearing those little sweaters. Figured I'd go back later, put up some posters, see if any of the owners wanted pictures. People who live in Rybridge, they can afford it."

The Feinsteins lived two blocks from the park. The homes on that street went for big bucks, not as fancy as the mansion Mila Carmody's parents lived in, but definitely in the "aspirational" rather than the "realistic" category for most people. Yes, the folks there had money.

But the cops had charged a man for taking photos of the sunset? No, I couldn't see it. Although the Richmond PD sure did have its problems. A little over a year ago, Blackwood had uncovered a child sex ring, and guess who'd been a member? That's right: Chief Garland himself. I used the past tense because he'd shot himself rather than face the consequences, and the new chief was rumoured to be cleaning house. But there'd been a *lot* of dirty cops in that department, so said Dan, who knew these things, and it stood to reason that he hadn't managed to sweep all of them out the door yet.

"Was Vonnie in any of the pictures, Micah?" I asked, and fear flashed in his eyes.

Nailed it.

"I never knew it was her, I swear! The cops said I followed her home, but I didn't."

"Where were you that night?"

"In my apartment."

"Fenika lives with you?"

"Yeah, but she was at a ballet camp that weekend." Pride crept into his voice. "She's an amazing dancer, my sister. One day, she's gonna be on stage. And she's smart. Pretends she isn't, but she's got brains."

"Why would she pretend she isn't smart?"

"Bullies, they don't like the clever kids. Year before last, she had to change schools because it got so bad, so now she stays under the radar if you know what I mean."

I thought back to the bullies in my old high school. "I do know what you mean."

But what the bullies hadn't realised was that I'd grown up in a trailer park in the rough end of town. The unofficial motto of Aspen Meadows—which was a bullshit name because there were no trees and no grass either—was fight or die. So when a bunch of kids cornered me in the hallway two weeks into the new term, I'd punched the biggest one in the face and broken her nose. Earned me a trip to the principal's office, but they left me alone after that. When Mom found out, she'd just shrugged. Didn't care. She didn't much care about anything but where her next drink was coming from.

"So you took pictures of Vonnie the day before she disappeared, and you have no alibi for the night of her abduction," Dan summarised. "What else? I can see them questioning you for that, but not charging you. There must be something else."

Now Micah shifted uncomfortably. "They searched the apartment. My car too."

"And what did they find?"

"Trash bags," he mumbled. "And twine, and a spade, and gloves. And a knife in the glove compartment." So basically a kidnap kit. Sheesh. "Probably shouldn't've had the knife, but I do yard work on the side. Course I'm gonna have that shit in my car. They said there was a hair too, a blonde hair, but I only bought the car two months ago, and getting it detailed would've took money I don't have. Who knows where the damn hair came from?"

"Was the former owner a woman?"

"A man, but he could've had a girlfriend, right? The cops keep asking me where I buried her. The girl, I mean. Over, and over and over." Micah raised his hands to his head and raked at his scalp. "Can't tell them what I don't know, but they won't stop."

"When you say 'they,' who are you talking about?" Dan asked. "Which detectives have the case?"

"Said their names were Duncan and Prestia. Duncan's a real asshole."

Dan snorted softly at the last comment, and I figured she was acquainted with Duncan. I'd avoided much interaction with the Richmond PD so far myself, but I suspected that was going to change real soon.

"We'll speak to them, find out what we can. And I

understand you have a public defender representing you? Del Farmer?"

"He said that if I just told him the truth, said what I'd done with the body, then the prosecutor would work out some kind of a deal. I thought the lawyer was meant to be on my side? He won't listen to a word I say."

That didn't surprise me—I'd looked up Farmer before we left the office this morning, and his speciality was plea bargains. Of the handful of cases that had actually made it as far as a trial, he'd lost three-quarters of them. If Micah was telling the truth, then that didn't bode well.

Dan sat back in her chair, legs crossed at the ankles, looking more comfortable than she had a right to since it was made from metal and bolted to the floor.

"Got any other skeletons in your closet? If we're gonna check into this, we need to know everything."

Micah closed his eyes, and from the way he sucked in a breath, I knew something bad was coming. Just how awful would it be?

"When I was seventeen, I was dating this girl, and we started sexting. You know, pictures of—"

"I know what sexting is."

"Her mom found the pictures, and she didn't much like me, so she reported it to the cops and they charged me with distribution of child pornography."

Seriously? If that was a crime, then half of the kids I went to high school with would be in jail. There were probably pictures of me in my underwear floating around in cyberspace. I wasn't proud of them now, but sixteen-year-old me had thought my C-cups were splendid and therefore a gift that should be shared with the world. Eight years on, I understood just how evil that world could be.

"Were you convicted?" Dan asked.

Micah shook his head. "I was wearing track pants, just—"

His cheeks darkened. "Just, you know, hard, and my attorney argued that the images weren't sexually explicit. But it'll be on my record."

And most people wouldn't care about the details. They'd see child pornography plus abduction of a minor, put two and two together, and make first-degree murder. Micah Ganaway was in a whole world of trouble.

"This is gonna get out."

"I understand that." He put his head in his hands. "I understand that, and whatever happens to me, I need to protect my sister. Even if that means pleading guilty to something I didn't do, I need to protect her. I'm not stupid—I know they'll throw everything my way to get their conviction, I've seen it a hundred times—but Fen's done nothing wrong. I have to know she'll be okay."

The anguish in his voice couldn't be faked, and at that moment, I felt genuinely sorry for him. Knox said Micah had put his own dreams on hold so Fenika wouldn't have to go into the foster system, and it had to be killing him that she'd ended up there anyway.

"I saw her last night, and I'll meet with her again tonight," I told him. "If there's anything we can do to help her, then we will, and in the meantime, we'll take a look through the evidence."

"What happened to the photos you took that day?" Dan asked.

"The cops have my camera. I worked for a damn year to buy the body, another year for the lens. They got my laptop too."

"Before they took them, did you save the pictures? Put them on your website? Upload them to cloud storage?"

"No, but Fen might've. She helps me out with that side of things—image processing, printing, mailing orders. I'm not sure whether she did that batch yet."

"We'll ask her. Now, I want you to run me through that night you went to Rybridge. Start to finish, and don't skip any details. Somebody abducted Vonnie Feinstein, and if it wasn't you, then maybe you're a witness."

"But I didn't see anything."

"You're a photographer. You saw plenty, and it's our job to work out whether any of it was important. Now, from the top…"

3

_____

HALLIE

"A part from the hair, which may or may not be Vonnie's, the evidence is all circumstantial," I said to Dan as we rode back to Blackwood's headquarters. Even though we were in Dan's Camaro, I was driving because only people with a death wish climbed into a car with her behind the wheel.

"It is, but there's still something I'm not getting."

If that was the case, then I also wasn't getting it.

"Like what?"

"Statistically, who's most likely to murder a child?"

Finally, a question I could answer. "A parent."

"Or somebody they know. And who's way down the list?"

"A stranger."

"Exactly. So why did the cops jump to Micah Ganaway so fast?"

"The parents were out that evening, so they probably had an alibi. We need to look at the babysitter?"

"Yeah, we need to look at the babysitter. Did you babysit as a teenager?"

"Didn't everybody?"

Although most folks at Aspen Meadows had seen childcare as an unnecessary expense. Why pay someone to watch a kid when the kid could watch TV instead? Learning to cook dinner had been a rite of passage for every tweenager who lived there. But in the suburbs nearby, parents saw the benefits of hiring a babysitter, and I'd picked up steady work from the age of sixteen. Mostly, it had been easy money, but I'd never forget the day I assumed responsibility for Satan's twin daughters—one ran out the front door, one ran out the back door, and when I tried to find them, they snuck inside, locked me out, and turned the sprinklers on.

"Ever invite a boy over after the kid went to bed?"

"Once or twice."

"What if Vonnie's babysitter had a friend? Add it to the list. Also relatives—uncles, aunts, cousins, grandparents. Find out if there's been animosity between them and Vonnie's parents, or whether any of them have a record. Check into finances too. Remember that case in the UK where the mom faked the abduction of her own kid to make money from the publicity?"

I'd listened to the podcast, horrified. "Yup."

"There're some sick, sick people out there. We need to talk to the cops too." Dan grimaced. "Micah's right: Duncan *is* an asshole. Try Prestia first."

"He's okay?"

"I've never crossed paths with him before, so maybe he's new? Whatever, he can't be worse than Duncan. And here's another angle to try—could Micah have been framed? Not long after I started at Blackwood, Duncan got caught planting a baggie of heroin on a kid at a traffic stop, and hair's easier to get hold of than dope."

"How does he still have a job?"

"Because the whole damn department was corrupt,

remember? Now it's more like half-corrupt, but I still don't trust those cops as far as I can throw them, and I'm pretty short and also not great at pitching."

"Are you sure I can't go back to investigating corporate fraud? I'm good at that."

Dan patted me on the arm. "Have faith in yourself, sister. Enjoy the challenge."

"What I'd enjoy is a week in the Caribbean."

"Then let's make a deal. Prove who did this, one way or the other, and I'll strong-arm Emmy into lending you her private island for a week."

Good luck to anyone that tried to strong-arm Emmy into anything, but I didn't doubt that she'd agree to Dan's terms. She might be an actual freaking assassin, but once you got past the potty mouth, the prickly outer layers, and the fact that she could shoot a man in cold blood without flinching, she was weirdly nice. And her island was rumoured to be a tropical paradise. Seeing as I was saving to eventually buy my own home, my finances ran to "three stars in Virginia Beach" rather than "billionaires' playground," so Dan's offer was a damn good one.

"I'll speak to Prestia."

"Attagirl."

"Can I interest you in our pre-weekend special? Any grande coffee and a muffin of your choice for half price."

Friday special. It was a Friday special. Why couldn't people just say what they meant? But I did like the idea of a chocolate muffin.

"Sure, why not?"

Since our meeting with Micah, we'd had two small breaks. The first came when Fenika told me that she had indeed uploaded the photos from that day to her brother's cloud drive. As I waited for my order at the Grindhouse, Blackwood's Cyber team was combing through every image for clues that might help us.

Of course, every silver lining had a cloud, and that cloud had been the bruise on Fenika's cheek. She'd tried to hide it, but it was the size of a nickel and the shape of Texas. Kids could be so cruel. When news of Micah's arrest came out, it hadn't taken long for Fenika's peers to start with the name-calling and worse. Once again, she'd begged Knox and me to take her home, but we couldn't. I'd wanted to, but we couldn't. Knox was going to speak with Cal, see if there was a way to get an advocate appointed for Fenika in her family's absence.

The second break? When I searched online for Detective Prestia, I'd recognised the oh-so-serious man staring back at me from the "Meet our newest members" post on the police department's social media feed. He'd been ahead of me in line when I picked up Emmy's coffee on Tuesday. I confess he'd caught my eye because he was hot—and as Dan said, even if a woman wasn't available, that didn't make her blind—but now that I knew he was a cop, any appeal he might have had vanished in a heartbeat. Why were the pretty ones always pricks?

Anyhow, I figured running into him by "chance" might have a better likelihood of success than me calling to request a meeting or stalking him home, and what better way to start documenting my thoughts on the case than over coffee and carbs in a reasonably upscale café? I only hoped Prestia was a regular.

Five coffees, four muffins, three bathroom breaks, and a

whole bunch of caffeine jitters later, he finally walked through the door. I'd almost given up hope. Now I just needed to convince him to talk to me without coming across like a manic idiot. Mental note: switch to decaf.

What would Dan do? Probably dazzle him with her boobs, which wasn't a possibility for me. And Emmy would hog-tie him, which wasn't an option either. I slipped into line behind him, pondering my options, only to get distracted by an idiot spitting on a panhandler sitting outside the window. What an asshole. The spitter, not the homeless guy. Chances were, he couldn't help his situation, and he'd been ready with a smile and a "Morning, ma'am" when I walked inside.

There were still three people in front of Prestia. I had a spare moment.

"I'm just gonna take this muffin to the guy outside," I called to the cashier. "I'll pay with my order."

Since I'd left my laptop on the table and tipped her well all morning, I figured she wouldn't mind. And it only took a second to put the smile back on the homeless man's face. So many people were only one paycheck away from the streets, and if Blackwood hadn't taken me in, I might have ended up there myself.

But when I got back inside, it seemed that not everyone felt the same way.

"Why do you waste your money on people like those?" a woman seated at a table near the door asked.

"People like what?"

"Vagrants."

"Everybody has to eat."

And what right did she have to judge people? Maybe if she'd just gone back to her frou-frou coffee and bran muffin, I'd have left it there, but of course, she didn't.

"You oughta be ashamed of yourself. It should be illegal."

"What should be illegal? Homelessness?"

"Enabling those people to clutter up the streets."

"Are you kidding me? Why don't you call the cops and tell them to arrest me for buying a snack?"

"I don't like your attitude, young lady."

"Well, I don't like yours. It's barely above freezing, and I took the guy a freaking muffin. If you had an ounce of compassion in that scrawny body of yours, you'd buy him a hot drink to go with it. But seeing as you don't, how about you get outta my face and shut your nasty mouth instead? Didn't your momma ever teach you to mind your own business?"

The entire café had fallen silent. Every single head was turned in our direction. *Congratulations, Hallie. A masterclass in how not to conduct an investigation.*

But then somebody at the back began to clap, and a girl called, "I'll get the guy a coffee."

Another voice, male this time. "You should pack up your bran muffin and leave, lady."

But the woman *still* wasn't done.

"Are you happy now that you've caused a scene? Attention seeking, that's what floozies like you are. Maybe I *will* call the police and report you for disturbing the peace."

I felt rather than saw Prestia step up behind me.

"Ma'am, I'm a police officer, and if you do that, I'll arrest you for filing a false report." Prestia's accent told me he wasn't from around here, so Dan might have been right about him being a transplant. His voice held a hint of the south but not a full-on drawl. "And just so we're clear here, being homeless isn't a crime. The gentleman at the back offered you good advice, so I suggest you take it."

She opened her mouth. Wisely closed it again, then wrapped the remains of the bran muffin in a napkin and scuttled out the door.

Whew.

Everyone in line bought something for the homeless guy —a sandwich, a bottle of juice, a cookie—and when Prestia reached the counter, he turned to me. Hoo boy. He was even hotter the second time around. Short hair the colour of molten chocolate, matching eyes with gold flecks that twinkled as he glanced at the door behind me. Kind eyes. Watchful eyes. His facial hair was too short for a beard, too long for a five o'clock shadow, but the not-quite-polished look suited him. And when he smiled... Oh, he could be in Hollywood with those teeth.

"What can I get you?" he asked.

"Me?"

"One good turn deserves another."

Well, this was an interesting development. "Uh, a decaf latte and an apple."

"Decaf? You drink decaf?" He sounded incredulous.

"Today, I do."

"And the apple?"

"I already ate my weekly allowance of carbs this morning."

Prestia gave me a slow once-over from head to toe, and that did nothing for my temperature. Forget undressing me with his eyes, he peeled me like a crawfish and tossed me into a pan of boiling water. Then his lips quirked.

"Give me a granola cup and an Americano, plus a decaf latte and an apple for the lady." He didn't look away from me as he spoke. "And put our homeless friend's muffin on my tab."

"I've got a table over there in the corner if you want to join me?"

"I usually get takeout."

Another stranger spoke up, a grey-haired lady eating a pink cupcake. "No wedding ring. You should join her, hun. She's a good one."

Prestia's twitching lips spread into a genuine smile, and damn, that was devastating.

"How can I argue with that?" He glanced at his watch and shrugged. "Lead the way."

4

FORD

F ord Prestia shouldn't have been taking a break from the Feinstein case to eat a mid-morning snack, and he definitely shouldn't have been taking a break from the Feinstein case to eat that snack with a pretty woman. But fuck it. Duncan was an asshole marking time while he waited to collect Social Security, at least, he had been until he saw one last shot at glory, and the fewer hours Ford had to spend with him, the better. Back in New Orleans, he'd have picked up a drink for his partner too, but Duncan could buy his own damn coffee.

The object of Ford's fascination sashayed to the table in the corner where she had a laptop set up. On the previous two occasions he'd seen her—this past Tuesday and early last week—she'd ordered to go. Why was she working in the café today? Didn't she have an office? Perhaps she wasn't from around here, which might explain the accent. She had a twang you didn't hear much in these parts, and it only became more pronounced when she was angry. *Angry*. The sight of the willowy blonde laying into that stuck-up bitch shouldn't have been a turn-on, but Ford couldn't deny how it had affected him. At least he hadn't been the target of her tongue today, although maybe in the future, he wouldn't mind becoming better acquainted.

For fuck's sake, Prestia.

Picking up women on duty was a no-no, and hadn't he decided to focus on his job for now? He'd just gotten out of a long-term relationship—much to his sister's relief because Sylvie had never gotten along with Eliette—and he was in no hurry to get tangled up again. But something casual...

"Do you come here often?" the blonde asked, sitting down and closing her laptop in one smooth motion. "Sorry, that sounded like a pickup line, and it definitely wasn't." Well, at least she'd cleared that up. "Thanks for your help back there."

"Just doing my civic duty." Ford took a seat opposite. "Cops don't appreciate having their time wasted. And in answer to your question, I come here most days. They seem to serve the best coffee in this part of town."

"They do. My boss's boss is a real coffee snob, and this is her favourite place."

"A coffee snob? Maybe you should introduce us."

"Uh..."

Why did she look so horrified?

"Relax, I'm kidding. I just like good coffee, that's all. Took about two weeks after I moved here for the assholes in the department to start calling me Esprestia."

Now she seemed puzzled. "Esprestia?"

"Shit, sorry, I should have introduced myself." Ford held out a hand. Usually he was smoother than this, but when she put her hand into his, he jolted as *something* passed between them. A connection. "Ford Prestia."

She had the most beautifully expressive face, but instead of the smile he'd hoped to see, there was a moment's pause, and then he got shock. Shock and—if he wasn't mistaken—a hint of nervousness.

"You okay?"

"We shouldn't be talking to each other."

What? Why? "If it's about the incident outside the wine bar on Seventeenth, I swear that was a one-off. I'd drunk too much, and I never normally sing in public."

"Huh? No, it's not that. You're investigating the Feinstein abduction, right?"

Prickles rose on the back of Ford's neck. The laptop, the endless carbs... "Ah, fuck. You're a reporter?"

"A reporter? No, no way."

"Then what...?"

"I'm investigating the case too."

"*You?*"

She snatched her hand away and faced up to him, arms akimbo. "Yes, on behalf of Micah Ganaway. And why not me? You think because I'm young and female that I'm incapable?"

Because she was female? No, that didn't come into it. But she *was* young. Hell, she barely looked old enough to have graduated college, which was another reason why Ford's dick shouldn't have been twitching in his pants.

"You're working for Ganaway? I didn't think he had enough money to hire his own investigator."

"His brother retained us."

"Us?"

"I work for Blackwood Security."

Blackwood Security. Two words that cast fear into the heart of the Richmond PD. The enemy, or at least, they were according to Duncan. The folks from Blackwood bent the rules regularly, straight-up broke them on occasion, and generally rode roughshod over the entire department. Ford had always figured their paths would cross eventually; he just hadn't expected it to be under these circumstances.

But he couldn't deny he was curious. Did everyone who

worked for Blackwood look like this girl? If they did, then maybe he was in the wrong damn job.

"Interesting."

"Interesting? Have you heard of Blackwood?"

"I'm aware of their reputation."

"Then why haven't you tossed your coffee over me and bolted out the door?"

"Waste good coffee? No, I don't think so. And I still don't know your name."

The tension in her shoulders eased a fraction. "Hallie. Hallie Chastain."

"Well, Hallie Chastain, you're right. I probably shouldn't be talking to you."

"And yet you are."

"And yet I am."

So, Micah Ganaway had a team of investigators working for him, and not just any old team of investigators, but one with a history of cracking cases, one way or another. And why shouldn't he? Everyone accused of a crime had the right to mount a defence. And in truth, Ford was glad Ganaway had people fighting his corner. Something about the case didn't sit right with him. Duncan was convinced they had their man, but everything Ford had seen so far told him Duncan was a sloppy detective. He took shortcuts. And for whatever reason, he had blinders on when it came to Micah Ganaway. As soon as they'd gotten the tip about his car being in the area, Duncan had latched onto the kid as a suspect and gone all out to fit the evidence to the crime rather than the other way around. And now he wanted to pin a second kidnapping on Ganaway as well.

But with Blackwood involved, it might not quite be the slam dunk Duncan wanted to believe it was. How long had Hallie been working on the case? What information did she have on that laptop of hers?

"Tell me, Hallie, why does the Richmond PD dislike Blackwood so intensely?"

She tilted her head to one side. "Don't you already know the answer?"

"I know *an* answer, but I want to hear your version."

"They don't like us because we shine a light on their mistakes. Uncover the issues they want to sweep under the rug, such as the fact that their former chief was a freaking child molester." Now Ford got his smile, but it was sly rather than sweet. "Tell me, Ford," she mimicked. "How many officers in the Richmond PD are still aligned with Chief Garland? How many rotten apples are still clinging to the tree?"

A question he'd asked himself many, many times. Even in New Orleans, they'd heard about the trouble surrounding the department and Chief Garland, and in all honesty, Ford hadn't wanted to work there. He'd liked his old job. He missed his old job.

So how did he end up as Duncan's sidekick?

Firstly, and most importantly, his sister needed his support, and she lived in Chesterfield, Virginia. Ford had applied for a deputy position at the Chesterfield County Sheriff's Office, and although he'd been offered the role, it would have meant a step down the ladder, career-wise.

Then Richmond's new police chief, Jerome Broussard, had heard of Ford's plans and given him a call personally. Would he be interested in a lateral move? Yes, the commute would be longer, but the pay would be better, and he'd keep his detective grade. Which meant that when Sylvie's divorce came through and the custody arrangements were finalised, it would be a hell of a lot easier to go back home.

Broussard had headed up the New Orleans PD before he was hired to clean house in Virginia, and Ford had a lot of respect for the man. At the start of Broussard's tenure, the NOPD had been rife with corruption, but through determination, diplomacy when required, and a general unwillingness to take shit from anyone, Broussard had built a culture of integrity. A real team. Ford had faith he'd do the same in Richmond, but the structural problems couldn't be fixed overnight. Not with officers like Detective Duncan hanging on by their fingernails.

"How many rotten apples?" He shrugged, not wanting to admit the depth of the problem to a woman who worked for the opposing side. "One or two."

She snorted. "And the rest."

"If you know the answer, then why ask the question?"

"Because I wanted to hear *your* version."

Ford liked this girl. Heaven help him, but he liked her. He blew on his Americano. Took a sip and stirred his granola, thinking. Blackwood got results, and from what he'd heard, those results were usually the right ones. They didn't have to play politics. Sure, they wanted to please their clients, but their founder was a billionaire—he wasn't going to lose sleep if one or two of those clients ended up disgruntled. Ford's partner, on the other hand, spent more time watching the news coverage than he did reviewing the evidence, and the media wanted someone—anyone—to hang for Vonnie Feinstein's disappearance. The talking heads shouldn't have influenced Duncan's actions, but they did. He longed for the accolades. Broussard had to be feeling the pressure too—the Feinsteins had donated a tidy sum to their congressman, and he'd called at least twice that Ford knew of.

"Hallie Chastain." Her name slipped from his lips before he could stop it, and she quirked an eyebrow. "Are you going to be a pain in my ass?"

"Probably."

At least she was honest. "Have you spoken with Micah Ganaway?"

"Yesterday."

"And do you think he did it?"

A poor PI would have said no. A lawyer would have said "no comment." But Hallie considered the question, then gave a one-shouldered shrug.

"Honestly? I don't know. I've only had the case for three days. But I do know that your case is thin as it stands at the moment." Couldn't argue with that. "I mean, he went for a walk, took some pictures, and had gardening equipment in his trunk."

"Don't forget the knife concealed in his glove compartment."

"He wasn't in the car when you found it, therefore it wasn't about his person." She made a noise like a game-show buzzer. "No crime."

"It's circumstantial evidence."

"Was there blood on the knife? Hair? Skin cells? Any other trace of Vonnie Feinstein?"

"No, but there was blood in the trunk."

She froze momentarily, and he realised he'd caught her off guard. That little snippet of information hadn't reached her delicate ears yet, probably because he'd only just heard the news himself. The forensics team had turned up a darkened spot on the very edge of the carpet. Preliminary indications suggested it was a bloodstain, although whose blood it was or whether it was even human were questions that still needed to be answered.

"Fresh blood?"

"It's still being tested."

"Micah bought the car second-hand."

"As I said, it's still being tested. Plus we found a footprint outside Vonnie's window from a size eleven sneaker. Micah Ganaway takes a size eleven."

"Did you match the print to a pair of shoes he owns?"

"We're working on that."

Hallie's turn to take a drink. This was the weirdest coffee date Ford had ever been on. Except it obviously wasn't a date, no siree, more of a...verbal duel.

"Why did you tell me about it?" she asked.

"That we found blood and a footprint? You'd find out from him in a day or two, anyway."

"But you told me today. Are you trying to help me? Or distract me?"

Truthfully, Ford had no fucking clue what he was doing. His sanity had taken a hike the moment he followed her to the table.

"I'm not trying to distract you." Now she had Ford off balance. "Ganaway should have somebody on his side other than Del Farmer."

"Do *you* think Micah did it?"

"I'm on the fence. And I guess I'm hoping that by throwing you a bone, I might get something in return."

Hallie smiled and held out the apple. Ford had to laugh.

"And deprive you of the only healthy thing you might eat today?"

"One of the muffins had blueberries in it."

"*One* of the muffins? If you work at Blackwood, why have you been exiled to the Grindhouse?"

"Maybe I was hoping a handsome cop would come in and charm me with whispers of inconclusive evidence and tenuous theories." She reached across and cupped Ford's cheek in her hand. "Plus maintenance is testing the emergency lighting system, and it was giving me a headache."

He removed her hand, but he didn't let it go. Nor did he break her gaze.

"You sure know how to sweet-talk a guy."

"Wait, aren't we meant to be at war?"

"I'm looking forward to the battle, as long as it's a fair fight."

And he truly was. Hallie was smart—their all-too-brief conversation had shown him that much. A breath of fresh air after Duncan's ham-fisted attempts at investigation. Three months as Duncan's partner, and Ford was already counting down the days until the man's retirement.

"I only want justice." When Hallie bit her lip and lowered her gaze, Ford's traitorous dick made its presence known. "But what if I like to fight dirty?"

"You already are. An apple? That's all I get?"

"It's all I have right now. But if you give me your number, maybe I'll throw you a bone sometime?"

"And maybe I'll throw you a nice, juicy steak."

Such as the eyewitness. Not a particularly reliable one seeing as she was only four years old, but an eyewitness nonetheless.

"You have more?"

"There's more," Ford confirmed. "But this isn't a one-way street. You show me yours, I'll show you mine."

"I want *everything*."

At that moment, Ford realised this case might just be the death of him.

5

HALLIE

What the heck had come over me? I'd intended to have a very serious and professional conversation with a man whom I should have disliked on principle. But instead, I'd lost my mind, gotten into a verbal altercation with a nasty-ass woman, and then spent twenty minutes flirting with my sworn enemy.

And I didn't *do* flirting, not outside of the office.

Back in my former life, I'd been forced to use seduction as a survival mechanism because if I didn't keep the men who raped me happy, there was a grave waiting with my name on it. Pouty lips meant fewer bruises. Fluttering eyelashes earned me food. Little touches allowed me alcohol to dull the pain. So when I finally escaped that hellhole after more than a year, even the thought of flirting with a stranger made me feel physically sick.

Except, it appeared, with Detective Prestia.

After the argument, I'd been momentarily at a loss as to how I should open the conversation. But then we'd shaken hands, and I'd felt it. A connection. A connection that shouldn't have been there, not in a million years, but I saw from the heat that had flared in Prestia's brown eyes that he'd felt it too. And then it hit me: use reverse psychology. Push him away and wait for him to get closer. He wouldn't leave, that much I knew, because if I'd been in his position, I couldn't have gone anywhere either.

And my spontaneous plan had worked. I'd reeled him in, and he'd gifted me a crumb of information.

Plus a whole lot of confusion.

And the headache I'd fibbed about.

"How did it go?" Dan called as I walked past. She had an office on the executive floor upstairs, but she spent half of her time at a hot desk in the Investigations section.

"Better than I hoped, I think."

"You think? Did you speak to Prestia?"

"Yes, but he didn't act like a Richmond cop."

"In what way?"

I told the story from the beginning but left out the whole touchy-feely-lingering-gazes part. That wasn't important to the case, right? "So he gave me his number, held the door open for me, and then dropped twenty bucks into the homeless guy's cup. I guess I owe him a tip."

"So give him a tip."

"But I don't have a tip."

"The bad thing about the Richmond PD is that it's still tainted, but for the moment, let's also view that as a good thing. Fifty percent of the staff are still bribable. And one of my pet snitches says that activity's ramping up around the Mila Carmody disappearance."

"They think there's a link?"

"The media thinks there's a link, so the police can't afford to ignore it. And I bet our file on Carmody is more comprehensive than theirs."

"But we never found her."

"We didn't, but they fired us while we were actively

following leads. I still say there was something off about the whole case."

"The family?"

I'd read the file from cover to cover half a dozen times, and although there were precious few leads present, there were also clues notable by their absence. Common wisdom said Mila had been taken through her open bedroom window, yet the maid-slash-nanny swore it had been closed when she put Mila to bed. And there were no footprints among the flowers outside. A tiny speck of blood had been found on the frame, but the DNA didn't match any known males.

Mila hadn't cried out, and in the kidnapper's silent escape, he'd managed to avoid the security cameras at the back and front of the house. The Carmodys' spaniel hadn't made a sound either, and apparently he *always* barked if a stranger came inside.

Also missing from the crime scene? Mila's beloved plush rabbit, a toy she'd adored so much it even wore matching pyjamas. Pink, always in pink. It had been Mila's favourite colour. Dan clicked files on her screen, and there she was. A cute little girl with wavy brown hair, grinning for the camera as she held a bunch of balloons. The picture had been taken at her seventh birthday party, held three weeks before her disappearance.

If the bunny had been on Mila's bed, then I could have seen her grabbing it and holding on as she was spirited away. But the bunny had its own bed—a four-poster, no less—and that was on the other side of the room. Had the kidnapper paused in whatever he was doing—binding her, gagging her— to let her fetch Biggles? Or had he known how much the bunny meant to her and picked it up himself?

"Yeah, the family." Dan leaned back in her chair. "Emmy got bad vibes from the grandfather. Said he was a skeevy son of a bitch, and I agreed with her, but he had an alibi."

And after that, we'd started looking at Mila's uncle, which was when her father told us our services were no longer required.

"You think I should share our file with Prestia?"

"Not the whole thing, not right away. If he's going to throttle the information flow, then we need to play that game too. Tit for tat. And you know what else you should do?"

Avoid drooling when the detective was around?

"What?"

"Toss the DNA profile from the Carmody case over to Valerie Jenest. See if she can do anything with it."

Valerie was a newcomer to the Blackwood team, a genetic genealogist that Emmy had met as part of Bradley's totally over-the-top Secret Santa project last year. Valerie acted as a consultant now, and Dan was right—we should ask her to go over the file. Advances in DNA technology since the time Mila vanished might shed new light on the sample.

"I'll call her."

"And there's another angle to consider. If the Carmody and Feinstein cases are linked, then what happened in between them? Let's assume whoever took the girls molested them and then killed them." My gut clenched at Dan's words. This was the part of the job I hated. Putting myself in the shoes of a psychopath, something Dan and Emmy were worryingly good at. "Five years is a long time for a man with those tendencies to lie dormant. How did he control those urges? Try speaking to Dr. Beaudin, see if she can help with a profile."

Dr. Rosalind Beaudin was another new hire, a psychologist and former profiler brought in to help staff with any mental health issues they wanted to work through, as well as assist with investigations when necessary. Now I had a to-do list that ran into double figures, but Dan wasn't done yet.

"And Nick uploaded the footage from his own cameras. He's a couple of blocks away from the Feinstein residence, but you never know. Plus Lara called around her friends, which must be half the people in Rybridge, and she's gathering up recordings as we speak. Nick promised to add them to the server this evening."

"I'll take a look when I get home."

Who needed sleep anyway?

"Shut your mouth, shut your mouth, shut your mouth. Stupid bird." Pinchy flew from the perch on top of his cage and landed on Mercy's shoulder, pirate-style. "Snack, snack, snack!"

He bobbed his head until she handed him an almond, and then we had a few moments of blessed peace while he ate it.

"How was your day?" I asked. "Is the pile of cash getting any smaller?"

She shook her head. "We issued two new grants, but... Well, I never realised this would be such a problem. The money grows faster than we can spend it."

Mercy and I had been roommates for six months now, although our initial meeting had been a little unconventional. How many roomies shared a history of sex slavery? Not in the same location—our captor had run quite the empire—but we'd experienced the same despair until a Blackwood team rescued us. They'd given us our lives back, and that wasn't all. The apartment belonged to Emmy and her husband, a man everyone just called Black, and they were letting us live there rent-free for two years so we could get back on our feet.

Not content with closing down the network of sex mansions, they'd gone after the main man and taken all his money and, I suspected, his life too. Forgive me if I struggled to shed a tear. Then, rather than hand the loot over to the government so they could spend it on new office furniture for the FBI or whatever, Emmy and Black had funnelled the cash into their charity foundation, where Mercy worked as an administrator along with our friend Cora, doing her very best to give the whole damn lot away.

"Maybe you should start a homeless shelter?" I suggested.

"We already did that."

"Yes, but it's in Colombia." That was where Mercy came from. "I'm thinking of a place near Blackwood HQ."

"Why there?"

I told her about this morning's meeting, and with Mercy, I didn't hold back. More than anybody, she understood what I'd been through in the house of horrors and why the way I'd behaved with Prestia was so out of character. The more I thought about it, the uneasier I felt.

"My therapist thinks that in time, I'll begin to feel comfortable around men again," she said. "For me, that won't happen anytime soon, but perhaps you're healing? It's a good sign that you weren't creeped out."

"I'm creeped out now."

"Buyer's remorse?"

"No, not that. More like... I don't understand why I acted that way. And if I don't understand it, then how do I stop it from happening again?"

"You said you'd been drinking coffee and eating muffins all morning? Maybe it was the caffeine? Or the sugar? How much sleep did you get last night? I make poor decisions when I'm tired."

Hmm... Perhaps Mercy was onto something? I'd been restless from thinking about the Ganaway case, and the first two coffees I'd ordered had been red eyes. Wasn't caffeine basically a drug? And drugs were bad, m'kay.

"Oh, hell. I'll have to give up regular coffee."

"Are you sure? That's a big step. Why don't you try cutting down to start with?"

"You weren't there. You didn't see what I was like. And I should quit eating so much sugar too."

"Does that mean you don't want the cocadas blancas I made for dessert?"

Uh, I definitely wanted the cocadas blancas. "I'll start my new diet tomorrow. Did you make dinner too?"

"Cora's grandma made empanadas and rice salad."

"I love her."

The best part about moving to Richmond was the new family I'd found here. Not only the team from Blackwood but Mercy and Cora and Cora's fiancé, Lee, and her brother, Rafael. Cora and Rafael's grandma, Marisol, and her boyfriend, Vicente. Bradley. Georgia and Xav. Izzy and her mom. Izzy had gotten rescued soon after us, but not before she'd been sold to a private buyer like a piece of meat. Mercy and I, we'd had others to lean on during our time in captivity, but Izzy had been all alone. Terrified. Six months on, she still couldn't leave the house on her own.

"Want to watch a movie afterward?" Mercy asked.

"As long as the movie consists of vehicles driving around Rybridge the night Vonnie Feinstein was abducted."

Mercy made a face. "Surveillance videos?"

"I have to."

"Good thing *I'm* not giving up caffeine. Here, take Pinchy while I get dinner."

"Hey, Pinchy. C'mere."

"Fuck you." He bobbed his head again, then flew across the room to my outstretched hand. "Fuck you, fuck you. Shit."

I didn't teach him to say that, I swear, and neither did Mercy. A beautiful African Grey, he'd come to us with most of the vocabulary, hardly any feathers, and a serious attitude problem. But he was smart. Potty training had been a breeze. The feathers had mostly grown back, and we were trying to teach him to be more polite, but the attitude still needed adjustment.

"Wanna watch TV, Pinchy?"

"*Beep-beep-beep.*" His imitation of the microwave was uncanny.

"That's what I thought."

"Snack?"

"You've had enough snacks already today."

"Asshole."

Tell me again why I adopted a parrot?

6

FORD

Four-year-old Amelie Buckler sat on the floor surrounded by big-eyed dolls dressed in cutesy colours. Dr. Debra Carey, a child psychologist with extensive experience in interviewing young witnesses, leaned back against the couch next to her, cross-legged, and Ford silently thanked Chief Broussard for vetoing Duncan's plan to interview Amelie himself.

As it stood, he was pacing the observation room, nitpicking every question Dr. Carey asked, and Ford sincerely hoped the one-way glass was soundproof.

"You said the man who took Vonnie was big?"

"Yes."

"What shape was he? Was he thin like Swiper? Or wide like Benny?"

"She should show the kid a picture of Ganaway," Duncan muttered. "Ask her if it was him. This is taking too long."

Ford blocked the man out and checked his phone again. Still no message from Hallie, but he took the opportunity to google Benny and Swiper and found they were characters from *Dora the Explorer*.

"Just big. Big like Gru. Big and black."

Big and black. That was the phrase Duncan had latched onto when they'd first spoken with Amelie on the day after Vonnie's abduction. Specifically, the "black" part, arguing that any man would seem big to a kid her age. Ford's counterargument that any man would look black in near-darkness had been met with a shrug as Duncan once again viewed the evidence through the lens of his own prejudices.

Amelie's initial statement was why he'd focused on Micah Ganaway as a suspect so early on, despite the fact that Ganaway stood only five feet nine with a build best described as wiry. Ford conceded that he could have been wearing a bulky jacket, but there'd been no blood, blonde hair, or female saliva on the only coat from his apartment that fit the bill. True, he could have discarded his clothing, but Occam's razor was looking pretty damn blunt at that point. Then Duncan found out Ganaway had once been charged with the distribution of child pornography, and as far as he was concerned, he had his man.

On the other side of the glass, Amelie picked up a doll and placed it in the toy bed on the table. Picked up another doll and laid it on the pint-sized couch opposite. Ford held his breath. She was recreating the crime scene, something Dr. Carey had been trying all morning to get her to do, but until now, she'd resisted.

The night Vonnie disappeared, her parents had gone to the theatre with a group of friends, and her regular babysitter, an eighteen-year-old student named Vikki Walton, had been on duty. Nothing out of the ordinary there. But at the last minute, another couple in the party, the Bucklers, had been let down by their own sitter and rather than letting them miss out on the show, the Feinsteins had offered up Vikki's services. A kindness that had led to Amelie being interrogated three times in as many weeks.

The little girl covered both dolls with blankets and tidied doll-Vonnie's hair. The two girls hadn't been close friends, but they went to the same church and sometimes saw each other at picnics and get-togethers. And when Amelie wouldn't settle alone in the guest room, Vikki had carried her through to Vonnie's room and tucked her onto the couch with a quilt and pillow. That was where she'd been when the man who took Vonnie climbed through the window.

At the end of September, the weather in Richmond had been unseasonably warm. The Wednesday before Vonnie disappeared, the Feinsteins' AC had developed a fault, and when the technician couldn't source the right part until the following week, they'd cracked the little girl's window open so the room wouldn't get stuffy. A fatal mistake.

As best as Ford and Duncan could ascertain, the intruder hadn't even noticed Amelie. He'd missed her bundled up in her shadowy corner. There'd been a partial moon that night, and the light would have allowed her to see his outline against the window on the other side of the room, but not necessarily vice versa. She'd been frozen in fear, still too scared to move or speak when her parents came to pick her up a little before two a.m. Now she was talking more, but would she reveal anything useful?

Amelie picked up a third doll, a boy dressed in black, and Ford noticed her hand was shaking now.

Dr. Carey watched her carefully. "Can you show me what the man did?"

"Why you ask me that?"

"Because we don't know."

"You don't know? You didn't be there?"

"No, we weren't there."

Amelie put the boy-doll down and stared into space, processing. She lived in a world where adults knew all the answers, and now she was being asked to provide them. A toy unicorn sat on the table, and she grabbed it, stood up, and walked around the room. She got distracted like this a lot, but she was doing her best.

"Where's my mommy?"

"Do you want to see her now?"

"Can I have a drink? Please?"

"What would you like to drink?"

"Milk. And a cookie? Please can I have a cookie?"

Somebody had prepared for that eventuality because a minute later, an assistant knocked on the door with a plastic cup of milk and a package of Oreos. Amelie twisted the cookies apart and ate the filling first while Duncan bitched that it was lunchtime and he was hungry.

"Why don't you go out and buy food?" Ford suggested.

"Because we're in the middle of the interview."

"They're recording it from two different angles, and I'll fill you in on whatever you miss." Plus he was serving no purpose by being here other than getting on Ford's last nerve. "Can you pick me up a sandwich?"

"Uh, yeah. Sure."

Ford handed his partner twenty bucks. "Take your time."

At least now he could focus on Amelie without feeling constantly on edge. He leaned forward as she lifted the boy-doll into the air where the window would have been, then walked him straight to the bed. Put his hand over doll-Vonnie's face. And waited.

And waited.

And waited.

"Did the man stand there like that?" Dr. Carey asked.

"Yes."

"Did Vonnie say anything?"

Amelie shook her head. "Not really."

Not really?

"Did she make any sounds?"

49

"Like *mmm-mmm-mmm*. But then she stopped."

"Did she move?"

"No."

The man wouldn't have killed her right then, surely? What would have been the point? Plus they'd have found evidence of that—her bladder and bowels would most likely have voided as her sphincter muscles relaxed at the moment of death. Yet she'd gone quiet. So...drugged?

"Did the man say anything?"

"Yes."

Holy shit, this was new.

"What did the man say, Amelie?"

"He said Vonnie was pretty."

"What words did he use?"

Amelie screwed her eyes shut, but she didn't cry, not this time. There'd been plenty of tears this morning, but she'd turned out to be damn brave for such a little thing.

"He touch her like this." Amelie demonstrated with the dolls, and rather than the sexual assault Ford had half expected —and dreaded—the intruder stroked Vonnie's hair. "Come on, my pretty."

She whispered the words, and that just made it even more fucking creepy.

"That's what he said? 'Come on, my pretty'?"

"Yes." A look of panic flashed in her eyes. "My mommy says I'm pretty. Will he take me now?"

"No, sweetie. Your mommy and daddy will keep you safe."

"You promise?"

"I promise."

"Because Mommy says you can't break a promise."

"I absolutely promise. What did the man do next? After he spoke to Vonnie?"

"He put her out the window."

"Did he drop her?"

Blank look.

"Did you hear a *thump*?"

"No."

"Can you show me how he held her? With the dolls?"

He'd used a bridal carry, then leaned out of the window and lowered her to the ground. Amelie squeaked in frustration because the boy-doll wouldn't bend in the right places, but Ford got the picture.

"And then he left too?"

"He went through the window."

"Did you see him again after that?"

"No."

"Did you get up and look through the window?"

"I didn't get up *at all*. Not until my mommy came." Now the tears were back, but she'd done well. "I go now. I want to go."

"We'll get your mommy, okay? She'll take you home."

"Will the man come?"

Ford sure hoped not. It was why they'd gone to such lengths to hide Amelie's existence from everyone but the tight inner circle of the detective's department. Broussard had threatened to shitcan anyone who leaked, and with a child's life on the line, for once the ship had stayed watertight. So why was he considering risking his job to tell Hallie?

He checked his phone again. Still nothing. Why hadn't he asked for her number in return? Because he'd been caught up in the moment, that was why. Ensnared by those big hazel eyes and a coy smile. He thought she'd felt the pull too, but what if he'd been wrong? Almost twenty-four hours, and she still hadn't gotten in touch.

On another day, he might have been tempted to go back to the Grindhouse, order a coffee, and wait. Although that might be classed as stalking. What if he called Blackwood? Could somebody on the switchboard patch him through? Would that come across as desperate? He was pondering his options when Duncan came back, and from the look on the man's face, he had something new.

Uh-oh.

Ford should have been fired up at the prospect of another lead, but instead, all he felt was an impending sense of trepidation.

"Guess who just called the tip line?" he asked.

"Who?"

"Micah Ganaway's old boss."

"From the fast-food place?"

"No, from five years ago. He runs a landscaping company, and whose home do you think was on his roster back then?"

Five years ago? There could only be one home that would have set Duncan drooling like Pavlov's dog.

"The Carmody place?"

Duncan clapped Ford on the back. "We'll make a detective out of you yet."

Asshole.

"Ganaway did yard work for the Carmodys?"

"Not on a regular basis, but sometimes the staff covered vacations and sick leave."

"So did Ganaway fill in at the Carmody home?"

"The guy couldn't remember, but he said it was definitely possible."

Possible. Yet another piece of circumstantial evidence, but to Duncan, it represented one more nail in the lid of Ganaway's coffin. Ford should warn Hallie. It wasn't quite the big juicy steak he'd promised her—it was more of a French fry —but she'd need to know the investigation was veering in that direction. Micah would have been, what, eighteen years old at the time? Barely more than a kid. Could he really have broken into a mansion, successfully evaded all security, snatched Mila, and gotten away with it? When Ford was that age, he'd been too busy playing football and partying to hatch something that complex.

His phone buzzed in his hand, and he didn't realise how much tension he'd been holding until it leaked out of him.

Unknown: I have a peach for you. H.

Hallelujah.

"What are you so happy about?" Duncan asked.

So the man did have an iota of observational skills, even if he chose not to use them most of the time.

"My nephew won a spelling bee."

Duncan just grunted, but at least he turned away. The smell of tuna filled the small room as he unwrapped his sandwich.

Ford: My favorite fruit. Meet me tonight?

Her reply was almost instantaneous. No more games.

H: Where?

A good question. Ford's place would be too forward, ditto for her place, plus that could come across as pushy. No way was he going to walk into the Blackwood offices, same as she couldn't go near the police department. Which left neutral territory. It was too cold for a stroll in the park, and they needed somewhere quiet to talk. So basically, that meant a restaurant.

But which restaurant? Too casual, and he risked looking like a tightwad, too expensive and he'd come across as a snob. Middle-of-the-road could be a minefield, especially when he hadn't lived in the city for long.

Easier to turn the question back to her.

Ford: What's your favorite restaurant?

H: Is that a good idea?

Shit, she'd gotten cold feet since yesterday?

Ford: We both have to eat.

In reality, the radio silence couldn't have lasted for more

than five minutes, but it felt like forever. Finally, *finally*, Ford's phone vibrated in his hand again.

H: Il Tramonto, 8 p.m. I've made a reservation.

He typed out *It's a date*, then quickly deleted it. It wasn't a date. It was a...business meeting? Not quite, but close.

Ford: I'll bring a banana.

HALLIE

I stared at the phone. *He'd bring a banana?* Was that a reference to my peach joke—the one I'd regretted making as soon as I pressed send—or was it a euphemism for something entirely different? I couldn't be totally sure, and my brain was struggling to function properly this afternoon. Caffeine withdrawal was a bitch, and so was I. I just couldn't help it. After I'd snapped at Knox, Dan had threatened to tie me down and pour espresso into me if I didn't lighten up.

When Prestia suggested dinner, I'd caught myself smiling for the first time all day. But the smile had quickly faded when I wondered what exactly dinner would mean. Not a date, surely? We didn't have that type of relationship. *Wait.* Wait, wait, wait. We didn't have a relationship, full stop. Did we? My palm prickled with the memory of his day-old scruff. During that conversation, the background had faded until it felt as if we were the only two people in the Grindhouse, the only two people in the world.

I couldn't afford a repeat of that. My sanity wouldn't take it.

But Prestia was right—we had to eat—and meeting him in

a restaurant was certainly preferable to, say, a cosy tête-à-tête in his apartment, an option I absolutely, definitely hadn't contemplated. So I'd called Giovanni at Il Tramonto and asked for my favourite table, which was tucked far enough out of the way to have a private conversation and public enough that I wouldn't be tempted to stroke the good detective, a move that wouldn't even have been a consideration until the events of yesterday. It was official: I'd lost my freaking marbles.

And now I had another problem. What was I meant to wear for a non-date at a reasonably upscale restaurant? Jeans seemed too casual, and a dress too...well...dressy. On a normal day, and by "normal" I meant one where my mind wasn't begging for caffeine and Detective Prestia wasn't hammering my synapses, I'd have simply worn a pair of smart pants, but because I'd gone crazy, I saw Bradley coming out of the second-floor kitchen with an empty vase and called him over.

"What's up, doll?" His face fell. "Is it the new drapes? You didn't like them?"

"What new drapes?"

"In your apartment. I hung them with Izzy on Monday."

That was how preoccupied I'd been—I hadn't even noticed. "Oh, *those* new drapes. They're amazing."

"You don't think the colour's too much?"

"Not at all." What colour *were* they? Whatever, it didn't matter—we were stuck with them now. "Uh, what should I wear for dinner at Il Tramonto with a guy who isn't really a friend and isn't really a business contact and definitely isn't a date?"

"If he isn't any of those, then why are you going?"

"He's kind of an...informant, I guess?"

"Is he hot?"

"What sort of a question is that?"

"He *is* hot! You're blushing. On a scale of skinny jeans to little black dress, how sexy is he?"

"Forget I asked, okay?"

"I never forget a thing." Bradley put down the vase and fished a glittery notepad out of his purse. "See? I write notes. Now, I think you went more scarlet than rose, which means he's lickable if not edible, so let's go with a dress."

What had I done?

"Maybe I'll just cancel."

Bradley gasped in horror. "Cancel? You can't do that. He'll be soooo disappointed. Do you have shoes? I'll bring shoes as well. You'll be here for a couple more hours, right?"

"Yes," I said weakly. No point in denying it. He'd hunt me down wherever I went. Honestly, I didn't know why it took the US so long to find Osama bin Laden—they should have just started a rumour he'd committed a crime against fashion and Bradley would have dragged him into Bloomingdale's by the beard.

"Fandabidozi. I'll fix your hair when I get back too."

"What's wrong with my hair?"

"What *isn't* wrong with it? Did you even use the coconut conditioning pack I left in your bathroom?"

"Uh, no?"

He tutted to himself and strode off, muttering. Okay, so there weren't many jobs that came with free makeovers as a perk, but some days, I simply didn't have the energy to deal with Bradley, and today was one of those days.

What a time to give up caffeine.

"Hallie... *Mi amore*." Giovanni shooed the maître d' out of the way and air-kissed me on both cheeks. "You look *bellissima*. Your date is a lucky man."

"Oh, I'm not here on a date."

"Then who is your friend? He works for Blackwood?"

It was a fair question. Giovanni had only ever seen me here with girlfriends or colleagues, and he liked to keep up with who was who at Blackwood on account of us getting a special discount. Emmy's lawyer, Oliver, was Giovanni's silent business partner, and he'd arranged the deal.

"No, he doesn't, he's, uh..." I couldn't tell Giovanni that Prestia was an informant. "He's just an acquaintance."

Giovanni gave me an exaggerated wink. "An acquaintance, *sì*. I will bring you *aperitivi*."

"It's not that kind of..." Oh, it was pointless arguing. One word from me, and Giovanni would believe what he pleased. "Thank you, but no alcohol for me. I don't want to end up with a DUI."

"*Sì, sì.*"

Far easier to tell people I was driving than admit the real reasons I avoided drinking. And I *did* have my car with me, so it wasn't a total lie.

Prestia was already seated at the table in the corner, and as I approached, he did that whole undressing-me-with-his-caustic-soda-eyes thing again, only this time, thanks to Bradley, there were fewer clothes to remove. I'd lost the jewellery and done my best to tame my hair into a ponytail, but there hadn't been much I could do about the dress or the shoes.

"I didn't realise it was this sort of occasion," Prestia said as he stood to greet me. I stuck out a hand before he could kiss me on the cheek. Better to start as I meant to go on, right? Although when he did shake hands with a bemused smile, he held on for so long that heat burned up my arm. "Should've worn a tie."

He, of course, had gone super casual in faded blue jeans and a T-shirt emblazoned with the logo of Le Roux's Seafood Shack, so now I had two choices—either die of embarrassment or brazen it out. And if I was going to die, I could have done that a year ago in a Florida sex mansion.

"Do you even own a tie?"

"Several, in fact."

"How about a proper shirt?"

A smile played over his lips. "What's wrong with this shirt?"

It was two sizes too small, and it showed every bump of his six-pack, not that I'd been looking or anything.

"I meant with buttons and a collar."

"Sure, I own a dress shirt. I even own a tuxedo. Want me to catalogue the rest of my closet, or are you going to sit down?"

Right. Yes, I should sit because now a man from the next table was looking at me too. Bradley had brought three little black dresses for me to choose from, and I'd picked out the one that showed the least cleavage, but it also happened to be the shortest, and the hem rose up my thighs as I sat. I'd planned to run home between work and dinner to find a pair of pants, but a client had called, and then a colleague had begun asking questions about a previous case, and there were emails, and now I was pressing my thighs together so I didn't accidentally flash my underwear.

A part of me, the cautious part, hated wearing this outfit. Two years ago, I used to dress exactly the way I wanted, and I'd have loved everything that Bradley offered, but now I preferred to avoid attracting attention, just in case it turned out to be the wrong sort again. I could easily have followed Mercy's example and opted for all things baggy. But the stubborn part of me knew that if I gave in to the fear, the men who'd made my life hell would win. And I refused to give the ones still living the satisfaction.

"Dainty little peach you have there," Prestia said once I'd settled into my seat.

Really? So this was how we were gonna start? When had he checked out my ass?

"One could say the same about your banana."

I had to credit him with having a hearty laugh, but once he straightened his face again, he nodded toward my purse.

"Touché. But I just meant you can't fit much in there."

Ah, right. I felt myself blush.

"I can fit the essentials." Phone, debit card, cash, gun, tampons, knife, keys, lip gloss. What more did a girl need? "And I'm assuming we're talking about metaphorical fruit, anyway."

"Aw, and here was I..." He reached into the pocket of the jacket hanging over the back of the chair and produced an actual banana. And not any old banana. No, this was a monster. "Here was I thinking you just wanted to get your five a day."

I'd promised myself that there wouldn't be any more Grindhouse shenanigans this evening, but Prestia sure wasn't making this easy. Fortunately, Giovanni chose that moment to deliver us glasses of Crodino, and I sipped the bittersweet drink to buy myself time. Something about Detective Prestia left me off balance.

"I should have checked you like Italian food," I said, still stalling.

"I'll eat anything."

"That's good to know."

Gah!

The case. I needed to focus on the case.

"You mentioned a big juicy steak before, but now you've downgraded to a banana. Does that mean the Feinstein investigation isn't going as well as you hoped?"

"I could make a meat joke there, but I'm not going to." Thank goodness. "The investigation is...difficult. Did your peach involve a hair salon? That colour looks good on you."

"Uh, thanks?" I was surprised he'd noticed, but he *was* a detective. Trained to observe and all that. "But no salon. I got my hair done at work."

Bradley had brought his box of tricks to my desk and foiled my hair while I ran computer searches. He'd tried to paint my nails too, but I'd had to draw the line somewhere.

"At work? You have an office barber?"

"He prefers 'stylist.'"

"I'm in the wrong damn job."

"You could always come over to the dark side. We have cookies and a basketball court."

"I prefer football."

"The LA office has a football team, plus they have better weather."

"Been there, done that, got the T-shirt." Prestia glanced down at himself. "Not this T-shirt. My California T-shirt came from Big G's Surf Store."

"You surf as well?"

"Not since I was a kid. We moved from LA to New Orleans when I was thirteen."

California and Louisiana—both places on my bucket list to visit. So far, my travels had taken me from Kentucky to Virginia via Florida, and I wished I could erase the Florida part from my psyche. And the Kentucky part too.

"What made you move to Richmond?" When I thought of the way he'd flirted, a hint of bile rose in my throat. Prestia wasn't wearing a ring, but that didn't mean much nowadays. "A woman?"

"Why do you ask that?"

"Because nobody aspires to work for the Richmond PD, and the city doesn't have the same kerb appeal as LA or New Orleans."

Prestia kept me in suspense while he swallowed half of his drink. *Add "frustrating" to his list of attributes.*

"It *was* for a woman, but not in the way you think. My sister lives near here. Down in Chesterfield. She's having a rough time at the moment, and she needs some support."

"I'm so sorry. Is she... Is she sick?"

"Just sick of her soon-to-be ex-husband, and she's stuck in Virginia while they fight over custody."

"That sucks. So you're here playing the good brother?"

"For a couple of years, yeah. Figured it'd be interesting to see more of this great country. Might've been more fun if her prick of a husband lived in New York, but it is what it is. And what brought you to Virginia? You're not from around here either, are you?"

Oh, why had I steered the conversation down this path?

"I got offered the job at Blackwood, and I took it."

"Don't see many female PIs around. What made you pick that field?"

"Mysteries always fascinated me. I grew up reading true-crime books, then I got addicted to podcasts. And women can solve crimes every bit as well as men, thank you very much."

"Not saying they can't. Where'd you train?"

"Here. I'm, uh, I'm still training now."

"And they've let you loose on the Feinstein investigation?" Prestia gave a low whistle. "Talk about throwing you to the wolves."

"Are you saying you're a wolf?"

"I can be. Depends on whether there's a full moon or not. But seriously, Hallie, this is a big case."

"You think I don't know that?" Now his attitude was beginning to grate. Although that wasn't necessarily a bad thing—better for the heat in my veins to come from anger than from stupid, dumb lust. "And for your information, it's not only me looking at Vonnie Feinstein. Blackwood works as a team. I'm just the one who drew the short straw and had to take you out for dinner."

Rather than getting defensive, Prestia merely chuckled. "You're cute when you get riled up, tenderfoot. If it makes you feel better, we can say I'm taking you out for dinner."

"If you keep calling me 'tenderfoot,' we won't be having dinner at all."

"Should I assume that 'peach' is also unacceptable?"

I tried to suppress a smile. "You should."

"Plum?"

"You can call me 'plum' if I can call you 'frappé.'"

8

HALLIE

P restia considered my offer for a moment. "Frappé? I can live with that."

Well, that backfired. Great.

"Can we get back to the reason we're actually here? The Feinstein case?"

"Sure." He held up his glass. "*Laissez les bon temps rouler.*"

"Huh?"

"It's French for 'let the good times roll.' The waiter's coming—know what you want to eat?"

I ordered chicken provolone I wasn't sure I'd be able to stomach, and Prestia picked grilled langoustines plus a salad. Next time—if there was a next time—I'd offer to meet somewhere that didn't involve three courses and...

"Wine?" Prestia asked.

I shook my head. "Just water for me."

"You don't drink?"

"I only drink with friends."

"Ouch."

That had come out harsher than I'd intended, but really, what were we? Just two people wishing to trade information about a particularly nasty crime. As soon as the waiter moved out of earshot, I got to the point.

"The Feinstein case—what do you have?"

"What happened to 'ladies first'?"

"I made an executive decision, and it's your turn."

He gave a wolfish grin. "For the record, that's not how I usually operate. But for you, plum, I'll make an exception. There's a possible connection between Micah Ganaway and another abduction."

"Mila Carmody?"

"I see you've been reading the papers."

And the rest. "What's the connection?"

"Micah Ganaway used to work for the landscaping company the Carmodys used." Prestia watched me carefully. "You weren't expecting that."

No, although I wasn't sure what I *had* been expecting. But when I'd asked Micah about Mila Carmody this morning, he'd flat-out denied knowing her, and Prestia's revelation sent a chill through me. Had Micah held back? If so, why?

"You mean MowTown Lawn Care?"

Prestia's turn to look surprised. "You know of them?"

"The Carmody file's been on my desk for months. I don't have a full caseload yet, and I like to read through the cold cases in my spare time."

"Blackwood worked on the Carmody disappearance?"

"Her father hired us."

"And yet you didn't solve the mystery."

Thanks for the reminder.

"The family didn't like the direction we were headed in."

"Which was?"

Nice try. "Ganaway would have been a kid back then."

"You think teenagers can't harm people? What about Harvey Miguel Robinson, Craig Price, Jesse Pomeroy?"

"I'm not saying it's impossible, just...statistically less likely. How long did he spend at the Carmody place?"

"That's currently unknown."

"Did he work on the Carmody contract at all?"

"Again, unknown. We'll be asking him those questions tomorrow."

"What time?"

"You're gonna try and beat us to the punch?"

"Of course."

Prestia barked out a laugh. "Your honesty's refreshing, plum, but the detention centre's closed to visitors on Sundays. Breadstick?" Dammit. He held out the basket, and I took one, just one, careful not to let our hands touch. No carb overload for me this evening, and no feeling up the detective either. "Plus we're still on opposing teams here. What've *you* got?"

"Fine, *frappé*." I had to play the game too. "Micah says he knows nothing about the blood in his trunk."

"Figures. Is that it?"

I folded my arms. The surveillance footage hadn't yielded any breakthroughs, but thankfully, I'd been able to find a ripe peach or two elsewhere.

"Give me a little credit."

"I'm listening."

"Since Micah knew nothing, I got in touch with the vehicle's old owner. Micah bought the car on August nineteenth from a man named Jack Lucking over in Wyndham." When I called Fenika, she'd told us where Micah kept his papers, and Knox had let himself into their apartment and rummaged through the kitchen drawer until he found the receipt. "Mr. Lucking says that a year or so ago, his wife cut herself on the edge of a saw blade while they were unloading the car after a trip to Home Depot. There's every chance the blood belongs to her and not Vonnie Feinstein. And that blonde hair you found... Guess what colour her hair is?"

"Blonde?"

"Blonde, but bleached. I bet when your lab takes a closer look, they'll find evidence of cuticle damage."

"I'm impressed."

"And I'm not done yet. Ever hear of a girl called Donna Metgood?"

"Can't say I have."

Neither had I until this morning. But thanks to the cyber geniuses who practically lived on Blackwood's third floor, her name had pinged onto my radar as I sipped my second cup of decaf. They'd created a program called Providence, which was basically Google on steroids. Ask it a question in plain English, and it trawled through the internet plus Blackwood's internal databases and came up with answers in the blink of an eye. Plus it used advanced AI to make connections that might take a human months to put together.

"Donna Metgood lived on the outskirts of Lewisburg with her parents, and just over three years ago, she vanished from her bed in the middle of the night."

Prestia dropped the breadstick he was eating onto a side plate and leaned forward. "You think there's a connection to Feinstein and Carmody?"

Providence had thrown it up as a possibility. "They disappeared in nice, low-crime neighbourhoods, and in all three cases, the perpetrators came in through the window. Donna's parents were asleep in the next room, and nobody heard a sound. The only evidence noted in the media was a size eleven footprint outside her bedroom window. As far as I've been able to ascertain, nobody was ever arrested, let alone charged."

"Gone without a trace."

"Not exactly. A hiker stumbled over her body in a forest near Fairfield six months after she vanished."

"So that's one big difference to the Carmody case."

"Is it? Just because nobody's found Mila Carmody's body doesn't mean it's not out there. Somewhere."

The waiter bustled up with our food, his cheery smile at odds with the heavy silence that had fallen over our table.

"I have the chicken provolone for you..." He slid the plate in front of me, then turned to Prestia. "And for you, the langoustines. Can I get you anything else? Some wine?"

Prestia answered for both of us. "We're good here."

"*Buon appetito.*"

We stared at our food. The chicken looked perfect, but I had zero desire to pick up a fork.

"Lost my appetite," Prestia muttered. "How'd you come up with Donna Metgood? That another Blackwood case?"

"No, not ours, but we began wondering what the person who took Mila Carmody had been doing for the past five years, and there she was. The disappearance was a big story in West Virginia, but it didn't make much of an impact here, even when her body was found. Can you get the file?"

Better to ask nicely than admit that I'd already put in a request with Mackenzie Cain, Blackwood's top cyber geek and the architect of Providence. She had ways and means of getting ahold of information, ways and means that Detective Prestia definitely wouldn't approve of.

He pondered for a few moments, no doubt trying to work out whether my suggestion had merit. He'd also have to work out a way of explaining the hot tip to Detective Duncan.

Finally, he nodded. "I can try."

The coil of anxiety in my gut loosened a smidgen. Deep down, I'd been afraid Prestia would brush me off, especially after his "tenderfoot" comment. But he believed me, and maybe, just maybe, that was the first brick in a foundation of trust between us.

"Thank you. Is that enough of a peach for you? Or do I

have to deliver the whole damn fruit basket before I get the steak?"

"The steak... The steak could cost me my job, so forgive me if I'm a little hesitant about forking it onto your plate. Do you have anything more? A pear? An orange? One of those spiky pink-and-green things that I have no idea what to do with?"

"A dragon fruit?"

"Yeah, one of those."

"Try blending it into a smoothie. But the pear and the orange will have to wait. I have a psychologist working up a profile and a genetic genealogist looking at the DNA sample, and the results will take time to come back."

"What DNA sample?"

"The one from the Carmody crime scene."

"How the hell do you have that?"

"Because five years ago, you could buy any low-level employee of the Richmond PD for a six-pack and a pretzel." So Dan said, anyway.

Prestia groaned. "Tell me that's changed?"

"Now it would cost NFL tickets and a month's worth of pizza."

"You're joking?"

"There's a reason why Blackwood's hospitality budget is so large."

"Sheesh. Although NFL tickets..."

"You're a fan?"

"I still have season tickets for the Saints, although I don't suppose I'll get to use them much this year."

"Blackwood has a box at the Washington Football Team's stadium. I could ask—"

I could ask myself what the hell I'm doing. But before I got that chance, Prestia was already shaking his head, and he looked *pissed*.

"I'm not one of the men you can bribe, no matter how short your skirt is. Let's get that straight."

Gee, thanks for making me feel like a whore.

"I wasn't trying—"

"If I think it'll benefit a case, I'll trade information on occasion, but I am *not* a corrupt cop."

"I didn't mean it that way, I—"

"Then how did you mean it?"

"I—"

"How, Hallie?"

"I just... I thought... Maybe I just wanted to spend some time together, okay? When I got near you, I felt as if I was on a roller-coaster ride—light-headed and slightly sick, but it was also fun and weirdly addictive. But now you've fixed that by acting like a jerk, so I suppose I should be relieved." I shoved my chair back and stood, all too aware that people were staring at me. "Some detective you are. You saw things that weren't there and jumped to the wrong conclusions, kind of like you're doing with Micah."

"Hallie—"

I hurled the banana at him, and it hit him square in the chest. "Go stuff that where the sun don't shine."

"Plum..."

"Don't you 'plum' me."

I rifled through my purse and dropped a hundred-dollar bill onto the table, then marched out of the restaurant as fast as I could manage on Bradley's stupid shoes. Graceful I was not. At least I'd parked my car in the basement garage, so I didn't need to run along the damn street.

"Hurry up, hurry up." I jabbed at the elevator button once, twice, three times. "Come *on*."

Prestia was heading toward me with a face like a winter storm, but the doors opened and I leapt inside. Pushed the button for the basement.

"Stay away from me!"

He checked his stride for a second, long enough for the doors to close. Then I was gliding downward, and my tears began to fall. This was such a mess. *I* was a mess. And perhaps Prestia had been right to call me a tenderfoot because I had no idea what I was doing. How the hell was I meant to explain this to Dan? To Knox? I needed to come up with an explanation fast because Giovanni would probably call Oliver, and he'd call Dan because they were friends, and for once, I hated the speed at which Blackwood managed to disseminate information.

I fished in my purse for my key, and the second I emerged into the parking garage, I bleeped my car unlocked. But then a loud *bang* sent my heart leaping into my throat, and when I wheeled around, Prestia was running out of the stairwell. Instinct took over. True, the last two times I'd been abducted, men had slipped drugs into my drink, but terror gripped me with eagle claws and I fumbled for my purse again, for something to protect myself—my switchblade, or the gun I'd spent so many hours on the range learning how to use—but in the panic of the moment, I pulled out a freaking tampon and aimed it at his chest.

"Stop!"

He skidded to a halt and stared, incredulous, then slowly raised his hands.

"You sure do know how to strike fear into a man's heart, plum."

9

FORD

After Hallie stormed out, it took Ford two seconds to realise he'd been an asshole. Eight years as a cop had made him quick to see the worst in people, and that comment about her skirt had been completely uncalled for. Which meant he needed to apologise, and quickly, because if he were in her impressively high shoes, what's the first thing he'd have done? That's right—block his number.

She made it into the elevator, but Ford ran five mornings a week, so the stairs would be almost as fast.

He was six steps away from her when she turned.

Then his chest seized.

Because what he saw in her eyes wasn't frustration or annoyance or even disgust, it was sheer fucking terror, and *he'd* been the man to put it there. She went for her purse, and if anyone on the street had done that, he'd have been reaching for the gun strapped to his ankle, but this was Hallie. *His pretty little fruitcake.* The way he'd snapped at her, he deserved everything he got.

And what he got was...a tampon?

"You sure do know how to strike fear into a man's heart, plum."

He meant that sincerely, because what if she never spoke to him again?

"I told you to s-s-stay away."

Shit, her voice was shaking as badly as her hands.

"I'm staying right here. Don't suppose you'd consider putting that, uh, weapon down?"

"Go to hell."

"I'll show myself to the ninth circle after I've apologised. Hallie, I'm sorry I jumped to the wrong conclusions. I'm sorry I bit your head off and wouldn't let you speak. And I'm sorry I disparaged your choice of clothing, especially when I think you look abso-fucking-lutely beautiful tonight."

She didn't move, didn't say anything, just stood there staring as tears left sooty tracks on her cheeks.

"Hallie, is there someone I can call for you? A friend?"

"No." It came out as a croak, and she tried again. "No."

"A cab?"

She shook her head. "I-I-I can drive."

"Will you wait here while I get my car? I need to know you get home safely."

"But then you'll know where I l-l-live."

"I'm a cop. I could find that information out in two minutes anyway."

"You're n-n-not meant to do that."

"We both know I break the rules from time to time. Hallie, I'm worried about you." She was still frozen to the spot, her gaze fixed on his chest rather than his face. Weirdly submissive, and nothing like the woman he'd been getting to know. "Plum, who hurt you?"

For a long minute, he thought she wasn't going to answer, but then her lips moved, the whisper barely audible.

"Everyone."

She sank to the floor, and he felt like the biggest dick in the world for putting three condoms in his wallet tonight. This evening hadn't turned out the way he'd expected at all.

Fortunately, he'd grabbed his sport coat before he left the restaurant, and now he shrugged out of it and tucked it around her shoulders. She let him help her to her feet. What next? She couldn't drive like this. Hell, she wouldn't even be able to see the road properly.

"Come sit in your car, okay? This way."

She'd dropped the key, so Ford scooped it up, then guided her to the Honda compact whose lights had flashed as he exited the stairwell. Her dress rode up as she slumped into the passenger seat, but she didn't seem to notice, and he wasn't about to risk tugging it down for her.

"Don't take me back there," she murmured, eyes unfocused. Her mind was somewhere else entirely. But where?

"The only place you're going is home, Hallie. You can't stay here in the parking garage all night. Should I call someone from Blackwood?"

"No!"

Well, that was emphatic. No friends, no colleagues. "In that case, I'm just gonna sit here with you until you feel better, okay?"

Ford settled onto the concrete and leaned against the car, facing into the cavernous garage. Watching for any visitors and also studiously avoiding getting an eyeful of Hallie's panties. How long would she stay upset like this? Not that it truly mattered; he'd sit here until morning if he needed to.

Ten minutes of quiet sobbing later, the elevator pinged, and the male who exited headed straight toward them, no hesitation. Security? Ford scrambled to his feet. The newcomer was wearing black pants and a dress shirt but no tie, and despite the steel-grey hair, he wasn't old. Ford put him at about thirty-five. He carried something in his hand. A phone?

"Move along, nothing to see here."

"The hell I will," he snapped back.

"I'm a cop with the Richmond PD, and everything's under control."

"I don't care if you're Chief Broussard himself. Why is Hallie upset?"

This guy knew her?

At the sound of her name, Hallie shifted in her seat. "Oliver?"

"What happened?" The man elbowed Ford out of the way, and he didn't argue. The last thing he needed tonight was another fight. Businesslike, the man reached out and pulled down the hem of Hallie's dress, then crouched in front of her. "Do you want me to call Dan? Black? Emmy?"

"I'm o-o-okay. There was a m-m-misunderstanding."

"A misunderstanding? Do you want this man here?"

Translation: should he try to remove Ford from the building?

She shrugged. Well, it was better than a straight-up "no," although she still wouldn't look at him. How had things gone so wrong, so fast? Half an hour ago, he'd been enjoying the battle of wits with the first woman to interest him since he moved to Richmond. A rival, yes, but she intrigued him like no other.

And then everything that was building between them had imploded.

Oliver turned to Ford. "Leave us for a moment."

An order, not a question, and his tone told Ford that he was used to being obeyed. But again, Ford wasn't going to quibble. And it was a smart move on Oliver's part—if Hallie was feeling intimidated, the space would allow him to find that out.

But Hallie's hand shot out and grabbed his.

"He can stay."

"You want to talk about what happened?"

She shook her head. "My past just crept up on me, that's all. I want to go home."

The next challenge.

"I offered to call her a cab," Ford told Oliver.

"Hallie doesn't take cabs." Oliver offered her a handkerchief, watched with concern as she wiped her face. "Sweetheart, I'd drive you myself, but Stef's having a rare night out, and I'm on Dad duty."

He glanced at the phone in his hand, and Ford realised it wasn't a phone at all; it was a hi-tech baby monitor. A picture filled the screen, a sleeping infant bundled up in one of those pyjama things with the feet. Hallie turned the unit so she could see and smiled for the first time since their aborted dinner.

"Aw, she's so cute."

"And also louder than I ever thought possible."

"How's Stefanie?"

"Happy, but exhausted. Even though we have Bridget to help, she's still trying to do everything herself."

"You should probably go back upstairs."

"Not until I know you're okay." Oliver looked up at Ford. "Can you take her home?"

"She didn't like that idea either."

"Sweetheart, either this cop sees you home, or I'll call a car from Blackwood. You can't stay here all night, and I don't think it's a good idea for you to drive yourself."

Hallie was still holding on to Ford's hand, and now her grip tightened, her fingernails digging into his palm. What was it to be?

"Ford can take me home." She finally met his eyes. "Will you?"

"Already said I would."

Oliver nodded once. "Good. I'm going to need your full name. Do you have a card?"

"Ford Prestia. Detective Ford Prestia."

Ford handed over a business card and got presented with one in return. The guy carried a supply in his pants pocket. *Oliver Rhodes, Attorney at Law.* Ford recognised the name if not the man. He'd made the national news for switching sides to prosecute not only a notorious serial killer but a problematic ex-DA.

"Don't tell Dan. Please, don't tell Dan," Hallie begged.

"As long as you get home safely, there's nothing to tell. Call me when you arrive." The baby cried, and Oliver cursed under his breath. "I need to go."

"Thank you," Hallie called as he jogged back across the garage, leaving the two of them alone again.

"I'm sorry," they both said at the same time.

"You have nothing to apologise for." Ford tried to flex his fingers. "But I'd appreciate if you could loosen your grip a little."

She let go as if she'd been stung. After yesterday's coffee at the Grindhouse, Ford had pegged her as a bon vivant, but now he realised it had all been an act. A fragile woman masquerading as a good-time girl. And what had she meant when she said her past had crept up on her?

That was a question for another day. Tonight, his priority was to get her home.

"How do you want to do this? I can drive your car, or you can ride in mine."

"If you drive my car, how will you get home?"

"Let me worry about that." He could walk back or take a cab if she lived farther away. And at least she'd have her car with her for the morning. "You need to swing your legs inside and put on your seat belt."

"I... Okay."

"Where do you live?"

"Over in the Fan." She managed a tiny smile. "South Plum Street."

Plum Street. Ford had to smile at that too. And it was a nice neighbourhood from what he'd seen so far.

"I should have guessed."

Once she was ready, he closed the door and got behind the wheel. Moved the seat back three inches and started the engine.

"You live on your own?"

"No, I have a roommate. Do you live far away? I don't recall seeing a Frappé Street."

"Around thirty minutes south of the city."

"In Meadowbrook? Bellwood?"

"No, in the River Bend Yacht Basin."

"Huh?"

"I live on a boat."

"That's...that's...interesting? Did the city run out of apartments?"

"Not a fan of boats, then?"

"I don't know; I've never been on one."

"*Never*? Not even one of those little pedal boats you find on lakes?"

"Nope. Why did you decide to *live* on one?"

Did Ford want to tell her the details? At least she'd settled into having a proper conversation again, and if they spent more time together, then she'd find out eventually.

And yeah, he *needed* to spend more time with Hallie Chastain.

10

FORD

"**M**oving onto the boat wasn't my original plan," Ford said. "It was a...toy. Two years ago, I was renting a nice Creole townhouse in the French Quarter with my ex, and the thought of living on the water had never even entered my mind. But then I began to notice signs that things weren't quite right. She started working late. Her phone was always on silent. She spent more time on her hair and make-up, but every time I suggested going out, she had other plans. She started doing the laundry..." Ford barked out a laugh. "And Eliette *never* did laundry."

"She was cheating?"

"I convinced myself I was imagining it all. *Wanted* to believe I was imagining it all. But one night, we were...you know...and she called me Aiden."

Ford put the Honda in gear and headed for the exit. South Plum Street was less than two miles away, so at least he'd be able to get the hell out of the vehicle soon.

"I'm so sorry. I mean, that's the shittiest thing to do."

And there was the pity he hated. In truth, he was better off without Eliette, and even when she'd begged him to come back, he hadn't considered it, not for a moment. The cynic in him said she'd only cried once the rent fell due and her paycheck wouldn't cover it. What about Aiden? Well, he'd turned out to be a work-shy art student from the University of New Orleans, and the relationship had fizzled out soon after he realised he might have to contribute something other than dick.

When news of the break-up had reached Ford, sure as hell he'd laughed.

"Yeah, well, that's why I moved onto the boat. At short notice, it was the easiest place to go."

"But you're *still* on the boat?"

"Getting rid of most of my stuff was weirdly liberating. Paring my life down to the bare essentials, drawing the line between what was important and what I'd only been holding on to because I was too stubborn to throw it out."

"I've bought it, so I'll keep it?"

"Exactly. I've realised I don't need much to be happy. And when the time came to move to Richmond, the simplest thing to do was sail my home here."

"Wait, it's a *sail*boat? With, like, *sails*?"

"No flies on you, plum."

"Shut up. You sailed here from *New Orleans*?"

"Me and a buddy, yeah."

"That must've taken weeks."

"About a month and a half. Would've been quicker if we hadn't spent two weeks bar-hopping in Florida."

The garage door rolled up, and they pulled onto the street. A light rain was falling now, and Ford managed to put on the turn signal and accidentally flash the headlights before he found the windshield wipers. Shit.

"Are you going to get an apartment here?" Hallie asked. "Or stay on the boat forever?"

"I guess I wouldn't mind being closer to work, but I don't

want to sell the boat, and finances would be tight if I rented an apartment too."

"You could share with a roommate?"

"I've grown to appreciate my own company."

They'd gotten most of the way to her apartment before she spoke again, and that pretty head of hers had obviously been working overtime.

"If you live on a boat, how do you take a shower?"

He burst into laughter, and she twisted to glare at him, indignant.

"What? It's a valid question."

"The boat has a bathroom."

Three, actually.

"Oh. What about laundry?"

"I use the washing machine."

"Hmm. Sounds like quite a nice boat."

She seemed surprised, and she'd probably be more surprised if she found out how much the *Shore Thing* had cost, but that was a story for another day. As long as she didn't start muttering about corruption again.

"It *is* quite a nice boat." Ford turned onto South Plum Street. "Which place is yours?"

"Up ahead on the right."

His turn to be surprised. He'd expected an entry-level PI to live in a fairly utilitarian apartment block, but the building she pointed at was seriously swanky. Either her roommate was wealthy, or private work paid more than he thought. A ramp led down to an underground lot like the one they'd just left, and he was grateful to see the red eye of a camera over the entrance. He'd sleep better knowing she had good security in place.

"Want me to ask the concierge to call you a cab?" she asked once he'd parked in her allotted space.

There was a fucking concierge? "I'll walk, but first I'm seeing you to your door."

"You don't need to do that."

"Yes, I do. All part of the service."

When she didn't move to get out of the car, he thought that perhaps he'd pushed her too far, that she didn't want him near her home. But it wasn't as if he didn't know her apartment number—it was written in front of her parking space.

Once again, he was wrong.

"Ford?"

"Yeah?"

"I'm sorry. Sorry for the way I behaved earlier."

"Forget about it. I deserved the dressing-down."

"I mean afterward. In the basement. If the gun had come out of my purse first, I'd..." She closed her eyes for a long second. "I'd probably have pointed it at you."

"You carry a gun?"

"I have a permit."

"And you know how to shoot?"

"Blackwood has a range, and I go at least twice every week."

"That's something, at least. Plum, why were you so scared? I swear I wouldn't have touched you."

"I know. But...but not all men are like you."

The way she said that turned Ford's blood to ice.

"Hallie, *did* somebody touch you?"

"Not today. I can't do this today."

Cop or not, Ford would fucking kill him.

"Tell me who, and I'll fix it. Shit, wrong word." He dragged a hand through his hair as Hallie climbed out of the car. "I know I can never fix it, but I can damn well make him pay."

"It's already been handled. Please, can we just stop talking about this?"

Handled by who? And then Ford realised: Blackwood. Suddenly, they went up in his estimation. Seemed renegades and vigilantes like Daniela di Grassi did serve a purpose after all.

But now he didn't know what to do with Hallie. How to *handle* her. Yesterday, she'd touched him, cupped his ugly mug in her hand and stroked his damn cheek. But today, she'd kept her distance. When she stood, he'd been about to steady her with an arm around the waist, but now he rethought that plan.

"We can talk—or not talk—about whatever you want. And rest assured that when I've delivered you safely back to your roommate, I'll leave, okay?"

She gave a quick nod, and Ford took that as agreement. Hallie lived on the fifth floor, and there were no crammed-together units here. When they stepped out of the elevator, he could only see two doors, and she headed for 501.

"So, uh, thanks for seeing me home."

"Anytime. I mean that."

"I'll call you if I find another peach, okay?"

She cracked the door open, but he hadn't taken two steps back when he heard a man's voice coming from inside the apartment, and it didn't sound friendly.

"Fuck you."

Ford's gun was in his hand in a heartbeat, and he pulled Hallie behind him before he burst through the door, scanning the room. Who the hell was inside her home? Had an intruder broken in? Been lying in wait?

"Shut up, stupid bird. *Beep-beep-beep.*"

"What the...?"

The lights were on, but all Ford could see was a scrawny parrot. And all he could hear was Hallie's laughter.

"Oh my... Oh my gosh..." She actually snorted. "You thought... You thought Pinchy was a burglar. I can't believe... This is the funniest thing *ever*."

"Snack?"

"Asshole," Ford growled.

"Mercy, Mercy, Mercy."

"No, Hallie." She closed the apartment door and crossed to the cage, opened it, and let the feathered fiend climb out onto her arm. "Mercy's my roommate," she explained.

"No Hallie, no Hallie. *Beep-beep-beep*. Snack?"

"You have a pet parrot?" Ford said, stating the bleeding obvious.

"No flies on you, frappé."

Oh, thank fuck. Her sense of humour had come back. There was hope after all.

"I figured you were the cute-fluffy-dog type."

"You know I can still shoot you, right?"

But she was smiling now.

"He's called Pinchy?"

"It's short for *pinche vato*. That's Spanish for—"

"Fucking dude." Ford nodded to himself. "Yeah, I can see how that suits him."

"Mercy named him. She comes from Colombia, so she speaks Spanish, although *pinche vato* is more Mexican."

Hallie opened a small plastic box on the table, took out an almond, and handed the nut to the bird. Flakes dropped onto the rug as he crunched it up with his beak.

"Who taught him to speak? Is he bilingual?"

"Trilingual. He's picked up a few words of Spanish since we got him, but whoever owned him before was responsible for his potty mouth."

"And what's the third language?"

"Pirate."

Sheesh.

"A second-hand, foul-mouthed parrot. You surprise me every day, Hallie Chastain."

"You only met me yesterday."

"And I bet you'll surprise me tomorrow too. What made you choose a parrot?"

"We didn't exactly choose him. Animal Control found him half-dead and took him to Hope for Hounds as an emergency case—that's a rescue centre for dogs—and when he began feeling a little better, he cursed out a group of elementary school kids there on an educational visit."

"Yeah, I see how that could be a problem."

"The teacher wasn't impressed. But Georgia, one of the volunteers, she knows Emmy Black. And I don't know if you've met Emmy, but she swears like the love child of a sailor and a trooper, plus she's fond of animals, and Georgia thought the two of them would be a perfect match."

"What went wrong?"

"Emmy's cat kept eyeing Pinchy up like he was lunch."

"That doesn't explain how he ended up with you."

"I met him at Emmy's place and thought he was funny. When I was a kid, I used to enjoy watching cartoons, and Iago from *Aladdin* always made me laugh, so I figured that maybe Mercy and I could take care of Pinchy while his feathers grew back. But now it looks as if he's staying. Don't you think he's cute?"

"What's not to love?" Ford couldn't keep the sarcasm out of his voice.

"Most of the time, he's no trouble, and he's been so good for Mercy. But I wouldn't complain if he stopped imitating the microwave. Here, you want to give him a nut?"

Ford took the almond and gingerly held it out. Pinchy leaned forward and grabbed it with his talons.

"What do you say, Pinchy?" Hallie asked.

"Asshole."

Ford had to laugh. "You're welcome."

"You should be honoured—he only calls people 'asshole' if he likes them."

"Don't shoot Mike," the bird squawked, sounding decidedly female this time. "*Pew-pew-pew.*"

"Who's Mike?"

"Who knows? But Pinchy's a big fan of CSI, so he probably heard it on TV. Plus he can sing several lines of 'Jolene,' so I hope you're a Dolly Parton fan."

Did that mean Hallie planned on Ford spending more time around Pinchy? He sincerely hoped so because that meant he'd be here at the apartment, and she would be too. Although it didn't look particularly lived-in. The vast great room was spotless apart from the remnants of food on the floor around Pinchy's giant cage, and painfully neat too. The furniture looked new—pale-grey leather couches, a fluffy cream rug under a glass coffee table, filmy drapes in a light shade of purple. Fresh flowers on a sideboard. Abstract art on the walls. The mother of all flat-screen TVs hanging above a stainless-steel fireplace. It reminded Ford of his father's home —tasteful yet soulless—although the parrot did add a certain something.

"Maybe I should try teaching him about the musical genius that is Bruce Springsteen? Got another nut?"

Hallie passed one over, and this time when Ford held his offering out, Pinchy took off and made a jerky circuit of the room before landing on his shoulder.

"Ahoy, Cap'n. Arrrr. Snack?"

"He's cute in a cantankerous kind of way. Glad you're not a fluffy-dog person, plum. The parrot's more fun. Can you say 'dipshit,' buddy? Go on, say 'dipshit.'"

"Asshole."

"Guess we'll have to work on that." That drew a half-smile from Hallie, but now she looked nervous again. Why? Had

Ford overstayed his welcome? "You want me to leave? I never meant to stay."

"I was... Uh..." She moved to shove her hands into her pockets, but she didn't have any pockets in the dress, so she clasped her hands together instead. "Actually, I was wondering if you'd like coffee? I owe you dinner too, but I'm not a great cook, and I'm not sure if I could even stomach food tonight, but..."

"For the avoidance of doubt, we are talking just coffee here? Not coffee as a euphemism for anything else?"

Her look of absolute horror gave him his answer. "Just coffee. The drink. Nothing else."

"Hey, don't back away. You never need to back away from me. If you want space, stand your ground and tell *me* to move."

Hallie stopped in her tracks. "I don't know what's wrong with me today."

"You got shaken up, that's all. Want me to make the coffee while you take a load off?"

"I...uh..."

"Yes or no, Hallie."

She bit her lip, which did nothing for Ford's self-control, then gasped and gave her head an emphatic shake.

"No. No! What was I thinking?"

"That you wanted a coffee?"

"I'll make it. I always make the drinks. *Always*."

She bolted into the kitchen before he could say another word. What just happened?

11

HALLIE

Had I lost my damn mind?

Ford Prestia had offered to make me a drink, and I'd actually considered accepting. And I *never* took food or drink from people I didn't trust. In the evenings, I frequented two restaurants—Il Tramonto and Rhodium—because Oliver part-owned them, and I knew he got Blackwood to vet the staff. If I wanted a night out, the only club I'd go to was Black's, and that was because it belonged to Emmy. I always went with friends or colleagues, and even then, I didn't take my eyes off my drink.

Prestia was a virtual stranger.

He was in my apartment.

And for reasons I didn't understand, I hadn't totally freaked out yet.

I'd gone through every possible emotion this evening, and now I settled on bewilderment. Ford Prestia was in my living room with my parrot. Take a load off, he said, but I had so much nervous energy I couldn't bear to sit down. I didn't bring men home with me, and if Mercy saw him here, she'd freak. I grabbed my phone and typed out a quick message.

Me: Any idea what time you're coming back tonight?

How soon would I need to get rid of Prestia? The reply appeared almost immediately.

Mercy: I'm going to stay over—Bradley's here, and we're having a movie marathon. Want to come? We made obleas.

By "here," Mercy meant Cora's place, and although thinking of obleas—crispy wafers filled with dulce de leche and jam—made my mouth water, I couldn't face the idea of Bradley's boundless energy this evening. Not when I wanted to curl up and cry.

Me: Thanks, but I'll pass. Need to sleep.

I filled the kettle and set it to boil. Until a month ago, we'd had a pretty red stove-top kettle, but since it would only have been a matter of time before Pinchy copied its whistle, we'd packed it away in a cupboard and bought a shiny silver electric kettle instead. It took ages to boil, but at least we wouldn't need earplugs.

Why didn't I just use the coffee machine, you ask? Because at some point over the past three days, our old drip machine had vanished, and in its place was a small spaceship. At least, that's what it looked like. I couldn't even work out where the beans went. At this time of night, instant decaf was the way to go.

I spooned granules into two mugs, wondering what to say to Prestia. I couldn't just ditch him. After everything that had happened this evening, he was still with me, and that in itself was a miracle. Never had I been so grateful for Pinchy's big mouth. He was carrying the conversation for me. Even now, I could hear him cursing Prestia out in the living room.

Why did I feel so uncomfortable with Prestia here? So out of sorts? Knox often came over for dinner, as well as Ryder, who worked in Special Projects with him, plus Kellan, who'd started in Investigations a month before me. But they all knew about my past, about Mercy's past, and they stayed on their best behaviour, probably because they'd have Emmy or Rafael to answer to otherwise.

But Prestia... He didn't know the rules. Didn't even know there *were* rules.

And even if somebody enlightened him, how could he be expected to stick to them when I'd already breached the "no touching" edict myself?

I had no idea what to anticipate next, and that left me jittery.

"Do you take sugar?" I asked. Prestia was standing by the window, looking out at the street below. "Milk? Cream? Uh, I don't even know if we have cream. Maybe half-and-half?"

"Black is fine. Did you call Oliver?"

"Uh, no." Dammit. "I'll do it now."

"Need a hand with the drinks?"

"I'm okay."

But once I checked in with Oliver, then poured the water and tried to pick up the mugs, I found I wasn't okay at all. My hands wouldn't stop shaking.

"Actually, could you just..."

Prestia picked up both mugs and carried them through to the living room coffee table with Pinchy still riding on his shoulder. I had to hand it to the bird—at least he had taste. When Prestia settled onto the couch, I paused to watch him for a moment. Despite the drama, he'd been good to me. Treated me well. Shared snippets about the investigation and acted like a gentleman. And now I had a decision to make.

Did I make the easy choice? Keep him at arm's length for the remainder of the case, then back away? Or should I let him in? Explain why I'd melted down tonight and hope he understood? Blackwood had done their best to clean up my past, to make sure the dirty details were swept under the rug, never to see the light of day, but even they couldn't erase an entire police investigation. If Prestia dug deep enough, he'd be able to find little threads.

When it came down to it, the question was simple—did I want him in my life?

And the answer...was yes.

Which meant I had to tell the truth. If not the whole truth, then most of it.

"Penny for them?" he asked.

"We need to talk."

"Now I'm worried."

That made two of us. "*I* need to talk."

"I'm listening."

I couldn't sit. I couldn't look at him. Instead, I took his spot by the window and stared at my reflection in the glass. I'd put on weight since I came to Richmond, filled out a little, and I liked my face better now. Before, I'd been gaunt. During my time as a prisoner in Florida, nervous energy had consumed every calorie I ate, and I'd felt too sick to face food most of the time.

"Earlier, you asked what made me become a PI, and I said because mysteries had always fascinated me. Which wasn't a lie, but it wasn't the whole truth either." I took a deep breath. "When I got accused of murder, the police refused to investigate properly, and I had no choice but to take matters into my own hands."

"Well, shit. That wasn't what I was expecting."

"Asshole," Pinchy put in. Thanks, dude.

"And what *were* you expecting?"

"I figured an ex knocked you around, and that's why you get jumpy. Who'd they think you killed?"

"A property developer from Kentucky. A guy I'd never even met until I woke up next to his body."

"What the hell...?"

"The killer drugged me. Drugged me in a club and

arranged my unconscious body next to a dead man to frame me. I guess that's why I find it easier to give Micah Ganaway the benefit of the doubt—because I know how it feels to be accused of a crime you didn't commit."

Prestia nodded toward my untouched mug. "And also why you make your own drinks."

"Right."

Perceptive, wasn't he?

"Sheesh. After what happened in the garage tonight, I knew you'd had a difficult past, but I didn't realise it was *that* bad."

"Oh, it gets worse."

I took a steadying breath. The only way I could talk about this, put the nightmare I'd lived into words, was to...kind of detach from my own mind. Otherwise, the breath stuck in my chest and I struggled to get enough air.

"The downside of doing everything yourself is that it costs money. Gas money, phone call money, lab testing money. So I had to take on extra work to pay for everything."

"What job did you do back then?"

"I was a waitress in a shitty diner. But I answered an ad looking for event staff, and the interview went real well. The guy hired me on the spot, even offered to give me a ride to the hospitality gig he wanted me to waitress at, and I woke up in a Florida brothel."

"A *brothel*? He drugged you?"

"Of course he freaking drugged me! You think I'd have gone there voluntarily?"

"No, but *fuck*." Now Prestia stood, took a step toward me, and then stopped. "Shit, I don't know what to do."

Join the freaking club.

"Welcome to my life."

12

HALLIE

Prestia looked genuinely distressed, which made me feel better about my decision to share. At least he didn't blame me for letting my guard down—twice—or try to brush off what had happened as a tall tale. When I'd gone to speak with the police in Kentucky, sixteen months after they first issued a warrant for my arrest, they'd accused me of engineering the whole "escapade" to evade charges. Black and Oliver had soon set them straight, but there'd been a terrifying moment when I thought the sergeant was going to march me straight to jail.

"I'm so sorry that happened to you. I'm so sorry that the Kentucky cops treated you that way. I'm so sorry that a bunch of assholes with dicks took advantage of you in the worst possible way."

Pinchy latched onto a familiar word. "Asshole."

"Shhh," I told him.

"Shut up, stupid bird."

At least he helped to lighten a heavy moment. "I used to be real outgoing. Happy hour was my favourite time of day, and I'd make friends with anyone. But now... Now, I second-guess everything. Is that man safe to sit next to? Should I touch this drink? What if that cab driver's a closet psychopath? I do my best to hide my nerves and act normal, and most of the time I pull it off, but then sometimes... sometimes my shields break down, and then...well, you already know what happens. Other than colleagues, you're the first man I've tried having dinner with since all the problems started, and I thought it would be okay—hoped it would be okay—but it was too soon."

Prestia met my gaze. Held it. "Thank you for trusting me enough to tell me your story. And one day, I'd like to take you out for dinner again, but only when you're ready."

I'd held the tears back for as long as I could, but his sweetness was my undoing. Salty rivulets tracked down my cheeks, and I didn't know whether to run or hide or brave it out.

"I'm such a freaking mess tonight."

"Normally I'd offer a hug, but I don't suppose that'd work too well. I have a handkerchief?"

"Thank you."

"Snack?" Pinchy asked, and a hysterical giggle burst out of my throat.

"Can he have another almond?"

"Sure."

"I'd offer to cook you a meal, but I see how that wouldn't work either. How about I order a pizza?"

"A pizza?" I wiped my eyes and stared at Prestia. "You want to eat pizza? I figured you'd run out the door the first chance you got."

"I'm not going anywhere, plum. Not unless you want me to, that is."

Did I want him to leave? When I took a moment to consider the question, I was surprised to find that no, I didn't.

Even though I was a snotty, teary wreck, I wanted Prestia to stay.

"It's up to you."

"What toppings do you want on your pizza?"

"I...uh...anything."

"Why don't you pick out a true-crime documentary while I put in the order?"

"A documentary?"

Now he wanted to watch TV?

"You look pretty much talked out to me, plum, and sitting in silence isn't really my thing."

How did he understand me better than I understood myself? It was a question I pondered as I nibbled on the edge of a deep-dish pizza with everything and half watched a deep dive into the psychology of the Golden State Killer. Prestia seemed relaxed, sitting next to me with his legs crossed at the ankles, focused on the TV rather than on me and my shortcomings. And slowly, slowly, the stress that had exploded from every pore earlier began to simmer down. It was unexpectedly nice having him there. Just *being*. As if we were two regular friends meeting up for death and dinner. And after the show had finished, Prestia deposited Pinchy onto his perch and tidied away the trash. He hadn't struck me as the domesticated type, and yet there he was, loading our mugs into the dishwasher.

"Will you call me tomorrow?" I asked.

"About the Feinstein case? Or just call you, call you?"

"I meant about the case, but I wouldn't object if you...you know."

"Called to shoot the breeze?"

"Something like that?"

He stepped closer, not crowding me, but his proximity made goosebumps pop out on my arms. My feet wanted to run, but I forced myself to stand my ground the way he'd told me to earlier.

"If I asked you to move back, would you do it?"

"This makes you uncomfortable?"

"A little."

"Try it and see."

"Can you give me more space?"

He stepped back in an instant, and relief coursed through me. But then I steeled myself and took a pace forward, closing the distance again. When he raised an eyebrow, I gave him a tight smile.

"I can't be scared my whole life."

His smile was wide and genuine. "So... Do you wanna do this again?"

"You mean sob my eyes out? Or TV and pizza?"

"Maybe we could try Chinese next time? A nice show about Jack the Ripper or Jim Jones... Something light."

"When?"

"Tomorrow?"

I found myself wanting to, but...

"I can't. This isn't me blowing you off, honestly, but Mercy will be home, and she came to Richmond from the same place as me."

"You mean the house in Florida?"

"They actually took her to the North Carolina branch, but—"

"Wait, you're telling me there was more than one of these places?"

"It was a small chain."

"Fuck me."

"We already established that was off the table, remember?"

Prestia scraped a hand through his hair. I'd noticed him do that once or twice when he got stressed, and the tousled effect made my heart skip in ways I couldn't explain. Ways I didn't want to explain.

"How many?" he asked, his voice hoarse.

"How many houses? Or how many women?"

"Both."

"Five houses. Hundreds of women, too many to count. Some died, and some were sold into private ownership, and they're still unravelling the details. It'll take years."

"Sold? Like fucking slaves?"

"Exactly like slaves. My friend Izzy, she got rescued, but she's doing the worst out of all of us."

"All of you?"

"Me, Mercy, Izzy, and Cora. Cora's bounced back real well. She's the strongest, plus she was there for the shortest time."

"How long were you there, Hallie?"

"About fifteen months."

Prestia slumped against the wall. "Fifteen months? Fifteen months and nobody looked for you? Nobody knew you were being held against your will?"

"The FBI knew, it turned out. But they wanted the man at the top, so they just...left us there."

Now Prestia looked positively stricken. "They *left you there*? Had they lost their fuckin' minds? Who? Who was in charge? Give me a name."

"It's been dealt with, okay? It's been dealt with. And we're doing okay, the four of us. We have homes. We have jobs. We have a support network."

"Blackwood?"

"They've been there for us every step of the way."

"How did they get involved, anyway?"

This was where I had to pick my words carefully. Blackwood protected me, and I'd always protect them.

"They were hired to find Cora, and I'd become friends

97

with Cora while she was in the Florida house. Then, after we were freed, they kept on helping. They're good people, despite what your colleagues might have told you."

"I understand now why you have such a low opinion of law enforcement."

"Cops haven't done me any favours over the years, that's for sure. Come to think of it, I'm not even sure why I like you."

The tension in his frame eased. "But you do like me?"

"Maybe."

"You do."

"Okay, I do. And when Mercy spends another evening out, I'd love to share Chinese with you, but she doesn't have much of a social life either. We're both still taking baby steps."

"If you ever feel inclined to take a slightly bigger step, you could come and visit with me on the boat. It's too cold to sit out on deck at this time of year, but there's a TV in the saloon."

"That might be a step too far at the moment."

"Figured it would be, but the offer's there, and it's not gonna expire." Prestia broke into a smile. "I like you too, plum."

I couldn't believe I was about to ask this, but, "Is that hug still on offer?"

"I'm the king of hugs, so my niece tells me."

Be brave, Hallie. Prestia opened his arms, and I stepped into them. Gingerly touched my hands to his back. He brushed my hair away from my face and arranged it so it hung between my shoulder blades in one smooth curtain, then wrapped his arms around me. And instead of feeling trapped, I felt...safe. Protected. I'd seen that guarding instinct when he leapt to save me from Pinchy, and now I breathed it in. The earthy scent of man with a hint of cologne. I laid my cheek against his shoulder. How long would it be reasonable to stay there?

"How old is your niece?" I mumbled.

"Five. And my nephew's three."

"Do you see them often?"

"Every weekend, plus evenings when I can. I'll spend the afternoon with them tomorrow after we wrap up with Ganaway. But yes, I'll call you first."

"If I don't answer right away, I'll call you back. I'm going to go door-to-door around the Feinstein house."

"On a Sunday?"

"As I said, I don't have much of a social life, and Blackwood works twenty-four-seven."

"Promise you'll be careful. Are you going alone?"

"Not totally on my own. Dan, Knox, and Kellan will be in the area too. Somebody saw something; we just have to find them. Plus there's a woman we want to look for. She was in three of Micah's photos, and her head was turned in the direction of the Feinsteins." Agatha, Mack's sidekick, had run downstairs with her laptop to show me while Bradley was chopping the split ends off my hair. Three photos taken over the course of a minute, each with a dark-haired woman and her dog in the background. Vonnie and her mom appeared in five pictures in total, although the focus seemed to be on the sunset rather than the people meandering through the shot. "There could be an innocent explanation, but we still need to get to the bottom of it."

Sure, she could simply have been taking the pooch out for its evening exercise, but we all knew a dog made the best cover if you wanted to perform surveillance unnoticed. Dan often borrowed one of Emmy's pets, plus there'd been talk of adopting a departmental support dog to assist on jobs.

"It wasn't a woman who took Vonnie," Prestia said.

"How do you know?" I loosened my arms and pulled

back far enough to look him in the eye. "Women are just as capable of evil as men are. The ring your chief was involved with—"

"If you're talking about Garland, he was never my chief."

"Okay, the Richmond PD's chief, the ring he was involved with used women for some of their dirty work. And a little girl probably wouldn't have been so scared if her abductor was female."

"It was a man."

"You don't—"

"We do." Prestia closed his eyes for a second, and when he opened them, he avoided looking at me. "There was a witness. Fuck, there was a witness, and if anyone finds out I told you, I'll lose my job."

"A witness? A freaking witness?" I wriggled out of Prestia's embrace. "There was a witness, and you're only telling me this now?"

"Shh, shh."

"I won't... I can't..." Fuming, I paced across the room. "You kept this from me. You kept this from *everyone*. What did they see? Did they see Ganaway? Is that why you and Duncan are gunning for him?"

"Firstly, it's Duncan who's gunning for Ganaway, not me. And secondly, quite apart from the fact that I'll be unceremoniously fired if the department finds out I'm leaking to Blackwood, the witness is a terrified kid."

"A kid?"

"Four years old. We don't know who this guy is, or where he is, but if he sees her as a loose end..."

The fight seeped out of me. A child. Another child wrapped up in this awful affair.

"It won't leak farther than Blackwood, I swear. Our team's watertight."

"Fuckin' better be."

I cupped Prestia's face in my hands. "You can trust me. I promise you can trust me."

"Okay." He raked his fingers through his hair again, then rested his hands over mine. "Okay, but remember trust goes both ways, plum."

It did. Prestia was absolutely right, and in two days, he'd done more to earn my trust than most men did in a lifetime. This guy wasn't about to drop a roofie into my drink.

"What's your favourite Chinese food?"

"Huh?"

"Answer the question, frappé."

He twined our fingers together and dropped our hands to his sides. "Crispy beef with steamed rice, egg rolls on the side."

"Then that's what I'll bring you when I come to your boat."

"You'll come to the boat?"

"You said the offer was always open."

"And it is. When do you want to come?"

"Tomorrow?"

"I'm having dinner with Sylvie tomorrow. My sister."

"Monday?"

"You want me to pick you up?"

"I'd rather drive myself."

"Then I'll send you directions." His voice hushed to a barely there whisper, and he trailed a fingertip down my cheek. "You're not the only one on a roller-coaster ride, plum."

That night, I barely slept. Prestia's feather-soft touch still burned into my cheek like a brand, and every time I closed my eyes, I saw his face. What was I doing? I honestly had no idea, but last Friday in the Grindhouse, when I'd laughed and flirted with a virtual stranger, I'd caught a glimpse of the girl I used to be. I liked that girl. I wanted to be her again. And if Prestia was the key to finding myself, then I wanted him too.

In the morning, I almost cracked and drank caffeine again. And maybe it wouldn't have been so bad if I did? My behaviour around Prestia couldn't have been entirely due to its effects because I'd felt that hop-skip-jump again yesterday evening.

I poured myself a mug of decaf, then jolted and slopped half of it onto the floor when the intercom buzzed. Was Mercy expecting a delivery? We never got visitors this early.

"Hello?"

"Ms. Chastain? It's Bernie at the front desk. A gentleman just left a package here for you."

I *definitely* wasn't expecting a package.

"Did he say where it was from?"

"No, but it smells like a croissant."

It wasn't a croissant; it was a Danish. A plum freaking Danish. How long had it taken Prestia to find that? He'd also left a decaf cappuccino and stolen a tiny piece of my heart.

Ford Prestia, what the hell am I meant to do about you?

13

HALLIE

A string of curses slipped from Dan's mouth as she shook her head in disbelief.

"A kid? There was another kid in the room? Fuck, she's gonna be traumatised for life."

How could she not be? "A fifty-fifty chance of being kidnapped. She lived, and her friend died."

"We don't know for certain that Vonnie's dead."

"If an abducted child is going to be killed, then eighty-five percent of the time, it happens within the first five hours."

"*If* a child is going to be killed."

"Almost every child is killed within the first twenty-four hours."

"*Almost* every child."

"But there haven't been any ransom demands. You really think Vonnie could still be alive?"

"Honestly?" Dan leaned back in her swivel chair. "It's extremely unlikely. But in this job, you can't afford to close your mind to any possibilities. Do that, and you might as well go join the Richmond PD. If it was up to them, Ethan would still be locked up in a supermax, and the man who nearly killed me would be out there trying to beat Samuel Little's murder record. And if the cops in Kentucky had gotten their way, where would you be?"

"Okay, okay, point taken. But I don't think Prestia's as short-sighted as Duncan and his buddies."

"Prestia this, Prestia that. The two of you seem quite pally."

My blush told her what my silence didn't. Why did my boss have to be a freaking detective?

"Oh, so you like him?"

"I... I... I'm mostly confused."

"In what way?"

"Generally, I don't like cops—the reasons are freaking obvious—so I *shouldn't* like Prestia. And I definitely shouldn't like Prestia in the middle of a kidnap investigation where we're on rival teams."

Dan just laughed. "You think that's awkward? Try falling for the suspect in the middle of a murder investigation."

I hadn't worked for Blackwood at that point, but I'd heard the stories, and yes, Dan had done exactly that.

"Okay, you win. But what should I do?"

"Are you asking for company policy? Or my personal opinion?"

"Both."

"Blackwood's policy is 'don't screw up the case.' My opinion..." Dan paused for a moment. "Sometimes you gotta follow your heart over your head. Just walk fuckin' carefully."

"But what if everything goes wrong? I don't trust my own judgment when it comes to men."

"I'd say it's unlikely Detective Prestia's gonna pin a murder on you." Dan patted me on the shoulder. "He has Micah Ganaway for that. And if he tries to sell you like a side of beef, rest assured that me and Emmy'll hunt him down and make a balloon animal out of his junk."

"Thanks, I think."

"You're welcome. Now, ready to go ask questions?"

Not really. "Bring it on."

We'd split the area surrounding the Feinstein house and Rybridge Fields into four, and I couldn't lie—our expectations were low. Usually in an investigation like this one, we could play on the heartstrings of potential witnesses by explaining that we wanted to catch a killer. But as far as the general public was concerned, the Richmond PD already had the man who'd taken Vonnie in custody, so why would we still be looking? And if we told the truth—that we were working as part of Micah Ganaway's defence team—the chances of cooperation fell even lower.

We'd tried our best to level the playing field by including Knox and Kellan on the team. True, Knox didn't generally work on investigations, but there were a lot of bored housewives in these parts, and he could charm their panties off. And Kellan had a quiet, confident manner that made you spill your secrets before you even realised what you were saying.

By lunchtime, we'd struck out fifty times over, and none of us had hit even a crumb of pay dirt. Most people flat-out refused to speak with us, and those that were willing to talk hadn't provided any useful information. Was Prestia at the detention centre right now? What was Micah saying?

I spotted a gardener working beside the gates of the next mansion and conjured up a smile. Prestia had promised to call. I just had to be patient.

Trust went both ways.

"Excuse me, do you have a moment to help?"

The gardener looked up, his hands covered in dirt. "You're lost?"

Were we talking physically or metaphorically?

"I'm actually a private investigator engaged to assist in the search for Vonnie Feinstein." It wasn't a lie. We *were* looking for the little girl. "She disappeared on Saturday night three weeks ago, and I was just wondering if you saw anything around that time."

"What do you mean by 'anything'?"

That was always hard to define. And we never asked for "anything suspicious" because any little piece of information could be significant, no matter how innocent it seemed, especially when looked at as part of the bigger picture.

"Were you in the area on that Friday? Or in the days preceding?"

"It was my daughter's birthday on the Thursday, and she wanted to go to Chuck E. Cheese with her friends. I took the Friday off to recover."

"What about before that?"

"I was here Monday through Wednesday, but I was working around the back. Don't recall seeing anything out of the ordinary when I was driving through either, and the week before, I was over in Wakefield."

"Well, thank you anyway. Do you know if anyone else is home today?"

"The Bradshaws are on vacation, and Consuela has the week off. Did the Feinsteins hire you?"

That question was the kiss of death, but what did it matter if I answered now?

"No, we're working on behalf of the current suspect."

Rather than offering the usual withering glare, the gardener just shrugged. "Figures."

Now I was curious. "Why do you say that?"

"Not like them to spend extra money when the cops are working for free."

"You know the Feinsteins?"

"Used to work for them a day a week."

"Why'd you quit?"

"Didn't quit. Got let go. Delia Feinstein and me, we had a difference of opinion over whether it was possible to grow canna lilies in the winter. You want a tip? It isn't. But the new guy, he planted them—saw them as I was passing—and they all died after the first frost. Guess he got let go too."

"Thanks for the info." I held back a smile. A disgruntled ex-employee was the perfect person to dish the dirt. "As far as I know, the Feinsteins haven't hired an investigator of their own. You think they're penny-pinchers?"

"I think they have the wrong priorities. They'll spend thousands on a new cabana for the swimming pool, but a few bucks to take their kid to the petting zoo? No way. And they wouldn't be caught dead at Chuck E. Cheese."

"They focus on appearances?"

"Yeah. Don't know why they even had the kid. They seemed to regard her as more of a nuisance than anything else. Always figured it was a 'keeping up with the Joneses' thing. All Delia's friends had kids, and she didn't want to get left out."

"She couldn't just have bought a puppy?"

"She did buy a puppy. Sold it again after it ate her favourite pair of shoes."

"How do you know that?"

Nobody else had mentioned issues with the Feinsteins' behaviour, including Prestia. Was the gardener merely bitter and trying to cause trouble? Or was there a grain of truth in his story?

"Rosalia told me. Their maid. But I doubt she'll say the same to you because she can't afford to lose that job. You want to see the real Delia Feinstein? Find the people she fell out with or fired."

"What about her husband?"

"Stu? Never saw much of him. But if I'd married that woman, I'd have spent most of my life at the office too."

"You think they could have harmed their own daughter?"

"Harmed her? Not on purpose. When I heard the kid was missing, I figured Delia had accidentally left her at the mall or someplace, but now they're saying she got taken. Watched Delia on the TV last night. All those crocodile tears. She cried more after someone scratched her fancy new BMW in a store parking lot. Felt damn sorry for that girl, having those two for parents."

If what the gardener said was true, then I felt sorry for Vonnie too. I knew what it was like to grow up with parents who didn't care. Well, parent. My father had walked out before I was even born.

"I really appreciate you telling me this." Even if it fell into the "interesting" rather than "useful" category. "If I have more questions, is there a number I can reach you on?"

"Got a card somewhere... Here you go."

Garry's Landscaping Services, no job too big or too small. Water features a specialty. I handed over a card in return and got a smile.

"Halina Chastain. Pretty name for a pretty girl. If you ever need any yard work done, give me a call."

"I live in an apartment, but if I ever get a house... I don't suppose you know who planted the canna lilies, do you?"

Could it have been MowTown Lawn Care?

"Can't help you there, I'm afraid." Garry turned back to his digging. "Good luck with the hunt."

I met Dan and Knox in a ritzy little café not too far from Nick's place. Kellan said he'd join us once he'd finished the next cluster of houses. A group of women by the window looked down their noses at Dan's outfit, even though she'd reined in her wilder side with jeans and a leather jacket today, but the irony was, she was probably wealthier than all of them put together. Plus she was practically married to a world-famous music producer. I wasn't jealous—she'd earned every cent of her money and every second of her happiness—but I couldn't help wishing I could find my own little slice of joy someday.

I stole one of Knox's fries while I waited for my panini to arrive, and dished Garry's dirt on the Feinsteins.

"But I'm not sure what it means, if anything. That Delia Feinstein's been crying for more sympathy than she deserves? We know a stranger took Vonnie."

Knox pointed his fork at me. "But was it a stranger to Vonnie or a stranger to the kid witness? The Feinsteins were out, but what if they came back a few minutes early, and Stu Feinstein climbed through the window to make it look like a third party was involved? What shoe size does he take?"

"I'm not sure."

"What's the motive?" Dan asked.

Knox shrugged. "Beats me."

I shook my head too. "From what Garry said, Stu just wasn't interested in his daughter. Why would he risk prison to make her disappear? And where is she?"

"Okay, so it's a stretch."

"Although the yard-work angle's worth following up on," Dan said. "We know the Carmodys used a service, and maybe the Metgoods did too? They were financially comfortable. Dual income, one kid."

"I'll see if Prestia has a list of tradesmen who visited the Feinstein house."

"When are you seeing him again?"

"Tomorrow evening." Knox started humming the "Wedding March," and I threw a wadded-up napkin at him. "I don't see you making personal sacrifices for the good of the case."

"Is that what women call dates now?" he asked, eyes twinkling. "'Sacrifices'?"

"Screw you."

"Any time, baby." He leaned in closer. "How about this? When we find the motherfucker who took Vonnie, I'll make a personal sacrifice by defenestrating him."

"De-what?"

"Throwing him out of a window," Dan supplied, then nodded over my shoulder. "The server's bringing your sandwich over."

But before the girl could put down the plate, Dan's phone rang, and when she answered, I knew from her satisfied smile that we had something good. My throat went dry, and I barely even noticed when Knox grabbed a handful of my potato chips.

"What happened?" I asked the instant Dan hung up.

"Kellan's on his way—he found our mystery woman."

14

HALLIE

Kellan had hit the motherlode in a small enclave of luxury homes a quarter-mile north of the Feinstein house. First, he'd been in the right place at the right time to assist Dorothy Ziegler, a wealthy widow who'd twisted her ankle while she was out for her morning constitutional. Kellan had helped her home, then partaken of tea and dainty cakes served by the maid while they waited for Dorothy's personal physician to arrive.

And Dorothy Ziegler didn't think much of the Feinsteins at all.

"They're part of the nouveau riche, according to her," Kellan told us. "But they barely qualify for the 'riche' part. And Delia Feinstein doesn't understand the difference between shiny baubles and class. Dorothy said she's a needy sort, always wants to be the centre of attention."

"Did Dorothy know anything about Delia's relationship with her daughter?" Dan asked.

"Dorothy didn't even know the Feinsteins had a daughter until she saw the news."

I didn't much like the picture we were building up. "It's

beginning to sound as if Vonnie was an inconvenience to her parents. Why didn't they just hire a nanny if they didn't want to spend time with her?"

As usual, Dan had the answer. "Dorothy was right about the lack of 'riche.' Mack's been looking into the Feinsteins' finances, and they're in debt up to their eyeballs."

"Could it be like the Carmody case? Are we back to the parents again?"

Did they somehow engineer Vonnie's disappearance? The thought made me shudder. The idea had sounded so farfetched when Knox suggested it, but who else had a motive? True stranger abductions were rare. But then there was Donna Metgood, and when I'd watched a recording of her parents' press conference, her mom's tears had seemed genuine. Her father had been more stoic, but he had a clear alibi for his daughter's disappearance. Norman Metgood had worked as an area manager for a chain of restaurants, and on that Friday night, he'd been dealing with a water leak at the branch in Lewisburg.

Dan shrugged. "Think of the case as a recipe. Right now, we've got a bunch of ingredients but no clear idea what we're making. Although nothing we've found so far suggests Micah Ganaway was involved, does it? Knox, have you spoken to Calvin recently?"

"Early this morning. I told him to hang in there and that we're doing everything we can."

Kellan took a sip of his Pepsi. "I doubt the cops are getting much further than we are, especially if they're fixated on the wrong suspect. Dorothy said she hasn't returned their call because she once met Chief Garland and he was—I quote—a slimy son of a bitch. I quite liked the old gal. Plus she offered to call around her friends and get back to me if they had any other snippets of information."

"What did she say about the woman with the dog?" I asked.

"Nothing." Kellan grimaced. "After I'd drunk tea with Dorothy, I made the mistake of knocking on Berta Michaelson's door."

When he mentioned the name, Dan nearly choked on her milkshake. "The Grand High Cougar of Glen Allen? I didn't realise she'd moved to Rybridge."

"I thought she was gonna rip my shirt off. We should've sent Knox in with body armour."

"She'd only have seen that as a challenge. What did she have to say?"

"Apart from inviting me to go skinny-dipping in her pool?"

Knox winced. "Tough draw, buddy."

"That was only the half of it. She's got a bunch of yappy little dogs that kept running around my feet, and I thought her perfume was gonna set off an asthma attack. Next time, I want hazard pay."

"I owe you a beer."

"You owe me at least a six-pack."

"Deal. Berta was the one who identified the mystery woman?"

"Yeah. She's Berta's dog trainer, and judging by the teeth marks in my ankle, I'd say she's not a particularly good one. But I have an address—she lives over in Montrose. Should I pay her a visit?"

Dan shook her head. "When you're having so much success here? No, I'll go with Hallie. But if you want to purchase your own set of body armour, I'll sign off on the expense."

"Gee, thanks."

But Kellan was smiling—he knew we were making

progress. I only hoped it would be enough to put the right man behind bars.

Linda Hurst lived in a modest duplex in an average part of town. Her yard was small but neat, and most of the driveway was taken up by a small van with tinted rear windows. A sign painted on the side told us we were in the right place. *Paw & Order Dog Training School*.

When I knocked on the door, a cacophony of barking sounded on the other side, but in an instant, the dogs fell silent as if on command. A moment later, a petite brunette cracked open the front door and peered out.

"Whatever you're selling, I'm afraid I don't want any."

Dan did the talking. "We're not selling anything."

"Are you sure? Not even religion?"

"We're actually private investigators."

"Private investigators? Are you here about the missing trash cans? Because I have no idea where they're going."

"No, we're here about the disappearance of Vonnie Feinstein. Do you have a spare moment?"

"Vonnie Feinstein? The little girl on the news? Because I definitely don't know her."

"But you were in Rybridge the day before she disappeared. Friday evening, three weeks ago."

Now Linda looked puzzled. "Yes, I was there. I take Mrs. Juneau's labradoodle to the park on Fridays. Loopy was so reactive to other dogs when I first started walking him, but he's gotten much better. Now we just need to work on his recall, and— That's not important, is it?"

"We're interested in what you saw in the park that day."

"But why? I thought the police already caught the man responsible?"

"There's some uncertainty over whether they have the right person in custody, and Vonnie's still missing. We're doing our best to find her."

"Oh, I see. Well, yes, of course, I'll tell you everything I can remember, but I don't recall seeing anything strange."

"Do you want to talk out here, or would it be easier if we came in? I notice your neighbour is watching us."

Dan had a sixth sense about these things. I glanced to the side in time to see the voile drapes at the bay window of the next house fall back into place.

Linda tutted. "She spends half her life nosing around. If anyone knows where those trash cans are going, it's her, and yet she denies everything. Come in, come in. The pups don't mind visitors."

Linda had three big dogs—Dobermans? I thought they were Dobermans—and perhaps her training skills weren't so bad after all. She told them to stay, and they did, watching attentively, then she dropped one hand and they sat down in perfect unison. Hmm. Did she work with parrots?

"Would you like a drink?"

Dan nodded. "I'll never say no to coffee."

Linda turned to me. "Coffee?"

"Uh, I only drink decaf."

Dan snorted, but the tables were quickly turned when Linda said, "Really? Me too. In fact, that's all I have."

Since I was with a colleague, I'd risk sipping a drink, and five minutes later, we settled onto comfortable leather couches with steaming mugs. No stray hair, so I figured the dogs weren't allowed on the furniture. They were starting to get a bit creepy now, just sitting there in silence, arranged in size order from small to large, staring at us with unblinking eyes.

Dan showed Micah's pictures of the park to Linda, but didn't tell her who had taken them.

"You look as if you saw something interesting there. Can you remember what it was?"

"Oh, sure, sure. There was a loose dog, which there really shouldn't have been because dogs are meant to be on leashes in Rybridge Fields, and it was running all over, doing as it pleased. There were other dogs around, and children too, and I remember thinking it was only a matter of time before somebody got hurt."

"And did they?"

"Well, no, not that day, but it did scare a teenage girl walking a chihuahua. The poor little thing slipped its collar and raced right out of the park with the girl running after it."

"Which direction did they go?"

"Toward the exit onto Willow Avenue."

Which was the exit nearest to the Feinstein home. I leaned forward to point out the Feinsteins in Micah's pictures.

"Did they leave before or after these people?"

"Sorry, but I just don't know. Is that the girl who disappeared?"

"It is."

"I don't..." Linda reached out and touched the picture as if that might form a connection. "I don't remember. When I'm out walking, I always pay more attention to dogs than people, but I guess I should change that, shouldn't I? I mean, I didn't even see the person with the camera. Is the girl dead? On the news, they say she's missing, but it's been weeks now."

My head told me the answer was yes, but Dan was right—there was always hope. "Nobody can say for sure."

"Her poor parents. I always feel safe when I'm walking Rocky, Ranger, and Royal..." She waved a hand toward the three statues on the other side of the room. "But Loopy

Juneau's such a friendly dog. Should I start carrying pepper spray?"

"That wouldn't hurt." Dan rummaged around in her oversized purse. "Here, take my spare."

"Wow, thank you so much."

"Don't suppose you know the name of the girl with the chihuahua?"

Linda shook her head. "But I've seen her before, so I think she lives in the area. Want me to ask around?"

"We'd appreciate that."

The more people on the lookout, the better. But this was yet another piece that might or might not have been part of the puzzle. Only time would tell.

"He was there."

Prestia's words sent a bolt of shock through me. He'd called after lunch as promised, but we'd ended up playing voicemail tennis all afternoon while I spoke with potential witnesses and he visited the science museum with his sister, niece, and nephew. Now I was home, and my feet were killing me. Pinchy had no sympathy whatsoever.

"Who was where?" I asked, just in case I'd misunderstood.

"Micah Ganaway was at the Carmody house."

Yes, I'd always known that was a possibility, but I'd never truly believed it.

"Are you sure?"

"He admitted it. First, he said he wasn't, claimed he didn't remember going there, but then Duncan showed him a picture of the place and he recognised the pool."

"Just like that?"

Detective Duncan had Micah in his sights, and Micah had handed him extra ammo?

"Surprised me too, and his lawyer. The lawyer tried to shut him up, but he said that firstly, he wasn't a liar, and secondly, if he said he wasn't there and it came out later that he was, he'd look even guiltier. Guess I can see his point."

"Did he mention Mila?"

"Swore blind that he didn't see her, let alone touch her, and he claims he only visited the house once or twice, covering for someone else. It wasn't one of his regular jobs."

"When did he go there? What dates?"

"He doesn't recall."

"So it could even have been after Mila's abduction? And there's still no proof he ever set foot on the Feinstein property, just that he was nearby. Do you have a list of people who *did* visit the Feinsteins?"

"You're trying to create reasonable doubt?"

"At least fifty people went through the Carmody home in the two weeks before Mila disappeared. I have a list Blackwood compiled at the time when people's memories were a lot fresher, and Micah's name isn't on it."

"Fifty? Was it a home or Grand Central Station?"

"The Carmodys never lifted a finger for themselves." With their wealth, they didn't need to. I suppose that's what surprised me the most about Emmy and Black—they had billions in the bank, but if a sink was blocked, one of them would still grab a plunger. "They hired people for everything. Landscapers, cleaners, a cook. A florist brought flowers every week, Mrs. Carmody had a personal stylist, and Mr. Carmody's golf buddies came over most weekends. They were having the driveway repaved and the guest cottage repainted. Then there were delivery drivers and repairmen, oh, and the window cleaner, and that fifty doesn't even include the guests at a party they held the previous week. You say Micah

Ganaway's a suspect, and I'll give you a hundred other people who should be on that list. Did you cross-reference?"

There was a long pause. "I don't have the list for Carmody."

"You *don't have the list*?"

"It appears that some of my predecessors weren't so hot at filing."

"You mean there was a list, and somebody lost it?"

"It's listed on the evidence log, but it's not in the box."

"How about a soft copy?"

"It's got six names on it."

"Are you kidding me? Was everyone asleep on the job?"

"Who the hell knows? Duncan said there was a server failure a few years ago, and they had to recover the Carmody files, but some of them were corrupted, and... I'll buy you dinner if you send me your list."

"Is this when I give my speech about being incorruptible?"

"What if I throw in dessert?"

"What if I trade my Carmody list for your Feinstein list?"

"You strike a hard bargain, plum."

"Is that a yes? And did you get ahold of the Metgood file yet?"

"It's a yes, but I'm still buying you dinner. And I've put in a call to the lead detective on the Metgood case."

"Is this dinner in addition to Chinese tomorrow night?"

"Do you want it to be?"

Do I want it to be? I took a moment to breathe. Every conversation with Prestia left my heart racing, and this was no exception.

"Are we talking a working dinner? Or...something else?"

"Take your pick." His tone softened. "I just like spending time with you, Hallie."

Freaking hell. What was I meant to say to that? Words stuck in my throat, and I was still trying to come up with an appropriate answer when I heard a small voice in the background.

"Uncle Ford? Uncle *Ford*! Mom says dinner's ready."

"I'll be there in a second."

"No, now. Mom says it's ready *now*."

"Guess I've gotta go, plum. I'll see you tomorrow, okay? And I'm buying the Chinese."

"Okay." The word came out as a croak, but before I could say it again, Prestia was gone.

And for the second night in a row, I barely slept a wink.

15

FORD

Ford had been on plenty of dates in his life, but he'd never felt as nervous as he did waiting for Hallie to show up at River Bend. And it wasn't even a date, for fuck's sake. Although that hadn't stopped him from spending half of last night cleaning the *Shore Thing*—mainly because he couldn't sleep—and he'd ordered food from the nearest Chinese restaurant to arrive at eight. He'd taken a shower. Brushed his teeth. Checked his watch ten times, and at five to seven, he climbed onto the dock to watch for Hallie's arrival.

The River Bend Yacht Basin wasn't as fancy as the marina he'd lived at in New Orleans, but it was tidy and well-maintained, and the folks who ran it were friendly. He missed the nightlife of the Southside Yacht Club—this time last year, he'd been able to step ashore into the clubhouse bar, take a swim in the pool, or work off steam in the gym—but his sister's happiness was more important than having the additional amenities.

When Hallie hadn't arrived ten minutes later, he began to fear that she'd gotten cold feet. Had it made her uncomfortable, driving to the middle of nowhere? He should have offered to meet her someplace else. Arranged a private dining room or something. But then her Honda rounded the trees into the small parking lot, and the tension that had knotted around his stomach released. She climbed out holding a laptop bag, a purse bigger than the one she'd used on Saturday, and a paper carrier bag.

"Hey."

She smiled back at him. "Hey. I brought information and fortune cookies. Which boat is yours?"

"At the far end."

Ford offered a hand, and she steadied herself as she stepped gingerly onto the dock, bracing as if she expected it to rock.

"It's fixed. Solid. It won't move."

"Phew."

He knew the moment she saw the *Shore Thing* because she looked up, and up, and up, then squeezed his hand tighter as her mouth dropped open. He understood. Even after eight years, he still occasionally felt the same way.

"That...no."

"Yes."

"That's not a boat, it's a freaking ship."

"She's a sixty-six-foot blue-water cruising yacht. Really, she shouldn't even be on this river, but needs must."

"When you said you lived on a boat, I imagined something like this one," Hallie said, pointing at a small cabin cruiser.

"I couldn't even stand up in that. Want to come aboard?"

"Okay. But the *Shore Thing*? Who came up with the name?"

"I did. After one shot of bourbon too many."

Hallie's nails dug into Ford's palm as she walked down the wide gangplank to the swim platform, but once they'd climbed up into the cockpit, she relaxed enough to look around, drinking in all the little details. The polished wood and chrome. The bench seats. The pair of cardboard boxes lined up on said seats.

"You're using the boat as an archive room?"

"That's a little light reading for after dinner."

"Huh?"

"I pulled every case file on every unsolved child abduction in Virginia for the last twenty years. Technically, I shouldn't have taken them out of the office, but..." Members of the department took case files home to work on from time to time. Yet another symptom of budget cuts—if cops stayed in the office to give every case the attention it deserved, nobody would ever leave. The brass turned a blind eye if a detective wanted to read through notes over dinner. "Don't say I never bring you gifts, plum."

"That's the best present ever." She lifted the lid off the first box and put a hand to her chest. "Be still my beating heart." Most women loved diamonds, his preferred dead bodies. Go figure. "But hasn't the Richmond PD ever heard of a scanner?"

"I'm an old-fashioned guy. My brain works better when I have paper in my hand."

"You should talk to Black. He's a fan of paper too. Nate shows up for meetings with a tablet and a laptop and a freaking hologram projector, and Black brings a notepad."

"Who's Nate?"

"One of Blackwood's directors." Hallie nodded toward the files. "Should we take them inside? It's meant to rain later."

"Yup, and then we can do the tour." Ford waggled an eyebrow. "Wanna see my washing machine?"

"You sure do know how to impress a girl."

He waved a hand at the saloon. "After you."

The saloon housed a dining table that comfortably seated six, plus a navigation station that doubled as Ford's desk when the boat was berthed. A galley to the side held the usual kitchen appliances, including the all-important coffee machine. Ford's double stateroom and en-suite were housed in the stern, and the bow yielded two more bedrooms—one a double with an en-suite, one with bunks—plus the guest bathroom. The only thing he truly missed about living in an apartment was a big, comfortable couch. In the summer, he'd stretch out on a bench seat in the cockpit, but in the winter, it was just too cold.

Like every other woman he'd shown around the boat, Hallie was fascinated by the tiny cupboards and storage spaces, by the dressing table with its swing-out stool and the compact but fully functioning bathrooms. The yacht's true strength lay out on the ocean waves—she was a dream to sail—but she didn't make a bad place to call home either.

"What do you think?" he asked once Hallie had ventured into the engine bay and come straight back out again.

"She's...beautiful. Definitely not what I'd imagined. But I have to ask—why the boat and not an apartment? I'll bet one of these doesn't come cheap."

Ah, they'd reached the awkward part of the night. After this conversation, fifty percent of women flashed dollar signs in their eyes, another forty percent wanted to know if he could get tickets to a movie premiere, and the remaining ten percent appeared to take the news in their stride. *Appeared* to. Roughly half of those were hiding their true nature, and too late, he'd realised Eliette had fallen into that five percent.

"The *Shore Thing* was a graduation gift from my father. I couldn't insult him by selling her, and in truth, I didn't want to. I've always loved sailing."

"That was real generous of him. My pop didn't stick around long enough to see me graduate kindergarten. But can you sail on the river? You said she didn't belong here, and don't sailboats kind of...zigzag?"

"Every so often, I take her out on engine power, but it's almost a hundred miles to the open ocean, and they need to raise two bridges for me to get there. I looked at renting a slip in Virginia Beach, but it's too far for a daily commute, and once I paid out for slip fees, I'd only have enough money left over for a really crappy apartment." Sylvie had offered to move both of the kids into one bedroom so he could stay with her, but his job meant he'd be coming and going in the middle of the night, and he wasn't always in a great mood when he finished a shift. "This was the best compromise for the moment."

No dollar signs. No questions about his father. Hallie fell into that rare ten percent. But would she turn out to be a closet gold digger? Ford had hope that she wouldn't, and part of that hope stemmed from the fact that she spoke about Charles and Emerson Black with such fierce affection. She already had friends with money, far more money than Denton Prestia would ever possess.

"Sometimes, we have to play the hand life deals us." She sidled up to him. "Did you say there'd be food?" Her stomach grumbled on cue, and she giggled. "My lunch was a chicken sandwich with low-fat mayo and a fruit salad. Emmy's nutritionist was on the rampage again, and he took all the candy away."

"The horror."

"It's not funny. Times like today, I need sugar to operate."

"Bad day?"

"Not bad, just difficult. We found Donna Metgood's mom, and those conversations are always the hardest."

"You spoke to her?"

"Yes, along with Dan. But what could we say that would make the situation any better? Three years have passed since Donna disappeared, and nobody's ever been brought to justice." Hallie slumped onto the seat that wrapped around the dining table. "She cried, and I cried too. Thank the stars we weren't on a video call."

"You want a drink? I figured alcohol was out, so I picked up a bunch of stuff in cans and bottles. They're all sealed, so you can open them yourself."

"You did? That's...that's..." She wiped her eyes with a sleeve. "Sorry, my emotions are still all over the place. I should learn to be tougher, like Dan."

"No, you shouldn't. Keeping your humanity is hard in this job, and the longer you can manage that, the better. I've got water, Pepsi, lemonade, iced tea, orange juice, or Dr. Pepper."

"Is the Pepsi diet?"

"I bought both kinds. You want the diet?"

"Yes, please."

Ford passed her a can, then popped the top on a bottle of beer. He figured he deserved one drink after the day he'd had. A four-year-old kid in Bon Air had found a loaded revolver in his parents' bedroom and shot his six-year-old sister, just like he'd seen in his big brother's video games. Couldn't work out why she wouldn't get up again.

"Cheers."

He held up the bottle, and Hallie clinked the can against it.

"Cheers. Is it bad form to eat the fortune cookies first?"

"I've got candy if you want it."

"Really?" She brightened. "What kind?"

"Skittles, Haribo, M&Ms, Sour Patch Kids, suckers, and Swedish Fish."

Her eyes narrowed. "How old are you?"

"Thirty. But don't forget I'm cool Uncle Ford. I have to keep something on hand to slip the kids when my sister isn't looking." He leaned his elbows on the table. "And also my sworn enemy. Which do you want?"

"The M&Ms."

Ford got up and rummaged through the cupboard beside the refrigerator. "Peanut or regular?"

"You have peanut ones? My hero."

He tossed the package in her direction, then checked his watch. The food would arrive at any minute, and the driver always waited in the parking lot.

"Back in a moment. Make yourself at home."

"Yes, sir."

At least Hallie was back to her sassy self tonight. After her heartfelt confession yesterday, he'd wondered whether the atmosphere on the boat might be uncomfortable, but she was smiling, which meant he had to do so as well. He'd never be able to forget about her past—how could he when the events had engraved themselves onto her psyche?—but he'd take his lead from her and tuck the issues to one side for now.

The food came right on time. He'd ordered twice as much as they could eat, but he hadn't been sure what she liked, and reheated leftovers were gourmet chow after a long shift anyway. But when he got back to the saloon, she was laughing. Not just the occasional giggle, but full-blown stitches.

"What happened?"

"Ohmigosh! There's a picture of your naked ass on the internet."

"What?" His heart stuttered. The photos from that bachelor party were never meant to see the light of day. "Where?"

"Right here."

She turned her laptop around, and he breathed a sigh of relief. That was his ten-month-old ass, not the twenty-two-year-old version.

"Oh, *those* pictures."

"You mean there are more?"

"I, uh... Not for public consumption." But wait a second... "You researched me?"

"Oh, come on... What did you expect? After you said your dad bought you the boat, I got curious. Nosiness is basically in my DNA. And your ass was *so* cute."

At least she didn't try to hide her snooping or casually slip hints about Hollywood into the conversation. In a way, the openness was refreshing.

"*Was* cute?"

Ah, now she turned beautifully pink. "Well, it still might be. It's not as if I've spent much time looking."

"*Much* time? So you have spent *some* time?"

"I wish I'd never started this conversation."

Ford took a seat opposite her. "I'm kinda glad you did. The longer I leave it, the more awkward it gets. So, you found out who my dad is?"

"I think I saw one of his movies once." Her expression turned sober. "Wikipedia said your parents got divorced. I'm so sorry."

"Don't be. It worked out better for everyone that way. Mom's new husband—Alain—is a great guy. It was him who helped me with my homework, him who drove me to soccer practice, him who bawled me out when I fucked up. Dad... He just wasn't cut out to be a family man."

"He didn't care?"

"He didn't abandon us or anything like that. But his one big passion in life is making movies. Ask him a question about lighting or camera angles or special effects, and he's basically an encyclopedia, but ask him when my birthday is, and he'll have to check with his PA. We never wanted for material things, but love... Dad understands how it looks from the outside—hell, he directed last year's hottest romance movie— but he just doesn't know how to feel it."

Ford hadn't meant to say all that. The last thing he wanted was sympathy, but Hallie laid a hand on his arm.

"It's hard, isn't it? When you're a kid, you think it's your fault. You spend hours wondering what you did wrong, trying to work out how to fix it, and it's only years later that you realise the failings weren't yours at all."

Now he had a lump in his throat because that was *exactly* how it had felt. Until his mom remarried and Alain took over the role of father, Ford had spent every damn night wondering how he could possibly please his dad. As a kid, he'd volunteered to be an extra in every damn scene just so he could spend time with the big man. Most of his childhood memories came from movie sets.

"You've thought about that a lot?" he asked.

"For more than a year, I had nothing to do but watch Netflix, spread my legs, and overanalyse everything and everyone. So yes, you could say I've thought about it a lot."

16

FORD

Fuck, that was blunt. And Hallie's words hit Ford right in the damn chest. But he was seeing a stronger version of her tonight, so he had to view that as a good thing.

"Want to hear a funny story? After I finished college, I took a trip to LA to visit Dad, and he asked what I planned to do with the rest of my life. I told him I wanted to be a detective. And his eyes just lit up. I thought finally, *finally*, I'd managed to do something right, and then he said, 'That's great, son, great—I'll speak to casting and make sure you get a few lines.'"

"What the hell?"

"He was shooting a cop movie at the time. When I broke the news that I mean an actual detective—bear in mind here that I'd just graduated magna cum laude with a degree in criminal justice—he rolled his eyes and said, 'Where did I go wrong?'"

"Wow."

Ford shrugged. "He is who he is. I've accepted it now. And he isn't a terrible father intentionally; he simply doesn't understand the requirements of the role. But enough about him—dinner's getting cold, and we have a stack of bedtime reading."

"Did you order egg rolls? Tell me you ordered egg rolls."

"Best part of the meal."

"Are we going formal here? Or can I work while I eat?"

"Be my guest. I'm gonna start with the Metgood file. Pete Sarba—Detective Sarba—emailed me the bones of it right before I left the station. What did Donna's mom have to say earlier?"

"We didn't ask many questions on the phone, but we're going to speak with her in person tomorrow."

"In Lewisburg?"

That was a seven-hour round trip. Hallie would be gone all day.

Or maybe not.

"She actually moved to White Sulphur Springs to live with her sister. I was planning to drive, but Dan wants to fit in some flight hours, so we're gonna borrow Emmy's helicopter instead."

Her *helicopter*? Okay, so Ford had to concede that working in the private sector did have its advantages. His assigned vehicle was a five-year-old Dodge Charger.

"Is Dan a good pilot?"

A nervous giggle burst out of Hallie's mouth. "I hope so."

"You hope so?"

"Emmy assured me that Dan's flying isn't as bad as her driving."

"You're not exactly filling me with confidence here, plum."

"We'll be fine." Why did Hallie seem as if she was trying to convince herself as well as Ford? "Yes, we'll be fine." She sliced the end off an egg roll, popped it into her mouth, sighed, and opened the first file. "To think I could have been watching Netflix this evening."

Now that Ford had escaped the Hollywood life, he

preferred a good book to a movie, but he understood the sentiment. He echoed Hallie's sigh and opened his laptop. The good news? The Metgood file wouldn't take long to get through. The bad news? There wasn't a whole lot in it. Reading between the lines, the detective in charge had been Duncan's brother from another mother, except he hadn't even found a suspect. When he retired, the case had been passed on to Sarba, but he was a recent transfer from the West Coast, newly promoted, unfamiliar with the locale and the folks involved. He'd never heard the name Mila Carmody either.

As Ford scanned the sparse details, a chill ran up his spine. Hallie had been right—the similarities were too significant to ignore. Donna had been asleep in a first-floor bedroom, and it appeared the suspect had climbed in through an open window. In August three years ago, the temperatures had been into the nineties, and they didn't drop below seventy overnight. Why had the window been open? Because the AC was out. Size eleven footprints criss-crossed the dirt outside. The neighbour's dog hadn't barked, and Donna hadn't made a sound.

Ford studied a photo of the little girl. She'd been ten years old at the time of her disappearance, clever according to her teacher, but small for her age and timid. In the picture, she wore a pink tracksuit and carried a soccer ball. Had pink been her favourite colour? She'd disappeared in a pair of pink pyjamas, but no clothes had been found near her remains. Her *remains*. Her skeleton had been picked clean by scavengers, the bones scattered over a thirty-yard radius. She'd been identified by dental records and X-rays, the latter taken when she'd broken her arm two years previously.

The details made the hair on the back of Ford's neck stand on end.

"How's it going?" he asked Hallie. A half-full plate of food sat at her elbow, and the fortune cookies remained untouched. "Lost your appetite?"

"After everything I've seen, I shouldn't be surprised at the amount of evil in the world, but this... They're just *kids*. Sorry I didn't eat much."

"Doesn't matter. Did you find anything interesting?"

Hallie had gotten a third of the way down the stack of files, and she'd been making notes on her laptop as she went. Should he have given her free rein like that? Officially, no, and Duncan would blow his top if he found out, but didn't Blackwood and the cops have the same ultimate goal? To solve the case? To stop more girls from disappearing?

When Ford first stepped into the Feinstein residence, he'd felt in his bones that she wasn't the first. The crime was too neat. Too audacious. Everybody made mistakes, so where and when had the perp made his? That was the key to solving this case, and by going back in time, maybe they could find out where he'd started.

"One more possible," Hallie said.

"How are you approaching this?"

Ford asked for two reasons. One, he was curious about Blackwood's methods, and two, he was all too aware of Hallie's greenness. She had instincts, but not the hours of experience to back them up. It wasn't his job to mentor her, but at the same time, he *wanted* to help her hone those skills.

"I'm reading through each file and entering the key points into our database. And while I work, Providence is plugging away in the background to add any supplemental information that might be relevant."

"Providence?"

"Blackwood's in-house search-and-analysis software."

"It's like an extra pair of hands?"

"Exactly like that."

Smart. "Can I see?"

Hallie hesitated for a moment, then angled her screen so he could see it.

"The information in black is user-entered. Notes in blue were added by Providence. And if I click on one, the reference pops up. See? Then I can confirm whether it's relevant or not, and Providence uses my choices to learn."

Ford did see. He saw that Blackwood's system was light years ahead of anything the Richmond PD had. He saw that Hallie had distilled the case of Michelle Moody, who'd vanished six years ago at the age of ten, into the pertinent facts and entered the details succinctly. He saw that Providence had trawled social media and found current posts from Michelle's birth father in Idaho. And in the background of a photo of a family cookout, he caught a glimpse of a teenage girl who bore a remarkable resemblance to the image of Michelle. The case had been languishing in the cold files for years, and Hallie had potentially cracked it in the time it took her to eat half a portion of chow mein.

Ford pointed at the screen. "Think that's Michelle?"

"Give me a minute..."

She opened up a new window and dragged all the photos they had of Michelle, her mom, and her biological father into it. Two minutes later, Providence provided an age-progressed image of Michelle and an assessment that the girl in the picture was eighty-three percent likely to be the same person.

Hallie shrugged. "I'm gonna go with 'probably.' Can you follow up?"

"I'll definitely follow up. Who's the possible you found?"

"Araceli Suarez. Nine years old, disappeared from Roanoke in August last year. Snatched from her bedroom, intruder came in through a window, size eleven footprints in the dirt outside, nobody ever saw her again. Sound familiar?"

"She's from a different demographic. Poor, Hispanic.

Donna and Vonnie could be twins, and apart from the hair colour, Mila fits that profile too."

"I'm not saying the cases are definitely linked. I just think it warrants a further look."

Yeah, it did. Hallie was absolutely right on that point. "Was the AC at the Suarez home broken, by any chance?"

"I haven't seen anything about AC."

"Why was the window open?"

"To cool the place down, I guess."

"Most people use AC for that."

"Looking at the pictures, the Suarez family didn't have much money. Maybe they couldn't afford AC?"

"Yeah, maybe. Do me a favour—when you speak with Mrs. Metgood, ask her about the AC. When it failed, whether a technician came, that kind of thing."

"Okay, but why?"

"Because the Feinsteins' AC wasn't working either. We already ruled out the tech who visited—he was at a family reunion when Vonnie was snatched—but I'm wondering whether there might have been sabotage involved."

"Break it in daylight, come back in the dark?"

"Something like that." It was a reach, but they had little else to go on. And the offender's method of selection bothered Ford. Vonnie's window could be seen from the ridge behind the house, true, but not from the road. "Want me to take some of those files?"

"I need to enter the data into Providence."

"Can you give me access?"

"Sorry, I just don't have the authority to set up an additional login. I could try speaking with Mack tomorrow, but tonight..."

"Let me read through them, and I'll note down the important points. Then you can type them in. Will that work?"

Hallie nodded. "I think I need a sugar hit first. Got any more M&Ms?"

"For you? Always."

By the time midnight struck, they'd found one more possible candidate—Janiya Thomas, nine years old, mixed race, taken from her bed in a run-down neighbourhood on the outskirts of Lynchburg. Size eleven prints in the dirt. If these cases really were linked, then the problem was far bigger than anyone had suspected. Five girls gone in six years.

Five girls.

Six years.

All in August or September.

The hotter months.

Open windows.

"We're missing one."

"Huh?" Hallie raised tired eyes. "We've done all the files now."

"One girl disappeared each summer, but there's a gap between Donna and Araceli. What happened that year?"

"I don't... I don't know. Maybe something went wrong?"

"Or maybe there's another girl. We need to expand the search. Donna came from West Virginia. So far, we believe our man's hunting ground spans from Richmond across to Lewisburg and down to Roanoke. What if he travelled farther west? Or south?"

"I'll..." Hallie covered a yawn. "I'll start looking."

"Tomorrow. We'll start looking tomorrow. You need to get some sleep, plum. We both need to get some sleep."

"What time is it?"

"After midnight. What time do you need to get up?"

"Six."

Another yawn. Was she even safe to drive? Back when Ford was a patrolman, he'd seen the aftermath when people fell asleep behind the wheel.

"Want me to give you a ride home?"

She managed a smile. "You're as tired as I am."

"I can load up on caffeine, and I don't need to get out of bed until seven." He hesitated, then raised her chin so she faced him. "Or I have a spare room you're welcome to use."

"I'm not sure..."

"I know you're not. It's a big step, and there's no pressure, but I figured it'd be rude if I didn't offer."

Hallie bit her lip, and Ford's cock twitched. That was the moment he realised he wanted her in *his* bed. Someday, no matter how long it took, even if he had to walk through fucking fire to get her there.

"There's a lock on the door," he murmured. "Promise I'm not gonna make a move until you want me to."

Now those beautiful hazel eyes narrowed. "*Until* I want you to?"

Sometimes, a man had to take a chance. "Yes."

Once, she'd looked at him with fear, but now he saw something else. Apprehension, and then acceptance.

"I should text Mercy," she murmured. "Let her know I won't be home."

"Call her, don't text. This is a new thing for you, and she'll need to hear your voice, understand that you're not under duress. Okay?"

"Okay."

"Should I find you a T-shirt to sleep in?"

A nod. A quiet, "Thank you."

And Ford knew nothing would ever be the same again.

17

HALLIE

Ford stayed true to his word. Apart from the gentle touches that had become his habit, he'd kept his hands off me. After I'd reassured Mercy that I was absolutely fine, that I hadn't been forced into anything, he'd found me a brand-new oversized T-shirt advertising the Corner House in New Orleans—his mom and stepdad's bar, he said—and told me to use whatever toiletries his sister kept in the bathroom.

Then he'd left me to sleep.

Sleep.

What a joke.

I'd spent the whole damn night wondering what it would be like when he finally did put his hands on me, alternating between freaking out and clenching my thighs together. Until I met Prestia, I'd viewed the possibility of having sex again with an unsettling mixture of panic and dread, but now...now I began to wonder if it would be as bad as I feared.

I mean, sex had never been *great*. Even before I got abducted, orgasms had come with fingers or mechanical assistance, not with cock, and I'd always assumed that good sex was a marketing concept invented by the porn industry. My past boyfriends had aspired to mediocrity and missed the mark in every possible way.

Prestia? Well, I very much suspected he'd be magna cum laude.

Dan snapped her fingers in my face. "Earth to Hallie." She glanced down at the ground far, far below us. "Okay, not earth, but whatever."

"Huh?"

"Are you listening to a word I'm saying?"

"Uh, would you mind repeating it?"

I couldn't even claim the rotor noise as an excuse. Dan's voice was crystal clear in my headset.

"He's really gotten under your skin, hasn't he?"

"What? Who?"

"Your cop."

"He's not *my* cop."

Dan turned to look at me. "You're blushing."

Shit.

"Could you please watch where we're flying?"

"Relax, we're not going to crash. You're also wearing the same jeans as yesterday, plus a T-shirt you got from the supply cupboard in the office. Pro-tip: keep spare underwear in your desk drawer."

How did she know I'd gone commando? Add "X-ray vision" to Dan's list of superpowers. I'd intended to run home before I came to the office, but when Prestia knocked on my door at five thirty, he'd told me there'd be decaf waiting. And when I emerged after a shower, I found he'd made pancakes. Freaking pancakes with fresh fruit and cream and maple syrup. So I'd used up all my running-home time on breakfast, and now I was paying the price.

Prestia wasn't *my* cop.

But a small part of me wondered whether he'd be interested in the job.

"We were going through case files." I filled Dan in on what we'd found, including Ford's theory about an annual pattern. He'd also been able to fill in a couple of blanks for me—Stu Feinstein took a size nine shoe, not an eleven, and the Feinsteins had never used MowTown Lawn Care. "It got late, so I stayed on his boat, but nothing happened, okay?"

"On his *boat*?"

"He lives on a boat."

"Bet that's cosy."

"It's more of a yacht."

"He bought a yacht on a cop's salary?"

"No, his father has money." I closed my eyes and remembered how it had felt to be wrapped up in Prestia's arms this morning. His niece was right—he did give the best hugs. "Is it crazy that I like him? I mean, after everything in my past... And he's a *cop*."

"Not all men are assholes, although the Richmond PD's had more than its fair share of pricks. And when you find a good one, it can change your whole damn life."

"A good man? Or a good prick?"

Dan snorted a laugh. "Both, sweetie. If you think Prestia might be the man with the golden gonads, then no, it's not crazy. Grab him while you can. What did you find in the case files?"

I laid out the basics for Dan. The chance that this case was bigger than just Carmody, Metgood, and Feinstein. The possibility of an annual pattern. The similarities between the abductions, and the differences. Prestia's interest in why the windows were open. The question mark over how the victims —if they were indeed linked—had been selected.

And when I'd finished, Dan nodded thoughtfully. "That's good, solid work. When we land, call Kellan and get him started on the search for the missing victim. And tell him to go back further too. I can't believe Mila Carmody was the first—

everything about that scene was too neat. As far as I can recall, nobody ever mentioned an issue with the AC in the Carmody home, and don't forget the maid swore the window was closed when Mila went to bed. She could be covering her ass, but I interviewed her at the time, and even when I promised she wouldn't be in any trouble if the window *had* been open, she stuck to her story."

"What about the other windows in the house? Were they open?"

"Not on that floor."

I'd studied the photos and the layout, and the Carmodys lived in an "upside-down" home set on a slope, with the bedrooms on the first floor and the living areas above. Mila's bedroom had been on the north side of the house with a view across the backyard. At the time of her disappearance, only she and her parents had been on the lower floor—the maid slept in a room off the kitchen. Mila had been the only child of Derrick and Jeana Carmody, and although she did have an older half-sister from her mom's previous marriage, Cassandra had moved out years ago. Derrick reportedly slept through anything, and Jeana took sleeping pills as well as wearing earplugs to block out her husband's snoring.

"So much about this case doesn't make sense."

"We're finding pieces of the jigsaw, but we don't yet know how they fit together. Or even *if* they fit together."

"But there are a number of similarities between the disappearances."

"Agreed. Let's go talk to Patti Metgood, see what she has to say."

Patti Metgood was a tiny, birdlike woman with big blue eyes and flyaway blonde hair that she couldn't stop fidgeting with. Everything about her screamed "nervous." She'd agreed to the meeting readily enough, but now I wondered if she was hiding something. Her sister hovered protectively in the background, ready to swoop in if Dan or I asked the wrong question.

Dan took the lead. "Thank you for speaking with us today. I appreciate that this can't be easy, and we're very sorry for your loss."

"I'll do anything to help catch the man who killed Donna. Three years. It's been more than three years, and the police don't even have a suspect."

"Patti calls them every month," the sister said. "All they say is that they're 'working on it.' But what we don't understand is why you're here?"

Was the sister going to help or hinder?

"It's possible that Donna's death might be connected with another case we're investigating. We don't want to raise your hopes prematurely, but we do need to consider a link."

"What link?"

"The method of abduction is similar to that in two other cases we're looking at."

Patti clutched at the little gold cross that hung around her neck. "*Two* other cases?"

"I'm afraid so. Patti, could you talk us through what happened that night?"

"I... I..." She seemed to steel herself. "Yes. Yes, if you think it would help. Where should I start?"

"Right at the beginning. When did your AC fail?"

"The AC? I don't... Why does that matter?"

"We understand the suspect entered your home through Donna's window. Did you habitually leave it open at night?"

"No, no, only because...yes, the AC." Comprehension dawned. "It broke maybe three days before? Norm called the company, but they couldn't send anyone until the next week. He was so angry, and..." She trailed off. "He was upset, that's all."

The sister rolled her eyes. "Norm was always 'upset.'"

"Did Norm have issues with his temper?"

"He just liked to be treated right."

"Patti!" the sister chided. "You got divorced. You don't need to cover for that jerk, not now, not ever again." She turned to Dan. "You bet your ass Norm had anger issues. If he hadn't been asleep next to Patti when Donna disappeared, he'd have been number one at the top of my suspect list."

Interesting.

"Did he hurt you physically?" Dan asked Patti gently.

"Sometimes he just used to...lash out. But I learned to avoid him when he was in those moods."

"What about Donna? Did he touch her?"

"I..."

"Patti..." the sister warned.

"Hardly ever, but there were days when he'd been drinking, and... He hadn't laid a hand on her for months, I swear. And never in *that* way. He was getting help for the drinking, but after she died, everything just...fell apart again."

"Are you certain he was asleep in bed with you all night?"

Vigorous nodding. "I'm a very light sleeper."

"But you didn't hear anyone come into Donna's room?"

For a moment, Patti looked puzzled, but then her brow smoothed. "There was a fan. Norm put a fan in Donna's room because the AC was out, and it rattled."

"Was Donna a light sleeper too?"

"Oh, no, Donna slept like the dead." The memory brought a faint smile, but that smile morphed into horror when Patti realised what she'd said. "Oh my gosh, I... She's gone. My baby's gone."

Tears came, and the sister was quick with tissues and a

hug. It was clear she'd practised that move dozens of times, and it was also clear that we were getting more of the truth than the cops had gotten three years ago. Dan always said that hostile exes made the best witnesses.

She touched Patti lightly on the arm, bringing her back. "Donna didn't deserve to walk with the angels so soon."

"She was the sweetest"—sniff—"girl. Such an easy baby and so creative as she got older. Do you have children?"

"A son."

"Then you know what a big piece of your heart a child holds. Mine... It'll never be whole again."

"Let's see if we can get justice for Donna, okay? We were talking about the AC... You said Norm called a technician— can you remember the name of the company he used?"

"A local place. They installed the system, and it was still under warranty. I think that's why he was so mad, because it never should have broken that way, and the nights were sweltering. He kept tossing and turning..."

"Do you know where Norm lives now?"

The sister snorted. "Good luck with finding that jackass. He took off with the neighbour's wife and Patti's share of the proceeds from the house sale."

And still Patti tried to minimise the man's actions? Boy, he'd really done a number on her. But when I'd looked through the Metgood file last night, there'd been no mention of domestic violence whatsoever, so I suppose I had to view this as progress. At least she had her sister to help out.

"Sounds like a real treasure," Dan said.

"Don't get me started. Patti, tell the investigators what happened after the AC broke."

"Honestly, it was just a regular week."

"Donna was on summer vacation?"

"Class started the next Monday, so we went shopping for clothes and school supplies. Donna liked to have a new pencil case at the start of every term. Norm said she didn't need one, but there's always so much peer pressure among kids, isn't there? And I took her bowling, and to the hairstylist. We'd planned to head over to the park as well, but Donna didn't want to go without Cleo, and C-C-Cleo was away with her parents, so Donna spent a lot of time splashing around in the pool on her own."

"Who's Cleo?"

"Her best friend. She lived right next door, and...and..." More tears.

"It was Cleo's mom that Norm ran off with," the sister supplied.

"I-I-I didn't even realise he liked her, not in that way. He always said she talked too much."

What an absolute car crash of a relationship that had been. Dan had been right earlier, hadn't she? When you found a good man, you had to grab him while you could. Prestia's words echoed in my ears. *Promise I'm not gonna make a move until you want me to.*

"Sometimes, you don't see the worst in men until it's too late. During that week, do you recall getting any visitors? Not necessarily social calls, but tradespeople, delivery drivers, door-to-door salesmen? A cleaner? A gardener?"

"You had a gardener," Patti's sister prompted. "That retired guy."

"Doug? No, he wouldn't have hurt Donna. He was always so kind to her."

"Why don't you give us his details and let us have a chat with him?" I asked. "He might have seen something useful."

"He...he passed away over a year ago. It was so sudden. One week, he was fine and digging in the yard, the next week, he was a little short of breath, and a month later, he was gone. Cancer's such a terrible disease. I went to the funeral, and his wife asked everyone to bring flowers from their yard, and there were so many bunches in every colour, and— Yes, it was a real tragedy."

"What about a cleaner?" Dan asked.

"I did all the housework myself. Norm never liked the idea of a stranger poking around in our home."

"Tradespeople?"

"I don't think so, not that month. The year before, we had the kitchen remodelled, and before that, there were painters, and Norm hired a guy to build one of those big brick grills in the yard."

"Do you have details of the contractors?"

Patti gave a helpless shrug. "Norm arranged everything."

Behind Patti, her sister rolled her eyes, but I had to sympathise. Back when I'd rented an apartment from somebody other than Blackwood, on the rare occasions I'd managed to convince the landlord to fix something, I couldn't have named any of the people he sent. I'd never checked ID, never ensured they had the proper credentials. Now I knew better, but I'd learned the lesson in the worst possible way.

Beside me, Dan changed tack. "I'm going to show you a set of pictures. Can you tell me if you recognise any of the men?"

Patti sat up straighter. "A suspect? You have a suspect?"

"At the moment, we don't know whether he's a suspect or not, but his name's been mentioned in connection with the two other disappearances I spoke about."

Dan had printed out a headshot of Micah Ganaway—I recognised it from his Facebook page, although she'd cropped out the background—and added five other photos to make a line-up. I saw one of the men from Emmy's Special Projects team, and I assumed the other four were Blackwood employees too. Patti took the page and studied it carefully. I didn't see any sudden spark of recognition, but finally, she tapped the picture of Isaiah.

"I think maybe this guy used to work in the grocery store?"

In between travelling the world with Emmy and her band of merry men? No. Nuh-uh. And she clearly wasn't familiar with Micah, which added another check to his "innocent" column.

"We'll take a look into that," Dan said. "One last question —could you see Donna's bedroom window from the road?"

"Not from the road, no. There was a tree in the way, and bushes. But I guess if someone walked a short distance down the drive..."

"Thank you so much for your help today. Can we call if we have more questions?"

"Any time." Patti bobbed her head. "I just want the man who took Donna to pay."

18

HALLIE

Outside, I jumped behind the wheel of the rented SUV before Dan offered to drive. I'd survived her piloting skills with minor palpitations, but only a suicidal stuntman could ride shotgun in her car without hyperventilating.

"Back to the airport?" I asked.

Greenbrier Valley Airport lay just north of Lewisburg, a fifteen-minute drive from White Sulphur Springs. We could be back in Richmond in time for lunch. Or possibly end up in a smoking pile of wreckage.

"Let's make a detour first."

"A detour where?"

"I want to see where the Metgoods used to live. Get a feel for the area. I spent time at the Carmody place, and I drove past the Feinstein home on the weekend. If the cases *are* linked, and I'll agree that the signature looks similar, then the victims must have something in common. Why those particular girls? How were they targeted?"

The old Metgood home was far smaller than both the Carmody and Feinstein residences, a tidy ranch-style house with a separate two-car garage on a half-acre lot. Patti was right

—from the road, we couldn't see either side of the building, but not to be deterred, Dan strolled up the driveway.

"What are you doing?"

"Looks as if somebody's home. There's a TV on in the living room." Halfway to the front door, she paused, and I followed her gaze. The driveway was offset, the L-shaped house on a slight angle, and from our vantage point, we could see the right-hand wall. "Which room was Donna's?"

I'd studied the floor plan last night, and I counted the windows. "Blue drapes, second from the back."

"No security cameras, just lights, and those are poorly positioned. See the motion sensor by the left one? It's set too low. Won't pick up anyone until they're virtually at the house. And the right one's beside a tree. If those branches get overgrown, it'll blink on and off all night long."

"The Metgoods' gardener was a retired guy with health problems, so I'll bet he didn't spend too much time climbing ladders."

"Exactly." Dan carried on along the driveway and rang the doorbell. "Physical security and tech are only as good as the people setting up the system. All those bushes would make good hiding places too. When I get a yard, I'm just gonna have grass. Grass and a pool and maybe one of those laser grids with booby traps."

"Are you thinking of moving?"

Dan lived in an apartment at the moment. A penthouse not too far from Mercy and me, but she'd bought it when she was still single.

"I always said that when I grew up, I'd swap the party pad for a we-can-grow-old-here home, and the other day, Ethan was trying to measure my finger while he thought I was asleep, so I guess that time's coming soon."

"Oh my gosh! Does he know you were awake?"

"Nah, I figured I'd just act surprised if he asks."

"*If* he asks? Don't you mean *when* he asks?"

I'd seen the way Ethan looked at her. Like he was starving and she was a chocolate fudge cake with sprinkles. But before I could interrogate Dan any further, the front door opened to reveal a brunette with a puffy, mascara-streaked face and a petulant expression. She was younger than me. Perhaps sixteen?

"Look, if you're from the truant squad or whatever, you'll have to arrest me because I'm not going back to school."

Uh-oh.

"We're not from the truant squad," Dan assured her.

"Then who are you?"

Dan already had her Blackwood ID card in her hand. "My name's Daniela, and I'm a private investigator. This is Hallie, one of my colleagues."

"I swear I didn't know the car was stolen when that guy offered me a ride. Like, I barely knew him anyway."

She sounded just the way I had ten years ago. "We're not here about the car, but you shouldn't accept rides with people you don't know. It's not safe."

"Who are you? My mom?"

"No, I'm the girl who accepted a ride with a guy I barely knew and got sold to a sex trafficker."

"You're kidding," she said, but doubt crept into her eyes. "You're kidding, right? Because that's not even funny."

"I only wish I was kidding."

Incredulity turned to uncertainty. "So how did you escape?"

"The Mafia had a shoot-out with the traffickers, and I snuck through the back door while no one was looking."

"No way."

"Yes way."

"It's true," Dan said. "And you shouldn't take rides with strangers, just like you shouldn't have opened your front door before you asked to see our ID. But that's not why we're here. Did you know the people who used to live in your house?"

"Hey, is it about that kid? The one who got murdered?"

"That's right."

"The realtor told my parents the story. Mom says it's creepy, but it's kind of cool, don't you think?"

"I'm not sure 'cool' is the best word for it."

"Well, it's not like she died *here*. D'you wanna look around or something?"

"If that's okay with you. What's your name?"

"Sure, sure. Wait, I need to put shoes on." Great, we were gonna have an audience, but at least she hadn't told us to get lost. "I'm Apple."

"Apple?" Was that better or worse than plum?

"Don't bother with the jokes—I've heard them all already. Apple pie, apple sauce, apple strudel. No, my favourite restaurant is *not* Applebee's, and my phone's a Samsung. What are you looking for?"

"We're trying to understand why Donna Metgood was taken," Dan said. "Is this a busy neighbourhood?"

"No, it's *lame*. I didn't want to move, but Mom said the traffic was too loud at our old place. Like, nothing ever happens around here."

"Do you get many people walking past?"

"Kids before and after school. People jogging and walking dogs. But this street doesn't really lead anywhere, so everyone just drives if they want to go out."

"Do you recall if the hedges at the front were lower when you moved in?"

"They were higher. The whole yard was overgrown. But there was a massive hole right there—" Apple waved an arm toward the fence that separated the former Metgood home from the neighbouring house. "And the realtor said the guy next door got mad and drove his wife's BMW into our swimming pool. Like, why would somebody do that? D'you think he was drunk?"

Possibly, but that wasn't the main reason for his actions. "His wife had an affair with the man who used to live here."

"Oh, wow. That's *stinky*. Okay, now I totally get the car thing. Did he go to jail?"

"I don't believe so."

"Hmm, that's good."

The way she said that... "It's not a good idea to drive a car into a pool."

"But what if the person totally deserves it?"

Was this connected to those puffy eyes? "Did something happen earlier?"

"Yeah, *something* happened. My boyfriend made out with Amber Kennedy from the cheerleading squad, and when I threw my book bag at him, he acted like *I* was the unreasonable one. And then Amber pushed me, so I shoved her back, and then she ripped my shirt and everyone saw my bra and now I can never go back to school ever again."

Ouch. I felt her pain. Really, I did. Except I'd been a majorette, and my high-school boyfriend had ditched me for a tuba player. I'd quit band practice that day and never returned, and in hindsight, that had been the start of my downward spiral. I'd lost the structure in my life.

"I know it's not easy, but you should go back to school. He'll go back, and she'll go back, and the only thing that'll suffer is your education."

"But everyone will laugh at me."

Fortunately, Dan had the answer. "Let them laugh. The best revenge is to hold your head high and live well. Study hard, get good grades, and in a couple of months, they'll have forgotten all about it. But if the asshole keeps jerking you around, that's when you tip the bottle of soda into his gas tank."

"Soda?"

"It won't kill the car, but it'll block up the fuel system until he gets it cleaned out."

"And don't forget to wear gloves," I added. "But Dan's right—success is the best revenge. There was a time in my life when I wanted to shove a tuba up my ex's ass, but if I was still dating him today, I'd probably never have left the town where I was born. I'm in a much better place now. Do you have a goal?"

"Like, for the future?"

"Exactly."

"Yeah, I want to study cookery in Paris and then work in a Michelin-starred restaurant."

Well, that wasn't quite what I'd been expecting, but in a good way.

"That's an excellent goal."

"My parents don't think so. They want me to join their accounting firm, and I *hate* math."

"Have you tried telling them how much cookery means to you?"

"Yeah, and they don't care."

"Then at some point in the future, there may come a time when you have to decide whose dreams to follow—yours or theirs. Neither will be easy, but the best thing you can do right now is to ensure you get a good education."

"*Parlez-vous français?*" Dan asked Apple.

"*Oui, un peu, mais je n'ai personne avec qui pratiquer.*"

"What if we found a French speaker for you to practise with?"

"You could do that?"

"Give me your number before we leave, and I'll try to set something up online, okay? I know a lot of people. But getting back to the reason we're here..."

"Right, the little girl."

"Have you had any problems with the AC in this place?"

"The AC? It broke right after we moved in, but some guy came out to fix it, like, a week later."

"Is the condenser unit around here?"

"Uh, is that the big box thing? It's behind that wall over there."

The condenser unit was whirring away, and better yet, it had a sticker on the side with the name of the firm who'd installed it. Jentech Heat and Air. I photographed the details for later, then thought back to our earlier conversation with Patti Metgood.

"Does anyone ever mention the Metgoods around here?" I asked. "Talk about what happened?"

"Not really. But my friend Lauren, she lives opposite, and she said Mr. Metgood was a real jerk. Like, he used to yell *all* the time. Lauren thought Donna ran away, but then they found her body, so I guess she didn't. And Lauren's mom said Mrs. Metgood wore sunglasses indoors even in winter, and there's only one reason for that, isn't there?"

"It doesn't seem as if they had the happiest of marriages."

"Why do girls even like boys? They're all asshats anyway."

"Another of life's mysteries."

"Do you need to look inside the house? I just made cookies."

Who could say no to a cookie? "Sure, let's look inside."

"What do you think?" I asked Dan on the flight back. "Could Donna have run away? Run away and then been picked up elsewhere by a stranger?"

"Possible, but unlikely. If she'd run away, she'd have taken stuff with her. A bag. Clothing. A favourite toy. There was nothing missing apart from her, and don't forget the footprint outside her window. What we need to do is establish whether there's a link between all the cases or not. Mila, Janiya, Donna, Araceli, Vonnie... And we need to find out what Micah was doing on the days they disappeared. We already know about Mila and Vonnie, but if he has a strong alibi for one of the other three and they *are* linked, then that's what's gonna set him free."

"But it won't get us any closer to finding the real culprit."

"Technically, finding the culprit is Detective Prestia's job, not ours. Blackwood's agreement is with Calvin Ganaway, and our task is to get Micah out of jail if that's appropriate."

"What about Mila Carmody?"

"We were fired, remember? The case stayed in the cold pile for curiosity's sake, but again, not officially our job."

This was where I began to see Prestia's argument for being a cop. Once he got a case, he was free to follow it through to the bitter end, no matter where the journey took him.

"So you're saying we shouldn't care about finding these girls?"

"No, we *should* care. We wouldn't be human if we didn't. But we can't neglect the rest of our clients to focus on work that isn't ours. Help Prestia, give him what we've got. We'll all do what we can. But if Ganaway isn't the man the cops are looking for, our paths are gonna diverge at some point."

"That sucks."

"We're not giving up. We just won't be able to spend every hour of every day on the case."

"I guess I understand."

"Prestia has other cases too. Life is a juggling act."

True, but I hated when the balls were innocent children. Who knew when another one might get tossed into the air?

"What do we do now?"

"We need to establish a timeline for Micah."

"Okay, but we can't speak with him until tomorrow."

With Prestia channelling me information, I hadn't made it a priority to go back to the jail before. Divide and conquer.

"No, but we can try Fenika. See if she keeps a diary or some kind of schedule. You have her number?"

"I'll call her."

But when I dialled her number, it wasn't Fenika who picked up. It was a supervisor at the residential home, and she sounded frantic.

"Are you a friend of Fenika's?"

"More of an acquaintance, really."

"Have you spoken with her today?"

"No, why?"

"Because we can't find her anywhere."

Terrific. Was today the day for teenager trouble?

19

HALLIE

Couldn't find her anywhere? Well, they hadn't looked very hard, had they?

Fenika was in the remains of her apartment, crying. Every room had been trashed, and someone had spray-painted *PEDO SCUM* across the living room wall in turquoise paint, along with a few racial slurs that made my blood boil.

"Aw, hell," Dan muttered, hurrying over.

"They broke everything," Fenika sobbed.

Stuffing spewed from the couch, the TV had a baseball bat rammed through the screen, and the drapes had been slashed to ribbons. The stink of spilled food rolled through from the kitchen, and when I stepped on the carpet near the bathroom, it squelched because the intruders had blocked the sink and left the taps running. More delightful messages dripped in shaving foam on the mirror.

I crouched on the other side of Fenika. "I'm so sorry. We'll help you to clean up, but... Where are the trash bags?"

"I know a guy who can install a new door," Dan said. "But we need to take you back to the residential centre now."

"No. No, I'm not going."

I made an attempt to convince her. "Sweetheart, you can't stay here. There's so much damage, and..." I waved a hand toward the graffiti. "That."

"You think this is bad? You should hear what the other kids at the home have been saying. If you take me back there, I'll just leave again."

"You can't stay here alone."

"Fine, then I'll stay somewhere else."

Dan took a calming breath. "We're doing our best to help Micah, but if we're running around Richmond looking for you, that'll only make our work take longer."

Still Fenika shook her head. "I can't go back there. I can't." She rose gracefully and pulled down her waistband, turning to the light so we could see the purple bruise on her hip. The one on her cheek had faded now, but this was fresh. "My roommate did this right before she ripped up my homework. She said my brother's a kiddy killer, and I must've known what was happening."

"We'll get you a new roommate."

"They're all the damn same. The staff too. A couple are okay, but most of them look at me like I'm trash." A tear ran down her face. "They won't let me go to my ballet classes, and I *need* to dance. It's...it's part of me. And I can't afford to miss the due dates on my assignments. If I don't make it as a dancer, then I need good grades to fall back on."

"We've got a spare room..." I started, but Dan shook her head.

"They don't let just anyone take kids. Has to be either a relative or a long-standing family friend, or you need to be approved as a foster parent. The training goes on for weeks." She cursed softly. "It'll have to be me. I went through the process last year so I could take Caleb." Another curse. "Help clean up this mess while I make some calls, okay?"

Sure, but where did we start? Actual cleaning was

impossible because the vacuum cleaner had been broken into three pieces, and judging by the smell of bleach, the cleaning products had been poured all over the bathroom.

"Do you have trash bags?" I asked again.

"I don't know. I don't know anymore."

"If you did, where would they be?"

"In the kitchen."

We found a roll of black plastic bags under the sink, miraculously untouched, and set about picking up the spilled food. Every jar had been broken, every bottle emptied.

"Should we report this to the police?" I asked Dan. "They could check for fingerprints?"

Fenika snorted. "They won't do nothin' except laugh. Truth. And who do you think made half of this mess? The cops didn't tidy up after themselves when they turned the place over."

"She's right," Dan said.

"But Prestia—"

"Is one good apple in a bowlful of rotten fruit. I hear the new chief is trying to replant the orchard, but not much is ripe yet. If we call this in, Blackwood reporting a crime involving Ganaway, they're not gonna send their best. Keep your eyes on the goal, Hallie."

The goal. Right. Clear Micah Ganaway, and then let the Richmond PD deal with the fallout. Dan's phone rang, and she turned away. I didn't envy her having to deal with this at the end of the working day.

"Why don't we take a look at your bedroom?" I suggested to Fenika. Wherever she ended up, she'd want to salvage as much of her stuff as possible. "We can get your clothes laundered if they're dirty."

Except they weren't just dirty; they were destroyed. Torn, cut, stained, even burned with holes from a lit cigarette. Fenika clutched the remains of a pale-pink tutu to her chest and sniffed. What gave somebody the right to destroy another person's entire world? Especially a totally innocent girl's? The stain on her bed looked suspiciously like urine, and broken dance trophies littered the floor. I stooped to pick up a ripped paperback. *La Fille Qui Danse*. Wait. Was that French? I only spoke English and a little Spanish, but I thought maybe it could be.

"Do you speak French?"

"When I was a kid, I saw *An American in Paris*, and after that, all I ever wanted to do was dance. I had this dream of going to L'École de Ballet de Paris next year, but even if I pass the entrance exam, there's no hope now, is there?"

"There's always hope."

And there was also the possibility we could hook Fenika up with Apple and solve at least one of today's problems.

By the time Dan came back, we'd divided the contents of the room into two piles—salvageable and dumpster-worthy. The dumpster pile was three times bigger. Fenika needed a whole new wardrobe, but luckily, I knew just the man for the job.

"Everything's set," Dan said. "Fenika can stay with me until Micah gets out or Calvin gets back, whichever happens sooner. Don't even ask how many favours I had to call in to arrange that. But..." She turned to Fenika. "There are conditions. If you have a problem, you talk to me, and if I'm not available, you call my assistant or Ethan."

"Who's Ethan?"

"My boyfriend. I'm responsible for your safety, so I need to know where you are at all times, and if there's an issue at school, I'll deal with it. You don't run off. Got it?"

Fenika nodded. "Can I go back to dance classes?"

"I'll get a driver to take you."

"Thank you. Someday, I'll make this up to you. I don't know how, but I will."

Hmm...

"Actually, there's a way you could help right now," I said.

"Really?"

"How do you feel about some extra French practice?"

"French practice?"

"Earlier today, we met a girl named Apple..."

We left Fenika at Dan's place with Ethan and Caleb, plus she had Apple's phone number and she'd promised to call her. Bradley was booked for a shopping trip tomorrow morning, and he'd also volunteered to arrange a clean-up crew for the rest of the Ganaways' apartment.

Dan still had a meeting to attend, two conference calls to join, several reports to review before they were released to clients, and a case file to read over. Grudgingly, I had to admit that she'd been right earlier. No matter how much we wanted to do it all, there just weren't enough hours in the day. Which wouldn't stop me from working my evenings to help Prestia, but we needed to pay the bills.

And speaking of Prestia, I had to call him. No, I *wanted* to call him. Usually, I loved walking into my beautiful apartment at the end of each day, spending time with Mercy and Pinchy and catching up with whatever show I happened to be watching. Sometimes, I'd go to the gym first, or head out for dinner with Mercy, Cora, and Izzy, or meet with Sky— Emmy's protégé—for a chat, but I always looked forward to going home.

But now I found myself wanting to drive south, to share the sunset on a big-ass yacht in the middle of nowhere.

Grab him while you can, Dan had said.

I picked up the phone.

20

FORD

"How was your day, frappé?"
Better for hearing your voice.

"Could've gone more smoothly than it did," Ford admitted.

"Want to talk about it?"

In his old life, Ford would have been in the bar by now, but he didn't have the same relationship with his colleagues in Richmond as he'd enjoyed in NOLA. Yes, he'd been out a time or two at Duncan's invitation when he first moved to Virginia, but the drinking-slash-bragging sessions weren't his thing, and he hadn't much liked himself when he woke up in the mornings afterward. Especially the times there'd been a cop groupie lying beside him.

So he'd stopped going out, and damned if he hadn't gotten lonely.

Until now.

"Yeah, it'd be good to talk."

"In person?" Hallie asked. "It's my turn to buy dinner, and don't start with some bullshit about corruption because we both know I'm interested in more than your case notes."

Suddenly, the evening was looking up.

"Want to come over? Or I can come to you?"

"Mercy still gets nervous around men she doesn't know, so I think it's better if I come over. Is that okay?"

It was more than okay. Ford liked that Hallie was comfortable enough on the *Shore Thing* to visit two days running.

"I've already stocked up on peanut M&Ms."

"I love you!" There was a sudden gasp. "I mean, I don't, not in that way, not yet..." Hallie cursed under her breath. "I'm making this worse, aren't I? What I meant is that I *really* like peanut M&Ms, and I quite like you too."

Ford had to smile. How could he not? With Hallie, what he saw and heard was what he got. She didn't play games the way Eliette had, and even though her past had left her fragile, she faced her fears head-on. He wanted to help her conquer every last one of them.

"And I quite like *you*, plum. Come whenever you're ready."

"Are you still at work?"

"Just left."

When he'd walked out of the building, it had felt as if there were a target painted on his back. Today had been the day when Ford's differences of opinion with Duncan had finally come to a head. Until this afternoon, Duncan had encouraged Ford to pursue links to other abductions, to hunt for patterns and evidence. But that was because he thought he could pin those crimes on Micah Ganaway.

First thing this morning, Ford had laid out the details of the five cases he and Hallie suspected might be linked, and Duncan had agreed the theory had merit. Then the phone company had finally come through with Micah Ganaway's call records. During the Carmody, Thomas, Metgood, and Feinstein abductions, his phone had been quiet. No calls made or received, no pings on cell towers. But in the middle of the time period when Araceli Suarez had been snatched, the phone registered to Ganaway had made a one-hour-and-forty-seven-minute call to a lady named Latasha Daynes.

When Ford had contacted Latasha, she'd remembered the conversation, although it had taken some convincing for her to explain why. August sixth, the day Araceli had disappeared, was Latasha's birthday, and a year ago, Micah Ganaway, an old friend and occasional booty call, had taken her out for dinner. Always responsible, he'd left after dessert to go home to Fenika, but the night hadn't ended there. No, he'd engaged in a little late-night phone sex with Ms. Daynes, and judging by her coy giggles, she'd be up for a repeat. Incidentally, she'd also scoffed at the idea of Micah being involved with any abduction and not-so-politely told Ford that all cops were assholes.

Right now, he had to agree with that sentiment.

Latasha's evidence had sealed the deal.

Ganaway wasn't their man.

But Detective Duncan? Well, he'd twisted himself into a pretzel as he tried to break apart the links he'd agreed had merit earlier, and then he'd accused Ford of trying to sabotage the case.

Out of the bullpen and into the doghouse...

But Hallie was coming over, so the day could only improve.

"Italian?" she suggested. "Should I bring Italian, or will that jinx things?"

"That depends—are you gonna threaten me with hygiene products again?"

"Shut up."

Ford just laughed. "See you later, plum."

Hallie messaged when she left the office and again when she arrived in the parking lot at River Bend, and when Ford climbed onto the swim platform, she was already striding along the dock with a large paper carrier bag in her hand and a giant purse slung over one shoulder. When he offered her a hand to cross the gangplank, she didn't hesitate. Another step in the right direction.

"We might need to reheat this. I picked it up from Il Tramonto half an hour ago."

"I'll turn on the oven. The drive over was okay?"

"There's rain headed in this direction."

"Then it's a good thing we're not having a cookout."

"Do you know how to grill?"

"I'm a man. Of course I know how to grill."

"My ex said that, and then he set fire to the fence."

Ford ran a fingertip down Hallie's cheek. "Then it's a good thing I'm not your ex."

No, he was her future.

She leaned into his touch for a second, then shimmied past him into the saloon. "Did you bring me gifts?" Her eyes lit up when she spotted the papers on the table. "Ooh, you did."

"You only want me for my files," he grumbled, and she spun to face him, grinning, and pressed one hand to his chest. It was the first time she'd touched his body that way, and heat radiated through his torso.

"But, honey, you have such *big* files."

"Only for you, sugar pie." Ford took the bag of food and arranged the foil containers in the oven. "I picked up a bottle of wine, just in case."

"In case of what? Is there something bad in those files?"

"In case you don't plan on driving home. Plus I stocked your bathroom with shampoo and shit."

"*My* bathroom?"

"You're welcome to stay here any night, plum. The front stateroom's yours, but I won't object if you want to try out my bed sometime."

"I..."

Ford brushed her hair away from her face. "Whatever happens between us, it happens on your terms. I'm not gonna push you. But I'm not gonna leave you under any doubt as to how I feel either."

Hallie bit her lip and shrank back an inch, and not for the first time, Ford wondered if he'd gone too far. But he meant what he'd said—he didn't play around. And once Hallie had taken a moment to consider, she managed a small smile.

"I like you, Ford. I really like you, maybe even more than peanut M&Ms. But I need time. Until we met, the thought of going to bed with a man again left me physically sick, but now... Now, I'm coming around to the idea."

"We've got all the time in the world. I'll take my cues from you, okay? And I swear I won't let anyone else hurt you, not ever again."

Ford spoke the truth, or so he thought. At that moment, he didn't know just how hard his promise would be to keep. No, he simply uncorked the wine and poured a glass for each of them. Ignorance was bliss, so the old saying went, and that evening, he was happier than he'd been in a year, despite the problems at work.

"I have an overnight bag in my trunk. *Just in case.*"

"Are we on the same page here, plum?"

She glanced away. Blushed. "Yes."

Thank fuck for that. Ford wanted Hallie more than he'd wanted any other woman in his life, but only in the right way. She had to be comfortable with anything they did together. And her smiles... They were better than a damn orgasm anyway.

"How was your trip to West Virginia?"

"It was...interesting. Do you want me to go over the details while the food heats?"

"Take a seat and spill. Can I tempt you with candy?"

"And ruin my appetite?"

Ford leaned forward. "You have a big mouth."

"By rights, I should slap you for that."

He waggled his eyebrows. "Who knows, maybe I'd enjoy it? Do you want the candy or not?"

"Of course I want the candy."

Ford poured peanut M&Ms into a bowl and added a handful of the regular variety for good measure. Then he settled onto the seat opposite Hallie and waited while she opened her laptop. The news about the Metgoods' unhappy marriage surprised him because that hadn't been mentioned in the file, and the AC company used by the family was different from the repair guy used by the Feinsteins—he came from Premiair Cooling. Neither revelation took the case further forward. His heart went out to Fenika Ganaway, but at least he could offer some good news there.

"If we can establish a firmer link between Suarez and Feinstein, then Ganaway's in the clear."

"Are you serious?"

"Duncan doesn't like it, but he can't argue with the facts."

"But how...?"

"Phone records. The night Suarez disappeared, Ganaway spent nearly two hours engaging in coitus telephonicus with a young lady named Latasha."

"Two hours? That's...that's..."

"A hell of a lot of dirty talk?"

"I was going to say 'impressive,' but your way works too. And you're certain it rules him out?"

"According to the file, Suarez's mom checked on her just

after midnight when she got back from her evening job, and her dad found her missing when he went to kiss her goodbye at five a.m."

"That early?"

"He worked as a short-order cook at the local diner. Had to catch the before-work crowd. I'm planning on visiting them tomorrow, which will also have the added bonus of keeping me away from Duncan."

"He's that bad?"

"I've spent months wishing I'd stayed in New Orleans." Ford reached out for Hallie's hand and gave it a light squeeze. "But it turns out Richmond isn't so bad after all."

"Seriously, is he going to cause you problems?"

"Maybe." Ford sighed. "Probably. But I can't avoid doing what's right just because my partner's a prejudiced, short-sighted prick."

"Why don't you tell me how you really feel?"

Hallie had a way of lightening the mood and the weight on his shoulders too. Ford got up and grabbed a kitchen towel to take the food out of the oven, pleased his appetite had come back after the run-in with Duncan earlier.

"If I speak with the Suarez family, would you be able to take the Thomases?"

"Tomorrow?"

"Yeah." Once, he'd have wanted her to wait, but now that he'd seen the way she worked, he trusted her to speak with them first. Trusted her more than half the detectives in the squad. "They're still near Lynchburg, in the same home. I've got a number."

"If they'll see me, I can go, probably with Kellan."

"He's experienced?"

"He was a cop in Maine for eight years before he joined Blackwood." Ford slid a plate in front of Hallie, and she picked up a dough ball. "Why did *you* become a cop? Did you always want to be a detective?"

"Nah, I wanted to play football. Being a cop was my backup career."

"So what happened?"

"A ruptured Achilles tendon when I was in college."

"Ouch."

"It healed pretty well after the surgery, but I missed most of the season, and I never managed to get back to the level I was playing at before."

"What position did you play?"

"Cornerback."

Hallie grinned. "Got pictures?"

"Possibly."

"Aw, are you gonna make me hunt them out on the internet?"

"I'm surprised you haven't already."

"Perhaps I just prefer the real thing."

Ford couldn't hold back his groan. "Are you trying to kill me?"

"At least it'll be a pleasurable death. Lasagne and M&Ms —what more could a man want?"

"That's an inappropriate conversation for the dinner table, but it does involve eating."

Ford waited for Hallie to blanch at the innuendo, but she covered her momentary choke well. This was getting easier for her.

"You never did answer my question. Why did you become a cop?"

"When I was sixteen, I saw a woman get mugged in the French Quarter. I was too far away to step in, but these two cops suddenly appeared out of nowhere, chased the guy down, and tackled him. Everyone on the street started applauding, and I thought, 'Yeah, that looks like fun.' Plus cops get handcuffs and a uniform, and I heard the ladies get excited about that."

"Don't you ever stop?"

"Trust me, I can go all night."

The dough ball hit him square in the chest, but thankfully, Hallie hadn't dipped it in butter yet. He picked it out of his lap and took a bite.

"You want more wine?" he asked. "Or a glass of water? Or soda?"

"Water, please. Tell me more about New Orleans. Was it hard to leave?"

"It's got a vibe all of its own. A heartbeat. Jazz on the corner; hot, humid evenings; Creole food made from recipes passed down through the generations. But it's more than just parties every night. There's a real sense of community. Folks take care of each other."

"I bet you miss it a lot, huh?"

Ford nodded. "Especially the people. The NOPD had its fair share of problems, but we were still a team. I could hang out with those guys. In Richmond, not so much. More people lived on boats in NOLA too. The marina was always buzzing. Don't get me wrong, the neighbours here are friendly, but when I moved in, I brought the average age down by a decade."

"You're lonely," Hallie said, putting into words what Ford had been reluctant to admit.

"I guess I am."

He spent at least one day a week with Sylvie and the kids, and stepped in whenever her ex came over to make a nuisance of himself, which averaged out at three times a month. Less now that he'd realised Ford was around. The rest of the time... Ford had tried going to bars, but they didn't have the same relaxed atmosphere. Everyone assumed you were there to either drink or hook up, and even if he picked a quiet corner, a stray woman always managed to find him. Go to a restaurant alone, and folks figured he'd been stood up. The pitying glances made him squirm, so now he got takeout or cooked for himself. He'd yet to identify where his kind of people hung out.

"You can share my friends if you want. I think they'd like you, but you might prefer to leave your badge at home."

What had he done to deserve this woman? He had to swallow the lump in his throat before he could speak.

"So I guess that's dinner at your place, then?"

"It's a date."

"An actual date? Or a figure-of-speech date?"

Those beguiling eyes were going to be his undoing, especially if Hallie kept biting her lip that way.

"An actual date?"

Hallelujah. "Just tell me when, and I'll be there. Uh, do I need to cook?"

"*Can* you cook?"

"I'm the official heir to my step-grandma's recipe collection, so I can make precisely seven dishes. Is there any food you don't like?"

"Celery."

Ford rolled his eyes to the ceiling. "Okay, I can make precisely one dish. I hope you're a fan of shrimp casserole."

"Uh..."

"Should we order in?"

"That might be a good idea. But I'd better warn you that Pinchy loves get-togethers. He never shuts up."

"I'll deal. Is he okay tonight? I mean, with you being here?"

"Izzy's at my place with Mercy, binge-watching TV, so he's fine. Izzy's a soft touch when it comes to snacks, plus he's quite the fan of telenovelas. He's halfway there with the theme song from *Maria la del Barrio*."

"I don't know what that is."

"Hold on to that thought while you can. Is it time for dessert yet?"

"Thought you ate dessert first?"

"You know damn well there was a tiramisu at the bottom of that bag. Dessert and a movie? Or dessert and a TV show? I'm not sure this seat is comfortable enough for a whole movie. How do you not spend half your life at the chiropractor?"

"Simple. I watch movies in bed."

"Oh."

"It'd be antisocial of me to do that tonight, though. I never abandon my guests. But if you'd prefer, your room also has a TV."

"It does?"

"It's hidden behind the mirror. Use the remote on the nightstand. And stop biting that lip unless you want me to do it for you."

She released her teeth, but they left tiny dents in the plump flesh. Fuck and damn. Ford loved having Hallie on the boat, but it sure wasn't easy to keep his hands to himself.

"So the choices are we watch a movie here together, or I watch a movie in my room?"

"Yes."

"But earlier, you said that you wouldn't object if I tried out your bed, so couldn't we both watch a movie in your room?"

"You *are* trying to kill me."

"I'm talking fully clothed here. On top of the covers, not under them. Think of it as a more elongated version of a couch."

How could he say no? Hadn't he wanted this? For her to feel comfortable enough around him to inch herself closer?

The answer was yes, but he wasn't sure he'd be able to focus on the damn movie.

"Sure, plum, we can share the bed. Just make sure you keep your hands to yourself, okay?"

And Ford would have to take a cold shower in the morning.

21

HALLIE

W here was I?

Two seconds, and I remembered I was on Ford's boat.

Another two seconds, and I realised I wasn't in the room I'd slept in last night. "My" room, he'd said. Vague memories flittered back—of dinner, of flirting and innuendos, of my brilliant idea to watch a movie in his bed.

Shit. I'd fallen asleep in his damn bed.

But where was he? I reached out, feeling blindly in the dark, but the space beside me was empty. After a quick inventory, I worked out that I was still fully clothed and he'd laid a fluffy blanket over me. It smelled of him—the musk of man mixed with woodsy cologne.

Should I stay here? Go back to my room? Wait, perhaps Ford was in my room? Should I check? What if he slept naked?

Damn, shouldn't have had that thought...

The man might not have played football anymore, but he still had muscles. I'd felt the solid bulk of him when I put my hand on his chest last night.

I'm trapped on a yacht with the Hulk's baby brother.

No, not trapped. I wanted to be there. But honestly, if someone had described this situation to me a month ago, I'd have freaked out. If they'd told me I'd be considering sex, and with a cop no less, I'd have freaked out. And if they'd suggested I might contemplate having sex on a boat with a cop who looked like an extra from *Baywatch*, I'd have freaked *the hell* out.

And it wasn't just sex, was it? I'd spent months learning how to please a man—or else—from a physical perspective, but Prestia wanted more. This wasn't some meaningless fling. We ate dinner together. I had *a room*. He was coming over to have dinner with my friends.

And I had to stop calling him Prestia, for crying out loud. His name was *Ford*. And Ford was looking for a girlfriend, not a hook-up. A *girlfriend*. I knew next to nothing about being a girlfriend. My previous record for a relationship was six weeks. No way could I get enough of Ford in six weeks, and back then, I'd been able to put a man's cock in my mouth without heaving. What the fudging fuck was I meant to do? Hyperventilate? Oh, that was a great start.

I forced myself to focus on my breathing. *In and out, in and out, in and out.* Maybe I was reading this wrong? Perhaps he saw me as a challenge, and once he'd gotten me into bed, he'd lose interest?

But I didn't think so.

He was the real deal.

Wasn't he?

I closed my eyes again, but sleep was impossible, and when the dawn crept over the horizon, I gave up. Kellan could take the first driving stint later, and I'd get some rest then. For now, I might as well use the time to read through the Thomas file. How did a madman select his victims?

In the living room—the saloon—I flipped open my laptop

and set to work. The Carmodys were obscenely rich, the Feinsteins gave the illusion of being well off, and the Metgoods had been comfortable, but the Thomases, they were dirt poor. Home was a trailer park, and not even a nice one. Just looking at the pictures took me back to my childhood. To days spent amusing myself outside while my mom sprawled drunk on the couch, to nights hiding under the covers while she fought with whatever waste of space she'd dragged home that week. Had Janiya Thomas experienced the same sense of hopelessness that I'd once felt?

"Hey."

I looked up to find Prestia—*Ford*—watching me. He'd swapped his jeans for shorts and his boots for sneakers.

"Sorry I stole your bed."

"Doesn't matter. You looked peaceful sleeping, so I didn't want to wake you. Figured trying to carry you back to your own room wouldn't be a smart idea either."

"You could have stayed."

"No, I couldn't. That wasn't what you agreed to, plum. You have boundaries, walls, and I'm not gonna climb over them while you're looking the other way."

Until that moment, I'd been half wishing he'd stayed, but now I was glad he hadn't because it showed me the type of man he really was. A gentleman who took consent seriously. I was in safe hands. Or not in safe hands because he wouldn't touch me, but you get the point.

"Thank you. I mean that, but next time, you can stay. If there is a next time. I don't want to assume..."

"There'll be a next time, but it's my turn to pick the movie."

"You don't like dinosaurs?"

"I don't mind dinosaurs, but my dad directed that movie, and I know the diplodocuses—diplodoci?—whatever, they were three feet tall and made out of plastic. He sent me one as a souvenir, but I gave it to a buddy when I moved onto the boat."

We really did come from two different worlds, didn't we? Although a baby diplodocus would have been super cute.

"Why didn't you say something before we started watching?"

"Because you picked it out, and you were looking forward to it."

"But if you'd seen it already..."

"Okay, look at it this way—my dad probably got paid a royalty when we streamed it, so now my inheritance is three cents bigger. I watched the movie for purely selfish reasons. Feel better now?"

I pushed him playfully and used it as an excuse to get another feel of those muscles.

"You're a dick."

"I know, but I'm your dick now, so get over it."

Oh. Uh, wait. Whoa. He was mine? Or was he joking? No, he had his serious face on. I'd kind of hoped we were heading in that direction, but I'd never expected him to just come out and announce it like that. Ford was so...so straightforward. The butterflies in my stomach might have disagreed, but my head was grateful for his candidness.

"So what does ownership of a dick get me? And don't say I can pee standing up because we both know that'd be messy."

Ford laughed, a deep chuckle that sent vibrations through my core. "Well, firstly, it's a package deal. You get the dick, but you have to put up with the rest of me too."

"I can cope with that. And secondly?"

"Hmm... That'll be more fun to work out as we go along." He nodded past me to the laptop. "Starting work early?"

"I kept tossing and turning. You're going jogging? Couldn't you sleep either?"

"I usually run at this time in the morning."

"Do you go to the gym as well?"

"Not at the moment."

"So these muscles, they all come from the running?"

I ran my fingertips down his chest, but this time, I carried on to his abs. Six-pack. Or maybe an eight-pack. I'd need a better look to work out which.

"No, I do bodyweight exercises on the way. Push-ups, pull-ups, burpees, squats, lunges, that sort of thing. I joined a gym when I moved to Richmond, but it was too far from the station, so I cancelled the membership when I didn't use it."

"There's a gym in our building, and I have a spare pass. Uh, just saying." Nerves got the better of me. "Is it weird of me to offer that? Are we moving too fast? I mean, we've known each other for less than a week, and I already have stuff in your bathroom, and I'm not sure if that's normal because I really have no frame of reference, and..."

"Do *you* think we're moving too fast?"

"How should I freaking know?"

"Let me put it another way: do you want to slow down?"

Did I? "No."

"There, that was easy, wasn't it? And maybe I *could* use that spare gym pass from time to time."

My pulse slowed. Ford, he had this steady presence, and it calmed me. No stress, no drama, just a sensible answer for everything.

"Okay. Okay, I'll get the pass. And can you send me your licence plate number? I'll ask building security to give you access to the parking garage."

Was this what a proper, grown-up relationship was like? You just shared your stuff and then your bodies and then your lives until you became a couple? No longer Hallie and Ford but Hallie-and-Ford, a single unit? Cora had managed it with Lee, and they were getting married. Sky and Asher were living together, and they were both younger than me. Emmy-and-

Black, Dan-and-Ethan, Mack-and-Luke. When I escaped from the house of horrors, I always figured I'd stay alone, that the only person I'd ever trust would be myself, and sometimes I had to remind myself that relationships were nothing unusual.

I could do this.

We could do this.

I stood on tiptoes, steadied myself with my hands on Ford's biceps, and kissed him on the cheek.

"Have a good run, frappé."

22

HALLIE

"This is the place?" Kellan asked.

Nerves buzzing, I'd made the call to Mrs. Thomas myself. I loved the investigation side of things, following the clues and solving mysteries, but speaking to people I didn't know still left me twitchy, and it was worse on the phone. At least in person, you were able to feed off their body language.

When I'd told Mrs. Thomas why I was calling, there'd been a long silence, followed by the unmistakable sound of sniffling. Then she told me nobody had called about Janiya in years. That she'd almost given up hope of ever laying her daughter to rest. She waited tables during the day and worked evenings as a janitor, but when I'd asked to visit, she'd quickly agreed to find someone to cover her shift at the diner so she could speak with us.

"Yup, this is it. Whispering Pines." With no pine trees in sight, whispering or otherwise. A dog barked in the distance, and two people having a shouting match drowned out the sound of a lawnmower to our left. *Just like home.* "Mrs. Thomas said to carry on driving until we see a turquoise pickup on bricks, then take a right."

We trundled past run-down trailers with eighty-thousand-dollar trucks parked outside, neat-as-a-pin homes with pots of plastic flowers on wooden decks, patches of scrubby lawn with rusting swing sets, pumpkins and plastic skeletons as folks got ready for Halloween, and boarded-up residences that had seen better days. A proud tabby cat stalked past, tail in the air, as two kids with a death wish ran across in front of our car. Shouldn't they have been in school? The Stars and Stripes fluttered in the breeze on a nearby flagpole, and the smell of burned toast permeated the air. A microcosm of the American dream.

Kellan gave the slightest nod toward two men in their early twenties standing on a nearby porch. "Dealer."

"Which one?"

"The blond guy."

"How do you know?"

"Poorly concealed sleight of hand and a guilty expression. There's the turquoise pickup."

The Thomas home was one of the tidier abodes, an old but obviously well-cared-for single-wide, white with a dark-blue stripe at waist height. The door opened before we had a chance to knock.

"Hallie Chastain?"

"Yes, and you're Mrs. Thomas? This is Kellan Gilmore, my colleague."

"Please, call me Dori. Come in?"

Inside, the home was as neat as the outside had suggested, and spotless too. I took a seat on an afghan-covered couch while Dori fussed around making coffee. Now I wasn't reminded so much of my previous life—my own mother hadn't been much of a housekeeper.

"Thank you," I said when Dori handed a mug over. It probably wasn't decaf, but I'd live with the caffeine today. "I appreciate you agreeing to see us."

"I was real surprised to get your call. It's been four years now, and after the first six months, the police went quiet. A cold case, they called it. Why are you here if you're not the police? We sure can't afford any investigator."

"Another girl vanished recently. We're working for a client connected with that incident, and as part of our efforts, we're reviewing past disappearances in the Virginia area in case there's a connection."

Dori sat, but barely. She perched right on the edge of a wooden chair from the dining set in the corner. "And you think there might be a connection with Janiya?"

"We're not sure at the moment, but we need to consider the possibility. I understand Janiya was taken through her bedroom window?"

"Someone climbed right in and grabbed her. The police found footprints, big footprints right outside."

"Was the window open? Or had it been forced?"

"It was open." Tears glistened in Dori's eyes. "We thought it was safe. I know what this place looks like, and I won't pretend everyone who lives here is a saint, but my neighbours wouldn't harm a *child*. Not a little girl."

"I'm so sorry she was taken." Dori looked as if she needed a hug, but I wasn't sure whether that would be appropriate. "Why was the window open?"

"It was hot, so hot that night, and humid too, I remember."

"What about the AC?"

"Back then, we didn't have AC. Couldn't afford it."

Well, shit. That blew our number-one theory out of the water. "I see. Did you often leave the window open?"

"In the summer, yes, but it's right around the back. If we'd ever imagined what would happen, we'd have closed the place up tight and moved heaven and earth to fit AC, but back then, I was sick, and even with assistance, the medical bills were crippling us. Darin—my husband—he worked three jobs just to put food on the table."

"Could you talk us through what happened that night? As best you can recall?"

"Darin and I were out—we both worked the graveyard shift in those days—and we put Janiya to bed before we left."

"She was alone?"

"No, no, my momma lived nearby, and she'd come over each night, just in case Janiya needed something. But Momma fell asleep on the couch, and when we got home, Janiya was gone. Momma didn't hear a thing."

"Is it possible to speak with your mom? Sometimes the smallest things can be important, even if they don't seem that way at first."

Now the tears fell. "Momma passed away not six months after Janiya was taken. The doctors said it was a stroke, but I know it was guilt. Guilt and a broken heart. She always blamed herself for not waking up."

"I'm sorry for your loss. For both of your losses."

"I know Janiya's gone. I feel it in my heart—call it a mom's instinct. But more than anything, I want to find her so we can lay her to rest."

"We'll do our best to help you with that, I promise."

Even if I had to work every evening and every weekend on this case, I would help. What else did I have to do? Apart from maybe hanging out with Ford? Kellan nodded too, and I knew I could count on him to assist in some capacity at least.

"In the weeks before Janiya disappeared, do you recall anyone loitering around the area?" he asked. "Any strangers? New neighbours? Tradespeople?"

"No new neighbours, and we didn't have the money to pay people to fix our stuff. Darin used to do it himself or barter favours."

"What about strangers?"

"We didn't see anyone, but I can't say for certain that there was nobody around. Darin and me, we both work multiple jobs, always have, so we don't spend as much time here as we'd like. My momma was a godsend. She was on disability, but she'd always watch Janiya while we were gone."

"Does Janiya have any siblings?"

The sadness in Dori's voice made my heart ache. "No, just her, and she was a gift. After the first round of cancer treatment, the doctors said I'd never have kids, but then she came along, and like I said...a gift. We couldn't have asked for a better child. Before Janiya disappeared, Momma always said that everything happened for a reason, but this... Why? Why her? Why did somebody take my baby?"

That was the sixty-four-thousand-dollar question, wasn't it? Why had somebody taken *any* of these girls? Once we understood the motive, we'd be closer to finding the perpetrator. Five little girls, all from different backgrounds. Why *them*? Kellan went through Janiya's history, asking about her school, her friends, her relatives, extracurricular activities, hobbies, interests. Every so often, Dori would comment that, "Nobody ever asked that before," and I began to wonder what the police had been doing four years ago.

But there were no "Aha" moments. Nothing jumped out, although it was invaluable to hear Kellan's approach to the questioning. Careful and methodical, calm and sympathetic. In some ways, he reminded me of Ford.

"Could we see Janiya's room?" he asked finally.

Dori nodded. "We haven't changed it. Even though I know she's not coming back, I can't bear to throw her things out."

Janiya's bedroom was tiny, barely big enough to fit the single bed, the narrow closet, and the toy box it contained. A pink teddy bear still sat on the patchwork quilt, books were stacked on a shelf, and Janiya's drawings were stuck to the walls. The window was single width and slid up from the bottom. If a man was careful, he could have climbed through and landed in the small space at the foot of the bed. But the window wasn't big. We were looking for a man with a light build, but reasonably tall. The size eleven footprints suggested a height of just under six feet.

But what was outside the window interested me more.

The view was nothing to shout about—a tiny yard squashed between the Thomases' trailer and the next home, patchy grass with a rotary dryer in the middle. But the neighbours had AC.

I pointed at the box attached to the outside wall of the next trailer. "Has the AC unit always been there?"

Dori followed my gaze. "Yes. I mean, I think so? I don't ever recall it *not* being there."

"Do you still have the same neighbours as you had back then?"

"Mizz Fleming? She was a friend of Momma's. She's been there forever."

"Think she'd talk to us?"

Another nod. "I can come with you, make the introductions. The police talked to her as well back then, but she didn't hear anything."

When we got to Ms. Fleming's home, I understood why. Even with the door closed, every word from the TV was crystal clear, and Dori had to knock three times before the noise finally shut off.

"Oh, sure," Ms. Fleming said when I asked about the AC. Actually, "yelled" was the more appropriate verb. She yelled in a New York accent that was even stronger than Dan's. Dan always said you could take a girl out of New York but you couldn't take New York out of the girl, and it seemed she was right. "Sure, the unit's always been there, but it got replaced three years ago. Darn thing was always breaking before that.

Every other month, there was a problem, and I could've bought a new unit twice over with all the repairs I paid for."

"I don't suppose you can remember who came out to fix it?"

"Not the name, but I got a card somewhere. They must've come a dozen times, and they still didn't get it right. Come in, come in."

Ms. Fleming was as untidy as Dori was neat. I hesitated to use the word "hoarder," but there really wasn't much space left.

"Won't be a minute. You just make yourselves at home."

"Should've brought lunch," Kellan murmured. "Looks like we're gonna be here for a while."

Dori excused herself after the first hour because she had to go get ready for her next job, and my ass was going to sleep on the lumpy couch. Kellan worked on his tablet, and I texted Ford with an update.

Me: The neighbor's AC unit is RIGHT OUTSIDE Janiya's bedroom window. Broke several times before Janiya was abducted.

Hot Cop: AC also broken at the Suarez place. Got a name for the tech?

Wait. I didn't save Ford as Hot freaking Cop. Who had borrowed my phone? I cycled through the possibilities and came up with a plausible answer: the girl from New York.

Me: Did you change Ford's name in my phone?

Dan: Not guilty. But I can take a guess who did.

Me: Who?

Dan: You're an investigator—figure it out.

Dammit. Okay, he'd definitely been "Prestia" when he messaged me yesterday. I'd meant to change it to "Ford," but I hadn't gotten around to it. Could *he* have done it? No, that wasn't his style. I'd been in the office this morning, and my phone had been with me the whole time, apart from when I went to make a coffee, and... The badass from England had been sitting on my desk when I got back. I'd assumed she'd been waiting for her husband to finish his meeting, but what if she'd had more nefarious deeds in mind?

Me: Did you touch my phone?

Emmy: Took you long enough to notice. Are you going over to the dark side?

Take a deep breath, Hallie. Reply to Hot Cop—shit—Ford first.

Me: The neighbor's hunting out the details right now. And I mean HUNTING. Her place is FULL of stuff.

Me: You're the freaking dark side! You can't just mess with people's stuff!

Emmy: Can't or shouldn't?

Me: My messages are private.

Emmy: Chill, I didn't read any of them, just changed the contact name. And am I lying? Dan showed me his picture.

Hot Cop: Tech here is Smart Climate. Let me know if there's a match.

Me: Okay, FINE. He IS hot. And sweet and sexy and kind. Happy now? But you still shouldn't mess with people's stuff.

Hot Cop: Hope that's me you're talking about, plum. Who messed with your stuff?

Shit, shit, shit! I stared at the screen in horror. I. Was. Going. To. Kill. Her. Or possibly myself. Yes, that would be easier since Emmy was basically invincible.

"Why the groan?" Kellan asked, and I groaned again. Why did my colleagues have to be so perceptive?

"I accidentally told Detective Prestia he was hot, and now I want to jump off a cliff."

"Relax—guys like getting told they're hot. Unless, of course, you don't think he's hot, and then it could be awkward." Kellan raised an eyebrow, expectant.

"Guys really don't mind if women objectify them?"

"This guy doesn't. Are we talking about the man you hooked up with the other night?"

Give me strength. "Why would you think I hooked up with anyone? Did Dan start that rumour?"

Because if she did, I'd have to kill her too.

"No, that was Carter. He noticed you wore the same clothes two days running, and on day two, you were smiling more than usual."

At this rate, I was going to run out of bullets.

"We did not 'hook up.' We were working on the case, and I fell asleep at his place."

"But you like him?"

And people said women were gossips?

"No comment."

Kellan grinned. "I'll take that as a yes. Say, I wonder if anyone's started a pool yet."

Did I mention the old Blackwood tradition of betting on people's love lives? Not that I was in love, no siree. Sex lives? No, that sounded so sordid. Ford was more than just a dick. As he said, I got the rest of him too. His smart mind, his quick wit, his thoughtfulness, those arms that were so good at hugging. Okay, perhaps I *was* a little bit in love with him.

Holy shit.

I was falling in love with Ford Prestia.

"Now what's wrong?" Kellan asked. "You look as if you got hit by a Mack truck."

Fortunately, Ms. Fleming saved me. She bustled in with a look of triumph on her face, holding a small red card aloft like a trophy.

"Here you go, hun. Eezy Breezy, those are the folks who made such a mess of the old unit. I've switched to a different company now. You want their name too?"

Not if it meant waiting for another two hours. "How

about we call you if we need it? We wouldn't want to take up more of your time than is strictly necessary."

She seemed almost disappointed. "Let me just write down my number."

Back in the car, I leaned back in the passenger seat and closed my eyes. Working on a complex case at the same time as I tried to navigate a possible relationship with Ford was exhausting. But I couldn't simply step away. Not from either of them.

My phone buzzed in my hand.

Hot Cop: You gonna leave me hanging?

Me: Maybe I think you're hot. And all that other stuff.

Hot Cop: Who do I need to have words with?

Me: Emmy Black. Good luck with that.

Hot Cop: How's about if I just buy you a new one of whatever it was she messed with?

This man... No wonder I'd been smiling in the office. He always made me smile.

Me: How's about it's your turn to buy dinner tonight?

Hot Cop: Come whenever you're ready.

Oh... I wasn't ready yet, but I was definitely getting there.

23

FORD

Ford smothered a laugh as a red-faced Hallie stood in the boat's galley and explained her "Hot Cop" faux pas. He'd nearly spit his coffee when he received that message.

"I swear I'll never leave my phone unlocked on my desk again," she said. "Lesson learned."

"What if I change your contact name to 'Hot PI'? Would that make you feel better?"

"You think I'm hot?"

"We don't need to put these burritos in the oven. You could just hold them for a while."

She pushed him good-naturedly, but he caught her hand and brought it to his lips.

"I speak the truth. Hallie, you're more than hot. You're smart and sensitive and even if we spent every day together for the rest of our lives, I'd never get enough of you. Does that help to clarify things?"

She swallowed hard, but she didn't pull her hand away.

"Uh, yes?"

"Good. Do you want dinner before or after we do our homework?"

"Before. But first...first, I want to kiss you."

First time he'd ever had a woman notify him of her intentions like that, but this was Hallie. She wasn't just any woman, and it was seven shades of sweet.

"You go right ahead, plum. I'm all yours."

When she took a tentative step closer and cupped his face in her hands, he wasn't sure what to expect. A peck on the lips? A chaste smooch? Tongues? Whatever, he'd let her take the lead. She stood on tiptoes and leaned in. Her lips were soft, and once she'd committed, she didn't back away. Skittish with a core of steel, that was his girl. As the kiss deepened, her lips parted with a soft moan, and Ford placed a hand on her back. The last thing he wanted was for her to feel trapped, but he needed that connection. Hallie kept her eyes closed, and he wished he could read her mind. Was she into this as much as he was? Or simply bracing herself for the challenge?

"Look at me, plum."

Her eyes popped open. "Huh?"

"I need to see you're okay."

"I'm okay." She wrapped her arms around his neck and leaned her cheek against his shoulder. "I'm more okay than I've been in a long time."

This time, he kissed her, and with every one of her breathy little gasps, his cock grew harder. Hallie tasted of candy and cola and hopes and dreams. A girl with a sweet tooth and a sweeter soul. He was halfway in love with her, no denying it. In less than a week, she'd stolen his heart, and now she had the power to crush it or give him hers in return.

This wasn't at all what he'd expected when he came to Richmond.

Hallie pressed closer, and he knew the exact moment she felt the effect she was having on him. Her eyes widened in shock, and her arms fell away as she took a hurried step back.

Then she glanced down, and those hazel eyes practically saucered.

"I'm sorry, I didn't mean..."

"Sorry for what? Fuckin' thing's got a mind of its own."

"For starting something I can't finish."

"Firstly, there's nothing to apologise for. And it's *we*. *We're* not gonna take things any further today, but when we do, it'll be worth the wait."

"But men have needs."

"Yeah, and I need you to be comfortable with anything and everything we do together."

"*Physical* needs."

"Plum, I have a hand, and I know how to use it. Now kiss me again, and then we can eat."

She obliged, not quite as hungrily as before, but it was still early days. Two steps forward, one step back, but that was all right. They were making progress. Ford had picked up Mexican food on the way out of Richmond—nachos and burritos, plus churros for Hallie and her sugar addiction. She'd already helped herself to M&Ms. She was finding her way around his kitchen now, and he liked that. He liked it a lot.

"Beer? Are you staying again tonight?"

"Yes, and yes."

"I'll let you do the honours with the bottle opener while I dish up the food."

She didn't worry about her drinks now, he'd noticed. Those hang-ups were gradually fading, at least on the boat. He wanted to take her on a proper date, and soon, but the folks at work would undoubtedly hear about it, and things were awkward enough in the bullpen as it was. Duncan had already questioned where some of the information was coming from. In Ford's opinion, solving the case took priority over departmental politics, but his consorting with the enemy wouldn't go down too well among his colleagues.

Still, that was tomorrow's problem. Tonight, he'd enjoy dinner with Hallie and see where the evening took them, both with the case and with whatever came afterward.

"So, the Thomas family's neighbour used Eezy Breezy?" Ford asked once the food was on the table. Hallie had sent him the name earlier. "That's five girls and five AC techs."

"Five AC techs?"

"I spoke with Jeana Carmody. The AC was working at the time of Mila's abduction, but the system was serviced regularly by CoolClime Air. What do you suppose the staff turnover's like in those companies?"

"You think a rogue AC tech could be behind this?"

"I keep coming back to the 'how?' *How* did the offender know all of those kids would have open windows on those particular nights? One kid, and someone might've overheard the parents talking, but two, three, four?"

"Mila Carmody? The AC wasn't broken?"

"That's where the theory falls apart," Ford admitted, taking a bite of his burrito. "Maybe she was ground zero? Our man could've acted on impulse, then refined his methods as time went on."

"Did you go back further to see if there were earlier victims?"

"Yeah, and I haven't found any likely matches, not yet. But there's a possible candidate for the gap between Metgood and Suarez."

"Who? Where?"

"Maria Rodas near Greensboro, North Carolina. Her parents reported that she'd been snatched through a window, but the file's thin. Real thin."

There was a theme, Ford had noticed. Kids like Mila Carmody and Vonnie Feinstein garnered endless column inches and spots on the national news. Task forces were formed. Vast amounts of overtime were approved, and everyone knew their names. The Janiya Thomases of this world, the Araceli Suarezes, they were lucky to get a vaguely competent detective and an article in the local paper.

"Are Maria's parents still in North Carolina? I could go visit with Kellan if you're not able to."

"No, because after they made the report, ICE got involved and deported the whole family to Guatemala."

"That's...that's..."

"That's a job I could never do. Ripping people's lives apart. They already lost their kid, and then they lost their home as well. Welcome to the American fucking dream."

Did Ford sound bitter? That's because he was. No parent uprooted their family from their homeland and undertook a perilous journey unless they were desperate. And rather than helping, too many of Ford's fellow countrymen punished those parents for trying to provide their kids with a safer life and kicked them back to face the same dangers they'd fought to escape.

Only this time, the new life hadn't been safer, and the Rodas family been sent home minus one of their children.

"We have to find out what happened to her." Hallie's voice dropped to a whisper. "We have to. Could we speak to the lead investigator on her case?"

"He passed away last year. But we're getting closer; I can feel it. If we go through the personnel records from each AC company and cross-reference, we might find our link."

"Obtaining those records will be faster for the police than for Blackwood. White-collar workers are easier to dig into because they all have LinkedIn profiles and websites and online résumés, but blue-collar workers don't tend to have such a wide digital presence. Can you get a warrant?"

"I can try."

"How are things going with Duncan?"

"Painfully."

Detective Duncan had let it be known that his partner was an incompetent renegade. Now most of the cops in the squad room were avoiding him, the sergeant had sided with Duncan, the captain was pissed, and there were rumours flying that Ford would be receiving a visit from the chief soon.

Good.

Bring it on.

Ford would do a show-and-tell with his evidence, and Duncan could present his story. Chief Broussard wasn't a fool. But the situation would require Ford to present the solidest case possible, and that meant more work.

"How long until Duncan retires? It has to be soon, right?"

"Approximately seven months, six days, and twenty-one hours."

"Guess you're looking forward to that."

"Those detective instincts of yours are working overtime, plum. Hell, maybe I'll even buy him a leaving gift."

"A sightseeing tour in the Arctic Circle? It's always good to experience new things."

"I was thinking of a bargain-basement skydiving adventure, but hypothermia works."

"I'll wish him bon voyage." Hallie picked up a set of cutlery. "But I won't send flowers to the funeral."

"What's with the knife and fork?"

"I want to enter some of this data into Providence while I eat, but I hate having a greasy keyboard. Don't you dare laugh."

The first nacho broke, the second slipped off her fork, and Ford struggled to keep a straight face.

"Next time, I'll just order canapés." He'd meant it as a joke, so why did the colour drain out of her face? Fuck. "Hallie? What's wrong? What did I say?"

"Nothing. Everything's fine."

"Then why do you look as if someone ate your last M&M?"

"I... I just hate canapés, okay? When I was in that...that *place*, we weren't allowed cutlery in case we used it as a weapon, so every meal was finger food." She tried a smile, managed half of one. "You have no idea how much I love forks. Mercy bought me a fancy one for my birthday last month, and it was the best gift ever."

"Your birthday... I don't even know how old you are."

"Twenty-four. And you said you were thirty?"

"Hit the big three-oh right after I moved to Richmond. Maybe we should play twenty questions? Get the basics out of the way. My sister asked me what your favourite food was, and I had no idea."

"You told your sister about me?"

"Well...yeah. And she wants you to come over for dinner." When Hallie hesitated, Ford wondered if he should have kept his mouth shut. "Too much, too soon?"

"I... What if she doesn't like me?"

"Plum, she's gonna love you."

Which would be a pleasant change. When, soon after he moved in with Eliette, Ford had asked Sylvie why she hadn't warmed to her, his sister had told him straight: she thought Eliette was a two-faced sponger with expensive taste who expected Ford to pay for everything. At the time, he'd brushed off her concerns, but in hindsight, she'd been absolutely right. Eliette had declared her love after a month and asked Ford to move in with her, and caught up in the heady rush of a new relationship, he'd packed a bag. Now he understood that she'd only needed someone to pay half the rent after her previous roommate moved out.

But those concerns didn't apply to Hallie. What you saw was what you got, and she seemed more enamoured with candy and cutlery than with diamonds. They were still moving fast, but it was a different sort of speed. More feelings, less finance.

Hallie gave a nervous smile. "I hope so. Will your niece and nephew be there?"

"Unless it's their father's turn to have them."

"That would be easier, I think. I mean, if they were there. Less attention on me and more people to talk to. I could bring dessert? I'm not the best cook, but Izzy and Mercy have been teaching me."

Another difference from Eliette's "let's go to a restaurant and your sister can hire a babysitter" approach.

"Anything you make will go down well."

"Is it my turn to ask a question?"

"You still didn't tell me your favourite food."

"Oh... Uh, lasagne."

"Not candy?"

"I can't live on candy. At least, that's what Emmy's nutritionist says. What's *your* favourite food?" Hallie suddenly stiffened. "Holy shit!"

"Pretty sure you can't live on that either. What happened?"

"The link. I think that maybe...maybe Providence found the link."

"What? Where?" Ford moved to the other side of the table so he could see her screen. "Show me."

"Eezy Breezy, Jentech Heat and Air, Smart Climate, Premiair... They're all subsidiaries of the same company. See?" She pointed at a bunch of blue text. "Brand Holdings, Inc."

"What about CoolClime?"

"Not listed. But as you said, Mila Carmody could have been a starting point. What if the guy worked for CoolClime, and then he moved to Brand Holdings? So he doesn't keep transferring to a new company every year, he just gets shuffled around within the group?"

Ford stared at the screen. There it was, in blue and white. The connection they'd tried so hard to find. In a way, it would have been easier if the culprit had kept moving around—what were the chances of two people having worked at the same five companies in five years? But with this theory, he'd only have to get two warrants—one for CoolClime and one for Brand Holdings. And a big group like that, there'd have to be good records. A central billing department. A paper trail of who'd visited which customer.

He leaned over and planted a smacker on Hallie's lips. "You're brilliant. Don't ever let anyone tell you otherwise."

"Actually, it's Mack's program that's brilliant, but I don't recommend kissing her. She's married. And also I might get jealous."

Jealous? Really? He liked that idea. *Possessive Hallie.*

"Is sending candy appropriate?"

"I might allow that."

They had a link.

By the end of the evening, they'd learned that Brand Holdings, Inc. was a family-run company headquartered on the outskirts of Richmond. Not a million miles from Blackwood, in fact. The group had been started forty years ago out of Laurence Brand's garage, with him taking on the technical work while his wife handled the back-office side of things, and grown throughout the years. Organically at first, but over the past decade, they'd embraced a strategy of acquisition. They'd buy smaller AC service companies in Virginia and the surrounding states, keep the name and logo because that was what customers were familiar with, and centralise the admin functions to save on costs. The group's website listed over thirty subsidiaries. And if the admin functions were shared, then maybe the staff were too?

Laurence Brand was still listed as CEO, but he was also president of the local golf club, and judging by his handicap, three of his kids ran the family business now. Melissa was VP of finance, Jack oversaw operations, and Alton was head of training and technical. Who would be the best person to speak with? Jack? Did HR fall under operations? Hallie covered a yawn, and Ford realised how late it was. But at least they had their starting point.

"Ready for bed?" he asked.

"Can we watch a movie?"

"It's nearly midnight."

"A show, then? I need to unwind. My head's full of corporate jargon and search terms."

"Sure, plum." If Hallie planned on inviting herself into Ford's bed again, then he didn't much care how little sleep he got. "Why don't you pick something out while I clean up here?"

"I can help—"

"By picking a show."

"Okay." She pressed a soft kiss to his lips. "And thanks."

When she headed straight for his stateroom without hesitation, he wanted to pump his fist. Hallie was getting over those fears faster than he'd dared to hope. And when he stretched out beside her, there was more good news.

"Ford?"

"Mmm?"

"If I fall asleep here tonight, will you stay?"

"You sure you want me to?"

"I'm sure." Her cheeks turned pink in the light from the TV. "Actually, I'd kind of planned on falling asleep here tonight."

Oh yeah, she was definitely his girl.

24

FORD

Laurence Brand might have started from humble beginnings, but he'd finished with an AC empire. Brand Holdings, Inc. occupied a sprawling grey warehouse on the edge of an industrial area, and through the open roller doors on the first floor, Ford spotted rack upon rack of AC units and spare parts. Vans painted with the logos of a dozen different companies dotted a neatly landscaped parking lot, and staff strode back and forth, loading and unloading equipment.

Signs directed visitors to a lobby at the far end of the building. Here, the offices rose three storeys, and a receptionist smiled a greeting.

"Can I help you, sir?"

"Detective Ford Prestia. I have a two o'clock appointment with Jack Brand."

"Can I ask what it's concerning?"

"I'm afraid not."

Ford had kept it vague on the phone. Just told Brand's executive assistant that there was a potential issue with an employee, and he needed to speak with the boss. Was the receptionist merely being nosy? Or had she been told to fish?

Her smile slipped a fraction. "Please take a seat, and I'll let him know you're here."

The lobby was like a hundred others that Ford had been in. Uncomfortable cream leather seats, a coffee table but no coffee, corporate brochures scattered around just in case he got the urge to upgrade his AC system while he waited. At two o'clock precisely, the elevator doors opened and a curvy blonde appeared.

"Mr. Brand will see you now."

Ford followed her to a third-floor corner office, where a smartly dressed man sat behind a sleek glass desk. Jack Brand. Ford recognised him from his photo on the group's website, although the picture had been either taken a decade ago or heavily edited. Brand looked years older in person. Ford put him in his early forties, with thinning salt-and-pepper hair and furrows etched into his forehead. No laughter lines around the eyes, though. He wore a good suit with a sensible tie and cared enough to polish his shoes. Ford felt mildly underdressed in khakis and a sport jacket.

"Detective Prestia?" Brand rose and offered a hand. "I don't quite understand why you're here?"

"I appreciate you making the time to see me." Ford shook hands, then took a seat in the visitor's chair on the other side of Brand's desk. "I'm here because we've identified a possible link between your company and a case I'm working on."

"What case? What link?"

"I can't go into too many details right now, but I'm interested in the service records for five properties your group has worked at." Although they'd crossed the Carmody property off the Brand Holdings list, Ford had added the Rodas home on a hunch. "Do you keep those records?"

"For seven years, yes."

"Can you provide them to me?"

"I'll have to run the request past our lawyers, but I should imagine they'll ask for a warrant. Which properties?"

"We'll include the list with the warrant, and I have to ask that you keep this request confidential. We don't want to risk tipping anybody off."

There was a chance word would get out anyway, but the less warning a potential suspect received, the better.

"Of course, but if there's an issue with one of our employees, then I want to know about it. We put a lot of trust in them when they go into our customers' homes."

"Do you have many problems with employees?"

"No, not at all. In an enterprise this size, the occasional matter crops up, but we vet potential joiners thoroughly and monitor performance with regular internal audits."

"What issues *have* you experienced?"

"Mainly pilfering. Usually from the warehouse, but once or twice from customers' homes. Those employees are no longer with the group."

"Other than theft, have there been any complaints from customers regarding employee behaviour?"

"The usual grumbles about systems not getting fixed fast enough, parts not being available, that kind of thing. A lady called last week to criticise one of our men for leaving the toilet seat up when he used the bathroom." Brand looked as if he wanted to roll his eyes, but he held steady. Practice? "Most issues stem from customers not having read the service-level agreement properly. We run our own training program here, and we're very clear on what we expect from our staff, which means grievances are kept to a minimum."

So if a technician did have a taste for kiddies, he kept his urges well-hidden.

"Does HR fall under your remit?"

"An HR manager reports to me, but overall, yes."

"Do you know offhand if you took on any staff from CoolClime Air?"

"CoolClime? Not that I'm aware of. They're a small outfit —a good reputation, yes, but not serious competitors."

"Can you check? Or do we need to include that in the warrant?"

"We keep scans of résumés, but those won't be searchable. We'll have to go through them manually. Do you have a time frame?"

"Let's say between four and six years ago."

"I can't give you a name without a warrant, but if the answer is no, I can inform you of that. Good enough?"

"For now, yes. Here's my card. Thank you for your time, and I'll be in touch."

The meeting had gone as well as Ford hoped. In truth, he hadn't expected to get the information he'd needed without a warrant—corporate types liked to cover their asses so they didn't get sued later—but he'd wanted to get a feel for the place. The operation came across as slick. Organised. And Jack Brand's concern over the possibility of a rogue employee had seemed genuine.

Back at the station, the conversation with the CEO of CoolClime Air went more smoothly. Actually, he was CEO, head of HR, AC technician, and chief coffee maker, so he said. CoolClime Air only had four employees—two brothers, their buddy from high school, and the buddy's sister. Nobody else had worked for them since they started the business, and they didn't use any contractors.

Two steps forward, one step back. That was the story of Ford's life at the moment.

Where was the Carmody link?

Was there even a link?

Ford was still puzzling over that question when Chief Broussard appeared in the bullpen, grim-faced. He looked around until he spotted his person of interest, and then beckoned.

Fuck.

Make that five steps back.

The whispers started before Ford made it out the door, detectives gossiping like kids in a schoolyard.

Ford followed Broussard along the hallway to his office. The chief hadn't added many personal touches since he arrived, just a photo of his kids—no wife on account of him getting divorced—and a few pictures of New Orleans, including one of his favourite bar in the French Quarter. The Corner House.

"Jerome."

"Ford. Hearing rumours about you being at odds with your partner."

"Figured you would."

"Lay it out for me."

So Ford did. From start to finish, from Carmody to Ganaway to Brand Holdings, he laid out the bones of the case and his thought process. The evidence, the supposition, the links he'd found with Hallie. His interpretation of their young witness's testimony versus Duncan's. The question everything came back to: why *those* girls?

"And how does Blackwood fit into this?" Broussard asked. "Keep hearing their name mentioned too, and there's an element that's unhappy about it."

"I ran across one of their investigators near the start of things. They're working the case too, from a slightly different angle."

"What angle?"

"Ganaway's brother approached them."

"So they want him cleared?"

"Not necessarily. They said they'd look into the matter pro bono, and their goal is the same as ours—to make sure the man who's snatching little girls receives the punishment he deserves. Blackwood also worked for the Carmody family back in the day, and I gather the fact that they didn't solve the case is a sore point. This is round two for them. And they came up with the Metgood link."

"What about the others? Thomas, Suarez, Rodas?"

"I found those."

"Interesting."

"Blackwood isn't the enemy here. They're a source of information."

"Is that information flowing both ways?"

Ford considered lying, but he didn't want to bullshit Broussard. Not only was the chief a friend of his stepfather's, but he was also an observant son of a bitch.

"Where I believe it will benefit us, I've worked with them rather than against them. I've seen their technology, and it's light years ahead of ours. Plus they're better funded and have available manpower. Think of it this way—why would we not do everything possible to get a monster off the streets?"

"Word says they don't just bend the law, they break it when that suits them."

"I can't comment on other areas of their business, but that's not happening in this case. They're using good old-fashioned legwork and publicly available information. It's how they're putting it together that's been key. I get that there's been bad blood between Blackwood and the department in the past, but we have to consider the context—the Richmond PD was a fucking mess, so Blackwood picked up the slack and made us look like fools in the process. And then there was this Ring business that Chief Garland was involved in..."

Broussard sat back and sighed. "Can't say I disagree. Not with any of it. But I'm walking a fine line here—I'm the new guy, and I need to build trust within my team as well as improving the solve rate."

"Duncan has his own agenda."

"Again, I'm not disagreeing. We've worked together

before, Ford. You're a good detective, and I trust your instincts."

"But..."

"But I can't turn a blind eye to the tensions in the detective squad."

"I understand." Ford really did. Nobody should have to work in that environment. The question was, what did Broussard plan to do about it? Ford had known the issue would come to a head, sooner or later. Come to terms with it. Yes, he wanted to be a detective, but the infighting wasn't making an already stressful job any easier. He'd also started wondering whether Hallie had been serious when she'd suggested stepping over to the dark side. "But Duncan's due to retire in seven months, and I can't stand by and watch while he does everything possible to keep an innocent man in jail."

"You believe Ganaway's innocent?"

"I do. And his life's been turned upside down. Did you know his sister was taken into foster care because he's her legal guardian? And their apartment got trashed as well. If nothing else, that's a lawsuit waiting to happen."

"All valid points." Broussard picked up the picture of the Corner House and studied it for a moment. "When I partnered you with Duncan, I hoped your influence might turn him into a better cop, but we don't always get what we wish for. Can I speak candidly?"

"Always. I prefer it."

"Good. Duncan's a known troublemaker, and he only survived the departmental clear-out because he's so close to retirement. He was a borderline case, and HR believed it would be easier to let him keep his pension and fade quietly into the night rather than risk him kicking up a stink. But it seems he's not on board with that plan." Broussard stared past Ford for a moment, then came to a decision. "Fuck it. Do whatever you need to do to get that warrant. I'll deal with

Duncan and your captain. The detective sergeant..." Broussard just shook his head. "The less said about him, the better."

"I need to take formal statements from the witnesses. One of them was interviewed by Blackwood, not me."

"Get it done ASAP, and we'll line up a judge."

"And Ganaway?"

"The links between those girls need to be stronger, then Ganaway will get out based on his alibi for the Suarez case. Carmody?"

"The media and Duncan made that link based on the superficial facts available, and the timeline fits. But there are subtle differences between the cases."

"You think Carmody's separate?"

"Right now, I wouldn't want to say either way."

Broussard nodded. "That's better than the bullshit I got from Detective Duncan. Well, why are you still sitting there? Get to work."

"What about Blackwood? Is working with them going to be a problem?"

"Keep it legal, Prestia. Do not jeopardise a future prosecution."

"Understood." Ford had to smile as he stood and saluted the chief. "Getting to work, sir."

He was almost at the door when Broussard spoke again.

"I should also say good work on the Michelle Moody case. How did you work out the girl was with her biological father?"

That had been the easiest case Ford had ever solved. Maybe he should send the cyber gurus at Blackwood a fruit basket as well as a box of candy? Based on the tip Hallie had come up with, he'd gotten in touch with the authorities in Idaho, and the local sheriff's department had done the legwork for him.

"Tip from a source."

"And would that source work for Blackwood?"

Ford's smile gave Broussard his answer.

"Do you want the good news or the bad news?" Hallie asked.

"Funny, that was gonna be my line."

"Why?" Ford didn't miss the nervous hitch in her voice. She was a natural pessimist, although he could hardly blame her for that, given her past. "What happened?"

"I'm still at work. Meet you in the usual place?"

"Uh, would you be able to come to my apartment?"

"Why? What's wrong?"

Now who was the damn pessimist?

"You know how we spoke about you coming over for dinner someday? To meet my friends?"

"Yes?"

"I mentioned it to Knox over lunch today, but I made the mistake of not checking behind me first, and Bradley overheard, so long story short, there's a party at my place tomorrow and we're both expected to be there. If you don't want to come, I totally understand, and I can make an excuse, but it'll only be a temporary reprieve, unless of course this *thing* between us isn't serious, and then—"

"One question—what time do you want me to come over tonight? Is this to meet Mercy?"

"Exactly. Uh, just whenever you finish work?"

"Seven?"

"Cora's grandma said she'd make dinner. Is that okay?"

"As long as she doesn't try to poison me."

Hallie giggled nervously. What did that mean?

"Her cooking's that bad?"

"No, no, her cooking's *great*. I'll see you later."

"I do have one more question. Who the hell is Bradley?"

"Emmy's assistant. He can be a little...over."

"Over?"

"Overenthusiastic, overdramatic, overwhelming, overexuberant... Just...over."

"Hey, do *you* need to make an excuse not to go? I could—" Fuck. Ford hastily stopped himself before he made a joke about kidnapping her. "I could tell him we have dinner reservations. In, say, Maryland."

"Better to get it over with. When Bradley makes a plan for a party, you can't cancel it, only delay. Are you okay with that?"

How bad could it be? Ford did need to improve his social life, and he hadn't been to a proper party—not for grown-ups, anyway—since he left New Orleans.

"Sure, plum. I'll be there." He lowered his voice. Most of the detective squad was treating him like a leper, which wasn't necessarily a bad thing given the current situation, but the folks around here sure were fond of sticking their noses into other people's business. "About tonight—do I need to bring a toothbrush? I'm easy either way, just want to be prepared."

If she said yes, he could swing by the store and pick up whatever he needed rather than driving home. And he hoped she did say yes. Waking up this morning wrapped up in Hallie had been an experience, and one he wanted to repeat. Often.

"I have a spare toothbrush and shampoo, but not underwear. Well, of course I do have spare underwear, but... Dammit, now I can't get that image out of my head."

Ford imagined her cheeks turning delightfully pink and couldn't resist joking with her. Very, very quietly.

"Plum, are you saying you want me to wear your panties?"

"No! Hell, no! I... Oh, shut up."

"I'll see you at seven. Pick out something lacy for me."

25

HALLIE

"I'm so sorry about this."

At least by apologising to Mercy, I could get in some practice for apologising to Ford later. And to all the people who got coerced into attending the party tomorrow night.

She waved a hand. "It's no problem. You're sure this guy is okay, *sí*? You haven't known him for long."

"He's more than okay. And it's true that things are moving quickly, kind of, but he's being a real gentleman about it."

"Kind of quickly? Have you...?"

"No! I mean, not yet. We're... I guess we're working up to it. He's letting me set the pace."

Which meant I could breathe, but also that I was way, way out of my depth because before the whole kidnapping thing, I was totally the girl who'd do it on the first date. Come to think of it, this had already lasted longer than most of my relationships. Taking things slow was a foreign concept.

"That's good, right?"

"Definitely, but it means I don't have the first freaking clue what I'm doing. What if I get it wrong?"

Mercy shrugged. "What do I know? My only serious

boyfriend sold me for profit, so I wouldn't take advice from me anyway. But Ford's coming at seven? We should heat up dinner. Marisol made sudado de pollo."

"That's chicken stew, right?"

"*Sí*, with rice."

"Snack?" Pinchy asked hopefully from his perch in the corner of the room.

"You just had a snack. Now you have to wait until dinner."

"Snack?"

"Not yet."

He flew a circuit of the room, squawking, then settled on top of a speaker. "Arrr arrr asshole."

Gee, thanks.

I followed Mercy into the kitchen and set about finding plates and cutlery, and once I'd laid the table, I sent a quick text to Marisol to thank her for cooking again. She'd basically adopted Mercy and me as extra granddaughters, which was all kinds of sweet but also a tiny bit strange on account of Marisol having once been involved in the family business.

Which was assassination.

But I couldn't deny Marisol made an excellent substitute grandma. She always had a hug when I needed one, she made delicious desserts, and if I needed to talk, she'd always listen. Mercy spent a lot of time with her, Izzy too, and slowly, slowly, they were growing stronger. Braver. So was I, but it was a long journey. After we escaped from our respective prisons, I'd overheard Black telling Marisol that I was the tough one, and maybe relatively speaking, that was true, but there were still days when I felt broken.

Dinner was almost ready when the intercom buzzed, and I checked the camera before I let Ford in. Once again, I thanked the stars for bringing Emmy and Black into my life. I could never have afforded to live in a place like this otherwise. They hadn't been under any obligation to provide us with an apartment, and certainly not one with security and a concierge, and yet they had. Because they wanted us to feel safe. And Black had assured us that even after the rent-free period was up, they'd offer enough discount that we'd be able to carry on living here.

"Hey." Ford greeted me with a kiss on the cheek when I opened the door, then held up a paper carrier bag from the fanciest French restaurant in town. "I didn't want to come empty-handed."

"Dessert?"

"Macarons and a tarte tatin."

"I'm definitely keeping you around."

He cupped my cheek with one hand, and my heart skipped. "Count on it."

"Come and meet Mercy."

Ford understood. He didn't try to hug her or kiss her or even shake hands, he just smiled and said, "Good to finally meet you, need a hand in the kitchen?" and Mercy looked more relieved than anything else and said, "Nice to meet you too. No help needed, but thanks." And then Pinchy said, "*Cabrón*," and everybody laughed.

Mercy clapped her hands together too. "Hey, he learned another new word. Izzy's been trying to teach him that for weeks."

Ford put the bag from Claude's on the kitchen counter. "Is it actually a new word? Or a word he already knows, just in a different language?"

"I suppose to him it's a new word?"

The ice was broken, and Pinchy flew a lap of the kitchen to celebrate. I motioned toward Ford's backpack.

"Want me to put that in my bedroom?"

"Let me get my laptop out first. When do you want to go over the case? Before dinner? After dinner?"

"Before? During?"

Ford glanced sideways at Mercy, and I knew what he was asking.

"Mercy won't say a word."

"Chief Broussard's already twitchy about me working with Blackwood."

"He knows?"

"Spoke with him earlier. Duncan won't be an issue anymore, but I promised we'd keep things legal and avoid doing anything that might jeopardise a prosecution."

I couldn't swear to abide by the first part, especially if Dan was involved because she preferred to take the expedient route over the lawful one on occasion. But we had the same goal, and that was to put a child-killer in jail.

"We won't jeopardise a prosecution."

"I notice you avoided mentioning the 'legal' part."

"If we skirt the law, you won't find out about it. Good enough?"

"I'm a cop, Hallie."

"You mean that's a badge on your belt? I thought you were just happy to see me."

Ford sucked in a long breath. "I'm always happy to see you, plum. Fuck, just don't tell me when you break the damn law."

Hmm. He wasn't thrilled, but he'd taken that better than I expected. And I wasn't going to lie to him and tell him everything we did was squeaky clean.

"My lips are sealed." Since Mercy was busy getting dishes out of the oven, I leaned in to kiss Ford properly. "Mostly."

"What did I do to deserve this?"

"Do you mean that in a good way or a bad way?"

"At the moment, I'm not sure."

Okay, on to the next subject... "You said you had good

news and bad news earlier? I'm assuming the Duncan thing is the good news, so what's the bad news?"

"The AC company that worked at the Carmody home has nothing to do with Brand Holdings. Zip. No staff in common whatsoever."

"They couldn't have contracted out?"

"Nope. The link doesn't work."

"Dammit, I was so sure..."

"Hey..." Ford tucked a stray lock of hair behind my ear. "We've still got five other missing girls. Carmody never quite fit in terms of the method."

"So what are we talking about here? A copycat?"

"Now there's a horrible thought..."

Could it be? Mila Carmody's disappearance had been all over the news for weeks. What if somebody had taken over the reins, gone bigger and better? We both stood there in silence for a moment, contemplating the fact that we might be looking for not one abductor, but two.

"What the hell do we do?" I whispered.

"For now, we carry on as we are. I'm dotting the i's and crossing the t's before I apply for the Brand Holdings warrant, and then we see where that takes us. It's possible the Carmodys' neighbour used a different AC tech, the same as happened at the Thomas place. Or our man could have come into contact with the Carmodys a different way. Maybe he was still refining his methods at that point? Right now, we have more questions than answers. You said you had good news and bad news earlier as well. What's the good news?"

"Blackwood hired a psychologist recently, and she put together a profile based on the information we have available so far. Want to take a look?"

Ford nodded toward Mercy. "Dinner's almost ready."

"I can finish here," she said. "Do what you need to do."

Sometimes when I looked back at my life, I thought fate

had been tripping on acid when she dealt my cards. My childhood had been rough, but at least I'd had a roof over my head and food in my belly. At twenty-two, I'd been kicked into the fiery pits of hell—twice—and when I clawed my way out, I'd climbed the whole way to the Pearly Gates. All of which meant I'd lucked out in the roommate stakes too. Mercy and I had been flung together by circumstances, but now we'd become the closest of friends.

"I'll clear the table afterward, okay?"

"Deal. Could you take Pinchy with you? He keeps trying to steal the rice."

"Sure."

Pinchy protested with a foul-mouthed tirade, told me not to shoot Mike, and eventually climbed onto my arm. Ford just stood there laughing, so at that point, I had to agree with the parrot when he called him an asshole.

Dr. Beaudin—she always told us to call her Ros—had emailed the psych profile to me earlier, and I'd gone downstairs to speak with her. There were still so many unknowns, including the offender's primary intent. Was his motive sexual? Or did he have some kind of emotional or selfish reason for taking young girls? Only Donna Metgood's body had ever been found, and she'd been a skeleton by that point, but there'd been no damage to her bones beyond the breaks she'd already suffered as a child. He hadn't beaten her, or at least not badly enough to cause fractures.

Ros had started with a general profile of a child abductor —male, unmarried, a social outcast. Interestingly, they weren't usually considered paedophiles and had little contact with children in their regular lives. Rather, they resorted to young girls because their lack of social skills made it difficult for them to attract an adult female. They typically had few friends and were viewed as losers.

Our man was an organised offender. He planned his

crimes carefully and selected his targets in advance. The crime scenes reflected his self-control, and he was patient, as demonstrated by the yearly pattern. He used restraints—in our case chemical—and that led Ros to believe that he'd demand submission from his victims once he took them to his lair. Plus she thought he'd met the girls in person prior to their abductions. Perhaps even had a conversation with them.

Which also made him smart.

"When we do finally catch this motherfucker, the interview's gonna be a challenge," Ford said.

"Ros said he'd anticipate your questions, and it's better to be direct."

"I'll take that on board. He doesn't quite fit into the boxes, though. He's organised, but the nature of his crimes suggests he's a social outcast. Most organised offenders tend to mix well."

"Ros noted that too. She suggested that his social issues might be more obvious when he's around women than when he's speaking with men."

"That makes sense. What's this part about him having a bolthole?"

"She thinks he has a specific place to take them. He waits a whole year to get his fix, and he doesn't want it to be over before he's had a chance to enjoy himself."

"Fuck, I feel sick."

Join the club. "And he's too well-prepared to risk being caught, so he takes them to a place where he's certain he won't be seen."

"Like a cabin in the woods?"

"Maybe."

"Or maybe not." Mercy spoke up. "When we were prisoners, we weren't always isolated, only controlled. Most of the time, I was held in a hideous mansion in North Carolina, but for a few weeks, they took me to a place in Chicago, and I could see the next house from my bedroom window. I used to wave at the old lady who lived there, trying to get help, and she just used to wave back."

Ford cursed under his breath. "You're kidding me?"

"It's true, but I don't blame her. She didn't understand."

I could go one better. "Our place was on a regular street. The FBI rented the house opposite, although we didn't find that out until later." Ford's mouth set into a hard line, and I put a hand on his arm. "Please, don't get stressed. It's over. I'm just telling you in case it's relevant to this case. What we're saying is that our perpetrator could live in a normal suburban neighbourhood."

"I'm not stressed. I'm trying to figure out if I can get away with murder."

"You're a cop, remember? Protect and serve, uphold the law."

"Some laws are bullshit."

"We can both agree on that, which is why Blackwood ignored those parts when they rescued Mercy and Cora. You should eat before your dinner gets cold."

"Think I lost my appetite."

"Marisol's food is too good to throw away."

"As Hallie says, it's over," Mercy added. "We're here, and talking about things helps. If we bury the pain and pretend it doesn't exist, it only burns us from the inside."

"Speaking of pain, do you know who's coming to the party tomorrow?" I asked.

"Izzy, Cora, and Lee."

"Rafael?"

"Depends on whether he can come up with a good enough excuse."

"I bet he says his dog's sick again."

"Bradley already thought of that and sent a bag of the

expensive dog food. The kind that stops the stomach ache. What's it called?"

"Hypoallergenic?"

"*Sí*, I always forget the word."

"What about Sky and Asher?"

"He invited them. He invited *everyone*."

Speak of the devil. My phone buzzed on the table, and it was Sky.

Sky: This party... Are we meant to bring stuff? Like a gift? No fucking clue here. And is it fancy dress?

An anxious laugh escaped. Why on earth would she think it was fancy dress? I showed the text to Mercy, and she shrugged.

"Nobody mentioned costumes to me."

"Costumes?" Ford asked.

I fired a message back to Sky.

Me: No gift needed. What do you mean, fancy dress?

Sky: I just saw the piñatas and the sombreros and wondered...

What piñatas? *What freaking piñatas?*

"Do you know anything about piñatas?" I asked Mercy.

She made the sign of the cross. "Please, no."

"Want to spend the night on the boat?" Ford asked me. "We could anchor up downriver. Nobody would ever know." He turned to Mercy. "That offer goes for you too—we have spare bunks and plenty of candy."

"Bradley will hunt us down and make us drink margaritas. And then next week, he'll hunt us down again for Halloween."

Hell, with all the work on the Ganaway case, I'd forgotten about the Halloween ball. "Tell me it's not true."

"You'll *definitely* need a costume for that night. Izzy will help—she loves making stuff."

Ford blew out a breath. "Thank fuck I'm not invited."

"Oh, you think? You're invited, buster. Consider yourself

my plus-one." Did I sound too pushy? "Uh, only if you want to."

"How can I let you suffer alone?"

I sent another message to Sky.

Me: Absolutely no fancy dress. And if you can disappear the piñatas, I'll love you forever.

Sky: Do you think I have a death wish?

Well, it was worth a try. And the evening hadn't been a complete bust—Mercy seemed comfortable around Ford, which was a big step for her. Plus he'd agreed to spend the night. At first, I hadn't been sure whether to ask him, but Mercy said that if I could cope with it, then she would too. Actually, her exact words were, "Just rip off the Band-Aid, okay?" and I figured she wanted to prove something to herself.

This morning, I'd woken to find myself using Ford's chest as a pillow, one leg hooked over his thigh and my arm around his waist. When he opened his eyes, he hadn't said anything, merely kissed my hair and asked if I wanted coffee. As if everything was normal.

As if I hadn't just reached a huge milestone in the quest to get my life back.

Tonight, we were in my bed, which was bigger than Ford's queen-size. I had a whole drawer full of silk pyjamas to choose from, courtesy of Bradley—he wasn't all bad—while Ford was sleeping in...jeans?

"You're wearing those?"

"Didn't have time to pick up a pair of track pants."

He couldn't sleep in jeans. Firstly, they had rivets, and secondly, he'd overheat. "You could take them off?"

"Only if you're comfortable with that."

I'd be more uncomfortable with him sweating next to me. "You're not commando, are you?"

"I'm an underwear guy."

"Then I'm okay with it."

"Are we gonna pretend to watch a movie?"

"Why break with tradition?" Plus it would cover up the sound of our make-out session. *Make-out session.* I sounded like a freaking teenager. "It's your turn to pick."

The movie could have been a romcom or a thriller or a slasher flick—I had no idea. The opening credits were still rolling when I turned my attention to the man next to me, and when I finally closed my eyes, my lips stung from his kisses.

As I drifted off, I had one final thought: *I could so easily love Ford Prestia.*

26

FORD

Without Duncan breathing down his neck, Ford found a weight had been lifted. *A good partner boosts you, a bad one drags you under.* He spent most of Friday on paperwork, taking formal statements and summarising the case notes so far. Dori Thomas and Ms. Fleming—he didn't yet know her first name—had agreed to give their statements to Ford and a detective from the Lynchburg PD tomorrow, and then Ford could request the warrant on Monday morning. Execute it in the afternoon. Working weekends wasn't his favourite thing, but he'd signed up to be a detective and criminals didn't respect the nine-to-five. Overtime was part of the job.

But before he spoke with the last two witnesses, he had a party to attend. Hallie didn't seem enthused, but it couldn't be that bad, right? And a Halloween ball sounded kinda fun. He'd always loved trick-or-treating as a kid, even when his dad took over the costume arrangements. He'd been the only kid on the block—hell, in the whole damn neighbourhood—wearing layers of special FX latex.

Tonight, he put on jeans and a dress shirt, then swapped

his tactical boots for a pair of brown suede shoes. And yeah, he knew Hallie had said no gifts, but when he'd walked past a jewellery store earlier and seen a pair of tiny maraca earrings, he hadn't been able to resist buying them.

The first indication that he'd vastly underestimated Bradley's capabilities came when he neared Hallie's building and saw a group of people standing on the sidewalk, looking up. He slowed and rolled down the car window. Was that... Was that a mariachi band on the balcony?

The second indication came in the lobby. He didn't have an elevator pass to take him directly to Hallie's floor, so he had to go via the concierge.

"You here for the party?" the man asked.

"On the fifth floor? Yeah."

"Take a hat." The guy pointed at a stack of sombreros on the end of the desk. "You want a poncho too?"

"I'm good without the hat or the poncho."

"You ever met Bradley?"

"Can't say I've had the pleasure."

"Trust me and take a hat."

Ford took the hat.

Three men stood in the hallway on the fifth floor, beers in hand and sombreros at their feet. One of them scanned Ford from head to foot as he approached.

"You Ford? Hallie's Ford?"

He liked the idea of being "Hallie's Ford."

"That's right."

"Take my advice and run from this shitshow while you can."

"She in there?"

"Yup."

"Then I've gotta stay."

"Don't say I didn't warn you." The man stuck out a hand. "Knox. And these assholes are Kellan and Ryder."

"Assholes? Have they met the parrot?"

"The parrot's calling everyone motherfuckers tonight. Guess he doesn't like being stuck in a cage. Good luck, buddy."

There had to be twenty people in the living room, and every single head swivelled to look at Ford when he walked through the door. This felt like being the new kid at school. He spotted Hallie on the far side of the room with Mercy and a smaller girl with similar colouring who he'd hazard a guess was Izzy. But before he could get to them, a man with lilac hair intercepted him.

"Drink! You don't have a drink! And where's your poncho?"

This must be Bradley. "I was told the ponchos were optional."

"By who?"

"The guy downstairs."

"Some people just don't understand the party spirit." Was he talking about Ford or the concierge? A waiter passed with a tray, and Bradley grabbed a bottle of beer. "Here, drink this. The caterers are almost ready with the food."

Caterers? Now Ford understood exactly what Hallie had meant when she described Bradley as "over."

Piñatas hung from stands, a couple of kids were playing hoopla with a plastic cactus, and another group was playing "pin the tail on the life-size donkey." And yeah, there really was a mariachi band on the balcony. They were actually pretty good.

He greeted Hallie with a kiss on the cheek. "This is...something."

"I'm so sorry."

"Hey, I've survived worse. At least the kids are having a good time."

"Dan and Carmen worked out that if they bring their sons to these things, they have an excuse to leave earlier."

"Sounds like a plan." Shit. Ford realised what he'd said. "I didn't mean that, not the way it sounded. At least not yet. Not that I'm averse to the idea of kids, but I... I'm gonna stop talking now."

This was going well.

But at least Izzy was smiling, and Hallie had warned him that out of the four of them who'd been imprisoned, Izzy was the one who'd had the hardest time. She took a while to warm up to strangers.

"I'm Ford," he said. "You've probably worked that out."

"*Sí.*" Now she turned shy. "Yes."

A man materialised at her elbow, and he was huge. Six and a half feet tall at least, and with a build to match the height. His hair was dark, his eyes were dark, in fact, everything about him was dark. A boyfriend? No, Izzy didn't date.

Thankfully, Hallie stepped in. "Meet Izzy and Rafael. Rafael, this is Ford."

"I know."

Ford proffered a hand, and although Rafael didn't crush it, he did issue a warning. "If you hurt Hallie, I'm the person you'll have to deal with."

"I have no intention of hurting Hallie."

"Good. Then enjoy your evening."

The giant vanished as quickly as he'd appeared, and Ford mentally crossed Rafael off his Christmas card list.

"He seems nice."

Hallie gave a nervous laugh. "He can be a little overprotective."

"I guess I have to view that as a good thing." Because who would want to risk the wrath of a man who probably sprinkled steroids on his cornflakes? "How did you cross paths with him? Does he work for Blackwood?"

"He's Cora's brother, and I guess you could call him a contractor. I was going to introduce you to Kellan, but he's disappeared."

"He's hiding out in the hallway with Knox and Ryder."

Lucky bastards.

"That's not fair. If— Oh, actually it looks as if Bradley found them."

The three of them slunk in, and judging by the gesticulating going on, Bradley was setting boundaries. Balcony okay, hallway not okay.

"Does everyone just...give in like that?"

"Most people. It's easier in the long run."

"But wasn't Kellan a cop?"

"Yes, and Knox and Ryder used to be special forces. Trust me, it makes no difference."

Bradley approached a group in the corner and tapped a man on the shoulder. For a moment, Ford thought the giant was Rafael, but when he turned, he was older, early forties at a guess. Bradley asked a question, and the man just shrugged. Brushed him off. Returned to his conversation.

"Guessing that guy's not one of the 'most people'? Who is he?"

"That's Black."

"As in Charles Black?"

A billionaire had shown up to this train wreck? That was something of a surprise. When Ford heard Blackwood was involved in the Ganaway case, he'd tried looking up the Blacks out of curiosity, but they had zero online presence. Zip. Nada. He hadn't found so much as a picture of Charles Black. Ditto for the wife. Opinion was split on her—some of his colleagues insisted she was a brainless bimbo, but others said she was... more. And those others, the ones who thought she wasn't quite what she first appeared to be, tended to fall into the group whose opinions Ford respected. Plus hadn't Hallie mentioned that Emerson Black swore like a sailor? Ford couldn't imagine a trophy wife spewing curses.

"Nobody calls Black by his first name," Hallie said.

"Noted. Is his wife here? Emerson?"

"Emmy. She was around earlier. I think Bradley's looking for her. And Black was totally lying when he said he didn't know where she was because he always knows everything."

Bradley worked his way around the room until he reached a younger guy with a tan complexion and sandy-blond hair. More gesturing, a glance toward the guest bedroom, and a lot of head shaking. Then the worst happened. Bradley set his sights on Hallie.

"Emmy's in the bathroom. You have to get her out."

"What? Why me?"

"Because you're a girl, and this is your apartment."

Hallie didn't look thrilled by that idea, and Ford didn't like the way Bradley tried to steamroller her, so he figured he'd better step in. How bad could it be?

"Those aren't valid reasons."

"Okay, fine, then you get Emmy out of the bathroom. Quick-quick, we need to do the piñatas."

"Why don't you just leave her out of the piñata thing?"

"Because there are gifts for everyone, including her, duh. And they're *fabulous* gifts. Plus we need an even number for the other party games."

There were more games? Fuck.

"I'll try talking to her," Hallie offered. "Okay?"

"What if we lock ourselves in a different bathroom?" Ford suggested once Bradley had turned on his heel. "We could take snacks and make out."

"Oh, if only..." Hallie straightened and squared her shoulders. "Just give me a minute."

27

FORD

Hallie headed for the guest bathroom and Ford followed, more out of curiosity than anything else. Who exactly was Emmy Black?

"Emmy?" Hallie knocked softly. "Bradley says you have to come out."

"He can't roust people from a fucking bathroom. That's against the rules."

The English accent was unexpected. So was the F-bomb.

"Bradley doesn't play by regular rules."

"Fine, tell him I'm busy having kinky sex."

"With who? Black's out here."

"Three-way with Dan and Sky."

Dan? Hallie's boss was in there too?

Someone moaned and said, "Harder, harder," then laughed.

"I don't have a fucking dick, Sky. That's not how girls do it."

"Well, how should I know? I've never bumped uglies with a woman before."

"Then maybe you should try it sometime? It can be quite pleasurable."

"What about a strap-on?" another voice asked, this one with a New York accent. Dan? What the hell had Ford walked into the middle of?

Hallie put her hands on her hips. "Just come and break the damn piñatas, would you?"

"Fine." A bolt shot back. "Got any tequila?"

Ford was still smiling at Hallie's assertiveness when he got his first look at Emmy Black. And yeah, she was a stunner. Waves of blonde hair, great body, face of a fuckin' angel... But when she skewered Ford with her gaze, he realised he'd rather juggle live hand grenades than get any closer. There was a toughness about her, an intensity that made him swallow hard.

"You must be Ford." She held out a hand, and as she did so, she...softened. Gone was the dark aura, replaced by something more insipid. A smile tugged at the corners of her mouth, and her stance loosened. The transformation was unnerving. "Emmy Black. I'd tell you not to hurt Hallie, but I'm sure somebody's already done the honours."

"That would be Rafael."

"Give the boy a gold star. Have you met Dan and Sky?"

Ford shook hands out of politeness, and Emmy's grip was oddly weak. An act? Had to be. Hallie's boss was a shorter woman with outstanding tits, a matching ass, and a dress to show them both off. She too exuded toughness, and he hoped some of that strength would rub off on Hallie. Not that he didn't like her softer side, but he also wanted her to have the confidence to handle anything and everything life threw at her.

Sky was a surprise. Younger than the other two, still a teenager if he had to guess, almost a junior version of Emmy with a hint of swagger. If these were Hallie's friends, he didn't know whether to be pleased or worried.

Dan gave Hallie a hug. "Sorry about this nightmare. We're gonna try hog-tying Bradley next time. We have a plan."

"He means well. I guess it's sweet that he threw us a party, but why the theme? Why are we wearing sombreros?"

Emmy adjusted her poncho. "Carmen just got back from visiting her family in Mexico City, and her mamá sent gifts for everyone. One of her friends just started a business making the ponchos, and the hats are handwoven by a women's collective near Temamatla that the Blackwood Foundation provided start-up funding for. Mamá Hernandez is expecting pictures of us wearing the outfits, by the way. And Carmen found the band—her neighbour's son is on the guitar, and this is their first paid gig. Mariachi with a modern twist. But the rest..."

"Yeah, Bradley has no idea what the word 'moderation' means." Dan looped her arm through Hallie's. "C'mon, let's get this over with. Who's gonna smash the piñatas?"

Emmy rolled a pair of the most striking eyes Ford had ever seen. What colour would you call them? They were a dark blue, almost purple.

"Go on, I'll do one. Sky?"

"Whatever."

Dan checked her watch. "Caleb'll probably take a third, but heads-up, in twenty-seven minutes, he's gonna say he's tired and we need to go home."

This was turning out to be among the strangest evenings of Ford's life, and considering he'd grown up in Hollywood, that was saying something.

"Is it always like this?" he whispered to Hallie.

She stopped mid-stride and let the others carry on.

"Pretty much. When I first came here, I thought I'd walked into crazy town, and I got so nervous at the first big gathering that I could hardly breathe, but then Rafael took me aside and we talked. Really talked. He asked what scared me about the situation. What caused the panic to well up inside and choke me. And I realised I was terrified of being blindsided again. That I wouldn't see where the threat was coming from. So he asked me who was in the room that I thought might want to hurt me? Who didn't have my back?"

"And what was the answer?"

"Nobody. Not one of these people would hurt me, and every single one of them has my back. Even Bradley. I might not love the party games, but we'll play half of them to keep him happy, and then we can relax while he cleans up the mess."

When she put it like that, it didn't sound so bad after all.

Outside in the living room, Emmy was wearing a blindfold while Bradley spun her around in circles. Despite the high heels, she managed to stay upright, which was impressive in itself.

"Okay, *lista*!"

Emmy stopped. Paused. Seemed to orient herself, then took four long strides toward the nearest piñata, wielded the stick like a katana, and sliced. The multicoloured donkey exploded, showering everyone with small turquoise boxes.

"You cheated, Emmy!" Bradley squealed.

"How is having good spatial awareness cheating?"

"You could see through the blindfold."

She pulled it off and tossed it to him. "Here—check it."

A dark-haired woman stooped to pick up one of the many boxes. She appeared to be the mother of the other child in the room, which by process of elimination made her Carmen. And was that Nate watching her? Another of the Blackwood directors? Hallie had said they were married.

"Did the piñata fillers come from Tiffany's?" Carmen asked.

Bradley folded his arms. "I wanted to get nice gifts, okay? Don't worry; there's boy stuff too."

Ford wasn't sure what he'd do with a pair of sterling silver ice tongs, but Hallie seemed happy with her necklace, a heart-shaped pendant in rose gold with a diamond on one edge.

"Can you put it on for me?" she asked.

He swept her hair to one side and hung it around her neck, leaning in closer so he could whisper in her ear.

"I wish I'd been the one to buy this for you."

"The only gift I want is your company."

Hallie twisted in his arms and kissed him softly. In the background, someone whistled, but they both ignored it.

Ford grinned. "That's the gift that keeps on giving. But I did bring you another present, just a small thing." He fished in his pants pocket for the tiny pouch containing the earrings and pressed it into her hand. "I know it's only been a week, but I'm gone for you, plum."

"I...I...I don't know what to say."

"You don't need to say anything." Ford hadn't expected her to, not yet. "Just laying my cards on the table. Aren't you going to open your gift?"

Eliette would have been poking through the pouch already, no doubt disappointed because the earrings weren't gold or platinum. But Hallie simply wrapped her arms around his waist and stood on tiptoes so they were eye to eye.

"After I've said thank you. Thank you for the gift, and thank you for making all of *this* so easy." Another kiss, and only then did she look at the earrings. "Oh, these are so cute!"

Behind them, Bradley huffed. "You people need to get a room."

"They have a room," Emmy pointed out. "You put everyone's coats in there."

"Stop talking and put the blindfold back on. I need a scarf. Who has a scarf? Emmy isn't allowed to cheat again."

Emmy looked like a mummy by the time Bradley had finished winding scarves around her head. If she could still breathe, it was a miracle. And Ford noticed that although she fidgeted and protested while Bradley did his worst, her feet didn't move.

"You think she's cheating?" he murmured to Hallie.

"She's not above it, but in this case, I don't think she has to. Sky told me Emmy practises hand-to-hand combat in the dark."

Different piñata—a watermelon this time—but the same result. Emmy smirked as Bradley examined the blindfold, still complaining about sportsmanship, and Caleb and Sky beat the final two piñatas into submission. Hallie spotted a package of M&Ms among the confetti on the floor and grabbed it.

"Treasure!"

Ford was the one who'd struck gold.

And it turned out Hallie was right about the craziness. After the piñatas were destroyed and folks had played a few games of hoopla, everyone piled plates high and settled down to eat. This was what he'd missed most about New Orleans— good food and good conversation. A handful of people left— mainly those who had to work the next day—but Dan came back after she'd taken Caleb home. Izzy fell asleep with her head on Rafael's shoulder, and Emmy lay on the floor with her head in Black's lap as Bradley tweezered confetti out of the rug alongside her.

Talk ranged from sports to politics, from history to current affairs, from relaxation techniques to fitness training, from vacation destinations to war zones, from fashion tips to costumes for the Halloween party they were all meant to be attending. Even Pinchy joined in, and evidently he was a quick learner because his new favourite phrase was, "You cheated, Emmy!" He even managed to convey Bradley's righteous indignation.

Although after the hundredth accusation, Bradley began to get sulky, and Ford couldn't entirely blame him.

"Doesn't that bird have an 'off' button?" Bradley complained.

Mercy giggled. She'd curled up against Rafael's other side, and Ford struggled to understand what had turned the grouchy giant into a chick magnet. Did women go for tall, dark, and surly these days?

"There is no button. He just keeps talking and talking and talking. Right, Pinchy?"

"Asshole. Snack?"

Hallie wriggled out from under Ford's arm, crawled across to the giant cage, and let the parrot out. He flapped back and forth, considering his options, before he finally settled on Black's head.

"Tell me the bird's house-trained," he growled.

"Oh, he is," Mercy assured him. "Mostly."

Black muttered what sounded like, "Fuck my life," and Pinchy called him a *cabrón*. Ford bet not many people got away with that. And Black clearly spoke Spanish because he responded with a few choice words of his own.

"Don't shoot Mike, don't shoot Mike, *pew-pew-pew*."

"Anyone worked out who Mike is yet?" Kellan asked.

Hallie shook her head. "The vet estimated Pinchy's age at somewhere between fifteen and twenty years old, so we reviewed all the crimes we could find for the last two decades with a gunshot victim named Mike."

"In what area?"

"The whole of Virginia. But we couldn't connect a parrot to any of the cases."

"Well, duh," Bradley said from his spot on the floor. "You probably did it wrong. That bird doesn't understand punctuation."

Black smiled, and that was a first. "Bradley's right."

Emmy groaned. "Don't tell him that. We'll never hear the end of it."

Ford thought about it. Saw that he got the answer at the same time as Dan and a fraction ahead of Hallie and Kellan.

Bradley enlightened those who hadn't picked up on his admittedly good theory. "The parrot doesn't say, 'You cheated, Emmy.' He says, 'You cheated Emmy,' which is actually quite insulting."

"And also accurate," she pointed out. "Whose credit card did you use to buy all that shit in the piñatas?"

"I got a bulk discount. And it's not shit, it's excellent quality."

Didn't that pair ever stop?

"Don't shoot, Mike," Ford said. "Add a comma. What if Mike's the offender, not the victim?"

"You really think the bird overheard a crime?" Knox asked.

There was only one way to find out, wasn't there? "Guess we'll add that mystery to the list."

One more puzzle to solve, but Ford felt he'd gotten a ways to figuring out the Blackwood dynamic that evening. These people had a bond, stronger than blood in many cases. And they each played a role in the family. Black and Rafael sat at the top of the pecking order, for example, both exuding the same dangerous vibe. They had to be related, right? Nobody had said as much, but the similarities were too great to ignore. Emmy was a woman who wore a lot of masks, but in an environment where she felt comfortable, she let her true self show. And that true self was a woman Ford wouldn't want to get on the wrong side of. Bradley was a force of nature, and everyone bitched and pretended to hate his unwavering cheerfulness and dedication to fun, but secretly, they didn't mind it. Hell, when he went overboard on the tequila, Emmy just rolled her eyes and carried him to the elevator at the end of the evening.

Ford was glad Hallie had these people in her corner, and he wouldn't mind sticking around either. He'd already agreed to go for beers with Kellan and Knox once the storm of the abduction case blew over.

And for the first time since he arrived in Richmond, he began to wonder whether a return to New Orleans was in the cards after all.

28

HALLIE

"Did you get it?"

"Sure I got it." Ford held up a bag from the deli near my apartment. "Turkey sub, right?"

"You know exactly what I'm talking about."

The warrant. Ford had spent hours at the weekend finalising the details so the request could go to the judge this morning, and I'd been on edge since he left for work. At least he hadn't had so far to travel. On Saturday night, we'd stayed on his boat, and last night, we'd switched to my apartment in the city. I kept waiting for the honeymoon period to end, either for him to get sick of me and my foibles or for me to discover he had some gross habit like collecting toenail clippings or scratching his balls in public. But so far...nothing. His ex must have been the dumbest woman in the world for letting him go.

We still hadn't slept together. Well, we had *slept* together, really, really well actually, but we were still stuck on first base. And the better everything else got, the more nervous I became about messing up the sex, which was crazy because I used to be good at that part. I'd needed to be—if we didn't please the clients, the punishments had ranged from sleeping on a concrete floor to being beaten with sandbags, which hurt like hell but didn't leave ugly bruises. And if we were no longer deemed to be useful, death had always been an option.

So yes, I knew I was perfectly capable in bed, but I was still wearing pyjamas around Ford.

"The warrant?" He broke into a grin as he dumped the deli bag on the dining table and shucked his leather jacket. "Yeah, I got that too."

"And? Is there a name in common?"

"Patience, plum. I spoke with Jack Brand, and he promised to have the information with me by mid-afternoon. Apparently, everything's scanned into the system already, and they just need to curate it. So let's enjoy lunch."

He didn't need to tell me twice. I'd meant to eat breakfast at the office, but Kellan had asked me to lend a hand with some property searches, and I owed him. Plus I'd followed up on the girl with the chihuahua who'd been in the park at the same time as Micah—Linda the dog trainer had come through with a name—but the only thing she remembered about that evening was chasing her dog for two full blocks and then getting a cramp in her calf. My stomach grumbled as I unwrapped my sandwich.

"Thanks for picking up the food."

"Your turn to get dinner?" he asked, and that answered the question of whether or not we'd see each other in the evening.

"How do you feel about Thai?"

"Thai works."

"Here?"

"As long as I'm not overstaying my welcome."

Ford set up his laptop, ready for the afternoon session. Even though Chief Broussard was aware that we were working on the same case and probably suspected we were trading information, I couldn't stroll into the police station and Ford didn't feel comfortable walking into Blackwood HQ. Not yet. This case represented a fragile truce and hope for the future, but we had to solve it before a professional working relationship between Blackwood and the cops would be accepted. Hence having lunch together on neutral-ish ground.

"You're always welcome here." And it was true—I'd had a heart-to-heart with Mercy, and she'd said she was comfortable with Ford being around, even if I was out. "How's your sister today?"

"A little calmer."

On Friday, Ford's nephew had tripped over in the schoolyard and grazed his knee. Yesterday, her ex had called to basically accuse Sylvie of child abuse. He'd taken photos of the injury, even had the kid hold up a ruler as if it were a freaking crime scene, no doubt so he could use the "evidence" in the upcoming custody case. Sylvie had been sobbing down the phone because she was terrified of losing her kids, and then the asshole had the gall to tell her that if she just went back to him, all the problems would disappear. She'd left him because of his controlling ways, but he hadn't changed. Now he tried to manipulate her from a distance.

While Ford went to comfort Sylvie, I'd headed to the Riverley estate—Emmy and Black's home—to fit in some time on the range with Sky, which had morphed into a self-defence lesson with Rafael and then a discussion about Halloween costumes with Izzy and Bradley. And thank goodness for that, because it turned out my candy habit hadn't gone unnoticed and Bradley wanted to dress me up as a jellybean. Yes, I'd told him I didn't want a risqué costume, but a *jellybean*?

"I'm glad she's feeling better. Her ex sounds like a real asshole."

"We should introduce him to Pinchy."

"Speaking of parrots, is a pirate costume okay for Halloween? It was Izzy's idea, but if you hate it, we can go back to the drawing board."

"What are you going as?"

"A gingerbread woman."

It had been a compromise.

"If you're a gingerbread woman, then shouldn't I be a gingerbread man? Or a baker or something?"

"A couple's costume? I wasn't sure you'd want to do that."

"We're a couple." A flicker of uncertainty crossed his face. "Aren't we?"

"Uh..."

"Shit." Ford raked a hand through his hair, a gesture I hadn't seen for a while. "I said I wouldn't push you, and now I'm sitting here making assumptions. Hell, I haven't even taken you on a proper date yet."

"That doesn't matter."

"Yeah, it does. As long as the shit doesn't hit the fan tomorrow evening, can I buy you dinner in an actual restaurant?"

"I'd like that." I scooted closer to kiss him softly. "And I'll tell Izzy you want a baker costume, okay?" Should I broach the trickier subject? Yes. Yes, I had to. "Uh, while we're discussing the 'couple' thing, would you mind, you know, putting your hands on me a bit more?"

"But I thought... You're sure you want that?"

"I'm still nervous as hell that I'll puke, but..." I put my head in my hands. "What am I even saying? That is *not* sexy."

Ford ran his fingertips lightly down my arms, fighting a smile. "I'll follow your lead, plum."

"Don't you get it? I have no freaking lead. I'm fumbling around in the dark here. What am I meant to do? Break off a kiss to ask you to squeeze my boob?"

He started laughing. The asshole actually started laughing, but thankfully, Pinchy was on my side.

"*Cabrón, cabrón.*"

"Yeah, you tell him."

Ford grew serious again. "I don't want to overstep."

"Can we assume I want to get to second base? And you could just..."

"Take us there?"

"Yes, exactly."

"Only if you promise to put the brakes on any time you feel uncomfortable."

No, because I knew for sure that I'd feel uncomfortable, but if I let that fear rule me, I might as well get measured up for a chastity belt and join a convent.

"If I want you to stop, I'll make that clear." I cupped his face the way I had on that first fateful meeting at the Grindhouse. "And I trust you to take us there in the best way possible."

Ford made a show of looking at his watch. "Now? Because technically, I'm still on my lunch break."

"Might as well get it over with." I clapped a hand over my mouth. "Shit. Shit! I didn't mean that the way it came out."

"Plum?"

"Mmm?"

"Stop talking."

It was at that moment I realised just how much Ford had been holding back. How much strength lurked in those muscles, how much heat coursed through those veins, and how much filth lurked at the back of his mind. He lifted me effortlessly, and a heartbeat later, I found myself straddling him. One hand came to rest on my ass, and the other fisted in my hair.

Then his lips touched mine, and they were fire.

Flames licked up my insides, and he burned that fear right

up as his tongue clashed with mine. I'd been worried that moving on would remind me of my past, but how could it when no man had ever kissed me so thoroughly before? Instinct took over and I wrapped my arms around Ford's neck, tunnelled my fingers through his hair, pressed myself against him.

"Snack?" Pinchy asked, and it should have ruined the mood, but Ford just shifted his grip and said, "Don't mind if I do."

Then his mouth was on my neck, soft, fluttery kisses alternating with hot and heavy and a hint of teeth. I tilted my head, giving him access to the parts he wanted.

More.

I'd give him everything.

His cock hardened between my thighs, and even though I knew we weren't going there yet, a small lump of fear pushed into my throat. But I swallowed, forcing it down. It had no right to ruin my happiness.

"Still okay?" Ford murmured, and I took the opportunity to snatch a breath.

"What happened to Ford the gentleman?"

The change was instantaneous. His hands dropped away, and he put space between us, or at least, as much space as he could with me still sitting on his knees.

"You want him back?"

"No, no, I don't, but..." I fanned myself with a hand. "Great balls of fire."

He glanced down, and when he looked up again, he wore a smirky grin. "Not yet, but do you have a sprinkler system in this place?"

"Actually, we do." I took a moment to study him. He'd worn a dress shirt and khakis this morning, his version of smart-casual. "Do you have a spare shirt here?"

"Yeah, why?"

"Because I always wanted to try something." I grabbed the edges of his shirt and pulled, but instead of the buttons popping off the way they did in the movies, one slipped through a buttonhole and the fabric tore a bit. "Well, that didn't work out the way I hoped. I swear I'll buy you a new shirt."

Ford guffawed. There wasn't another word for it—he freaking *guffawed*.

"Forget the new shirt, plum. This is the best laugh I've had in years."

"Oh, you think? I'd like to see you do better."

He took a good hold of my plaid shirt and yanked, and buttons pinged everywhere. Show-off. Thank the stars I'd put on good underwear this morning, except...

"*That's* how you do shirts." He paused, then took a closer look. "Is that a switchblade in your bra?"

Standard Blackwood issue, and only slightly illegal to carry concealed. Oops.

"Uh..." I blocked out the bad memories threatening to return, took a deep breath, and slid the remains of the shirt off my shoulders. "May I offer a distraction?"

Ford plucked the knife free and studied it for a moment, then set it on the coffee table. "I'm just going to forget I saw that."

Phew. And he didn't even give me a lecture. I held my ground, fought the nausea as his thumbs skated over my breasts. *This is Ford. This is good.* To distract myself, I unbuttoned the rest of his shirt and took my first good look at his naked chest. A smattering of light-brown hair, no tattoos, well-defined pecs.

"What else are you hiding?" I murmured.

"All in good time."

Goosebumps prickled my arms as he pulled down my bra cups and went to work with his tongue, gentle at first, but as I relaxed, he let his teeth graze my nipples, and I felt it right *there*. I wanted to reach between my legs, to release the ache, but...but...was that even acceptable? I had no idea. In the Florida house, men had liked to see that kind of thing, but I'd faked it every single time. Even before that, I'd never had an orgasm that wasn't self-induced, but Ford was about to tip me over the edge from second freaking base.

"I..." In a split second, I felt him start to pull away. "Do. Not. Stop. Don't you *dare* stop."

"Then what?"

"I need...a hand."

"With what?"

"A freaking hand!" I grabbed his wrist and guided him to where I needed him to be. "Just...a hand."

He got it right away, and no surprises, he knew exactly what he was doing. Even through a layer of denim, he found the right spot and applied just enough pressure to detonate me. Thank goodness the apartment had good soundproofing, because when I cried Ford's name, it caught even me by surprise. Years' worth of tension rushed out between my lips, and the release was followed by sobs I couldn't hold back.

"Fuck, what's wrong? Hallie, what's wrong?"

"Nothing! This...this is relief."

Relief that I hadn't vomited. Relief that I'd gotten to second base with the man I was falling in love with. Relief that I wasn't as broken as I'd thought.

He held me up, peppering my cheeks with sweet kisses and wiping away my tears. I'd never forget this. Never.

No, really.

Because it had slipped my mind that Pinchy was in the room, and as I borrowed the edge of Ford's torn shirt to dry my face, the damned parrot let out a cry that was uncannily similar to the one I'd choked out not thirty seconds before.

Oh.

My.

Goodness.

"Nooooooo," I groaned.

"I have a gun," Ford offered. "We could throw the body down the trash chute. Nobody would ever know."

"Mercy would know, you idiot."

"What if we just taped his beak shut?"

"Everyone will find out what happened."

"That your man got you off? Hate to break it to you, but that's not gonna be a surprise to anybody."

Hold on. Hold on a second, Ford was right. Hell, yes, he was right. And was it honestly so bad if people knew we had a normal, healthy relationship? Well, normal-ish. Call it a work in progress.

"Okay. Okay, I can deal with this." *Deep breaths, Hallie.* "I can cope."

"That's my girl."

And I was. I was very much his girl. He was stuck with me now. I buried my face in the crook of his neck and sent silent thanks to fate for bringing us together. Except it hadn't been fate, had it? A wrongful arrest, an engineered meeting, and six abductions we were still to solve, that was what had brought us together.

"I wish we could stay here like this all day, but I think our lunch break's over." Not that we'd gotten to the "lunch" part. "I'll find you another shirt."

He caught my hand before I could walk away. "To be continued."

"Tonight?"

"Your place or mine?"

"Yours? No parrot," I explained.

"What do you want for dinner?" A *ping* from his laptop caught his attention. "Damn, that was quick."

"What was quick?"

"Jack Brand—he's sent me the service files already."

Food was forgotten. Clothing—or the lack of it—was forgotten. Pinchy the pain-in-the-ass parrot was forgotten. I took a seat next to Ford and got ready to take the next step in solving this mystery.

29

FORD

From the highest highs to the lowest lows...

What happened on Ford's lunch break had been more than a surprise. Hallie had shocked the hell out of him, but in a good way. Second fucking base... Forget football; baseball was his new favourite game.

But now he was sitting on the couch with an aching dick and a deepening sense of disappointment. Brand had sent five sets of service reports, which included the Rodas home. Each time a technician—or technicians—visited a property, they filled out a record of the time spent, the work done, and the parts used. A separate column let the finance department check off the times and costs as they were entered into the billing system, and Brand had included the invoices too. Everything matched between the two sets of paperwork.

What didn't match?

The technicians.

Five properties, twenty-seven visits between them, eleven different AC techs. Nobody listed had visited more than one of the properties, and several of the visits had occurred after the relevant girl was abducted.

The link... It wasn't a link at all.

"This is impossible," Hallie muttered, scrolling through the pages for the tenth time. "There has to be something here. Something we're missing."

"I'll start speaking to these men tomorrow, find out what they remember and see if I get strange vibes from any of them."

"I could take half with Kellan?"

"Wish you could." Ford wasn't lying about that—if Blackwood's profile was right, the offender would act differently around women than men. "But these are suspects, not just witnesses, so I need to take them all. We can't risk fucking up a future prosecution. But you and Kellan can start running background—you've probably got better resources for that than we do."

Hallie slumped back, arms wrapped around herself. Ford had fetched her a sweater, an oversized thing with purple-and-white stripes, and she'd pulled it on over the remains of her shirt. Now he added an arm around her shoulders.

"We'll solve this. We will. It might just take longer than we hoped."

"What if Brand Holdings faked the reports?"

"Why would they do that? Jack Brand seemed as concerned by the thought that one of his employees could be a kidnapper as I am."

"I don't know why," Hallie admitted.

"We'll corroborate the information, just in case. You want coffee?"

"Not really."

"I'll make coffee. Don't forget to eat your sandwich."

"I'm not hungry anymore."

Neither was Ford, but he'd forced down half of a cold meatball marinara sub because he knew his body needed the fuel. In the kitchen, he set the kettle to boil. Ford's former partner in New Orleans had come up with a theory that everyone was allocated a finite amount of joy, and that joy had to be spread over every aspect of their life. So if work was going well, then other parts of a person's life would be shit, and vice versa. It was why Ignace hadn't cared when his girlfriends treated him like crap—he'd just said it was a good omen when it came to their solve rate.

Ford had never been one for superstitious bullshit, even when Mama Irma put the gris-gris on him for skateboarding too late at night and he fell off the damn thing and broke his arm, so he'd always discounted Ignace's theory. But the day after he left Eliette, they'd turned up a new witness in a long-running murder case, and now *this*. Maybe it was time to admit there was a greater power at work?

"Hey, c'mere."

Hallie's tone was enough to send Ford hurrying through the door.

"What is it?"

"Did you see this little box?"

"What little box?"

"Down at the bottom, hidden away in the technical gobbledegook. It says 'internal audit,' and it's ticked in at least one instance for each of the properties." She was sitting cross-legged on the couch now, his laptop balanced on her thighs. "Back in Kentucky, I worked for a chain of sports bars for a while, and an internal audit meant some creeper from head office followed us around all day and then wrote us up for not showing enough cleavage."

"I don't think AC technicians have to show cleavage."

"My point is that there might have been a second person there."

"And that, plum, is why I'm in deep here. You're the whole fucking package. Sweet, sexy, and seriously smart." Ford squashed next to her and nudged the laptop into the middle. "Does it give any names?"

"No names, just the checkboxes."

"I'll speak to Brand, get him to send over the reports."

Except once again, Jack Brand hid behind his lawyers. Things started off hopeful, and Ford heard him punching keys in the background, but then he got cagey.

"I'm not sure whether we'll need another warrant for this."

"It's the same information. Part of the service record."

"But we use a different form, and the internal audit department is separate from the service teams. I'd really feel happier if I ran it by someone."

Give me strength.

"Mr. Brand, this is a murder case. Any delays could result in another death."

In truth, that would be doubtful if the once-a-year pattern held, but Ford needed leverage. As long as there was a psycho roaming the streets and trailer parks of Virginia and the surrounding states, kids wouldn't be safe.

"Yes, yes, I understand, but we can't risk a lawsuit. I'll try to hurry things through."

"Make it today."

Ford threw the phone down, and it bounced off one of the couches. Where did all of those cushions come from? Damn things seemed to breed overnight.

"And breathe," Hallie said.

"I hate bureaucracy. Whole fuckin' country's run by lawyers and accountants."

"Don't forget social media influencers. They're important too. Is Brand insisting on another warrant?"

"Says he needs to check, which probably means yes."

But Ford had the number of the tech who'd worked at the

Feinstein home. He could speak with the man directly, see if he'd disclose the information.

Or at least, he could if the man answered the phone.

Hallie pulled out her own phone, tapped at the screen, and then fidgeted. "Feel like taking a walk?"

"Together?"

"No, just you."

"Why? What are you planning to do?"

"Well, as you know, Blackwood doesn't use warrants or follow rules or worry about what pesky lawyers might or might not have to say. So I thought I'd try, uh, circumventing."

Ah, fuck it. If Broussard asked, Ford would have to hide behind the old "anonymous source" excuse.

"Go right ahead."

"Oh, gee, no pressure."

But Hallie dialled a number, put the phone on speaker, and settled into the armchair opposite. Four rings, and a man picked up.

"You're through to Smart Climate, how can I help ya?"

"Okay, this is so..." Hallie let out a giggle. "So awkward. Like, a month ago, one of your technicians came out to service my AC unit, and we kind of got chatting, uh, but he didn't waste time on the job or anything, I swear. Anyhow, he gave me his number. Ohmigosh, he was real cute, but I had a boyfriend at the time, and I'm not a cheater, no way, so I didn't call him. Except yesterday, I found out my boyfriend was sleeping with my sister's best friend's dog groomer, so now I'm totally single, but I lost Angelo's number. I don't suppose you could refresh my memory?"

"Sorry, ma'am, but we're not meant to give out personal details."

"Oh, I totally understand. So could I book a service visit?" Another giggle. "With Angelo, of course. There's nothing wrong with my unit, I mean, he did a *great* job, but it's such a small price to pay for what could be true love, don't you think? Or do you have rules against that too?"

"Uh, I don't think so. Let me take a… Uh… Angelo's on vacation this week."

"Right, I remember he told me about that. It's his little girl's birthday. He showed me her picture, and isn't she the absolute cutest? Hey, could you call him and give him *my* number? Tell him it's Becky with the 'Wine me, dine me, sixty-nine me' T-shirt."

"You know what? Maybe I could make an exception to the rules just this one time."

"I'd *really* appreciate that."

Hallie fought a grin as she jotted down the number, and once she'd hung up, she held it out of reach, teasing.

"Okay, frappé. What do I get for this?"

"I'll wine you, dine you, sixty-nine you?"

A week and a half ago, Hallie would have paled if he'd said that, but today, she didn't even flinch.

"Definite on the first two, rain check on the third?"

"Hell, I'll buy you champagne." The good stuff. Would a trip to Paris be insane? "But how did you know that guy wasn't happily married? That he had a kid?"

Again, she held up the phone. "Somebody needs to learn about the privacy settings on his social media accounts. Are you going to call him? Or do you want me to do it?"

She fluttered her eyelashes, just a joke, but Ford felt a spike of jealousy. "I'll do it."

One chance… He couldn't afford to fuck it up, otherwise they'd be at the mercy of Jack Brand's lawyer for another day or two, and patience had never been one of Ford's strengths. He'd seen too much bad shit happen while he waited for the wheels of bureaucracy to turn. At least Ruiz answered the phone.

"Angelo Ruiz?"

"Yeah."

"This is Detective Ford with the Richmond PD. I'm hoping you can help me with a few questions."

"Yeah?" Wary this time.

"A little over two years ago, you made a service call to the home of Ernesto and Lona Suarez in south-east Roanoke. I have the notes here—they say you replaced a blower motor. Lona Suarez was home with her young daughter at the time."

Lona had barely recalled the visit. She'd been busy in the kitchen, baking cakes for the new business she'd started in the hope of providing a better life for her family. Two birthday cakes and her very first commercial wedding cake—she'd checked back in her order book—so her mind had been anywhere but on the men working on the AC unit in her yard. She hadn't even realised there were two of them.

"So what's your question?"

"Do you remember the job?"

"Any idea how many jobs I do in a year? Hundreds. And a bunch of them are replacement blower motors."

"On this particular job, you would've had a member of the internal audit team with you. Can you tell me his name?"

A pause.

"Okay, so I remember. Real dump of a house, mould on the walls. What'd he do?"

Interesting question.

"Why do you think he did anything?"

"Well, you're a cop, and I know *I* didn't do anything."

"Can you tell me his name?" Ford asked again.

"Alton. Alton Brand. The big boss. C'mon, what'd he do?"

Alton Brand.

Now they had their name, but where would it lead them?

30

FORD

*A*lton Brand.

Click, click, click. All those little pieces suddenly slotted into place. No wonder Jack Brand had gotten cagey on the phone. He'd looked up the audit records while they were talking and seen his brother's name on them. And *fuck*, now they'd tipped him off because what man wouldn't give his bro a heads-up that cops were sniffing around? Hell, perhaps he'd already found out after the first request? But the family would want to keep things quiet. Hush them up.

Once Ford started asking questions of employees, friends, and neighbours, word would get out, and once word got out, the media would create a shitstorm. Actually, scratch that. When they found out there were six kids involved, it would be more like a shit tornado.

So Ford had a decision to make: wade in or tread softly.

Choices, choices...

Then Ruiz took the decision out of his hands.

"Did he do something to that kid? The little girl?"

"Why would you think that?"

Another pause, longer this time.

"Alton's the boss, and I need the job. Maybe I shouldn't be talking to you."

"Nobody's gonna hear about this conversation from me."

"It's a good place to work."

"You got kids?" Ford asked, knowing damn well that Ruiz did, thanks to Hallie's research.

"A girl."

"Araceli Suarez went missing in August last year, and nobody's found a trace of her since. Recent developments have led us to look at Mr. Brand in connection with her disappearance."

"Oh, man..."

"Tell me what you know about Alton Brand."

Footsteps sounded. Shuffling, as if Ruiz was moving to another room. "He's just an odd guy, that's all."

"Odd in what way?"

"Shy. Not really sociable. The women in the office, they think it's funny because he can't make eye contact. Like, if they're having a conversation, he'll be looking all over the place —the ceiling, the walls, the floor."

Now Hallie had this big stupid grin on her face, and she mouthed, "We've got him."

Damn, I hoped she wasn't celebrating prematurely. But this felt right. Ruiz's description of Alton Brand's mannerisms matched up to the Blackwood shrink's profile, and the other pieces fit too.

"Do you recall seeing Araceli while you were there?" Ford asked.

"Sure, she was playing out in the yard. There was a climbing frame. Kind of rusty, and I tightened up a couple of the bolts while I had my tools out because the thing didn't look so safe. Probably I shouldn't have done that, but..."

"You were worried a little girl might get hurt."

"Yeah, exactly, and as I said, I got a daughter. But my prints are gonna be on that frame. I mean, if somebody checked it..."

Nobody had.

"I'll make a note of the explanation. Did you notice Mr. Brand paying any attention to Araceli?"

"You know, maybe that's why I remember the visit? Because he was down there, like crouching, talking to her. And this is a guy who never talks to anyone unless he has to. But then we left, and he didn't say another word, so I just... pushed it to the back of my mind, I guess."

"You didn't want to make trouble," Ford surmised.

"Couldn't afford to. But I'll tell you one thing for free—I wouldn't let Alton near my kid."

Nervous energy vibrated through Ford. Hallie was right —they had their man. But now came the hard part: proving it.

"How many people work in the internal audit team for the whole of the Brand group? Ballpark?"

"Four."

"Four? That's it?"

"Unless they get complaints, they only check up on us a couple of times a year. We know how to do our jobs."

"Do they cover specific areas? Or is it pot luck which auditor accompanies you?"

"Nobody ever told me, but I've worked for the Brands for nearly a decade, and I've met all of the internal auditors at one time or another."

"Any of the others give you weird vibes?"

"Nope. And one of them's a woman, so I don't suppose she'll be on your list of suspects. Always did wonder how Alton manages to communicate with her, but she said he mostly emails."

"You asked her?"

"She's cool. Laughed when she told me about the email thing."

True, they could rule her out as a suspect, but not necessarily as a witness. If she worked closely with Alton, she might have insights that others didn't.

"How do your jobs get allocated? Is that done centrally?"

"The bookings team sits in Richmond, and they email a schedule for each day. Or sometimes they call if there's an emergency. You know, like a breakdown at a hospital or a care facility, someplace where temperature swings could cause a problem for people's health."

"I need to speak with several of your colleagues, other technicians who were audited by Alton Brand. Is there a central directory you could access?" It was worth a try. "We have a warrant, but Jack Brand is delaying."

Ruiz snorted. "Bet he is, if you've got his brother in your sights. Jack's a smart guy."

"The directory? Is there one?"

"Not that a drone like me got access to, but I know a girl who works in the booking office. You want I should give her a call?"

"Will she talk to Alton Brand? It's important that we keep this quiet for the moment."

"Naw, man, not if I tell her why. Nina don't take no bullshit, and she's got a kid too."

Fuck it. They needed those contact details, and they needed them yesterday.

"I'd be grateful if you could pass her my number."

Things moved quickly after that. Hallie kept Ford's mug topped off with coffee in between doing her own research, and

Blackwood was on the case too. At the end of the afternoon, they pooled their findings.

Ruiz's friend in scheduling had provided the contact information they needed, plus the detail that the women of Brand Holdings had nicknamed Alton "Hubble" because he always stared into space when they were around.

Hubble had definitely been present at the Thomas-slash-Fleming, Metgood, and Rodas homes. There was a question mark over Feinstein—the tech whose work had been audited two years previously was no longer with the group, and although Ruiz's friend had provided a number, it was out of service. Blackwood was hunting for an alternative method of contact.

The Rodas tech thought Alton was "a bit odd" but "a great technician, really knows his stuff." The guy who'd attempted to fix Ms. Fleming's unit multiple times said Alton had seemed more interested in chatting with Janiya, who'd been leaning out of her window asking, "Whatcha doing?" and a million other questions, than in the job they were meant to be carrying out. He'd thought Alton was simply being friendly. Said he'd given the little girl candy and made her laugh. Didn't parents warn their children about that sort of thing anymore?

Because they should.

The AC tech from the Metgood home had an interesting tale. He'd been replacing fan coils at the house when he heard yelling followed by crying as Norm Metgood berated his daughter for leaving a toy where he could trip over it.

"Way over the top," the tech had said. "She was just a kid. What kid doesn't leave toys lying around the place?"

Norm's temper had been bad enough that the tech considered calling Child Protective Services, but Alton had talked him out of it. Told him to "believe in karma."

What the hell was that supposed to mean?

Because karma had struck the wrong damn person—Donna was dead while Norm was living it up with his neighbour's wife.

Hallie picked another M&M out of the dish on the dining table. "Alton was bullied in high school. Girls made fun of him because he carried a few extra pounds, and also because his mom was a real stickler for smartness and made him wear a tie every day."

"Who told you that?"

"A girl from his class. She said she felt sorry for him, but not sorry enough to turn herself into a target by breaking out the sympathy. He just withdrew. Got involved in math club and the robotics team and the science fair and avoided all social interaction."

"What about Jack? Didn't he wear a tie too?"

"Yes, but Jack *owned* it. Apparently, he got the charm and Alton got the IQ. Case in point—what do you think he's doing right now?"

"Who, Alton?"

"Mmm-hmm."

"Is this a hypothetical?"

"Uh, no?"

"Shit, Blackwood put a team on him?"

"Relax—he won't notice. And your colleagues won't know either unless you tell them. How long will it take you to get authorisation for surveillance, anyway?"

"Days," Ford admitted. If at all.

"Precisely. And by the time the bureaucrats have dithered around, you'll have missed the fact that Alton's in the cleaning aisle at the grocery store, picking out bleach."

"Tell me you're kidding?"

"Do you want to see the video feed?"

Ford cursed under his breath, but curiosity got the better of him. "Show me."

And there he was. A now-lean Alton Brand, standing next to a cart filled with buckets and mops and sponges as he studied the back of a bottle. The picture was surprisingly clear, and there was sound too. As Ford watched, the operative moved closer, closer. Too close.

"Excuse me?"

Brand glanced over his shoulder, then appeared to shrink an inch when he realised the question was aimed at him. Blackwood had a woman on their surveillance team?

"Uh..."

Damn, he really couldn't look her in the eye.

"Please could you pass me that bottle? The pink one? I can't reach it."

"Uh... Yeah, sure."

"Thanks a million."

"And now we have his fingerprints," Hallie murmured. "Thank goodness for self-checkout."

Fuck, they were slick.

"Who's that in the store? With the camera?"

"Sky. Don't worry; she's wearing a wig, and he didn't even look at her properly, so we can use her again later if we need to."

"Plum, this is a Richmond PD case. We need to take the lead here. Let us do our jobs."

"Well, Micah Ganaway's still in jail—which I think we can all now agree is a mistake of epic proportions—and as long as he's locked up, Blackwood's gonna be full steam ahead. We wouldn't be doing *our* jobs otherwise."

What could Ford say to that? It was true, every word of it. They'd screwed up with Ganaway, and his lawyer hadn't shouted loud enough or long enough to stop what had clearly been a serious error. Now they'd have to backtrack and convince a judge to issue new warrants for Alton Brand, a task

Ford was dreading because who liked to admit they were wrong?

He sighed and typed out an email to the chief. In light of the Duncan situation, Broussard had asked Ford to bypass the normal chain of command and report direct, and tomorrow's update was gonna be a zinger.

31

HALLIE

"So, Ganaway's being released today?" Black asked.

We were sitting in the office he shared with Emmy on the executive floor, together with Dan, Knox, and Kellan. Ford had called me an hour ago with the news about Ganaway, as well as reporting that a judge had signed off on a search warrant for Alton Brand's home in the suburbs. Ford planned to take Brand in for questioning while his property was being searched.

"They're finishing up the paperwork right now. Ganaway should be out this afternoon."

Dan took a sip of her coffee. "I won't tell Fen until he's actually out, just in case they manage to fuck things up at the last minute, but I'll arrange for transport."

"Transport to where?" Emmy asked. "Bradley gutted the Ganaways' bathroom, and as far as I know, he's still waiting for the new tiles to arrive."

"Can't he go to Lowe's?"

"This is Bradley we're talking about—he ordered them from Italy. Good thing you have another spare bedroom, huh?"

"Maybe I'll open a hotel."

Black ran a hand through his damp hair. He'd come to the meeting from the gym via the shower. "Are we confident the police will have the right man in custody this time?"

I nodded. "For the five most recent girls, yes—Janiya Thomas, Donna Metgood, Maria Rodas, Araceli Suarez, and Vonnie Feinstein. But the pieces for Mila Carmody don't quite fit. Brand Holdings never worked at the Carmody home, and the Carmody AC wasn't broken at the time of Mila's disappearance. Nobody even knows why her bedroom window was open."

"Shame. I'd have liked to get to the bottom of that one, if only to give the finger to Derrick Carmody."

"You didn't get along?"

"He claimed he wanted us to find the truth, but in reality, he only wanted that truth if it fit with his preconceptions. Hard to have respect for a man like that." Black leaned back in his fancy leather chair and steepled his hands. "But that's in the past. We've achieved our objective on Ganaway in less than two weeks, so good job."

"Cal's gonna be hella happy," Knox added.

But I wasn't happy. Not completely. Not yet. "I'm worried in case Alton Brand manages to wriggle out of this. The evidence is all circumstantial, and there's no way he'll rely on a public defender the way Micah did."

"You think wriggling is a possibility?" Black asked, sounding more curious than worried.

"I don't know. I hope not. But he's smart, and he's careful, and having gotten a glimpse of the inner workings of the Richmond PD, I realise there are still problems in the detective division. Ford's trying his best, and the new chief seems solid, but there are too many Duncans working there. And although the judge issued an arrest warrant for Brand, he was understandably concerned about signing the papers, I mean, in light of Micah being jailed for no good reason and all. As soon as the media finds out about the error, the headlines are gonna blow up. I just... I just..."

Ford said that Chief Broussard was bracing for riots. There were tensions between so many sectors of society, and at times, the country felt like a tinderbox waiting for a spark. And if trouble started, then police manpower would be stretched even thinner.

"You just what?" Black asked.

"Could I take the rest of the week off? I realise it's short notice, but I don't have anything else time-sensitive on my docket, and I want to be on hand to help."

"Because of the case? Or because of the lead detective?"

"Uh, both?"

"Things are serious between you and Prestia?"

"Totally unexpected, but I really freaking like him."

"Good." Black nodded once. "You deserve happiness. Take the time you need and get this case put to bed. Nobody wants to see a child-killer out on the streets."

"I'll do what I can as well," Kellan offered. "Around Blackwood commitments, obviously, but I've got evenings and weekends."

"Thanks."

"Same for me," Dan said. "I'll even work through Bradley's Halloween party. You know, if the need arises."

Knox grinned. "Me too. It's the least I can do after the effort you put in on Ganaway."

"We'll all bloody help." Emmy drained what had to be her sixth coffee of the day. Sometimes, I swore her veins were filled with caffeine because she never ran out of energy. "I might not be keen on kids when they're alive, but I like them even less when they're dead. Plus I'll volunteer Sky, which gets you Rafael too." She glanced sideways at Black, and one corner of his lips twitched. What did that mean? "Bump the case up to the top of the investigation list, for this week at least. But if anyone tries to skip out on the Halloween party, I'll personally hunt them down and drag them to Riverley by whatever body part I grab first. If one of us suffers, we all suffer, got it?"

I really did have the best of friends.

"Got it."

The waiting was almost unbearable. If I hadn't been so busy studying Alton Brand's neighbourhood, speaking with Dori Thomas, and coordinating with Ford and Blackwood, I'd have worn a hole in the rug through pacing. As it was, I'd barely slept last night, and now I was tanked up on coffee and sugar and jittery as a tap-dancing spider. Yes, I'd cracked and caffeinated myself.

The plan was simple. Ford would pick up Alton Brand at work, the place where he was least likely to cause a scene, and while he was—hopefully—answering questions, a team would be searching his property from top to bottom, grounds included. We were still missing four bodies, after all, five if we counted Mila Carmody. According to the satellite pictures Mack had provided, the yard was bigger than it looked from the road, stretching the whole way back to the woods behind, and there were several outbuildings.

As the police did their thing, Blackwood would be going door-to-door in the neighbourhood, working on behalf of Dori Thomas since we needed a good reason for being involved. We'd signed a contract yesterday. I'd offered to work pro bono, but Dori wanted to pay something, so Black joined the negotiations and we settled on the princely sum of one dollar. One dollar and, hopefully, the remains of her daughter so she could lay Janiya to rest. Morbid, maybe, but we had to be realistic.

Now I was on tenterhooks in the grocery store parking lot two miles from Alton Brand's home, waiting for Ford's signal to go. Kellan and Knox were next to me in Knox's SUV, and Dan would be joining us as soon as her meeting finished. Sky looked too young to be taken seriously for a task like this, so she was sitting today out, but Black had offered to help this afternoon.

My phone rang.

Ford.

Every muscle in me tensed.

"Are we a go?"

"You're a go."

Thank goodness. "Good luck."

"We'll fuckin' need it. The lawyer's already on his way. Keep me updated?"

"Absolutely."

In Virginia, voter registration lists were available for political purposes, and although investigating a murder-slash-kidnapping wasn't strictly political, Emmy said that all politicians should care about crime rates, shouldn't they? So she'd sweet-talked her friend James, who also happened to be the freaking President of the United States, and he'd called his campaign manager, and now we had a list of the voters in Alton Brand's neighbourhood.

We'd divided the properties up, and I'd been allocated those with single females or older couples. I couldn't say I loved going door-to-door on my own, but it was all part and parcel of becoming an investigator, and if getting closure for Dori wasn't an excellent reason for conquering my fears, then what was?

And Brand didn't live in a bad neighbourhood. In fact, it was a very nice neighbourhood indeed. Big houses on large lots set back from the road, with manicured lawns and expensive cars parked in the driveways. It wasn't quite Rybridge, but it didn't have the price tag to match either, and if it weren't for the possibility that one of the residents was a psycho, I wouldn't have minded living there myself.

Start at the centre and work out...

As I pulled into the driveway of the home directly opposite Alton's, the police were arriving outside. The lead team had gotten through the gates, and a woman in a maid's uniform was crying outside the house. Alton Brand had a maid? That was...unexpected. We'd thought that maybe since he lived alone, he used his McMansion as his lair, but would he really welcome staff in if that was the case?

I felt nauseated already, and I hadn't even spoken to anyone yet.

James's list showed a single resident at this address, a woman in her seventies named Phyllis Cooke. The yard was shabbier than many I'd driven past, but perhaps Phyllis wasn't as sprightly as she used to be? A dark-green compact was parked outside the front door, and I rang the bell.

A smiling nurse answered, neatly attired in a blue dress and sensible shoes. "Can I help you? I'm afraid Mrs. Cooke doesn't give money to cold-callers."

I held up my Blackwood ID card. "I'm actually a private investigator, and I was hoping she might have a moment to speak with me about one of her neighbours."

The nurse's ears pricked up. "Oh, come in. The guy across the street? Is he okay? What's going on there? Why all the police?"

"He's fine. The police are just speaking with him at the moment."

"Did he do something? What did he do?"

"I'm afraid I can't say."

"Are you with the police? Is that why you're here?"

"I'm not a police officer, but they're aware I'm here, and any information I obtain will be shared with them."

Chief Broussard wasn't happy with the situation, but he also knew he couldn't stop anyone from Blackwood from doing their job. And so far, he seemed to be taking a more pragmatic approach than his predecessor. Chief Garland had treated the relationship as a competition—us or them—and thrown up roadblocks at every possible opportunity, whereas Broussard placed more emphasis on getting criminals off the street by whatever means were appropriate. He wasn't going to help Blackwood, but he'd happily accept the fruits of our labour.

"Did the guy get arrested?"

"Do you know him?" Probably not if she kept calling him "the guy" instead of "Alton."

"I sometimes see him leaving for work in the mornings."

"Are you here all day?"

She shook her head. "I do the earlies. Other people do the lunchtime and evening shifts."

"Is Mrs. Cooke available for me to speak with?"

"Well, sure, she loves having visitors. But between you and me, she'd be better off in an assisted living facility. She can be a little...forgetful."

Forgetful?

I soon found out what the nurse meant.

"Phyllis? Look, you have a visitor."

The grey-haired lady turned from her spot on a chaise longue and focused rheumy eyes on me. The room was neat as a pin and smelled of furniture polish and fresh flowers with a hint of something medicinal. Matching velvet couches draped with lacy little covers and side tables full of knick-knacks were arranged around a fireplace at the far end.

Phyllis stared for a moment, face blank, and then her eyes lit up in recognition.

"Christine! You came. Golly, it's been so long. Come and sit down, sit down."

Who the heck was Christine?

"Her sister," the nurse mouthed in answer to my unasked question. "She died, like, twenty years ago."

Ah. Shit.

"Maybe I should…?" I lifted my chin toward the door.

"Easier to just go along with it. Phyllis lives in the past a lot of the time, but she's happier that way."

I didn't have time for this, but I couldn't blow off a sweet old dear. If I stayed for a minute or two, I could offer a few platitudes and then extricate myself from the situation gracefully.

"It's lovely to see you, Phyllis."

"Would you like tea? Let's have tea."

"No, really—"

Phyllis beckoned the nurse. "Helen, would you make us tea? Christine takes two sugars and plenty of milk."

"Actually, I'm short of—"

"Sure, I'll make tea."

Now what was I meant to do? I couldn't just walk out, could I? Helen bustled off, and I took a seat on the couch opposite a window that looked out on an empty swimming pool. How long would the cops take to search Brand's residence? It was a big place, a family home for a man without a family. The AC business must have been profitable.

"Do you know the man who lives opposite?" I asked.

Phyllis tilted her head to one side. "Man? That's Winnie's place. Winnie Brand. I play pinochle with Winnie on Thursdays, and she beats me nine times out of ten."

"What about Alton? Alton Brand?"

"Alton? Her grandson? Such a sweet boy. Always mows Winnie's lawn on the weekend, and mine too if I give him candy. Where's the candy?" Phyllis glanced around the room and spotted a box among the trinkets. "Could you…?"

"Sure." If I had to wait for Phyllis to get up, I'd be here for the rest of the day. "Here you go."

"Oh, nearly empty. I should get to the grocery store later. Take a piece, dear."

"Thank you. Do you know Alton well?"

"Winnie worries that he's lonely. So often, he has his head in a book, or he's helping his dad to fix things. How's that husband of yours? Still treating you right?"

Just go along with it, the nurse had said. "Uh, yes, everything's great."

"Good, good. And Bobby?"

Who the heck was Bobby? I scanned the photos over the fireplace, hoping for inspiration. Phyllis was in most of them, often with a dark-haired man but occasionally with a blonde woman. Christine? The blonde also appeared in another picture with a man her age and a small boy. Bobby?

"Bobby's doing well at school."

"He's going places, that boy."

The nurse returned with tea that had to be fifty percent milk, and I sent a silent thank you to the heavens as she turned her back and I managed to pour half of it into a potted plant. This could have been worse. Dan said that there were hiccups in every investigation, especially when people were involved, because people, by their very nature, were unpredictable. When the time came to leave, Phyllis gave me a surprisingly strong hug.

"You'll come back soon? I've missed you."

"Of course."

I'd have to because I needed to speak to the other two nurses, but it was nice to have an invitation.

"And Gregg? He'll come too?"

"I'm sure Gregg will visit soon." Whoever Gregg was. I

turned to the nurse. "Thanks for the tea, Helen."

"No problem." She lowered her voice to a whisper. "But my name's actually Blanka."

One down, only twenty-six more homes to go.

"His name's Alton? Oh, I never knew that. He's a quiet man, real quiet."

The speaker this time was a well-dressed woman in her late thirties, though her thoughts echoed the general consensus in the neighbourhood. Most people had seen Brand around but never spoken to him, just occasionally waved as he was passing. He was shy and a bit weird. Never rocked the boat. Most of the time, you'd never even know he was there.

A good neighbour.

"That's what most people say."

"Carol-Ann spoke with him once. Have you met Carol-Ann? She lives in the yellow house along the street."

"When I rang the bell, nobody answered."

"Oh, she's probably at her yoga class. She goes every morning, regular as clockwork. Anyhow, she was raising money for a new playground at the park, and he donated a thousand bucks. A thousand bucks! Said that supporting the younger generation was a cause close to his heart." I bet he did. "Don't you think that was kind of him?"

So many red flags. But without the benefit of hindsight, they'd all been viewed in black and white.

"Very generous."

"Carol-Ann offered him the chance to cut the ribbon at the opening ceremony, but he said he'd rather stay in the background. A shame, really, because he'd be a good catch. I mean, he has a steady job, a nice home, and plenty of money."

And tastes that ran significantly younger than the woman had ever suspected.

"Do you ever see him around the park?"

"He walks his alpaca on the weekends. The kids love it."

What? An *alpaca*? One of those things that looked like a mini llama?

"I didn't realise he had an alpaca."

"It used to belong to his grandma, but she passed several years ago, so I guess he inherited it. He keeps it behind his house in a little paddock. There's a pig too, so I've heard, and a few chickens, but I've never seen those. Why are you asking all these questions, anyway? What did the guy do?"

She'd find out soon enough.

"I'm afraid I can't divulge the details right now, but thank you for your time."

The picture Alton's neighbours painted was rosier than that of his colleagues, probably because they'd never gotten too close to him. As I meandered through the neighbourhood, I met a woman whose daughter sold Girl Scout cookies. Alton had bought thirty boxes because he admired the girl's entrepreneurial spirit. Another mom had actually taken her kids onto his property to visit the animals one day—she'd seen him in the yard and asked if it was okay, and he'd shrugged, looked anywhere but her face, and said that would be fine.

By mid-afternoon, I'd spoken to the occupants of nineteen of my assigned homes. Nobody answered at the other eight, which meant I'd have to try again tomorrow, plus I needed to go back to Phyllis's place. And there was no news from Ford, which wasn't entirely unexpected—he'd said that he'd most likely be on radio silence while he questioned Alton and coordinated with the searchers—but now I was twitchy because I didn't know whether there was good news or bad. It was time to regroup with the rest of the Blackwood team.

And where better to do that than the aforementioned

park? Well, anywhere really, seeing as it was freaking freezing today and the grey sky was threatening rain, but at least nobody could overhear us talking. I huddled closer to Knox and Kellan, using them as a windbreak.

"Any pertinent information?" Black asked.

Dan shook her head. "Keeps himself to himself, okay guy, good neighbour."

"That's what I got too. Brand appears to have followed the 'don't shit in your own house' rule."

Kellan piped up, "I found a guy who saw Brand speaking with his kid in the street—an eight-year-old girl—and the guy didn't like it, but Brand didn't do anything except talk. Brand claimed he saw the kid meandering around and wanted to take her back home, and the girl said he asked where she lived. But I also found another fellow who thought Brand was a genius because he helped him to repair his furnace gratis, so the views balance out."

"Not sociable, though," Knox said. "He's been invited to cookouts and get-togethers, and he never shows up."

Black nodded his agreement. "I heard that as well. But the neighbour to his left only moved in six months ago, so I need to follow up with the former residents. Nobody's ever seen him bring home a child."

Could we have gotten this wrong? If the man really had abducted a bunch of kids, surely there'd be some kind of *feeling* around the neighbourhood?

"Dammit, I was so sure—"

My phone buzzed, and my chest tightened when I saw Ford's name on the screen. Was there news?

There was.

Hot Cop: Cadaver dog just got a hit at the Brand property. On my way over.

Oh, hell.

I'd wanted to be right, but this was the worst possible way.

32

FORD

"I'm gonna be sick."

The good news was that Ford no longer had to put up with Detective Duncan. The bad news? Now he had Officer Matassa accompanying him. She'd introduced herself as Jayme but said everyone called her Tass, and she was so crazy keen to become a detective that she'd asked to shadow more experienced colleagues in her spare time. Or at least, she had been keen until the crime scene techs started digging.

"If you're gonna puke, don't puke on anything that might be evidence. And preferably avoid the cameras too."

The media had gotten word that something interesting was happening at 794 Kenton Lane, and they'd begun gathering outside the gates like flies on shit. No national news yet, just locals, but if this body was one of the missing kids, then that would soon change.

The smell was unbearable. Ford wrapped the scarf tighter over his nose and mouth and wished for a moment that he were hiding out in the restaurant beside the grocery store with Hallie and the rest of the Blackwood crew. They'd wanted to stay in the area, but it seemed Black was allergic to reporters, and Ford had stood firm on keeping them off the Brand property. He'd accept their help, but he wouldn't risk that all-important prosecution by inviting a bunch of civilians into a potential crime scene.

So they'd gone for a late lunch.

Ford wasn't sure whether he'd ever eat again.

But if this was what it took to finally stop Alton Brand, then he'd gladly starve.

Because without a body, they had nothing.

The house was clean—perhaps *too* clean, the techs said—although the maid they'd found at the property insisted Mr. Brand always kept things neat. She came via a housekeeping service, and she'd been cleaning for Brand three times per week —Mondays, Wednesdays, and Fridays, two hours each morning—for almost three years, apart from when she took vacation days, and then a colleague covered. A particular man, so she said, but not difficult to work for, although she rarely saw him. He disliked lemon-scented products, he hated his work papers being disturbed so she only vacuumed his den, never dusted it, and he left her notes if he wanted something specific, such as the plants watered or a suit dropped off at the dry-cleaner. She thought he did the yard work himself because she'd never seen anyone from a lawn care service there, but when Mr. Brand was away—he sometimes travelled for work —a guy came over to feed the animals. Oh, and he'd just installed a new bathroom upstairs. A man had shown up to do the tiling, but Mr. Brand did most of the plumbing himself because he was good at all that DIY stuff.

In short, Brand was socially awkward, but he wasn't a hermit.

The house wasn't a torture lair.

And the maid had been shocked at the very thought of Brand messing with small children.

The interview at the police station hadn't gone much better. Ford had figured Brand would hide behind his attorney with a series of "no comments," but he'd actually provided a response to most of the questions, even those where the attorney had tried to jump in first with a, "My client doesn't need to answer that."

Brand admitted he'd "probably" visited the homes in question—claiming he didn't actually remember most of them, but the computer records, records that Jack Brand had finally provided, wouldn't lie because Brand Holdings had excellent admin staff. He described the issues with the Feinsteins' AC system in great detail and said he recalled speaking with Araceli Suarez for "a few moments," but he was just being friendly, okay?

He sounded quiet but reasonable, and without access to all the other information, Ford might have believed him. But what didn't Brand have?

Alibis.

Not one alibi for any of the abductions.

On a whim, Ford had briefed Tass and brought her into the interview room, and then he'd witnessed the change in Brand for himself. The guy practically stuttered whenever she asked him the most basic of questions. Which wasn't a crime, but it backed up the information they already had. And so did Ford's gut. He'd met a lot of sick dudes in his time, the worst of the worst, including a serial killer who'd made his victims' toes into a necklace, and he'd developed an intuition for these things. A sixth sense. A prickle that started at the base of his spine and worked its way upward.

Alton Brand set off all the alarm bells.

But what they didn't have was enough evidence.

"What the hell?" the guy in the hole muttered.

The crime scene techs had spent an hour carefully digging and sifting through dirt over the spot the cadaver dog had indicated, and now they'd peeled back a layer of thick white plastic and uncovered... Yeah, "What the hell?" was a fair question.

The medical examiner crouched on the crumbling edge of the grave and peered down at the decomposing remains. A rose bush had been planted over the spot, and now it sat to the side, crooked and forlorn.

"I think it's a pig."

A pig? A motherfucking pig?

Another tech grimaced. "I guess that makes sense. There's an empty pen out the back beside the llama."

"It's an alpaca," someone else said. "Llamas are bigger."

Who cared whether it was a llama or an alpaca? "What about the dog? Why did the dog alert on a pig? I thought they were trained to find humans only?"

The handler stepped forward. "See, here's the thing. The scent of a human and the scent of a pig, they're actually very similar." He gave a chuckle. "After they're dead, anyway. In fact, we train the dogs to find human remains using the remains of pigs."

"And nobody thought to tell us this?"

Another chuckle, nervous this time. "How many crime scenes have dead pigs?"

Ford had to give him that one. Eight years as a cop, including three as a detective, and he'd never stumbled across a dead pig before. A dead sheep once, a dead sheep being violated by a drunk guy, and on second thought, maybe that had been worse than the sight before him today.

"Not many."

"Did you know that koala fingerprints can be confused with human fingerprints?" a nearby CSI asked.

"How many messed-up crime scenes have koala fingerprints?"

"Probably fewer than have dead pigs," the guy conceded.

"What about *under* the pig?" Brand was a sneaky son of a bitch. "Check beneath it."

Half an hour later, they'd hauled the stinking remains of the pig and its plastic shroud onto a tarpaulin, and the techs were back in the hole. Damn thing must have weighed over two hundred pounds when it was alive. Much of the flesh had decayed now, leaving skin, bone, and a corpse crawling with insects. A tech helpfully explained that soil came in layers, and if there was anything buried below the pig, those layers would have been disturbed deeper than they were. They dug until they hit hard-packed dirt, and then they shook their heads.

Fuck.

Ford pulled out his phone to give Hallie the bad news. A part of him was beginning to fear this case would never be resolved, but he wouldn't give up.

"Yes, Martha passed away at the beginning of June." Brand shifted in his seat, visibly uncomfortable. Worried about the search? Or had a stint in a cell taken its toll? "One day, she seemed fine, and the next... I think she had a seizure. Her skin was scraped up, and... What have you done with her?"

"We haven't done anything with her."

The Richmond PD was already facing a lawsuit from Micah Ganaway. Nobody wanted to get sued for desecrating a fucking pig.

"Good. She deserved a proper burial."

"My client is also concerned about his other animals. What provisions have been made for their care tonight? Or should we make our own arrangements?"

"No third parties will be allowed onto the property tonight."

"So, back to my first question…"

"They'll be fed." Ford could delegate that task to Tass. "I'm going to need a list of any other properties and vehicles your client owns or has access to."

"Why? So you can damage those too?"

"This is a murder investigation, and Mr. Brand's cooperation would be appreciated."

Brand and the lawyer whispered for a moment before the lawyer spoke again. "My client owns a cabin near Lexington—"

"Lexington, Virginia, or Lexington, Kentucky?"

"Lexington, Virginia." Which was damn close to Fairfield, where Donna Metgood's body had been found. "He'll grant access without a warrant because he just wants to get this misunderstanding cleared up." Which most likely meant he'd never taken Donna or any other girl to the cabin. "He also has access to any vehicle owned or leased by Brand Holdings. There are currently two hundred and seventeen of those."

Ford had to hand it to the man—he was smart. They couldn't possibly search every vehicle, and even if they could, other drivers used them too. Although Hallie said she had access to security camera footage from Rybridge on the night Vonnie Feinstein was snatched—if they could somehow cross-reference, maybe using Blackwood's fancy software…

"I'll need a list of all those vehicles. Licence number, make, model, and colour for each one."

"It will be provided. My client also wishes to convey his deepest sympathy to the families involved. While he dislikes being made a scapegoat, he understands their pain."

Cocky little fucker, wasn't he?

They needed to find something in that damn house, and

they only had a day left to do so before they'd have to either charge Alton Brand or let him go.

The clock was ticking.

Ignace's theory about the balance of joy was definitely on the money. Ford had no doubt now.

The little sleep he'd gotten last night, Hallie had been curled against his side, her breath whispering softly over his ear. They'd eaten a hurried breakfast together, and before he left her apartment, she'd leaned in to murmur, "You've got this. I have faith in you."

Halfway through the afternoon, she was the only one.

Brand had stuck to his story—he was very sorry for the situation, but he wasn't responsible for it—and Broussard was getting understandably frustrated with the lack of progress. They'd met for a catch-up half an hour ago, and Ford had summarised what they'd found so far.

"We know he was at every house except Carmody's. He had access to the central booking system, so he knew when the AC went out, and based on the weather, he could make a fair assumption that bedroom windows would be open. Plus he has no alibi for any of the nights in question. Several of his colleagues think he's odd, and one wouldn't let him near his kid. Brand takes a size eleven shoe, and we did find a pair of sneakers that matched the tread patterns left at the Feinstein scene, but they're mass-produced. We've got blood in a pigpen, but that might belong to the pig—the techs took a sample for DNA testing, but the results won't be back for days if not weeks."

The female auditor on Brand's team had said she wouldn't date him if she were paid, that they rarely saw each other in person, and it wouldn't *totally* surprise her if he turned out to be a pervert. But she'd never seen him around a child. Her feelings backed up Ford's thoughts, but she couldn't provide the evidence he'd hoped for.

"The DA won't indict based on that." Broussard told Ford what he already knew, deep down. "I called him this morning."

"I know. Dammit, I know."

"And the headlines this morning weren't kind. The words 'incompetent' and 'desperate' were mentioned in most of the articles, and they're saying we jumped the gun twice."

Ford had been avoiding the news. "What are we meant to do? Never arrest anyone in case we get it wrong?"

"With all the ambulance-chasing lawyers around, I'd say we're heading in that direction." Broussard sighed. "Tell me honestly—you still think Brand's the guy?"

It was only Ford's professional reputation on the line. No big deal.

"Yes, I do."

Now he had the choice of going to the cabin in the forest near Lexington or assisting with the search at Brand's home. The techs were crawling around in the attic now, but Ford didn't hold out much hope that they'd find anything. When he brought one of those girls home, he'd keep her somewhere convenient. Get his kicks, dispose of her quickly, then clean, clean, clean. But there *had* to be something. A hair, a speck of blood, a drop of saliva. They just needed to find it.

But Brand was clever. He covered his tracks. There were drop cloths in the double garage, but also paint cans. Knives in the kitchen, but also recipe books. Twine in the shed, but also plant stakes and secateurs. Seemed he and Ganaway had at least one hobby in common.

In the end, Ford headed back to the house, but it was a fruitless exercise. They might as well have inspected a model home. The car was clean, there were no nasties lurking in the yard apart from the pig, and even the forest behind the property checked out.

Brand walked out of the police station at five p.m., and Ford set off for the *Shore Thing*. He'd deal with the fallout tomorrow.

Tonight, he needed an alcoholic beverage, and he needed to lose himself in Hallie.

33

FORD

"He's out?" Hallie asked.

Ford had already finished a beer before she arrived, and now he poured himself a shot of vodka.

"Yup. Drink?"

She shook her head. "I didn't know if you had groceries here, so I picked up Italian. You never did tell me your favourite food."

On any other day, Ford's mouth would have watered, but pasta was the last thing he felt like eating.

"Right now, my favourite food comes in liquid form."

"What can I do to help?"

He downed the shot. "Pour me another drink?"

"Because a hangover will make everything better?"

"Can't make it any worse. This is the shittiest part of police work. Knowing a man's guilty but being unable to do a damn thing about it. Brand's lawyer threatened us with a harassment suit if we keep poking around in his client's business, and Broussard told me to back off."

"He didn't tell Blackwood to back off."

"You'll carry on?"

"Black wants to keep the surveillance going for another week at least. He says that sometimes criminals like to return to the scene of the crime, and he's got a theory that Brand might get tempted to visit his dump site, just to check everything's still hunky-dory."

Dump site.

Those kids weren't trash. They'd been living, breathing humans before Brand put his sick mind to work. Calling it a dump site minimised what they were, what they'd been. But none of this was Hallie's fault. She was only trying to help, so Ford bit his tongue.

"It's a possibility. Underneath the tongue-tied shyness, he's arrogant enough to do that."

"I suppose... Maybe there's a silver lining in all this, albeit a tarnished one? He knows you're onto him now, so you've saved any girls he might have planned to take in the future."

"Either that or he'll refine his methods, cover his tracks better, and start looking for his next victim. We didn't find his lair. We can't charge him with anything. And what's going on in his head, it's a disease. He can't switch it on and off like a light."

Hallie paled a shade, and she didn't have much colour to begin with. "You think he'll carry on going?"

"I think that the time for your surveillance will be next summer. That's his hunting season. He'll lie low for a while, wait for the heat to die down, and then he'll make his move."

"I'll talk to Black. See if we can get a team for next year. He may come across as cold, but he has a soft spot for children."

"And yet he doesn't have any of his own?"

"From what I understand, that's Emmy's decision, not his. Kids totally freak her out."

"What about you? Do you want kids?" Ford caught the look of shock on Hallie's face. "Ah, fuck. Too soon for this talk?"

"I... Are we that serious? I mean, I hoped, but at the moment, I can't even make it to third base."

Ford held out a hand to Hallie. She came willingly, and when he wrapped his arms around her waist, she leaned into him, her head resting on his shoulder.

"Yeah, plum, we're that serious. And two weeks ago, you tried to shoot me with a tampon in a parking garage, so I'd say we're making progress. Never thought I'd be consorting with the enemy, but I'm crazy about you."

Her arms tightened. "Until I went into that house in Florida, I always wanted kids, but I swore I'd wait until I was in a position to do it right. That means having the right man, financial security, and enough time to give a child the attention it deserves. I think... I *hope* that I've achieved objective number one, and number two is a work in progress, but number three... That'll take a few years. I enjoy my job, and I want to make something out of it." Hallie shifted, focused on Ford with those big hazel eyes. "Is this where you tell me you never liked the idea of being a father?"

Ford kissed her softly. "No, we're on the same wavelength here."

And just like that, he didn't feel quite so shitty anymore. That Brand was walking free still ate at him like a circling shark, but he couldn't afford to fuck up what he had with this amazing woman. He let her go—reluctantly—and stowed the bottle of vodka in the cupboard where it belonged.

"Let's get this food on the table." He kissed her on the forehead, squeezed her hands. "We both need to eat."

And they both needed to sleep, but it didn't come easy that night. Usually, the gentle rocking of the boat acted as a tranquilliser, but in the early hours, Ford was still buzzing with nervous energy. Hallie fidgeted in his arms.

"You awake?" he whispered.

"How can I sleep? I should've drunk some of that vodka."

"No, you shouldn't have. I shouldn't have either."

"Don't tell me to count freaking sheep."

He wouldn't. Or pigs. That fucking pig...

"Want a distraction?"

"What kind of a...?" He brushed her hair aside and kissed the back of her neck. "Oh..." A moment later, she'd twisted to face him. "I like that kind of a distraction, but... Ford, I can't return the favour. Not yet."

"What favour? You think this is a hardship for me?"

"Uh..."

"That was a rhetorical question. Every taste I get of you, I'm in heaven." To emphasise the point, he trailed the tip of his tongue along her jawline, and judging by her soft moan, she liked it. "How would you feel about *me* getting to third base? Just to be clear, I mean with my mouth."

She stiffened.

But then she relaxed.

"I... In Florida, that was the one thing I never had to endure." Ford didn't miss the quake in her voice. "The men there, they were all focused on their own pleasure, not mine. They took, took, took, never gave. So I think that maybe it would be okay? But I won't know until...until..."

"How about we try a few new things? If you want me to stop, you only have to say the word."

Hallie bit her lip as she nodded, and in a heartbeat, blood flowed straight to Ford's dick. She was wearing his T-shirt, not because she didn't have pyjamas of her own but because she liked it, and he liked it too. And when he slid the shirt up her thighs, he didn't miss the way she braced for impact. It hurt, seeing that. Hurt that she'd been used and abused by motherfuckers that Ford couldn't bring himself to call men.

He ignored third base—for now—and focused his attention on every other part of her body instead. Neck, arms, breasts, hands, the sensitive skin at the backs of her knees. When he reached her feet, she mumbled, "Thank goodness I took a shower before bed." She was still tense, but at least she hadn't lost her sense of humour.

And slowly, slowly, she began to relax. Her muscles softened. Her breathing grew heavier. Quiet little moans escaped from her throat. Fooling around with Hallie this way, taking his time, was...fascinating. In the past, he'd had a tendency to dive straight in, and now he realised just how much he'd been missing out on.

Ford traced a finger over a faint scar on her hip. "How did you get this?"

"Fell off the back of a pickup when I was eight."

"Do I want to know the full story?"

"A kid in the trailer park was giving people rides in his pop's truck, and he hit the gas when I was only halfway in."

"Someone should've taken his licence."

"Oh, he didn't have a licence. He was, like, eleven years old."

Sheesh. "Where was his pop?"

"Who knows? Probably passed out on the couch."

Ford placed a soft kiss on the scar. Part of Hallie's history. Part of who she was. She hadn't had the easiest life in the past, but he was determined to change that for the future.

Only when Hallie began writhing under him did Ford head for third. He suckled her through already-damp silk, and his heart soared when instead of stiffening, she arched off the bed with a gasp. That was a reward in itself.

He crawled up the bed to kiss her, only for her to push his head away.

"No, no, don't stop!"

Definitely progress. "Your wish is my command."

This time, he pushed her panties to the side, and fuck, she was soaked. He'd barely touched her with his tongue when she arched again and cried his name, her hands tangled in his hair. And it wasn't only his name he heard. As he wrapped her up in his arms and kissed her cheeks, she sobbed three quiet words.

"I love you."

Fuck, it was soon, but there was no denying the way he felt. "I love you too, plum."

34

HALLIE

When I lived in Kentucky, life had been hard. In Florida, it had been harder. But now I was coming to learn that life would never be easy, just difficult in different ways.

And if this case had been difficult for me, it had been a hundred times worse for Ford.

He was hurting.

He also loved me.

He *loved* me.

My stomach churned like a washing machine, my emotions a tangle of wet socks waiting to be unravelled. This was all new territory for me. How should I act? What should I say? Do? Somehow, I had to provide support and comfort, but my brain had turned into a weird, happy mush.

Yesterday—well, this morning—Ford had put his hands on me, and I'd enjoyed it. More than that... I'd freaking *adored* it. The lazy exploration, the sweet caresses, the tongue that got *everywhere*. And now... Now, I wanted to try the same with him. Yes, I could do that. Kiss every inch of him, find the hidden spots that made him groan with pleasure, maybe taste a little dick at the end...

"You with me, Hallie?" Kellan asked.

"Uh, yes?"

"You sure?"

Zoning out in a fast-food restaurant—that was a first for me.

"We should get back to work, huh?"

He nodded. "Right."

I still had three people in Brand's neighbourhood to speak with, and Kellan had four. Brand himself had gone to work as usual. Once he'd disappeared inside, Sky and Rafael had let themselves into an empty building opposite, and now they had line of sight into his office window. So far today, he'd spent a lot of time pacing, drunk more coffee than was healthy, and had an argument with his brother. Rafael had filmed the interaction, and now the clip was on its way to Elsa in Blackwood's admin team who, as well as being a formatting genius, had learned how to lip-read as a child.

I decided to tackle Phyllis's lunchtime nurse first. That property was the closest to the Brand house and therefore gave the greatest likelihood of success. I'd also picked up a box of cupcakes for Phyllis—it was the least I could do after she'd insisted on sharing her candy again yesterday evening. Someone had bought her another package, and it was nearly empty by the time I departed. The evening nurse told me that she often saw Brand arriving home, but she'd never seen him leave again afterward. He didn't seem to have much of a social life.

In truth, I wasn't expecting the afternoon nurse to have any vital snippets of information either, but if I didn't run down every possible lead, I'd always wonder "what if?" And Phyllis was sweet, even if she did think I was her dead sister.

Tea and chocolate was better than getting the door slammed in my face.

"Christine!" Phyllis greeted me like an old friend. "You came back."

"I promised I would."

"Ah, Blanka told me you might come." The afternoon nurse was male, a lightly built guy with a ready smile. "Callie?"

"Hallie. Hallie Chastain."

"I'm Nino. Sorry we missed you yesterday."

He'd taken Phyllis to the hospital. The evening nurse said they were worried about her balance, although she insisted she was fine. Her son was planning to install a stairlift.

"Did Blanka tell you what it was concerning?"

"Yeah, the weird guy across there." Nino jerked his thumb toward the front of the house. "The police searched the place?"

"They did, two days ago."

"But they didn't find anything?"

I shook my head. "Why do you say Mr. Brand is weird?"

"He has no wife, but he has a llama and a pig."

"I think it's actually an alpaca."

"Llama, alpaca..." Nino shrugged, then lowered his voice to a conspiratorial whisper. "And he dresses them up."

"As what?"

"Like, girlfriends?" He fussed around, tidying. "Phyllis, do you need more pillows?"

He began fluffing cushions, but I was more interested in his "girlfriends" comment. I mean, if Brand was screwing around with animals, that was gross. And also illegal. If Ford couldn't prove Brand had abducted a child, could he charge him with fucking an alpaca? And how would we get proof? That would be up to Sky and Rafael, and I could just imagine Sky's look of disgust when I broke the news to her.

"Could you elaborate on that? Girlfriends?"

"Sometimes we go for walks, don't we, Phyllis?"

She beamed. "All around the neighbourhood."

"And one time, we were walking past the weirdo's place, and I saw him get a dress out of his car. A pink dress?" Nino had a habit of speaking in questions, even when he wasn't asking one. "And he took it into the house with him."

"What kind of pink dress? Perhaps it was a gift for a girlfriend? Or he'd picked up her dry cleaning?"

"Naw, naw, it was too small for that. More alpaca-sized? A fancy, frilly dress in one of those clear plastic bags."

Nino was right—that *was* super weird. Even weirder considering Brand didn't have a girlfriend, not that we'd been able to find.

"How long ago did you see him with the dress?"

"Uh, six months? Maybe seven?"

Had Ford found a dress when they'd searched the house? If not, what had Brand done with it?

"Have you ever spoken with Alton Brand?"

"Never seen him speak with anyone. I said hello over the fence once, and he just ignored me."

The front door slammed, and footsteps approached. Another nurse? No, a man with blond hair. I took a step back on instinct, then realised I recognised him from one of the photos over the fireplace. Phyllis's son? Nino raised a hand in greeting, and Phyllis's face lit up.

"Gregg! Did you bring more candy?"

"I'll pick some up from the store later."

"Christine's here."

Curiosity turned to straight-up puzzlement, but Nino stepped in. "Her name's actually Hallie. She's an investigator looking into the weirdo across the road."

"Weirdo?"

"The guy with the pig and the lla— The alpaca."

"Ma doesn't need to be disturbed with any of that garbage."

"Nonsense, Phyllis loves the company. And Hallie brought cakes for everyone. I'll just get a plate. Who wants coffee? You all want coffee?"

"No, thank—"

Phyllis cut me off. "Coffee and cakes for everyone."

Gregg started to scowl, but turned it into a sigh. "Well, make it quick. I came to take Ma out for a drive. She likes to look at the scenery and visit a restaurant for lunch. Do you have many questions left?"

"No, not many." Since Nino had disappeared to the kitchen, I figured I might as well ask Gregg for his thoughts. "Do you ever speak with Alton Brand?"

"About as much as a man speaks to his ma's neighbour."

"Is that a yes?"

"Two little boys running around in the yard," Phyllis said, staring into space. "Alton can't keep the knees in his pants, and Gregg's no better. Winnie says she spends most of her time with a needle and thread in her hand."

"You knew Alton as a child?"

"We went to the same school," Gregg admitted grudgingly. "But I was in class with Jack, not Alton."

"What were your impressions of Alton?"

"Look, I'm not contributing to some witch-hunt. I heard the cops started harassing him, and yeah, he's not the most social guy, but that doesn't give them the right to pin a murder on him."

"If he didn't do anything, then he'll be cleared."

"Who even are you?"

"I'm a private investigator working for the parents of a little girl who died. They only want to find out what happened to their daughter."

"So you're not a cop?"

"No, I'm independent of the police."

"Okay, well, I still can't help you. All I know about Alton is that he's a shy guy who was good at math."

Phyllis chimed in, but she was still in the past. "Shy, so shy. Not so long ago, Winnie told me that Jack brought a girl home, and Alton was so tongue-tied he ran and hid in the basement."

Again, that fit with everything we'd learned so far. The complete inability to— Wait a second... What basement? Ford had given me a pretty detailed account of the search, and not once had he mentioned a freaking basement.

"Did that happen at the house over the road?" I asked.

"Poor little Alton." Her voice was almost sing-song. "Never has much luck with the ladies. Where's my candy? I need candy."

"If you could—"

"Ma's tired. She's not a suspect who needs to be interrogated."

"Where's my candy? Dennis always brings me candy. Where's Dennis? *Where's Dennis?*"

Nino came running as Phyllis stood and took a shaky step toward the door. "Now, now, my lovely. Come and sit back down."

"Where's Dennis? Where's my candy?"

Gregg searched the room with his eyes. "Where's the damn candy?"

"She ate it all."

"Where's Dennis?" Her voice was practically a screech now.

"I'll get more candy." Gregg herded me out of the room. "*You* need to leave. Don't you come back and upset my ma again."

"I'm so sorry. I didn't mean to—"

"Phyllis, you want a cake?" Nino asked from the living

room as I tripped over my feet in the hallway. "A nice pink cupcake?"

"Where's Dennis?"

Shit. I didn't know who Dennis was, but if I had to guess, I'd have said her late husband. The two of them appeared in most of the pictures on the mantelshelf, from old sepia snaps of them in their younger years to colour pictures of the two of them surrounded by grandchildren. Not Gregg's kids—he seemed to have two sisters who both had families. Hmm... Did either of them know Alton? They didn't look to be much younger, so perhaps they'd gone to the same school as well?

"Don't bother coming back," Gregg said as we walked outside. "Maybe you don't understand how fragile Ma is, but she can't deal with strangers bombarding her with questions."

Pointing out that she'd been happy to chat on my previous two visits wouldn't have helped matters, and I had to concede that Gregg knew his mom best.

"I really am sorry. Would *you* be willing to talk again?"

"For what reason? The neighbourhood's been through enough upheaval already without a busybody disturbing the peace. Just do me a favour and leave."

A busybody? Gee, thanks. Would Gregg have shown the same attitude if Ford were asking the questions? I seriously doubted that.

I fished in my pocket for my car key as I headed to the overgrown parking area on the far side of the two-car garage. Phyllis's home could be beautiful if somebody put a few bucks into it. A cushion of moss and weeds grew through the cracked asphalt of the drive, most of the window frames were rotten, and the roof had several tiles missing. Credit where credit was due—Alton Brand had done a great job of modernising his place. But had he hidden the entrance to a basement while he was at it? And how did the pink dress fit in? I needed to call Ford.

I didn't see the blow coming.

Barely heard it either, just the faintest rush of air at the last split second.

One second, I was fumbling for my phone, and the next, falling.

The world darkened as it faded to a tiny point and then...nothing.

35

HALLIE

My wrists hurt.
      My ankles hurt.
My head hurt.

What the hell happened?

My face was smushed into something soft—a blanket?—but when I tried to turn my neck, stars burst behind my eyelids and a grenade slammed into my left temple.

Slowly, painfully, snippets of memories filtered back... Cupcakes, candy, who the hell was Dennis? Nino, Gregg... *Gregg.* He'd been outside with me. Had *he* done this?

Why?

Was he that upset about me questioning his ma?

And where the heck was I?

I tried moving again, and this time, I managed to roll onto my side.

Could I open my eyes?

Did I even want to?

I wasn't in the dark, that much I could tell.

He hadn't buried me.

And I was alive. Alive and stuck in my worst nightmare.

Once again, I tried to open my eyes, forced the lids apart even as jagged lightning stabbed at my eyeballs. Then wished I hadn't bothered because now I was hallucinating. What other explanation could there be? On the other side of the room, three girls sat watching me, dressed in identical pink sweatsuits, and I knew I'd lost my mind because the smallest girl was Vonnie Feinstein's identical twin and the middle one bore more than a passing resemblance to Araceli Suarez. Who was the older girl? I didn't recognise her, but I estimated she was around fourteen. Maybe fifteen, if she was small for her age, and very, very pale.

I took in the room, what I could see of it. At first, I'd thought I was on a bed, but now I realised it was a couch. A couch covered in a fleecy pink throw. Matching armchairs sat at right angles opposite a flat-screen TV. *A living room?* A coffee table held a colouring book, a half-eaten package of cookies, what looked like a macramé project, and a doll with braided hair. Children's paintings were taped to one wall, and I spotted shelves filled with books and board games and soft toys and pots of coloured pens. *Yes, a living room.*

A living room with no windows.

There were drapes and frames, but instead of the great outdoors, somebody had painted a blue sky with fluffy white clouds.

The outside world was fake and it was silent.

Apart from the girls' breathing and the quiet hum of a refrigerator, there was no sound whatsoever. No traffic noise, no birds, no distant TV. Was the room soundproofed?

The horror kept unfolding as I realised that Gregg *had* buried me.

I was underground.

In a basement.

What basement?

I tried to slot the pieces of the puzzle together, but

nothing fit. How was Gregg connected to Alton Brand? *Was* he connected? He had to be. Didn't he? Was Gregg the man we'd been searching for? Did Alton tip him off about possible victims? Had he bought the information?

And more importantly, how the hell was I going to get out of here?

I focused on the girls again. *Could* they be real? This whole time, we'd assumed they were all dead like Donna Metgood, but some of them were still alive? Vonnie Feinstein was alive. Araceli Suarez was alive.

"Hi?" The first attempt came out as a croaky whisper. "Hi."

"Hi." The oldest one did the talking. "Do you want a drink?"

She sounded so...so unperturbed. So *normal*. I started to say "no" out of habit, because I never took drinks from strangers in case they were drugged and I got abducted again, but then I realised I was bound hand and foot and *in a freaking basement*. What did it matter if I took a drink? What did any of my stupid rules matter anymore? They couldn't keep me safe.

"Yes, please."

It seemed sensible to mind my manners. Behaving myself and biding my time had let me escape from the house in Florida instead of being tossed into a shallow grave, and I felt that survival instinct kicking in again. It had become second nature.

"Juice, milk, or water?"

"We're not allowed soda," Araceli told me, her voice robotic. "It's bad for our teeth."

They were being held prisoner, and their captor was worried about their damn teeth? That was *insane*.

Deep breaths, Hallie. "Juice would be good."

The older girl rose and walked through a door in the

farthest corner of the room, and while she was gone, I struggled up to sitting, my head throbbing with every movement. I heard the suck of a refrigerator door opening and closing, and a moment later, she came back with a juice box. Orange and pineapple with added vitamin C.

"Here. Uh, I'll get the straw."

"Can you untie my hands?"

Araceli piped up again. "He said we weren't allowed to do that."

"Who said?"

"Gregg."

So they knew his name.

"I'll tell him I got free myself. You won't get into trouble, I swear."

"We don't know who you are or why you're here," the older girl said.

"My name is Hallie Chastain, and I'm a private investigator. I guess I'm here because I asked too many questions. Who are you?"

"Starla. Starla Maple. And this is Araceli and Vonnie."

"I already recognised Araceli and Vonnie. Vonnie's picture's been all over the news." I nodded toward the TV. "You haven't seen the coverage?" My throat was as dry as the Sahara. "Please could I get that drink?"

Starla pierced the carton and angled the straw so I could drink.

"We only have DVDs."

Fuck, it was like being back in the Florida house, except we'd had a Netflix subscription. And also my roommates had graduated high school.

Vonnie spoke for the first time. "But he said nobody was looking for me."

"He said nobody was looking for any of us," Starla told

me. "Is that what you were investigating? Vonnie's kidnapping?"

"Not just hers—Araceli's too. Plus the disappearances of Mila Carmody, Janiya Thomas, Donna Metgood, and Maria Rodas. Are any of those names familiar to you?"

"You weren't looking for me?"

"I'm sorry, but your name never came up. There were similarities between the other abductions—mostly the method. Did you get taken from your bed?"

"No, from the park."

Which explained why we hadn't connected her name to the others. "Did any of the other girls come here?"

A nod. "Janiya, Donna, and Maria were here."

"But they aren't now?"

A shake. "They died."

Fuck. "You know that for sure? Gregg couldn't have taken them someplace else?"

"They all died right here. And Gregg didn't even come until after Donna was gone."

"Wait, wait. You're saying Gregg wasn't the man who snatched you?"

"No, that was Alton."

Ah, hell. The two of them were in cahoots?

"Alton and Gregg work together?"

"Kind of, I guess."

"You guess?"

"Alton doesn't like Gregg," Araceli told me. "That's what we think."

"Is that true?" I asked Starla.

"Gregg mostly comes to check on us while Alton's away. He travels for work—all over Virginia, he says, and sometimes other states too. And Alton says it's safer if another grown-up knows where we are, just in case something happens to him.

Like when he had to go into the hospital for an emergency and Cassy died."

Oh, fuck. Who was Cassy?

"What was Cassy's last name?"

Starla shrugged. "Just Cassy. I never met her, but I think she was the first. Alton said he learned a lot from her. Like, he only used to leave enough food and drink for one day, but now we have running water and plenty to eat, and a proper bathroom."

"How long have you been here, Starla?"

"Since I was ten."

"And how old are you now?"

"Fifteen."

"So you've been here for five years?"

"Four and a half."

And Mila Carmody had disappeared a little over five years ago. So it was still possible she *had* been here—especially as we now knew that Alton Brand had varied his method—but she was most likely dead now. And if I didn't get out of this basement prison, then I'd be following in her footsteps.

"Can you untie me?" I asked again. "Please?"

This time, Starla motioned for me to turn around, and I shifted so she could get to my hands. Thank goodness. Then I could tackle my feet, and they were already prickling with pins and needles because Gregg had bound them too tight with lilac cord. It looked as if he'd borrowed it from the macramé project.

"Gregg said we shouldn't—" Araceli started, but Starla cut her off.

"Alton always says that we should make new arrivals feel at home, and he's in charge, not Gregg."

"Do you know when they'll be back?" I asked. "Alton and Gregg? What time is it?"

Starla wore a watch, just a cheap pink digital model, but at least it let her keep track of the days. My own smartwatch had disappeared along with my phone, which meant that Gregg might have acted impulsively, but he wasn't a complete fool. Nobody could use them to locate me now. But my car... I'd used a pool car today, and all the pool cars had GPS monitoring. When somebody noticed I was missing—probably Kellan, maybe Ford—they'd find my car at Phyllis's home.

Or not.

Starla checked the time. "It's two o'clock." So I hadn't been out for long. "Gregg said he had to move your car, and I don't know what time he'll be back. Alton usually gets home around six."

Shit.

Shit, shit, shit.

Starla began to pick at the cord. Gregg had knotted it tightly, and she struggled to get it undone.

"I don't suppose you have scissors?"

"Only plastic safety scissors, and they won't cut this. If we want cord or ribbon cut for craft projects, Alton has to do it for us."

I shifted slightly, arching my back enough to feel the knife pressing into my breast. Gregg hadn't searched me too thoroughly, then. But I didn't want to divulge its existence to Starla, not yet, because I didn't know where her loyalties lay. Yes, she'd been kidnapped, but she seemed quite comfortable with the situation. Relaxed. They all did. Stockholm syndrome was a very real possibility.

While Starla worked, I forced myself to think through the problem. Blackwood could follow the car's route. Wherever the vehicle ended up, they'd know how it had gotten there, even if they didn't know who'd driven it. And if Gregg left it in the middle of nowhere, then Kellan and Dan and Ford would be smart enough to realise I hadn't abandoned it myself.

The question was, would they be able to work out where I'd ended up?

Yes, they'd have Phyllis's home as a starting point, and it was right opposite Brand's place, but they'd know it wasn't Brand who'd taken me. Sky and Rafael were watching him. And unless Phyllis let the information about the basement slip again, why would they look for me here?

The answer? They wouldn't. Which meant I was on my own. And while Alton Brand had kept three of his child victims alive, another four were dead, maybe five, and I had no idea how he'd react to an adult female who'd been sticking her nose into his business.

Finally, Starla got my hands untied, and I rubbed feeling back into my fingers.

"Thank you."

"You're welcome."

Starla was polite, and even though she'd been cut off from society since she was ten years old, she came across as articulate. Once I'd gotten my feet untied, I stood and flexed my ankles, then took a walk around the room. The books on the shelves surprised me. Yes, there were volumes of fairy tales and picture books and children's fiction, but there were also textbooks. Reading, writing, math, science... What looked like a whole homeschool curriculum.

Alton Brand cared about their education?

He kept them locked in a basement, but he encouraged them to learn geography? I couldn't get my head around it.

"Are you ever allowed out of here?" I asked.

Starla shook her head. "Never. Alton's stronger than all of us put together."

How did she know? That was the first indication he could have gotten physical with them.

"Nobody's ever tried to sneak past?"

"Donna did. And then he punished her."

A chill ran through me, despite the relatively comfortable temperature in the basement. It was strange—movies had people believe that kidnap victims got chained up in squalor, but here I was in what would have been a nice home if it only had windows. And the Florida house had been positively luxurious.

"What did he do to Donna?" Had Alton killed her in a fit of anger?

"He wouldn't let her eat dinner with us. She had to make her own food and eat alone in our bedroom, and I guess she didn't cook something properly because she got sick. Really sick, and he wouldn't take her to the hospital, and then she died." She'd died of food poisoning? *Food poisoning?* "And I can't leave anyway, because who would take care of the baby?"

I froze, and the chill turned to an icy stalactite hammering its way through my skull.

"What baby?"

"Janiya's baby. Alton called her Aliya. Like a mix of both their names?"

I was gonna puke. Seriously. The fries I'd eaten for lunch rose up my throat, and only sheer determination let me swallow the lumps down again. *That sick motherfucker.* Alton Brand had raped a child and gotten her pregnant, then she'd died. Janiya would have been, what, thirteen?

"How old is the baby?"

"Almost five months."

So near, yet so freaking far. Janiya had been alive half a year ago. How was I going to break the news to Dori Thomas? *Don't run before you can walk, Hallie.* I needed to get out of this hellhole first. There *had* to be a way. I couldn't accept that I'd be stuck in a basement until the day I died, however soon that day might come.

"Did Janiya die giving birth?"

"There was so much blood." Now Starla looked nauseated too. "It wouldn't stop."

"And Maria?"

"There was something wrong with her. She said her mom stuck her with a needle to stop her from getting sick, but Alton couldn't give her what she needed, and one day, she just went to sleep."

The police notes hadn't mentioned any illnesses, but the file had been so thin that it didn't even have current contact details for Maria's parents. Had she been diabetic? It was possible.

"Are you three okay? Physically, I mean."

Starla gave a one-shouldered shrug. "I guess. He makes us take vitamins."

"And the baby?"

"I feed her stuff from a bottle. Alton showed me how to make it."

"Can I see her?"

Starla headed for the door again, and I took that as a yes. The basement was roomier than I'd expected. We walked through a modern kitchen complete with a table large enough to seat six, and I noted there was an extractor hood above the stove. Did that mean there was some type of vent above ground? Or could those things use internal filters? Beyond the kitchen was a bathroom, and opposite the bathroom was a bedroom. A double bedroom with a man's clothes folded neatly over the back of a chair.

There had been times in the past when I'd questioned Emmy's life choices—not out loud, just in my head because I wasn't *that* stupid. And Black's, and Rafael's. They killed people, acted as executioner, sometimes as judge and jury too. I knew it didn't come easy to them, to Emmy in particular, but they could still look a man in the eyes and pull the trigger. I liked them, valued them as friends, but yes, I'd judged too. Asked how a person could be so cold.

Now I knew.

Alton Brand took children from their families and kept them as pets. He raped them and let them die, and no matter how comfortable he made their prison, he was still a monster. And Gregg stood by and let him do it.

Starla led me into another bedroom, this one laid out with two sets of bunks and a cot bed. An alcove held a treadmill and a stationary bicycle because, hey, exercise was important.

The baby was sleeping peacefully, swaddled in a pink blanket. She had a shock of dark hair and Janiya's nose, but Brand's lighter complexion. This whole arrangement was vile.

"Alton brought me books on what to do. Araceli tries to help, but she's so little, plus..." Starla grimaced. "Plus she's Alton's favourite now. That was always Janiya, but..." A single tear rolled down Starla's cheek, and she wiped it away. "I kind of wish it was me because hearing what goes on is sometimes harder than living it, you know?"

I did know. I knew exactly how that felt.

"Somehow, we'll get out of here, I promise we will. We can make a plan."

She took a step back. "I have a plan. When I'm eighteen, Alton says I can move into the house upstairs, and *then* I'll get help. Don't you dare do anything to mess that up."

"That's three years away."

"Two and a half years, and I've already survived nearly five."

"There are four of us and one of him."

"Oh, you think he'll just let us out?"

"We could rush him."

"Firstly, there's a camera in the living room. He makes sure we're not near the door before he opens it." Sick, but not stupid. "And secondly, the door's on one of those springs. It closes on its own, and it only opens again when Alton puts his finger on the scanner. He's not gonna do that."

Not voluntarily, but dead men couldn't argue. Although Starla's news did rule out my first idea of tossing boiling water in Alton's face. If any hit his hands, that could blister his fingertips and then we'd all be stuck.

And there were still so many unknowns... I'd been abducted by Gregg, not Alton, and I wasn't a member of the underage harem. What would Alton do with me? Was I disposable? If Starla was telling the truth, and she had no reason to lie, then Alton hadn't killed anyone deliberately, but he *had* let four girls die. Could *he* kill in cold blood? What if he saw me as a threat? And what about Gregg? How did he fit into the picture?

Only one thing was clear right now—I had to tread very, very carefully.

36

FORD

"There's a problem."

"Who is this?"

The question was more or less redundant. How many straight-talking Englishwomen did Ford know? But the call had come from an unknown number, and he didn't want to hear about a problem, especially when the caller was Emmy and he'd already been getting twitchy because Hallie hadn't answered his last text. He'd sent it an hour ago, asking whether it was his place or hers tonight, and she usually replied fast.

Ford stepped out into the hallway because this wasn't a conversation he wanted to have at his desk. Luckily, Tass had gone to find coffee.

"It's your friendly neighbourhood piñata slayer."

"And what's the problem?"

"Hallie didn't check in this afternoon, and we don't know where she is. Has she been in contact?"

Ford's heart seized. Emmy kept her tone businesslike, but there was no hiding the underlying worry.

"Not since lunchtime. I'll try calling her."

"Her phone's turned off, and the tracker in her smartwatch isn't responding."

"You track your employees?"

That was one hell of an invasion of privacy.

"Not habitually. But you know about Hallie's past—she asked for a tracker, and we provided one. We also have a GPS device in the Blackwood vehicle she was driving, and we found that in a grocery store parking lot near Brand's place."

"A grocery store parking lot? There might be cameras. We could—"

"Way ahead of you there, sport. There *are* cameras, but the store manager's a by-the-book asshole who doesn't understand the meaning of the word 'urgency.' We're trying to get the footage by other means, but—"

"What other means?"

"Electronic means."

"You mean illegal hacking?"

"Yes, I mean hacking. That's the difference between you and me, Prestia. If Hallie's in danger, I don't give a single flying fuck about playing by the rules."

Ford suspected that Emmy didn't give a fuck about the rules at any other time either, but when he was faced with a choice between his badge or Hallie's safety, there was no contest.

"Just cover your damn tracks."

This time, he heard the smile in her voice. "We always do. But you need to get over to that grocery store and put your badge in the manager's face. It might be quicker."

"Where's Brand? Hallie said you have a team on him?"

"He's at work."

"You're certain about that? What if he snuck out of the building?"

"We're certain."

"Okay. Okay, I'm on my way."

Should he tell someone where he was going? A colleague? Broussard? When it came down to it, who did Ford believe had the best chance of finding Hallie? His fellow detectives, whose hands would be tied by paperwork and procedures? Or Emmy and her bunch of renegades?

He glanced around the bullpen. Of the half-dozen people working, four were Duncan's drinking buddies, one was a rookie, and another was confined to desk duty with a broken ankle.

After a moment's hesitation, he headed for the exit. Easier to ask for forgiveness than permission.

He was almost at his car when he heard rapid footsteps followed by a breathless, "Where are we going?"

Ah, shit. Tass.

"I'm going home, and you're going back inside."

"Home?" She scrunched her lips to one side. "But the shift hasn't ended yet."

"Are you gonna go running to Broussard?"

"No, no, of course not. But..." Her face lit up. "I get it! You're going to meet an informant, aren't you?"

"What?"

"You're one of those super-dedicated detectives. There's no way you'd skip out early, so you must be doing some top-secret cop stuff. Right?"

"Top-secret cop stuff. Yeah. Can you do me a favour and forget you know anything about it?"

Ford had come to terms with tanking his own career, but he didn't want to take Tass down with him. Someday, she'd make a good detective.

"I'll just go right back inside. But if you need a hand, then call me, okay?"

"Sure I will."

But he wouldn't. He was heading over to the fucking dark side.

Emmy had been right—the grocery store manager *was* a by-the-book asshole. But after a brief verbal tussle and a reminder that a woman's life was in danger and customers wouldn't look upon his stalling too fondly if it happened to become public knowledge, he'd handed over the footage.

Too bad it hadn't provided the revelation they'd all been hoping for.

But it did confirm what they'd suspected: that Hallie hadn't driven the vehicle to the store herself. The suspect was male, average build, average height, and white. They'd caught the merest glimpse of his face beneath the oversized hoodie he wore as he strode out of the parking lot, head down and hands in his pockets. Blackwood's cyber team was working to enhance the picture, but Ford didn't hold out much hope.

The man had turned left along the street, and a Blackwood team was currently speaking with residents and workers in the area in the hope of piecing together the route he took. Meanwhile, Ford was with Kellan, working the other end of the problem. They knew Hallie had been at the Cooke home, but what had happened after she left?

Phyllis Cooke didn't know.

The evening nurse didn't know.

She'd called Nino, the care worker who visited Cooke in the afternoons, and he had no idea either. But Nino had been nearby, so he'd come back, and now he was standing in Cooke's kitchen, gesticulating with his hands as he explained just how little he knew about anything.

"Yes, yes, she was here, asking her questions. But she left. Phyllis got a little distressed—that happens sometimes—and when she's upset, candy helps to calm her down. So Hallie left,

ELISE NOBLE

and Gregg hurried out to buy Phyllis her candy on account of her finishing the last box."

"Gregg? Who's Gregg?"

"Phyllis's son."

"He was here? At the house?"

"Well, yes, he often comes to visit with his ma."

"Did he leave before or after Hallie?"

"Hmm... I guess at around the same time?"

"How do we contact him?"

"I have his number right here."

Nino scrolled through his phone and read out the digits. Was Gregg a witness? Or could he have been involved in Hallie's disappearance?

"Did Gregg come back with the candy?" Kellan asked.

"Now, I'm not sure. Phyllis tired herself out and fell asleep, and I had to move on to my next client."

"There's a box of cupcakes in the living room," the evening nurse offered.

"No, Hallie brought the cakes."

So Gregg Cooke had come to visit, rushed out to buy candy for his distressed mother, and then hadn't come back? Ford edged him over into the "suspect" column.

"I need to speak with this guy."

If Cooke picked up, Ford planned to play dirty and tell him there was a medical emergency with his mom. Probably another fireable offence, but he could apologise later, and anything was better than tipping off a potential kidnapper. But Cooke's number went straight to voicemail.

"Yello, this is Gregg. If you're a hot chick, leave a message and I'll call you back. If you're a friend, leave a message and I might call you back. If you're neither, you might as well go fishing."

What a jackass. Phyllis was no spring chicken, which meant Gregg had to be in his thirties at least, but he sounded like a horny teenager. Ford hung up and gave his head a shake.

"Phone on or off?" Kellan asked.

"Off or out of range."

Ford turned to the two nurses again. "Do either of you have an address for Gregg?"

Both shook their heads.

"But I don't think he lives far away," Nino said. "He drops by almost every day."

"I need you to go through everything that was said this afternoon. By Gregg, by Hallie, and by Phyllis."

"Well, I was barely in the room for any of it. I went to make coffee. But when Gregg and Hallie were leaving, Gregg complained about her upsetting his ma and told her not to come back again. And Phyllis was asking for Dennis—that's her late husband, not Gregg's father because he passed away when Gregg was a baby, but her second husband—and she usually does that when somebody asks questions that she doesn't know how to answer. She sort of...panics."

"Hallie found something," Kellan murmured.

Yeah, she did. She found something, and Gregg Cooke knew what it was. Did it concern him? Or had Phyllis spilled someone else's secret and Gregg tipped that person off?

And did they have one case or two?

Hallie had been asking about Brand.

Brand lived right across the street.

"Anyone know how long Phyllis has been at this address?"

Again, Nino answered. "She moved here when she married Dennis, so... Nearly forty years?"

And they already knew that Brand had a long-time connection with the area. He'd inherited his home from his grandma, and Hallie had said on Tuesday that Phyllis had known Grandma Brand. They'd been friends. But what about the boys? What was the age difference?

"How old is Gregg?"

"Maybe forty?" Nino suggested.

"Hard to tell," the evening nurse said. "He's a boy who never grew up, like a man-child. Late thirties?"

"On it," Kellan said. Since Blackwood had called what he termed a limited Code: Orange, he was wearing an earpiece, and somebody at Blackwood was monitoring the whole conversation. Probably recording it too, which was fine because Virginia was a one-party consent state, and... Who the fuck cared?

"Any idea what he does for a living?"

"He's one of those serial entrepreneurs." The evening nurse rolled her eyes. "If there's a way to lose money, he'll find it. Playing on the stock market, selling fake watches, and... What does he call himself now?"

Nino snickered. "A crypto dealer. Remember the fancy fish?"

"Oh, yes. He filled Phyllis's swimming pool with baby koi and they all died. And he keeps expecting her to bail him out, which is terrible because she really doesn't know what she's doing most of the time."

"Does he have power of attorney?"

"Phyllis's money came from Dennis's side of the family, and Dennis's daughter from *his* first marriage has control of it. Now, she doesn't see eye to eye with Gregg, but she lives in Portland, so mostly they just fight over the phone. Phyllis's care gets paid for, plus she gets a monthly allowance, so that's what Gregg tries to con out of her. But he's her son." The nurse shrugged. "What can we do?"

Kellan turned away, one hand over his ear as he listened. "They're close in age. Alton Brand is forty, Gregg Cooke is forty-one, and according to Cooke's social media, he went to the same school as Brand."

"Is he married? In a relationship?"

314

Kellan shook his head. "No evidence of that."

It was the evening nurse's turn to laugh. "Trust me, no woman would put up with him for long."

Son of a bitch. *That son of a bitch.* They were working together; they had to be. Gregg was the abductor, and Brand had, what, tipped him off about potential victims? Or did they share the load? Take it in turns?

And where? Where was their hideaway? At Cooke's home?

Fuck, he needed to get over there.

"Thank you both for your help. If we have more questions, we'll be in touch."

Was Hallie still alive? Dammit, she *had* to be alive. Ford had finally found the woman he wanted to spend the rest of his days with, and he wasn't willing to let her go now.

Outside, he said as much to Kellan—about visiting Cooke, not his plan to marry Hallie—but Kellan didn't see things the same way.

"You can't go steaming in there without a plan."

"I have a plan. I'm gonna make those motherfuckers talk."

"How? You're gonna knock on Cooke's front door, hold up your badge, and ask him to accompany you to the precinct?"

"What the hell else would I do? We can get a warrant, we can—"

Ford let out an unbecoming yelp as his arm was twisted up behind his back. He tried to reach for his weapon, but in a heartbeat, it was removed from his holster and pressed to his temple, plus his shoulder was halfway to being dislocated.

"What else can you do? You can sit quietly out of the way while my colleagues handle this unfortunate situation."

The accent was Spanish, the grip cast iron. In the garage window, Ford saw Rafael's face reflected over his shoulder and bit out a curse.

"That's assault on a police officer."

Rafael merely laughed.

"We can do this the easy way or the hard way."

"What's the easy way?"

"You can share coffee in the command post and enjoy the video feed."

"And the hard way?"

Rafael twisted harder, and fire burned through Ford's shoulder joint.

"Fine. Fine! We'll go to the damn command post."

Blackwood could do the dirty work, the same way as they always did. And at least Ford wouldn't get arrested for murder.

37

HALLIE

"Y ou shouldn't have brought her here."

Alton Brand paced the living room, muttering to himself. He hadn't looked me in the eye, not once, but he had glared at his partner in crime a number of times. Right now, I was sitting on the couch with the three girls while the men discussed the "problem," which was of course me.

"So, what would you have done?" Gregg whined. "Ma told her about the basement."

"Your ma's cuckoo for cocoa puffs. Who would have believed her?"

"*She* did." Gregg jerked a thumb in my direction. "I saw it in her eyes."

"The police have already searched the place once, and my lawyer will sue them for harassment if they try it again."

"And what if the judge sides with the cops?"

Alton didn't have an answer for that. Instead, he shrugged, philosophical. "Well, she's here now. She can help with Aliya. We have a spare bunk, and at least then Starla will be able to sleep through the night."

"You're not going to...you know?"

"You know what?"

"Get rid of her?"

Alton actually looked indignant. "I'm not a murderer."

Gregg snorted. "Four girls died already."

"Those were *accidents*. And besides, what would we do with the body? Martha passed away."

Who the heck was Martha?

"We can get another pig."

A pig? Why did that...? Oh my... They'd been disposing of bodies by feeding them to *the freaking pig*? My stomach threatened to heave up its contents, and beside me, Starla's lips quivered as she tried not to cry. Araceli didn't react, and Vonnie looked scared but not sick, so I had to hope the meaning of Alton's words had flown right over her head.

"If we get another pig, you'll have to learn to clean the pen properly."

"Whatever." Gregg rolled his eyes, and it was clear there was no love lost between him and Alton. How on earth had they ended up in this vile partnership? "You know, it might not be a bad thing, her being here." When he ran his slimy gaze over me, my skin crawled because I knew exactly what he was thinking. His eyes gave it away. That glittery lust made my guts churn. "Maybe I could have a little fun too?"

No. Oh, no. Cold fear gripped me, overlaid by desperate determination. *I will not be a victim again.* I'd made myself that promise.

Gregg came closer, and I noticed the change in his breathing. Heavier, raspier. Now that he'd had this idea, it excited him. And down here, he could do whatever he wanted to me. In the Florida house, there had been rudimentary rules with guards to enforce them. Yes, I'd been merchandise, but I'd had a value. Down here, the only thing standing between me and rape was Alton Brand, and although he curled his lip in disgust—what, was I too old for him?—he didn't veto Gregg's plan.

"Not in front of the pretties." That was what Alton called them. *The pretties.* And I'd noticed he made eye contact with the girls, too. When it came to minors, he didn't seem to suffer the same shyness that afflicted him around adult women. In the basement, he was the master of his domain. "You'll have to use the bedroom, but don't leave it messy."

Brand, he was unhinged. He genuinely sounded more peeved by the thought of the bedroom he shared *with a child* being untidy than by my potential rape. Gregg ran his fingers across my cheek, and I slapped him before he could block. I was *not* going down without a fight.

"You bitch!" He grabbed my hand and hit me twice as hard. "But hey, it'll be more fun if you fight back."

"Don't break anything," Alton reminded him. "And keep the noise down. Girls, have you done your schoolwork today?"

Gregg switched his grip to my arm and hauled me toward the bedroom. I dug my heels in, but he outweighed me and outmuscled me. Would he outsmart me too? Only time would tell, but not too much time. Originally, I'd planned to wait until only one of the men was in the basement, but when Gregg shoved me onto the bed, I knew I couldn't delay. Couldn't lie back and take it. Couldn't be a man's plaything, not again.

Not this time.

"Maybe this was fate." Gregg undid his belt buckle. Good. Let him pull his pants down; that way, it would be harder for him to run. "I've never been one for the kids because that's…" He screwed up his face. "That's gross. But now you're *my* pretty."

"If you don't like paedophilia, then why do you help him?"

"Because he pays me. Turn onto your back."

I only had one shot at this, but I'd had practice. Over and over in the gym at Riverley, usually with Rafael but sometimes with Black or Sky or even Georgia's boyfriend, Xav. Rafael's words repeated in my head: *If you're going to kill someone,* cariño, *you have to be committed. No hesitation, no holding back.* I wasn't certain I'd be able to take Gregg's life, but when he dragged me down the bed by my ankle, I knew that if I failed, it certainly wouldn't be due to a lack of effort.

I curled, pretending to cower while I reached into my bra for the switchblade that nestled there. Gregg had made a lot of mistakes in his life—partnering with Brand, abducting a woman trained in self-defence, failing to search me—but thinking he could violate with impunity was about to be his worst. My heart thumped as he loomed over me with a sick smile on his face.

Now or never.

The blade shot out with a quiet *snick*, and I stabbed upward with all my strength. Felt the give as the tip pierced skin, kept pushing, and then *ripped*. Gregg's howl was unearthly, a high-pitched scream that echoed off the walls of the small room. *Focus, focus...* I kicked with my feet, swore as a slick of blood made me lose my grip on the knife. He reached for it and pulled it out, curses dripping from his lips as more blood flowed from the wound. I prepared to defend myself, knowing that I'd get cut. What was it Emmy always said? Better to face a gun than a knife—most people were terrible shots, but in a knife fight, someone would always need stitches. But then Gregg's eyes widened as he looked at his stomach and saw the hole gape open. Now he had a choice— he could come after me and risk tripping over his own guts, or he could hold the mess in and pray for a miracle.

He chose the latter.

But it wasn't over yet.

Another jolt of adrenaline hit as footsteps pounded

toward me. Brand was coming, and although he wasn't as bulky as Gregg, he was tall, plus I'd lost the element of surprise. Where was the knife? Gregg had dropped it, but where had it gone?

I didn't have time to work that out because Brand was on me. Fear powered him, fear that his whole house of cards was about to come crashing down, and that gave him strength. I had the advantage of training, but a lack of practical experience when it came to fighting for my freaking life. I managed to knee him in the balls, but he couldn't have been blessed in that area because he only grunted a bit. And the move put me off balance. He flattened me on the bed and got his hands around my throat, squeezing, squeezing as I dug my thumbs into his eyes. He jerked back, but his arms were longer than mine and his weight still pinned me down.

Panic threatened to overwhelm me, but I heard Rafael's voice again.

Put a hand to my face and use the other to release an arm. One arm, not both, because you don't want my weight to collapse on you. Use the space to get your legs into play. Kick me. Hard. Harder. This isn't a game, cariño.

We both had bruises after those sessions, but the advice worked. I managed to get Brand off me for long enough to suck in half a ragged breath. His nose was bleeding, but he was fresher than me. Probably saw his dream slipping away as well as his life. But as he charged me again, I caught sight of a figure in the doorway.

Starla.

And her face was a mask of horror.

This time, Brand grabbed my ankle in the same way as Gregg had earlier, but I knifed up and headbutted him. Saw stars, but it was worth it when Brand staggered back and slipped in Gregg's blood. His nose was well and truly smashed now.

"You're crazy!" Starla yelled.

Now fury lit Brand's manic gaze, and ironically, he managed to look me in the eye. "You stupid whore. You've ruined everything."

"Good."

He roared as he leapt, and although I tried to roll out of the way, I wasn't quick enough. He landed with his full weight on me, and this time, he straddled my hips. Now it was time for the two-handed choke release. Then I could bridge my hips to destabilise him, and—

Brand's yowl made Gregg's sound restrained. His arms loosened and he collapsed forward, trying to crawl away as Starla plunged the knife into his back again, and I glimpsed the same anger in her eyes that I'd seen in his. But at least hers was aimed in the right direction.

Except now, his attention turned to her, and she wasn't trained. It only took him a second to grab the knife and begin slashing wildly, blinded by blood and rage and pain.

Fuck, fuck, fuck!

I pushed with my feet, wriggled backward up the bed, and grabbed the lamp from the nightstand. The cord tugged, but I had momentum on my side, and the plug pinged out of the socket as I smashed the thing over his head with every last ounce of strength I had left.

Only then did he finally go still.

Only then could I finally breathe again.

38

FORD

Ford expected to be driven to Blackwood Headquarters, but ten long, long minutes later, and with his shoulder still throbbing, Rafael ushered him through a plastic curtain and into a dirty truck emblazoned with a faded logo for Uncle Chuck's Frozen Seafood. But rather than the stink of shellfish and the chill of an oversized refrigerator, he found himself surrounded by several people and the quiet hum of electronics. Hell, this truck had more technology than the space shuttle.

A woman dressed in maroon jeans and a ski jacket watched him silently from one corner, and opposite her, Nate sat before a bank of monitors while Sky hopped around in her underwear, one foot in a pair of black leggings. Rafael's eyes lingered on her ass for a second before he turned his attention back to Ford.

"You've already met Nate and Sky." He nodded toward the woman in the black jacket. "That's Ana."

Even seated and seemingly relaxed, the "don't fuck with me" vibes rolled off her. Ford had no intention of getting any closer than he had to. A presence behind him made him turn, and he found himself staring down at a woman with mousy brown hair, chunky plastic-rimmed glasses, and a figure hidden by an ill-fitting navy-blue pantsuit. She held out a glossy pamphlet.

"I have a message from our Lord and Saviour." Her words were earnest, and her accent held a hint of the South. "Do you have a few moments to talk about the path to eternal life?"

Ford glanced at the booklet's title. "*The Blessed Light*?"

"I was all for calling it *Muzzle Flash*, but Dan thought we needed something more subtle."

This time, the accent was English, and Ford did a double take. "Emmy?"

She patted him on the shoulder a little harder than was necessary. "Well done. Keep that up, and someday you could make a detective."

"Xav's here," Nate announced.

The door opened a moment later. This guy was the male equivalent of Emmy, which was to say drably dressed and potentially deadly.

"Ready to go get doors slammed in our faces?" he asked.

"Five minutes. Sky, Rafael, and Ana need to get into position first."

"Who else is out there?"

"Cade's got eyes on the back, and Logan's watching the front. Dan and Knox are over at Brand's place in case he decides to leave."

Brand was home now? Ford's anxiety levels cranked up another notch.

"Where's Black tonight?" Xav asked.

"Washington."

"DC or state?"

"DC. National security, something, something. Sky, ready to go?"

She pulled on a leather jacket and tugged up the zipper. "Yup."

"What's the plan?" Ford asked. "Can you at least tell me that?"

And why did a teenager get to play an active part while he was shut out?

"We don't think Cooke's inside, but we can't be certain. There might be a basement or an interior room we can't see. So me and Xav are gonna ring the bell as a distraction while Ana, Rafael, and Sky sneak in the back. And if Cooke doesn't come to the door, we'll go in the front."

"How? It's not as if the guy's gonna leave his doors unlocked."

"Chill, we've got this. I've been taking lock-picking lessons from my ex-boyfriend's ex-boyfriend." Boy, there was a lot to unpack in that sentence. "Take a seat, have a coffee, and try not to stroke out while you're waiting."

Coffee? Was she serious? Ford never could tell, but sitting down was out of the question, even when Nate glared at him for fidgeting. Nate did have a cup beside him, Ford noticed, and there was an espresso machine in one corner.

Emmy and Xav started methodically at a small duplex several homes to the left of Cooke's, and they did indeed get doors slammed in their faces. One guy spit at them, and a woman informed them she had a concealed-carry permit, although Ford couldn't work out where she'd stash a gun in the bathrobe she was wearing.

"Why go through the eternal-life spiel?" he asked Nate. "I'd be asking what these folks knew about Cooke."

"First, your strategy would run the risk of a friend calling to warn him, and second, a deep dive into Cooke's psyche isn't our goal tonight. That comes later. We just need to get close to the house without risking a hostage situation."

"Right. What would Emmy do if someone really did want to talk about the Lord?"

"In six years, that's never happened."

"But if it did?"

"If it did, she's wearing an earpiece, and a researcher would feed her information on scripture." Nate patted the keyboard in front of him. "Thanks to the internet, we have a wealth of information at our fingertips." He switched his focus back to the team quietly approaching the house. "No sign of wireless cameras. Jamming cell-phone signals...now."

"What about wired cameras?" Ford whispered.

"Already took care of that."

Of course they did.

Ford had been in the background for many raids, but never one quite like this. There was no explosive entry, no shouting, no palpable tension, just a soft knock on Cooke's front door followed by a quiet *click* when he didn't answer. Then they were inside. It was fast, almost silent, and slightly scary, if Ford was honest. The way Emmy's team crept around, they could kill a man in bed and he'd only find out when he didn't wake up.

But despite all the sneaking, the raid was a bust.

There was no sign of Cooke, no sign of Hallie, and no sign she'd ever been there. The attached garage was empty, although there was space for a vehicle. Records showed that Cooke owned a late-model BMW SUV, which was interesting, Nate said, because it was an expensive import and not only had Cooke been losing money on his crypto trading, but he didn't have a steady job either. Nor did he make monthly payments—it appeared he'd purchased the vehicle outright. Ford didn't bother to ask how Nate knew any of that. If he found out the answer, he'd only have to lie about it later.

The team left the house as quietly as they'd entered it, and the coil of dread wound tighter around Ford's guts, a serpent hell-bent on squeezing the colour out of his world.

"What now?"

Nate drained the last of his coffee. "Now, we do Brand."

"In case Cooke's there?"

"Even if he's not, I'll bet you five bucks Brand knows where he is."

"And you honestly think he'll tell you?"

"He'll tell Emmy. You might want to close your eyes for that part. And your ears."

This wasn't just the dark side, was it? It was the fucking underworld.

And Emmy was the devil in disguise.

39

HALLIE

This wasn't just a nightmare, this was...what was worse? *A living hell.*

Not only were we still trapped, but Starla was bleeding. Badly. One of Brand's slashes had cut her thigh, and although I'd used his belt to make a tourniquet, blood was still oozing out of the wound. I kicked his unconscious body in frustration. Or maybe in the hope that he'd wake up and give us the code so we could get the heck out of there. Gregg was no help either. He might even have been dead by now—I wasn't about to waste time going back to check.

"Can we leave yet?" Araceli asked from the couch, cradling the baby. "Why can't we get out?"

"I'm trying, I promise. Just stay there with Vonnie for a little while longer, okay?"

Starla glared at me from the armchair. "Told you...we should've waited."

Her voice was getting weaker, which only scared me more. I needed tools. Something that could break through a metal door...

Initially, in the aftermath of the carnage in the bedroom,

I'd had hope. Making sure Brand stayed incapacitated had been my first priority, so I whacked him again to be on the safe side, then looked up in horror when I realised Vonnie and Araceli were standing in the doorway.

"Are they dead?" Araceli asked.

"Uh, no?" Not yet, anyway. "Could you take Vonnie back to the living room and then bring me some of the macramé cord? Please?"

Vonnie's face was white with shock, and I cursed Brand under my breath. No child should have to go through this. No adult either.

Araceli had found the cord while I used strips of bed sheet to bind the cut on Starla's leg, and together, we'd settled her onto the couch. Next, I'd tied Brand's ankles and secured one of his hands to his thigh. Why only one? Because I needed the other.

Dragging his dead weight through the underground apartment had sapped my strength, but the rush of elation I'd felt when I pressed his hand to the pad beside the door and the light blinked from red to green had made the effort worth it.

But that joy soon skittered away into the dark, dusty corners of the next room. A room Starla hadn't realised existed. Limbo? Purgatory? Was there a difference? Probably, but it didn't matter. If I couldn't find a way out, we'd all die there.

Shelving units sat against the left wall of the antechamber, and I took a quick inventory. Two new shower curtains, still in the packages. Several decorators' drop cloths. A saw. Claws of horror dug into me as the possible uses for those items became apparent, and I turned to face the opposite wall where two large chest freezers hummed quietly. I was *not* going near those freezers.

At the far end of the room, wooden stairs led up to the next floor. At the top of the stairs, there was a door, and beside the door was a black box, not another fingerprint scanner but a digital keypad. It needed a code.

And we didn't have the code.

Panic rose up my throat, but I couldn't afford to lose my head. I'd run back to Brand, but he was out for the count, so I'd tried Gregg. His guts were slithering out of him by then, but he was still awake.

"What's the code? The code to the door?"

His eyes struggled to focus.

"Tell me the code, and I'll call an ambulance. Maybe they can help."

He'd glanced down at the gelatinous snakes sitting in his lap and uttered two words.

"Fuck you."

And then he passed out.

No. No way. I was not giving up. I might have been bruised, exhausted, and covered in three people's blood, but I wasn't a quitter. My stomach churned as I searched through his pockets for a phone, but the momentary spark of hope I felt when I found a fancy new Samsung soon died when I realised there was no signal in the basement, not even Wi-Fi. Probably something to do with the layer of soundproofing in the ceiling.

Okay, onto plan C... I needed a solid object. A battering ram. But everything heavy enough—the stove, the kitchen table, the refrigerator—was either too big or too awkward to move. The hinge pins were on my side of the door, but I couldn't find anything to knock them out with. The cutlery in the kitchen was plastic—no use at all. I tried my own knife, but they didn't budge, and I couldn't afford to break the tip of the blade, not when there was the possibility of Brand waking up. I'd need to threaten him. To shave small pieces of his skin off until he told us what we needed to know. What about the wall? Could I break through that? Was it brick or Sheetrock?

I ran back to the antechamber, pausing to placate the girls as I went, which brought us to the current moment. Dammit, the wall was brick. Why did these old homes have to be so solid? And why had Alton Brand over-engineered *everything*?

Could I use the saw? Not necessarily to cut, but to pry? I grabbed it, tried to wedge it into the gap between the door and the frame, but it wouldn't fit. What if I broke the electronic panel? Would the lock release? I raised a fist, then hesitated. If the lock didn't release, we'd be in even more trouble.

Then I spotted it.

A wooden handle poking out from behind the nearest freezer.

An axe!

A heavy, solid axe. The blade was spotted with rust, but... Oh, fuck. That wasn't rust, it was blood, dried blood.

I puked bile onto the dirty floor and then gave myself a mental slap. I didn't have time to vomit.

No, I had to chop.

I grabbed the wooden handle and began swinging at the brick around the door frame. It was softer than the steel, and maybe, just maybe if I could loosen it enough...

40

FORD

Emmy opted for a different tactic when it came to entering Brand's home. Thanks to the comprehensive search earlier in the week, they knew that all he had in the way of security was deadbolts on the doors and locks on the downstairs windows. No cameras, no alarm. As Ford had said before, underneath the awkwardness, he was an arrogant fucker. He thought he was untouchable. So Emmy swapped her shapeless suit for skinny jeans and a turtleneck, added a gun and a tactical vest, and climbed up the outside of the fucking house to Brand's en-suite bathroom. He'd left a small window open for ventilation, and all she had to do was reach through to open a bigger window, then slide inside. The whole process took less than a minute.

Sky and Rafael had followed Brand home earlier, and the replacement team of Dan and Knox had taken over the vigil during the search of Cooke's place. The shades were drawn, and although light from a TV flickered in the living room, nobody could be sure that Brand was in there watching a show, so Emmy had to move slowly. The five minutes that passed as she made her way downstairs to open the back door for the rest of the team—Rafael, Sky, Ana, and Xav—were perhaps the longest of Ford's life. And fuck, he couldn't do what Emmy did. She just stayed so damn calm. One of the screens showed her vital stats, and apart from a brief spike while she scaled the building, her pulse hadn't risen out of the eighties.

Some kind of sign language went on, and the team inside headed toward the front of the house in two pairs—Emmy with Xav, Sky with Rafael. Ana stayed back, presumably covering the rear exit in case Brand made a run for it. All were wearing ski masks now, their faces hidden, and if Ford had encountered that group, he'd have told them whatever they wanted to know.

Nate had said Emmy would make Brand talk, and the more he watched her, the less he doubted that statement.

But where *was* Brand?

On screen, Emmy quietly asked the same question, but Ford couldn't mistake the annoyance in her voice. "Tell me that fucker didn't sneak out?"

"No way," Dan told her. "We've been watching the house, front and back. Haven't taken our eyes off it."

"Side window?"

"Got those covered too."

"Well, he's not here now."

"Did you check the closets?" Knox whispered.

"Please, don't insult me."

"The attic?" Rafael suggested.

"Hatch is bolted from the outside."

"So what does that leave? The roof? A tunnel?"

A slow grin crept over Emmy's face, and in the gloomy feed from Xav's body cam, the effect was unnerving, more Joker than joy. "A basement. A fucking basement. Check the floors. The walls downstairs. That psychopathic cuntcake's been hiding his lair, and I bet you a hundred bucks it's beneath our bloody feet."

"Nobody's gonna take that bet," Nate muttered. "She's always right."

"Knox, Dan, get inside and help. Look under rugs, behind paintings, mirrors."

"Bookshelves," Sky added. "Check the bookshelves. Does he have a piano?"

A piano?

"What's a piano got to do with anything?" Ford asked.

Nate gave a one-shouldered shrug. "That's a story for another day."

A memory stirred in the depths of Ford's brain, a conversation he'd had... The maid. Brand's maid had said he didn't like her to dust in his den, only vacuum. At the time, Ford had brushed it off as the quirk of a man who valued his personal space, but what if there had been a darker reason?

"Tell them to start in the den. The study. The shelves there."

Nate relayed the message, and Emmy headed in that direction with Sky as Rafael rolled up the rug they were walking over. Xav was already lifting prints from the walls.

"Den" was something of a misnomer because the room was reasonably large. Maybe "library" would have been a better word? Ford recalled flipping through a book or two as the tech guys checked Brand's computer, but he'd never suspected a hidden door. Had his carelessness cost Hallie her life? That thought was a punch to the gut.

In the den, Sky flipped on the light and moved to the first set of shelves, then began lifting books methodically, checking behind. But Emmy just stood still, thinking.

Or...listening?

"Shhh..."

"What?" Sky asked.

"Do you hear that?"

"Hear wh—" Then Ford heard it too. The faintest *thunk, thunk, thunk*. "Where's that coming from?"

"Over here."

Emmy moved to the shelves near the desk, but rather than pulling out books, she studied the tomes, her head moving from left to right. Then she reached for one volume on the top shelf and pulled.

What was the book?

Lolita.

The shelf slid to the side on hinges as silent as the grave.

Holy shit.

Ford had missed the hidden door on the first search. Missed the book, missed the significance. Missed the whole fucking basement.

Now Emmy stood before a steel door, and without the deadening effect of the books, the *thunk, thunk, thunk* took on a grittier tone. Was it digging? Was Brand digging? Ford's heart threatened to give out, because why would a man be digging a hole in his basement if not to bury something?

Emmy tilted her head to one side, and Ford couldn't imagine what was going through her mind. She was the one tasked with somehow getting through a hardened door into a basement occupied by a hostile, perhaps two if Cooke was down there with Brand. Nobody knew what sort of weapons they might have.

A digital panel was set into the wall beside the door, and Nate leaned closer to the screen as Emmy angled her camera for a better picture.

"I know the model," he said. "It requires a six-digit PIN, but there's a bug in the firmware. If you enter the first four digits, the display will either show an error code or wait for the other two. Long story short, I can brute-force it, but it'll take around an hour and a half."

Too long, too long. This was all taking too long.

Suddenly, Emmy stiffened and pressed her ear right against the door. What? What had she heard? She stepped back, thinking again as she wiped the door with a gloved hand. Clearly, she knew that an ear-print was as unique as a fingerprint, but the move seemed to be more of an ingrained habit than anything else. Covering her tracks came naturally to her.

Then she tapped on the door.

The thunking stopped, and Nate groaned.

"Why did she do that? Why give up the element of surprise?"

Emmy tapped again. *Tap-tap-tap, tap, tap, tap, tap-tap-tap.* Was that... Was that old-fashioned Morse code? Ford held his breath as the same pattern was repeated back, and then Emmy bellowed, "Hallie?"

"Emmy?"

Her voice was muffled, but the fear still came through, loud and clear.

Fuck Blackwood and their rules. Ford bolted out of the back door of the van and sprinted toward the house of horrors. His girl was alive. She was alive, and she was trapped underground with fuck knew who.

The whole Blackwood team was gathered in the den when Ford burst through the crowd. Rafael took one look and grabbed him before he could get to the door.

"Get the hell off me!"

"Shut up. Emmy's trying to talk."

"Stay calm and focus. We're gonna get you out of here. Nate's on his way to crack the lock—all you have to do is sit tight for a while longer."

"Where's Brand?" Ford hissed. "I'm gonna kill him."

Sky pointed at the floor. "Hallie might've already done that."

"Can't...no time," Hallie shouted, her words barely audible through the thick steel. "...bleeding...ambulance."

She was injured. Hell, Hallie was injured, and they didn't have ninety minutes for Nate to finesse the lock.

"Can't we break the door down? Knock it out of the wall?"

Again, Emmy studied. What was her pulse at now? Ninety? Ninety-five? "Fifty bucks says the frame's reinforced. Turn out the lights."

"What?"

But Sky obliged. The door had a crack of light around it, and Ford saw Emmy pull something from her pocket, then move in silhouette. When the lights blinked back on, there were three white crosses on the door. He'd given up trying to understand what she was doing. Far better to just let her carry on with the task.

"I feel like having a movie night," she said. "Ever seen *The Italian Job*?"

"What the hell does that have to do with anything? Aren't there more important things to think about right now?"

"What's the most famous line in that film?"

"You're only meant to— Fuck, you can't be serious."

"As an involuntary decapitation."

"Aren't all decapitations involuntary?" Knox asked.

"Now that I think about it, that's an excellent point. Unless someone decides to shoot themselves in the head with, say, a Desert Eagle. Or throws themselves under a train. Or—"

Ford was ready to have a coronary. "Will you just get on with it?"

Emmy held up a small velvet pouch. "Sure. Getting on."

And out of the pouch, she took...

"Is that a *tampon*? What in the world do you need that for?"

"Boy, you really listened in biology." She stripped off the plastic wrapper. "You've got no idea how many guys are scared of these things. My handbag's been searched at least ten times with these little widgets in, and not one man has ever had the balls to take a closer look."

"Then what...?"

Emmy mashed the "tampon" over one of the door hinges, then yanked the string out. "Might want to stand back. This thing's got a short fuse."

"Bit like you at the wrong time of the month," Rafael muttered.

"I fucking heard that." Emmy raised her voice. "Hallie, get back from the door. Right back, as far as you can. Do you understand?"

Hallie's voice came back, faint and high. "I understand."

Emmy repeated the process with two more "tampons," one for each of the crosses. *The hinges.* This was insane, and Ford would probably lose his job for going along with it, but at that moment, he didn't care. Love was more important than money. If the worst came to the worst, he'd just have to play a fictional detective in one of his dad's movies and earn a paycheck that way.

"Okay, everybody out," Emmy ordered.

"How do you detonate it?"

"I order pizza."

And she wasn't kidding. In the yard, Emmy took out her phone, scrolled down to the details for Papa Nate's Pizza Parlour, and selected "Share Contact."

"It's got biometric security, so don't get any ideas," she warned Ford.

"Trust me, I'm not getting any ideas."

She tapped in a long code from memory, then put her

fingers in her ears. Ford followed suit, just in time for the *boom*.

It was official: the woman was certifiable.

Ford's ears were still ringing when Emmy, Knox, Sky, Dan, Ana, and Rafael ran back into the house.

The door had fallen inward, and smoke curled into the den as Team Blackwood took the steps down to the basement with Emmy in the lead. Ford brought up the rear, wondering if he should take out his gun, feeling like the kid who got picked last for softball.

Then he saw her.

Hallie was covered in blood, so much blood, and she tripped into Rafael's arms. He caught her, held her steady as Ford pushed his way forward.

"Where are you hurt?" Rafael asked.

"Not me." Hallie choked back sobs. "Starla. Starla's hurt."

Who the hell was Starla?

They soon found out. Through the doorway beyond, Ford glimpsed three girls. Three *children*. And those cries... Was that a baby? This wasn't a basement; it was a war zone. Blood everywhere. A body lying on the floor...

"Take Hallie."

Rafael passed her over, and she was a dead weight, trembling from head to toe as Ford hung on to her.

"Plum, come and sit down, okay? Come and sit down."

"I thought I was going to d-d-die."

Under the blood, she was pale, so pale. "Has anyone called an ambulance?"

"Five minutes ago," Xav said.

"You're okay. Nobody can hurt you now, I promise." But Ford had sworn to protect her before, hadn't he? And look what had happened. "I love you."

She clung to him tighter. "I love you too."

Someone—Hallie?—had used a body to prop the door

339

open. Knox turned it over and checked the man's pulse. Brand.

"Still alive, unfortunately."

"How do we feel about that?" Emmy's question was phrased in general terms, but she was looking at Ford as she knelt beside the oldest of the girls. That had to be Starla. Ford recognised the other two as Vonnie Feinstein and Araceli Suarez.

Slowly, he processed Emmy's words. Realised what she was asking. Earlier, he'd threatened to kill Brand, but that had been in the heat of the moment. Could he take a life in cold blood? He had no doubt now that Emmy could. Probably half the people in this room could snuff the man out and not lose a second of sleep over it.

But at heart, Ford was still a cop.

"If he survives, then he should stand trial."

"Well, I hope you brought your handcuffs."

Ana and Emmy had Starla on the floor now, and first aid supplies had appeared from somewhere. Gauze, bandages, even an IV. Did Blackwood employees know how to do *everything*?

Knox saw him watching and answered his unasked question. "We all receive extensive medical training. Nothing fancy—we're not heart surgeons—but we can handle battlefield trauma."

Dan crouched in front of the two younger girls, talking softly while Xav rocked the baby in his arms. Did he have kids of his own? He looked as if he knew what he was doing, which was more than Ford did right now.

Sky reappeared through a door on the far side of the room. "There's another not-quite-dead guy through there." She wrinkled her nose. "Kind of gross."

"Ambulances are five minutes away," Emmy said. "Anyone who doesn't need to be here, clear out. Sky, Rafael, Xav, Ana."

"Wait, wait, wait." She couldn't just send people away from a crime scene. "They're witnesses. We need to take statements."

"They didn't see anything, they don't know anything, and they're not witnesses."

"But—"

"Here's what happened... You responded to a call from Mr. Gilmore—"

"Who?"

"Kellan. A call raising concerns over the safety of Ms. Halina Chastain, who hadn't reported in as she should, so you attended the home of Mrs. Phyllis Cooke to look into the matter. While leaving Mrs. Cooke's home, you spotted a suspicious character exiting Mr. Brand's residence and came to investigate. You found the front door open. Concerned for his safety, you entered the building and heard noises coming from the den. We followed, having been alerted by Mr. Gilmore, and offered assistance with the aftermath."

"Nice story, but that's not what the evidence shows."

"No, the evidence shows that the Richmond PD fucked up—again—and left three kidnap victims in a paedophile's basement. And because they fucked up, a fourth woman got abducted. Tell me, which story do you think Chief Broussard would rather see in the papers?"

"You're suggesting a cover-up?"

"Hey, at least this time, the chief'll be busting a child rapist rather than actively being one. Look, the Richmond PD's reputation is in the toilet, but I can see that Broussard's trying to change things. The last thing the department needs is more bad publicity."

"What about Blackwood? Don't you want the good publicity?" Ford spread his hands. "Think of the headlines— security firm finds three missing children." At least, he assumed Starla had been snatched at some point. "It could lead to new work."

"My team neither needs nor wants additional work. We turn jobs down every week. And I'm sure we can come to an arrangement with your media team regarding the initial investigation, but that's a discussion for later. Take care of Hallie."

"You're playing dirty."

"When did I ever give you the impression I'd do anything else?"

Years ago, Ford had taken one of those online personality tests, and it had described him as results-driven. And yeah, he was. For sure, he'd bent the rules on occasion, but he'd never broken them outright.

Not like this.

Ford looked around the room. At Dan, now holding the baby as she comforted Araceli and Vonnie. At Knox, standing guard over a groaning Alton Brand. At Emmy herself, playing nurse to Starla. She'd packed the wound with gauze, and the bleeding had begun to slow. And finally, Ford looked at Hallie, weeping softly in his arms. What would have happened if she'd spent a few more hours trapped in this basement?

Emmy had done the right thing. She might have given legality the bird in the rear-view mirror as she ran roughshod through rules, regulations, laws, norms, and whatever else she could break, but she'd done the right thing.

And Ford would go along with whatever damn story she cooked up.

Sky and Rafael had disappeared already, and Xav was walking out with Ana. As they passed through the antechamber, Ford saw Ana pause by one of the freezers and open the lid. She studied the contents for a moment, then her lip curled as she turned and crossed the room. When she reached Brand, she gave him a vicious kick in the kidney, muttering something in a language Ford didn't understand.

But he figured Brand probably deserved to be pissing blood.

Ford took a seat in the empty armchair and cradled Hallie on his lap. Yeah, he'd do whatever it took to make things right for her.

41

HALLIE

"How are you feeling?" Dr. Beech asked.

Numb.

I was still numb.

In the past twenty-four hours, I'd experienced every possible emotion. Happiness when I woke up with Ford. Frustration when it seemed as if the investigation had stalled. Elation and the thrill of the chase when I realised Alton Brand had a basement. Sheer terror when I woke up in it. Dread when Alton and Gregg had returned. Revulsion when Gregg tried to rape me, followed by anger, determination, and rising panic as I'd fought to save Starla and escape.

And finally, relief.

Relief that Blackwood had found me. Relief that Emmy carried explosives in her purse. Relief that Starla had gotten medical help. Relief that four children wouldn't have to spend years underground.

But what came out was a croaky, "I'm okay."

"Good, good. No pain anywhere?"

Only in my heart. Four other girls had lost their lives at

Brand's hands, and Janiya had died so recently. If only we'd started looking sooner...

"The others, how are they? Starla?"

"That was a nasty cut on her leg, but we're confident she'll make a complete recovery. Vonnie and Araceli don't appear to have suffered any physical harm."

Other than weeks and months of sexual assault, anyway. They'd bear scars from their ordeals for the rest of their lives.

"The baby?"

"She's in surprisingly good health. Other than a vitamin D deficiency, we haven't found any issues."

What would happen to Aliya? Her mom was dead, had still been a child herself, and the thought of Brand's family raising her brought the nausea back.

"And the two men?"

Ford squeezed my hand. He hadn't left my side since the team found me.

"You don't need to worry about them," he said.

"I want to know."

Part of me hoped they were dead, but another part, perhaps the bigger part, didn't want them to get off that easy. They deserved a trial, interrogation, everyone seeing them and judging them. Hating them. Knowing they were monsters.

Dr. Beech hemmed and hawed but finally told me, "Mr. Cooke didn't make it, and Mr. Brand is in surgery. One of the knife wounds punctured a lung."

Gregg was dead.

I'd killed him.

"Do you think Alton Brand will survive?"

"I'd say it's fifty-fifty right now."

When Dr. Beech left the room, Ford moved from the chair to the bed and took my hand.

"Cooke was self-defence, plum. He abducted you."

"I know."

345

"We'll get through this," he said, but there was doubt in his voice. He brought my hand to his lips. Kissed my knuckles. "Won't we?"

"I hope so?"

"Fuck, I'm so sorry. I missed the damn basement. This should have been over on Tuesday, and you should never have been put in this position."

"*Everybody* missed the basement. I only found out about it by accident."

"Phyllis Cooke told you?"

"She mentioned that Alton used to hide in there when he was a kid, but Gregg was there when she said it, and I didn't realise he was involved. So I went outside to call you, and I guess he must have hit me over the head because the next thing I remember is waking up in that living room with the girls."

"I let you down."

"Nobody let me down."

And I meant that. Everyone had done their best under difficult circumstances, and Brand had been a sneaky adversary. But most importantly, I realised, I hadn't let myself down. The last time I'd gotten abducted, I'd been Starla, toeing the line, waiting, waiting, waiting for an opportunity to escape to present itself. But this time, I'd made my own opportunity. I'd been given the tools to defend myself, and I'd damn well used them, and then when I'd needed a little extra help at the end, my team had been there.

If today had been a test, then I'd passed.

The numbness was receding, and instead, I felt...pretty freaking invincible, actually.

"But—" Ford started.

I twisted my grip, kissed his knuckles in return. "Really, I'm okay. I'm desperately sorry that Phyllis lost her son, and I wish Starla hadn't gotten cut, but I don't regret anything else. How can I? I stopped a man from raping me..." Ford blanched at my words. "And three girls are going home to their parents. Today, I didn't become a victim." I squeezed his hand tighter. "*Never again* will I become a victim."

"Bravo." I looked up to see Emmy in the doorway. "That's the spirit. There's no bigger buzz than staring death in the face and then kicking it in the arse. Or stabbing it in the back. That works too."

"That was actually Starla. She was trying to get Brand off me."

"Yeah, she said. Quite a kid."

"Are her parents coming? Did somebody find them?"

"No, and kind of."

My stomach lurched. "What does that mean?"

"Black took a look into her background. Starla Louise Maple disappeared from a park in Bloomfield, Missouri, four and a half years ago. There's no father named on her birth certificate, her mother died by suicide last year, and she was an only child."

For the first time since Ford carried me out of the dungeon, I felt tearful. Starla had no family? She'd finally managed to escape from hell, and there was nothing and nobody for her to go back to?

"What about other relatives? Aunts? Uncles?"

"Black's still digging."

"Is he here?"

"He's staying at James's place tonight."

Most days, I thought I'd adapted to my new life pretty well —having billionaires as friends, that kind of thing—but every so often, I got a reminder that these people played in a whole other league to me. Because by "James's place," Emmy meant the White House.

Even so, I tried to play it cool. "Say hi from me. Black will be back tomorrow?"

"First thing. How are you feeling tonight? Tired?"

I tried to make a joke. "Thanks to Gregg Cooke, I got some sleep earlier. What time is it?"

"Almost midnight, but Chief Broussard wants a chat. Are you up to that? Oliver's on his way, but I can put Broussard off until the morning if you want."

"I'd rather get it over with. Am I allowed to see Starla first?"

Would she even want me there? The last words she'd spoken to me had been in anger.

"I'll clear it. Dan's with her at the moment."

At least she wasn't alone.

Inside, I was feeling stronger, but my legs still threatened to collapse when I tried to get out of bed. Ford offered me his arm, but I'd only gotten halfway to the door when it flew open and Mercy rushed in.

"You're okay?" She flung her arms around me. "*Dios mio*, I heard what happened." She released her hold, then hugged me again. "That's from Cora. She wanted to come, but Lee said there would be a hundred people at the hospital already, so she's taking care of Pinchy."

Rafael appeared behind Mercy, and a lump came into my throat. If it hadn't been for his constant pushing, for all the painful sessions when he'd said, "One more time, *cariño*," I wouldn't be breathing right now.

"Thank you," I mouthed, and he flashed me a smile. Damn, he was handsome when he smiled.

Not that I cared, obviously, because I had Ford now.

I had everything.

"I'm sorry I got mad at you."

Oh, that poor girl. I sat on the edge of Starla's hospital bed and took her hand. "There's nothing to apologise for. What happened earlier... It was messy and stressful and neither of us was thinking straight. You did amazing."

"Will I get into trouble?" She seemed so young lying there. So fragile. "For...you know?"

"Absolutely not. You deserve a medal. And hey, look at us —out two and a half years early."

That drew the tiniest of smiles from her. "I can't wait until the morning. I just want to see the sunrise. The daylight. Trees, birds, clouds. I'm gonna stay outside all day, and I don't even care if it rains."

"I'm sure we can make that happen." Someone would have a spare coat and an umbrella. If I mentioned Starla's plan to Bradley, he'd show up with a transparent igloo and a heater too. "Did the doctor say how long you'd have to be here?"

"Till tomorrow, probably. What will happen to Aliya? They've taken her away, and I don't even know where."

Well, she could hardly go live with her father, could she? I deferred to Dan because she knew more about this stuff than me.

"The Department of Social Services will make sure she's cared for. Most likely, she'll be placed with a foster family."

"But I promised Janiya I'd take care of her. I *promised*."

"And you kept your promise. You took care of that little girl in a situation neither of you should ever have been placed in, and you did a terrific job. But, sweetie, you need to focus on yourself for the moment. Let other people take some of the load."

This had to be hell on her, and on Aliya too. For five months, Starla had acted as Aliya's mom, and now they'd been ripped away from each other.

"Is she okay?"

"She's doing well."

Starla swallowed, more of a gulp really. "When will my

mom come? When can I go home? I'd kill for pizza from Imo's." A sob burst out of her. "I didn't mean... I didn't mean, like, *kill*, just..."

"It's okay." But it wasn't, was it? Her mom was gone. I wanted to give her a hug, but she still had tubes sprouting from her hands. "We understand."

I locked eyes with Dan, and she gave a barely perceptible nod. She had this. Her shoulders stiffened as she prepared to deliver the news.

"Starla, your mom passed away last year. I'm so sorry."

It was the first time I'd seen her cry. She'd stayed unbelievably strong until now, but the news tipped her over the edge. Dan moved to the other side of the bed, and we tucked IV lines out of the way so we could both hold her. So we could absorb some of the pain.

"W-w-what will happen? W-w-where will I go?"

Dan pushed damp strands of hair away from Starla's eyes. "Let us worry about that. All you have to do is rest."

"Th-th-the whole time I was trapped, I only wanted to see my mom. Alton told me she didn't care, that she was never there and that was why he took me, but he lied. She *did* care. She just worked a lot, that was all."

Starla was absolutely right. Her mom had cared so much that she'd overdosed because she didn't want to live without her daughter. There'd been a note. Emmy had told me about it as we walked to Starla's room.

"Your mom loved you very much."

"He said he saved me. Saved all of us. I hope he dies."

Three hours later, Starla got her wish.

42

FORD

Broussard paced his office, spitting the occasional curse in his wake. Ford could hardly blame the man.

Mid-morning on Friday, and the media circus was camping outside the doors downstairs. The TV in the corner had been muted, but rumours of a serial killer who kept children as pets scrolled across the chyron at regular intervals. The talking heads were in full flow. With no press release available yet, the reporters were quoting anonymous sources and basically making stuff up, most of it inaccurate. Footage of the alpaca being collected by staff from an animal shelter was playing on a loop, and earlier, a reporter had been wondering on air whether or not alpacas were vegetarian.

Yes, there'd even been a mention of cannibalism, and having seen the neatly packaged lumps of Janiya Thomas in Brand's freezer, Ford had to concede it was a possibility. But Hallie thought he'd fed the missing kids to the pig. Was that better or worse? Right now, the CSIs were digging up the rotting remains of Martha—again—and this time, a veterinarian was on hand to perform an autopsy. Did animals have autopsies? Or was it a necropsy?

Ford had handwritten his resignation letter. It was sitting on Broussard's desk, but so far, he hadn't accepted it. He'd been too busy muttering.

"I came here to clean up this damn department, to improve public confidence, and now I'm expected to spin this damn case to the media? It was a goatfuck. A goatfuck from start to finish. First Ganaway, and now...this." He waved at the TV, where a cameraperson had zoomed in on the tent over the pig's grave. "Why didn't anyone find that damn basement during the first search?"

"It was well-hidden, sir."

"Nobody got plans for the house?"

"No, sir."

"And after I told you to back off, you just kept on going."

"Yes, I did. Because my girlfriend had disappeared, and I wasn't about to sit back and let an asshole like Duncan head up the investigation. What would you have done in that situation?"

Broussard paused mid-step and pondered for a second. "Probably the same thing as you did. But that doesn't make it right."

"I understand that, which is why I'm offering my resignation. But I can't regret what I did. I can't regret getting Hallie and those kids out of that basement or accepting Blackwood's assistance to do so."

"Shown up by Blackwood again."

"Yes, sir."

"A series of unfortunate errors." Broussard paused by the window. "Emmy Black's an interesting conundrum."

"She is."

"What do you make of her?"

"I think..." Where should Ford start? "I think she's a strong, loyal woman with a well-developed moral code.

However, that code isn't necessarily the same as ours. She has little regard for rules she disagrees with, and she won't hesitate to break them if it furthers her objectives. And those objectives generally involve righting what she sees as wrongs."

"That's more or less what I got, too. But I've heard her described as a mercenary."

"No, I can't see it, not in the conventional sense. I believe she gets paid to do jobs she'd do for free anyway, and because those jobs involve an element of danger, she probably gets paid very well. The money... For her, it's not about needing or even wanting piles of cash, but that the cash represents the respect she believes she's owed."

"An interesting theory."

"Just saying it the way I see it."

"If you were in my position, what would you do? Would you be economical with the truth when it comes to the media?"

"Honestly? Yes, I would. The only people who'd contradict whatever story we spin are dead anyway."

When Alton Brand had gotten out of surgery to repair the damage to his lungs, the doctors had increased his chances of survival to sixty-forty. But then his blood pressure had dropped, they'd discovered he had additional internal bleeding caused by a ruptured kidney, and he'd coded out in the early hours.

"That's true," Broussard said. "What about the kids?"

"Starla strikes me as the type who'd go along with Blackwood's version, and the two younger children witnessed neither the fight in the bedroom nor the action in the antechamber."

"And Blackwood themselves? What—" Broussard's phone rang, and he heaved a sigh before answering. "Patrice, I'm on 'do not disturb.'"

A pause.

"Is this a joke?" Broussard held the phone away, stared at it as if it'd been possessed, and then pressed it to his ear again. "Uh, yes, good morning, Mr. President."

The...president? President of what? The police union? Was he going to stick his nose into this case as well?

"Yes, yessir. ... Thank you, sir. ... I'll make sure I convey that message. ... An excellent job under difficult circumstances, yessir. ... Again, thank you, sir."

Once more, Broussard looked at the phone as if it could answer a question he hadn't asked.

"Did I just get Punk'd?"

Now Ford was also confused. "In what way?"

"That was a man claiming to be President Harrison. Do you have Twitter?"

"Yeah, but mostly for memes and—"

"Show me the president's account."

Ford did as instructed and scrolled through the feed. "He's getting a dog from a shelter in Virginia? Hope for Hounds? That's just up the road."

"Refresh it."

"What— Oh."

My thanks to members of the Richmond Police Department under the direction of Chief Jerome Broussard, whose diligent efforts in his new post yesterday resulted in the return of Vonnie Feinstein to her family, plus the liberation of two further kidnap victims. Justice has been served.

"Son of a gun." Broussard shook his head. "Guess we're going with the Blackwood version. How the hell did Harrison get to hear about the rescue so quickly?"

"I have no idea."

But Ford had lied; he did have an idea. Emmy's words

replayed in his head. *Black's still digging. He's staying at James's place tonight.* Son of a gun indeed.

"Emmy Black's a real piece of work."

Ford allowed himself a small smile. "You don't have to like her, but you sure as hell have to respect her."

Broussard's phone rang again, and he cautiously put it to his ear. "Yes?"

The news couldn't have been good because he paled a shade, a difficult feat with his Creole heritage.

"Keep that under wraps, for goodness' sake. The parents are distressed enough already."

Now what had happened? Hadn't this week been shit enough already?

Broussard sank into his leather swivel chair, picked up Ford's resignation letter, and tore it into pieces.

"If you ruin my girlfriend's birthday dinner again, I'll have you busted down to traffic, do you understand?"

"Yes, sir. Sorry, sir."

"Enough with the damn 'sir.' We've known each other too long for that."

"What was the news? Did they find something at Brand's place?"

"Apparently, the pig choked on part of a human femur. You know what? I'm glad we don't need to go through a three-ring circus of a trial. If we were back in Louisiana, this would've been a capital case, anyway."

"Better not say that in your press conference."

"Get back to the Brand home. Make sure they don't miss anything this time. And take Detective Matassa with you."

"*Detective* Matassa?"

"It's been in the works for a while, and she passed the exam with flying colours, plus she's smart and she's keen. I don't figure she can be a worse partner than Detective Duncan."

A baby alligator would've made a better partner than that asshole.

"I look forward to working with her."

"Well? What are you waiting for? I have a press conference to attend."

43

EPILOGUE - HALLIE

"**A**re you sure you're ready to go back to your apartment?" Ford asked.

I'd spent the weekend holed up at Riverley, recovering. Decompressing. On Friday night, I'd barely slept, but yesterday, Dr. Stanton had given me some pills to block the horrors, and I'd finally passed out. At least I wasn't the only person having nightmares. Apparently, Emmy had looked in the freezer after we left, and last night, she'd gone on one of her sleepwalking rampages. Black had a bruised face and a cut on his arm, which he said was an occupational hazard of sharing a bed with her, but I doubted he'd ever change the arrangement.

And Ford wouldn't change our arrangement either. He'd had to work, but when he came back, he didn't leave my side. Not even in the shower. He'd shampooed my hair, combed conditioner through to the ends, and then washed every inch of my body, carefully avoiding my many, many bruises. And after we'd gotten clean, he'd given me a massage that quickly turned dirty. At first, he'd been worried about touching me, but I'd urged him on. The new memories we were creating together could never erase the old ones, but they helped to push them into the background. And when Ford slid a finger inside me and found *that* spot, I'd been too busy moaning his name to consider freaking out. He'd held me up as my knees gave way, the tile cool against my back while the heat raged inside me.

And he did all of that in boxers because he didn't want me to feel uncomfortable. I hadn't even seen his freaking cock yet, but I loved him.

I'd always love him.

Plus we'd been through so much in our first few weeks together that the rest of our lives would be a breeze.

Earlier, we'd had lunch with his sister. He'd offered to cancel his usual Sunday visit, but family was important—not genes, not blood, but true family—so I'd pushed him to go. But then Emmy had suggested inviting Sylvie to Riverley so the kids could use the pool while the grown-ups talked, and that had seemed like a good compromise. The meeting had been slightly awkward as we both danced around the obvious elephants in the room, but we'd soon settled onto safer subjects. The decor at Riverley, the upcoming school concert (did I want to go?), Ford's sailing skills, that sort of thing. Not divorce, custody battles, or kidnap. Sylvie was sweet, easy to like. Maybe it was genetic?

While we chatted, Bradley fussed with Halloween decorations. The party should have been yesterday, but Emmy told him to cancel because we'd already had real-life Halloween and nobody needed to see any more gore this week. Bradley had gasped like a dying fish, and Izzy looked so sad that I'd suggested a compromise—postpone the celebrations by a week, and cut down on the blood. So now the party was next Saturday.

Weirdly, I was almost looking forward to it. Sure, everyone was bitching about the costumes, but that was normal.

And I needed normal.

The new normal.

"Yes, I'm sure I want to go back to my apartment." Riverley was spectacular and luxurious, but it was like staying in a hotel. "Take me home."

The details of the case kept unravelling throughout the week. Ford tried to keep the worst of the details quiet, but I made him tell me everything. Better the devil you know, especially when the media was making up so many stories. One "news" site said Brand had flayed the dead girls and made a coat from their skin, and when Sky showed us the article, Mack got a pissy look on her face and pulled out her laptop. An hour later, the web page was gone.

Ford did think they'd found a candidate for Cassy, though. Starla had spent hours with a team of specialist interviewers, going through every detail she could remember of her time in the basement. From little things Alton had said over the years, she thought Cassy had been around ten when she was taken, and also that she'd liked dogs. The plush puppy on the shelf in the living room had belonged to her. Brand had kept it as a kind of...creepy memorial, and none of the other girls were allowed to play with it.

Six years ago, animal-mad Cassy Hamill had vanished from her garden in Seymour, Tennessee, one sweltering summer afternoon, never to be seen again. Her puppy had been left behind, barking at the gate.

We thought we'd pieced together some of the specifics. Cassy had disappeared in August, and toward the end of September, Alton had collapsed with a burst appendix. Jack Brand was being remarkably forthcoming with information now. The ambulance had picked Alton up from work, and he'd spent two weeks in the hospital after complications—peritonitis followed by an abscess.

Alton had told Starla that before her arrival, he'd made modifications to the basement—added running water plus a full bathroom and kitchen. If Starla had been right about there being a limited supply of food and water prior to that, and Alton had been unable to return to Cassy for weeks... Well, I really didn't want to dwell on it. And all we could do was speculate, since her body had never been found. But the lab techs thought they could do something with DNA on the cuddly toy, so maybe with a little help from science, the family could get closure. Although Cassy's mom was in prison, the grandma who'd raised her was still alive and well.

Donna's body had been found, as well as parts of Janiya's, which left Maria Rodas. She'd arrived in the basement two years ago in August, and Starla said she hadn't been around for long. Neighbours recalled Alton buying the pig in September of that year.

I didn't much want to think about that either.

Although Starla thought the pig had been Gregg's idea. We'd built up a picture of him now, and former friends, teachers, and employers all said he'd been a lazy bum whose main goal in life was to make as much money as he could with as little effort as possible. So the pig fit. Why transport a body fifty miles and bury it if you could simply toss it out back and have an animal do the hard work?

That theory also went some way to explaining the weird relationship between Alton and Gregg. Gregg had come onto the scene at the same time as Maria, and Alton had been far from happy about it. Starla thought Gregg had caught Alton in the act—taking Maria out of a vehicle, carrying her into the house, something like that. And rather than do what any responsible person would have done and called the cops, he'd blackmailed Alton into giving him a "job."

Both men had been monsters, just in different ways.

And then there was Mila Carmody... Had she been another of Brand's victims? I recalled Gregg saying that four girls had died, but had Brand told him everything? Nobody could be sure. If we had the right Cassy, there was an eighteen-month gap between her abduction and Starla's. Had he snatched Mila during that window? It was certainly possible. How long had the basement been out of commission due to the renovations? Since Alton had done the work himself, there was no record.

Too many questions and not enough answers, but this was real life. Not everything got tied up in a neat little bow the way it did in the movies.

But there was one happy-ish ending. Okay, so it was still a work in progress, but when Fenika moved back home with Micah, that meant Dan had a spare room, so guess where Starla had ended up? The Department of Social Services was still looking for relatives, but if Blackwood couldn't find them, then there probably weren't any. Oh, sure, the arrangement with Dan was meant to be temporary, but somebody at the office had started a pool on when things would be made official, and Luther had picked next July, first week. Which meant that in approximately eight months, Starla Maple would be Starla di Grassi, with an outside chance at Starla White if Ethan got his act together and dropped to one knee before that.

Vonnie and Araceli had gone back home to their families. The Feinsteins had been all over the TV, a joyful reunion that might or might not have included crocodile tears, while the Suarezes were keeping a lower profile. Which left Aliya. The Thomas family had been approached, Ford said, but what a decision to have to make. Aliya was a tiny piece of their daughter but also of the man who'd taken Janiya from them.

How would I feel in their position?

I thought... I thought that I would want to keep the baby. None of this was Aliya's fault.

But fuck, being an adult was hard.

And so was Ford.

Every morning, he woke up with a tent in his boxers, but he didn't pressure me, not once.

Instead, I started to pressure myself. What if I never got over this stupid fear? What if I tried and panicked? Or what if he got sick of waiting?

On Saturday morning, I was in the middle of one of my second-guessing sessions on the boat when his eyelids fluttered open. A heartbeat later, those soft brown eyes registered concern.

"What's wrong?"

"Nothing."

"Don't bullshit me, plum. I'm a detective, remember?"

A detective, and too damn smart with it. "I'm just scared, that's all."

"We're going too fast? We can go slower. Anything you want."

"No, no, that's not it. I swear. I... I guess I'm...I'm scared you'll get frustrated. That you'll leave before...before..."

"Have you lost your mind?"

"Richmond isn't even your permanent home. You said you'd go back to New Orleans in a couple of years."

"I'm not going anywhere."

"Really?"

"What do you want me to do? Tattoo your name across my chest? Sign a lease on an apartment with you? Put a ring on your finger? All of the above? Because I'll do it. Yeah, I'm frustrated, but only because I don't know how else to show you that I love you. How to convince you that we're okay."

He just did. He spoke from the heart, and mine melted.

"A...ring? Do you mean...?"

"I didn't intend on asking you for a while because of the whole 'no pressure' thing, but yeah, consider yourself asked. When you're ready, you can let me know."

"And the apartment... Mercy..."

Ford tucked my hair behind my ears. "We've got all the time in the world. Does that mean I shouldn't rush out to the nearest tattoo parlour?"

"Would I need to get a matching one? Because I'm actually not a huge fan of tattoos, although I think that's probably because I'm not a huge fan of pain."

"So we'll cross the his 'n' hers tats off the list, then. How do you feel about piercings?"

"Again, pain."

"On me."

Something about the way he said it... "Ford? Do you have a piercing?"

He did, didn't he? Where the hell was it? Because I'd seen every part of him except for... Oh, whoa.

He took my hand and guided it downward, and I felt him for the first time. Eight inches of steel with a very definite bump. Curiosity got the better of me, and I slid down his underwear to get a better look. He had a little ring with a ball through the underside of his cock, near the tip.

"Why? I mean, when?"

"Seven years ago. My buddy Ignace's bachelor party. Yeah, alcohol was involved."

"Wow. I didn't think you were the type."

"Neither did I. I almost took it out the next day, but then I figured that since I'd gone to the trouble of letting a guy stick a needle through my dick, I should at least keep it for a few months."

"Does it hurt?"

"Not now."

"So is it...good?"

"For me? Fuck, yeah. Women either love it or hate it. If you hate it, then it's gone."

"Can I touch it?"

"You can do whatever you want with it. Just don't chip a tooth."

I wrapped my hand around him and flicked the little ball, which elicited a low groan from the bottom of his throat, and I realised that all the worry I'd been carrying around...it was gone. This wasn't so scary. Ford wore *dick jewellery*. My gosh, if Bradley knew, he'd probably stick a diamanté on it. The thought made me snort, and I clapped a hand over my mouth.

"What's so funny?"

"Nothing. Nothing at all."

"Plum?"

"Okay... I'm just thinking that if we don't keep this quiet, there'll be dick rings in the piñata next year."

Now Ford was laughing too. "I'm keeping my mouth shut for sure."

"Aw, that's a shame." I ran my thumb along his bottom lip until he gave in. "Twinkledick."

"The name's frappé, and don't you forget it."

"Twinkle, twinkle, little dick..."

"Little? You think this is little?"

"Sparkle, sparkle, giant cock?"

"Maybe I should just take it out..."

I pretended to pout. "But what if I'm one of the women who loves it?"

The atmosphere grew suddenly heavier.

"What if you are?" Ford whispered.

You know what? Screw this. *Screw this.* I could save myself from two monsters, but I couldn't make love to my own boyfriend—fiancé?—because I was nervous? No way. Fear could go fuck itself.

"Gimme the lube."

He had some in the bedside table, I knew he did, along with condoms, plus a package of M&Ms in case I got hungry during our movie sessions. He always came prepared.

"You're certain about this?"

"Absolutely."

I rolled on a condom, then squirted a generous amount of lube down his length like I was seasoning a hot dog. Not the most romantic gesture, but we could refine the technique later. This was getting *done*. Ford steadied my hips as I straddled him and slowly, slowly sank onto that generous cock. He filled me. Stretched me. But he'd never hurt me. I was still wearing his T-shirt, and I tore it off as I began to rock. The fear was gone now. I just needed to find the pleasure.

"The ball isn't doing much."

"When you're ready, try reverse cowgirl."

I repositioned myself, and oh, holy shit. Now I felt *everything*. I arched my back, hitting the right spot over and over and over as Ford helped me to find my rhythm.

"I can't see you," I choked. "I want to see you."

"Later. Take what you need first."

Take what I need... The orgasm ripped through me like a wildfire, searing every nerve ending in its wake. I collapsed backward, covered in a sheen of sweat as Ford wrapped his arms around me and peppered kisses across my shoulders. Now I knew how the boat got its name. Ford Prestia was definitely a sure thing.

"So, am I keeping the piercing?" he asked.

"Don't you even think about removing it." My legs were shaking as I rolled onto my back, pulling Ford with me. "Now it's your turn to take what you need."

What Ford needed, it turned out, was to make me come again. I was boneless on the mattress by the time he gave one final thrust and emptied himself into me, and I didn't much care if I never left his bed again.

Hallie Prestia. I liked the sound of that.

One day.

"I love you," I whispered. Maybe I cried a little as well, but they were the best kind of tears.

"Love you too, plum."

44

EPILOGUE - FORD

Ford could happily have stayed in bed for the whole weekend, but there came a point when they had to eat. Plus parts of him were a touch tender. After the dam had broken, Hallie had ridden his dick all morning, and some recovery time wasn't necessarily a bad thing.

Plus they had this party of Bradley's to go to.

Izzy and Cora had brought the costumes to Hallie's apartment yesterday, the baker and the gingerbread woman, and Ford figured he'd gotten off lightly with a hat and an apron. There was a rolling pin too, but he could dump that at the earliest opportunity.

"How do I look?" Hallie asked.

"Edible. Are you sure we have to go out?"

"We can sneak away early."

Sky had offered them one of her bedrooms for the night. Apparently, she lived in Emmy's spare house with her boyfriend because spare houses were a thing when you were a billionaire. Of all the people who worked for Blackwood, Sky had shocked Ford the most. She was so young to be doing what she did. When he was her age, he'd been sneaking kegs into parties and playing truth or dare, not hunting kidnappers. Apparently, she'd helped to bust a multi-million-dollar art theft ring earlier in the year too. An old head on young shoulders, as Ford's mom would have said.

Speaking of his mom, he wanted to take a trip to New Orleans to introduce Hallie to his parents. He'd almost gotten engaged this morning, and the three of them hadn't even met. They'd love her, but his mom wouldn't love him if he didn't get off his ass and arrange a visit. Hallie said taking time off wouldn't be a problem for her, so as soon as the Brand case died down, they'd go.

But first, they had to survive a late Halloween.

Just a few close friends, Emmy had said. There had to be a hundred and fifty people there. An interesting mix. When his father hosted a fancy shindig, the room was full of actors and singers with a sprinkling of politicians, so Ford had expected to see a handful of famous faces and perhaps some captains of industry sipping drinks as they networked. But no, this was more like a frat party, except with better food. And waitstaff. And...what the hell was that?

"Uh-oh. Emmy doesn't look happy," Hallie murmured.

No, she didn't. She had her hands on her hips as she squared up to Bradley, and Ford sidled closer with Hallie because nosiness ran through his veins.

"Which part of 'no blood' didn't you understand?"

"It's not blood; it's fondue."

"It's fucking red. A fountain of red. Like someone severed a bleedin' artery."

"It's opaque. Blood is translucent. And what else would we dip the fruit kabobs in?"

"Regular chocolate?"

"You're so boring."

Emmy spotted a passing waitress. "And what's that? It's red and translucent and it looks exactly like blood."

"Grenadine, and it doesn't *taste* like blood."

She flicked her gaze skyward and muttered something that could have been *give me strength*. "The fondue can stay, but lose the red cocktails."

"But—"

"We can drink them tomorrow. Starla's gonna be here in five."

Starla was coming? Was that a good idea?

Maybe it was. She walked in dressed as a ballerina with Dan and a man who had to be Ethan—Lydia and Betelgeuse tonight—plus Caleb and two other boys wearing pirate costumes who formed up around her protectively. Shit, was that Fenika Ganaway with them? Yeah, it was, plus Micah was behind her alongside a guy with bulky shoulders Ford assumed was his older brother.

Terrific.

"Who are the boys?" Ford asked Hallie. "Friends of Caleb?"

She nodded. "Trick and Vine—Trick's the taller one. They come as a trio. Dan adopted Caleb, but really, she ended up with all three of them."

Ford moved away before the Ganaways could spot him. Luckily, the ballroom was the size of a gridiron. But he watched the group from across the room, and those boys acted as pint-sized bodyguards, shepherding Starla around to get food and check out the carved pumpkins and watch the acrobats putting on a performance at the far end of the room.

Hallie grabbed glow-in-the-dark drinks from a passing server and handed one to Ford.

"Is this gonna irradiate my insides?"

"Relax, I'm pretty sure Emmy keeps the nukes in the basement."

"The...nukes?" Ford followed Hallie as she headed in

Mercy's direction. "Wait, you're kidding. You're kidding, right?"

"I *think* I'm kidding."

Ford gave his head a shake and then came to the conclusion that even if there was a nuke in the basement, he didn't want to know.

A server held out a tray. "Pastry snake?"

Hallie stiffened. "Uh..."

"Do you need a fork?" Ford opened the pocket of his apron to reveal a full set of cutlery. "I brought it in case there were canapés."

Now her lip quivered.

"Hey, hey, it's okay."

"I love you *so damn much*. But tonight, I'm going to eat the canapés with my fingers." She snatched a snake from the tray and bit off its head. "I can do this."

"Next stop, the fondue fountain?"

"Fruit skewers will never defeat me."

That was Ford's girl.

As with the previous party, once the initial chaos settled, the affair just became an evening of good friends and good food, albeit with a supernatural twist. Somebody—Bradley?—had placed wire sculptures on the lawn, and lit strategically, they gave the illusion of an army of ghosts heading toward the mansion. *Mansion*. This place made his father's home in LA look like a kid's playhouse.

Ford kept an eye on the Ganaway family as they mingled, because what was he meant to say to them? He'd been part of the process that put them through hell. And when they got close, he decided that moment was an excellent time for a bathroom break.

Except where was the bathroom? This place needed signage. Or maps. After five minutes of meandering through hallways and corridors, he had to face reality: he was lost. Now what? Should he call Hallie and ask for help? She'd never let him live that down.

A strange whomping noise began, quiet at first but growing steadily louder until it vibrated through his core. A helicopter? Was someone arriving by helicopter?

Yes, someone was. Ford found a window in time to see Marine fucking One and two decoys land in the backyard, and you know what? He wasn't even surprised.

No, the shock came five minutes later when he turned a corner and saw the president heading straight for him, surrounded by a phalanx of Secret Service agents. He shrank back into the shadows as Emmy and Black appeared from a nearby room. Tonight, Emmy was the ringmaster in a top hat, tailcoat, and high-heeled boots. Black had dressed as the Grim Reaper, which seemed appropriate.

"James," he said. "Diana."

When he reached out a hand, the First Lady came to him, standing on tiptoes to kiss him on the cheek. She'd dressed as a cat in a skintight black leotard with little black ears on a headband. If a picture of that outfit got into the papers, the media would have a field day.

The president was a vampire, and he hooked an arm around Emmy's waist.

"No biting," she warned. "And did you not read my text? We have a 'no blood' rule."

"It's not blood; it's corn syrup."

"Have you been talking to Bradley?"

"Not if I can help it."

Ford almost choked when she leaned in and licked his fucking face. He didn't miss the way Black's hands balled into fists, either.

"There, fixed. Now we can enjoy the party. Ford, are you lost?"

Ah, fuck. How had she known he was there? She didn't

turn, didn't so much as glance in his direction. The woman had a spooky sixth sense.

"Uh, yeah. I've been walking around in circles for ten minutes now."

"Know the feeling," President Harrison muttered. "This place is a maze."

"I keep telling Bradley we need maps, but they always get bumped down the priority list in favour of sparkly shit. You can follow us back to the ballroom. Have you met James?"

Of course Ford hadn't. The president held out a hand, and he hesitated. What was the protocol in a situation like this?

"Relax, he doesn't bite."

President Harrison grinned to reveal a pair of fangs. "Well, actually..."

Black clapped him on the back in what might have been a friendly gesture if he hadn't put so much force behind it. Harrison lurched forward.

"Need a better costume, buddy. That one's a fail."

"Says the man missing a horse."

Huh? "Does the Grim Reaper ride a horse?" Ford asked.

"He's a horseman of the apocalypse." Harrison thumped Black in return. "Seems you get an F too."

Black offered an arm to Diana. "Glass of wine, my darling?"

"Do you have a bottle from your vineyard? The white?"

"Of course."

Back in the ballroom, President Harrison's entrance caused barely a ripple, leading Ford to suspect that this wasn't the first time he'd shown up to a party at Riverley Hall. Nobody gawked, or asked for photos, or hovered to speak with him. He just helped himself to a drink and went to chat with a group in the corner.

"Did you know the president was coming?" Ford asked when he finally found Hallie again.

"Not for sure, but he shows up sometimes. Dan says that this is the one place he can let his guard down." Hallie giggled and took another swallow of rosé. "You know, I never used to think presidents had a social life, or friends, or fun. They were these distant, unapproachable people who appeared on TV. But James is human, just like us. Well, not *just* like us, but you know…"

"How did he get on the invite list?"

"School. He and Black went to school together. Where's the cake? I need cake."

Ford pulled her close, and his lips brushed her ear as he leaned in. "I need gingerbread."

"I haven't seen any—" Ah, now she realised, and that blush was hella cute. "Oh! Is it too early to sneak out?"

"I don't think so."

But he was wrong. They'd only made it halfway to the door when Calvin Ganaway blocked their path, and up close, his chest was a wall.

"You're Ford Prestia?"

What were the chances of denying it? Slim. But would Ganaway risk throwing a punch in front of the Secret Service?

"That's right."

Calvin's muscles bulged as he folded his arms. "My brother never should've been charged."

"No, he shouldn't. Questioned, yes, but it shouldn't have gone that far, and I'm sorry it did. If it would help, I'll apologise in person."

"Nah, he doesn't much feel like talking to you. But he asked me to tell you that he's dropping his lawsuit against the department."

Well, that was…unexpected. "Right. I mean, thanks, but… why? I realise I shouldn't say this, but he had a decent case."

"If Micah hadn't been arrested, then Blackwood wouldn't have gotten involved, and there's a good chance those girls wouldn't have been found. Our mom always believed in fate. Fate and karma."

"Blackwood played a bigger part in their rescue than the media would have you believe."

"So I've heard. Also heard you got a new partner."

"I did."

"Good. Do better next time."

"I intend to."

Calvin strode off, and Ford sent silent thanks skyward that his face was still intact. Then he pressed a soft kiss to Hallie's cheek.

"Thank you."

"For what?"

"For everything."

45

MORE EPILOGUE - HALLIE

"Orange juice?" I asked Emmy.

"Is it laced with Tylenol?"

"No?"

"Then why the fuck would I want it?" The sun popped out from behind a cloud, and a beam of light sliced through the kitchen window at Little Riverley and hit her full in the face. "But I'll love you forever if you pour me a coffee."

She'd staggered in ten minutes ago, complaining that Bradley was trying to kill her. How, you ask? By singing show tunes at the top of his voice while he directed the clean-up of last night's carnage. I still wasn't entirely sure how it happened, but somehow Ryder had ended up in the fondue fountain.

"Espresso?"

"Make it a triple."

The sun blinked out for a moment as Marine One flew past.

"Did Diana stop puking?" Sky asked.

"Eventually. Black sat with her until the early hours."

"Not James?"

"James needed the sleep more than Black did. He's off to a summit later, and nobody wants him to screw up the negotiations." Emmy cracked a smile. "And Diana's meant to be hosting the Egyptian girls' basketball team, so I guess she'll be doing that in sunglasses. But hey, we all survived Halloween, and I'm taking that as a win."

"Roll on Thanksgiving," Sky mumbled.

"Want to leave the country?"

"Give me five minutes to pack a bag."

"What happened to your go-bag? You should be packed already."

Mercy meandered in, still dressed as a worse-for-wear Cruella. She was meant to have stayed with Cora last night, but when we'd found her asleep on the couch, she'd looked so serene that we'd covered her up with a blanket and left her there. Kellan had skipped out the door wearing her Dalmatian puppy as a hat.

Emmy's phone vibrated across the table, and she glanced at the screen. Then her smile turned into an actual grin, which had to hurt at this time in the morning.

"What?" Sky asked.

"In five months, we'll be welcoming a little bundle of joy."

"*What*?" She snatched the phone from Emmy and checked the message, then threw a croissant at her. "You're such a moron."

"Who is pregnant?" Mercy asked.

"Nobody. Calvin Ganaway's not re-enlisting in the Navy. He's gonna join Emmy's team instead."

Emmy had caught the croissant, and now she took a bite. "He said he needed to sleep on the decision, and it seems he's woken up now."

"Knox will be happy. They're friends, yes?"

"Yup."

"Where is Knox? Did someone get him down from the roof?"

"I bloody hope so. He's meant to be flying to Antigua this morning."

"For a vacation?"

"Yeah, but not his. He's babysitting a royal pain in the ass while she goes on an Instagram-selfie tour of the Caribbean. Her father says somebody needs to keep her out of trouble, and since he's willing to pay our rates and Nick's team is rushed off its feet this month, Knox drew the short straw."

I raised my hand. "I'd be willing to overlook a rich brat's worst qualities for a week on the beach."

"Super. I'll remember that next time Nick's hunting for volunteers. But if you need a week on the beach, why don't you and Ford sail his boat down to Florida? Nobody's gonna mind if you take some time off."

"A vacation sounds good. But from what Ford's said, it's practically a military operation to get the *Shore Thing* along the James River because of the mast, so it might be easier to fly somewhere."

"Lorelei Cay's always an option. I understand Dan promised you a week there if you solved the Ganaway case."

Mercy tilted her head to one side. "Why does Ford have a really expensive sailboat that he can't sail?"

"Because he needs a place to live, and on his salary, it would be a stretch to pay for an apartment here plus mooring fees nearer to the ocean. But I guess someday we'll move in together, and then he can sail the boat again."

Mercy's face fell. "You're going to move out?"

Ah, rats. I hadn't planned on saying anything, not for a while. "Not right now. Probably not for months."

"Ford wouldn't want to share our apartment? It's big."

"You'd be okay with that? Having a man around?"

She shrugged. "He's already there half the time. Why not

make it three-quarters and spend weekends on the boat? And also, it's useful to have somebody at home who can open jars. And... And... He's nice. Kind." Mercy's eyes filled. "I'm so glad you found a good one. It gives me hope."

Awww. I got up to wipe her tears away and gave her a good hug while I was there. "Never give up hope."

The sound of a throat clearing made me look up.

"Uh, is this a good time?" Valerie asked from the doorway.

Emmy pushed a plate of pastries toward her. "Keep your voice down and don't make any sudden movements. Want a croissant?"

"The party went on late, huh?"

Valerie had offered what Bradley deemed an acceptable excuse for missing the get-together—her son had his first judo grading, and she wanted to be there to provide moral support. Last thing I heard, Dan was trying to sign Caleb up for martial arts classes.

"More like early. Do you need us for something? Or did you just come over to use the pool?"

Valerie took a mini pain au chocolat. "I came to swim, but then Bradley said Hallie was here, so I thought I could update her on that profile she wanted me to look at rather than waiting until tomorrow." She took a step toward the door. "But if you all have headaches, I can leave that."

"Profile?" I mumbled.

"The Carmody case? The blood spot on the windowsill?"

Now she had my attention, and Emmy's too. "Did you find a lead?"

"Maybe, but I'm not sure how it fits. The TV said that Brand guy took her?"

"It's possible but far from probable."

"Okay. Okay, so I used publicly available databases and started building a reverse family tree for the suspect. You know how that works?"

"You look for similarities in the DNA?"

"Exactly, a person inherits fifty percent of their DNA from each parent. Go back further, and you get twenty-five percent from each grandparent. The genetic similarity reduces to a quarter with each generation since people shared a common ancestor. So you share roughly twelve-and-a-half percent of your DNA with a first cousin, three-and-one-eighth percent with a second cousin, and less than one percent with a third cousin."

Mercy looked totally blank, but I kind of got it.

"It spreads out, like ripples in a pond?"

Valerie nodded. "Exactly."

Emmy merely groaned. "Just put my brain in the blender and turn it on. Cut out the middleman."

"What did you find?" I asked.

"Uh, I'll spare you the details, but I think his family lives in Scotland."

"Scotland?"

"Yup. We got lucky, and there was a second cousin in the mix. Plus a whole bunch of third cousins. And they all live in Scotland."

"But Mila Carmody vanished from Virginia."

"People move," Sky pointed out. "Me and Emmy both come from London."

"If you want to take a deeper look at this, I have a shortlist of names," Valerie said. "Possible branches of the family tree that we could check out to narrow down the search."

Emmy drained her coffee. "How short?"

"A half dozen."

"All in Scotland?"

"I believe so."

She turned to Sky. "How do you fancy a road trip?"

"To *Scotland*?"

"Nah, I thought we'd take a month off, drive Route 66. Of

course to fucking Scotland. We're flying to England the day after tomorrow anyway, so we can make a small detour and collect some DNA samples before we come back. And if we take our time, we might even miss Thanksgiving. You never know."

"I'd better buy a kilt. Hallie, are you coming?"

"Am I invited?"

We both looked to Emmy.

"Sure, why the hell not? I know fuck all about science." Not entirely true, but as she'd once told me, it was better to be an undercover expert than a cocksure fool. "And you'd better buy an umbrella too because I hear Scotland's cold, wet, and full of weird-ass cows."

"How will an umbrella help with cows?"

"If they're anything like my horse, they'll bolt at the sight of it."

Did I want to go to Scotland? My relationship with Ford, it was still so new... But I knew he'd understand. If he had the opportunity to get to the bottom of a puzzle, he'd take it too, and it would only be for a few days. He'd be working most of the time, anyway.

I thought back to the photos of Mila Carmody. Another little girl whose future had been stolen. Another victim.

"When do we leave?"

WHAT'S NEXT?

Mila Carmody's story continues in *Chimera*...

Evil wears many faces...

When Emmy Black, director of Special Projects for Blackwood Security, takes a trip to Edinburgh to collect DNA samples in a long-running cold case, a favour for a friend soon leads her to Glendoon Hall, a crumbling castle on the edge of the Highlands. Locals say a legendary beast walks the land, and Emmy's sidekick Sky wants to catch it.

Crazy.

Emmy's not one to pass up a challenge—or a bet—but the Beast of Glendoon definitely doesn't exist...does it?

For more details:
www.elise-noble.com/chimera

If you enjoyed *Pretties in Pink*, please consider leaving a review.

For an author, every review is incredibly important. Not

only do they make us feel warm and fuzzy inside, readers consider them when making their decision whether or not to buy a book. Even a line saying you enjoyed the book or what your favourite part was helps a lot.

WANT TO STALK ME?

For updates on my new releases, giveaways, and other random stuff, you can sign up for my newsletter on my website: www.elise-noble.com

If you're on Facebook, you might also like to join Team Blackwood for exclusive giveaways, sneak previews, and book-related chat. Be the first to find out about new stories, and you might even see your name or one of your suggestions make it into print!

And if you'd like to read my books for FREE, you can also find details of how to join my advance review team.

Would you like to join Team Blackwood?

www.elise-noble.com/team-blackwood

 facebook.com/EliseNobleAuthor
twitter.com/EliseANoble
instagram.com/elise_noble

END-OF-BOOK STUFF

Gosh, this book has been a long time coming! Over a year since the last Blackwood Security release, mainly because I got distracted by the Planes world and then Baldwin's Shore. Anyhow, I finally got to find out what happened to Mila Carmody. Ever since I wrote a few lines about her case in *Black is My Heart*, I knew that someday I'd revisit it in a bigger way. That bigger way turned out to be two books. Originally, I'd planned to write the end of her case as an epilogue, but as the story got more and more complicated, I realised it just wouldn't work. In the end, that adventure turned into a (short) novel in its own right.

My original plan with *Pretties* was to have Micah be Hallie's love interest, but I figured that would make the story too similar to *White Hot*, which I would have hated and probably you would have too. Then I considered Calvin... Thought, maybe? But I also felt guilty for always dunking on the Richmond PD so often, which I'm sure has plenty of fine, upstanding officers outside of my books, so I decided to write a good cop for a change. I like Ford. He'll be back in the future :) Maybe Broussard too—who knows?

As always, thanks to Nikki for editing and to Abi for working her Photoshop magic on the cover. If you have the paperback, did you spot the rogue AC unit on the back cover? Thanks also to Jeff, Renata, Terri, Musi, David, Stacia, Jessica, Nikita, Quenby, and Jody for beta reading, and to John, Lizbeth, and Debi for proof reading!

Elise

ALSO BY ELISE NOBLE

Blackwood Security

For the Love of Animals (Nate & Carmen - Prequel)

Black is My Heart (Diamond & Snow - Prequel)

Pitch Black

Into the Black

Forever Black

Gold Rush

Gray is My Heart

Neon (novella)

Out of the Blue

Ultraviolet

Glitter (novella)

Red Alert

White Hot

Sphere (novella)

The Scarlet Affair

Spirit (novella)

Quicksilver

The Girl with the Emerald Ring

Red After Dark

When the Shadows Fall

Pretties in Pink

Chimera (2022)

Secret Weapon (Crossover with Baldwin's Shore) (2022)

Blackwood Elements

Oxygen

Lithium

Carbon

Rhodium

Platinum

Lead

Copper

Bronze

Nickel

Hydrogen (2022)

Blackwood UK

Joker in the Pack

Cherry on Top

Roses are Dead

Shallow Graves

Indigo Rain

Pass the Parcel (TBA)

Blackwood Casefiles

Stolen Hearts

Burning Love (TBA)

Baldwin's Shore

Dirty Little Secrets

Secrets, Lies, and Family Ties

Buried Secrets

Secret Weapon (Crossover with Blackwood Security) (2022)

Blackstone House

Hard Lines (2022)

Hard Tide (TBA)

The Electi

Cursed

Spooked

Possessed

Demented

Judged

The Planes

A Vampire in Vegas

A Devil in the Dark (TBA)

The Trouble Series

Trouble in Paradise

Nothing but Trouble

24 Hours of Trouble

Standalone

Life

Coco du Ciel

A Very Happy Christmas (novella)

Twisted (short stories)

Books with clean versions available (no swearing and no on-

the-page sex)

Pitch Black

Into the Black

Forever Black

Gold Rush

Gray is My Heart

Audiobooks

Black is My Heart (Diamond & Snow - Prequel)

Pitch Black

Into the Black

Forever Black

Gold Rush

Gray is My Heart

Neon (novella)

Printed in Great Britain
by Amazon